THE ST. NICHOLAS
MURDERS

BY R. L. CHERRY

ISBN-13: 978-0999473900

ISBN-10: 0999473905

Wild Cherry Enterprise, LLC, Nevada City, CA

Cover Designed by Duong Covers

Books by R.L. Cherry

Historical Fiction

Three Legs of the Cauldron

Suspense

Foul Shot

Morg Mahoney Mysteries

Christmas Cracker

It's Bad Business

Father Bruce Mysteries

St. Nicholas Murders

St. Christopher Murders (2018 release date)

ACKNOWLEDGEMENTS

While the town of Buggy Springs and Pike County may not appear on any map of California, they exist in the spirit of the Sierra Nevada Foothills. They capture the zeitgeist of the region. Admittedly, Buggy Springs was inspired by Nevada City, moved to the isolation of Downieville, but is neither. Not one of the people in this book exists in the real world.. If you think you know who any of the people in the book really are, you are wrong. They are only figments of my rather fertile imagination. Only Blue is given his real name in this book and he has given permission. That being said, real people helped me make this book a reality. First and foremost, artist Paula DeGiorgis granted me permission to use her painting, "Trinity Church in Winter," for this cover. Then, the fiction writing group of Sierra Writers has listened to me read it and offered many wise criticisms. My fine editors, Cindy Grubbs and Dave Hershberger laboriously went through the manuscript, finding many more errors than I wish to admit. Father Chistopher Seal gave me some helpful input. Last and definitely not least, my wife and muse not only edited this work, but has supported and encouraged my writing efforts for many, many years.

Dedicated to my dear friend, the late Father Rich DeGiorgis.

"A fellow of most infinite jest"

Chapter 1

Sometimes little things we do, or don't do, lead to events in our lives that can have grave consequences for others. When I answered the phone on that November Saturday, I had no idea of the twisted tale that would follow.

"St. Nicholas of Myra Episcopal Church, Father Robert speaking. How may I help you?"

A low, throaty voice whispered, "Bless me, for I have sinned."

It sounded like a joke and my first reaction was to say, "Come to church and we'll talk." But I didn't. I was a little bored and leaned back in my chair, giving the proper response. "The Lord be in your heart and upon your lips that you may humbly confess your sins: In the name of the Father, and of the Son and of the Holy Spirit. Amen."

My caller had recited the opening line for The Reconciliation of a Penitent from *The Book of Common Prayer*, Form One. As an Episcopal priest, I didn't hear a lot of confessions, but some people still do make them. True, I had never done a confession by phone, but anything goes in California. And what would be next? I mean, I read that even the Vatican has approved a Confessional cell phone app. Is texting or tweeting Hail Marys on the way? However, even in such an out-of-the-way town as Buggy Springs, I do try to be up-to-date.

Silence. Had I lost my caller?

"You called for confession and reconciliation?"

"You might say that, Father."

"So, my . . ." The voice sounded male and was raspy, like a heavy smoker. Still, I had heard women who sounded like that after many years puffing cigarettes. ". . . child, what are your sins?"

A short, humorless laugh. "Many. But only one I want to confess now."

Okay, this is the granola state: the home of nuts and flakes. Evidently one of them had decided to call me. But it was a slow day. I was at the church alone, trying to write a relevant sermon for our

Kirkin' of the Tartan on Sunday afternoon. As chaplain of the local Celtic Society, I was expected to give a short homily during the service that was prosaic, pithy and profound. Not easy to do in eight minutes or less. It was late on an unseasonably warm, autumn afternoon and I was close to dozing off, so I took a break and played along with my mystery caller.

"And what is this sin?" Then I added, "But you know forgiveness demands that you try not to repeat your sins. That shows a penitent heart. If you're planning to do it again, you're not really sorry."

"The sin is theft. You should take special pity on me. After all, isn't that who your church is named after? The patron saint of thieves?"

This piqued my interest. Most people only identified St. Nicholas with Christmas as the patron saint of children. Whoever this was knew his saints, or at least how to research them. But then, the Internet made that easy.

"So, you stole something from somebody. Tell me about it, uh, sir." I paused. "Do I know you?"

"Can't tell?" A laugh. "Why would you think you do? Yes, I stole. But it was a crime of justice, so that shouldn't be a crime, should it?"

"That's not my call. I'm concerned about God's law, not man's. So what do you wish to confess?"

"Cut to the chase, huh? Okay, Father. Read 2 Samuel 1:25."

I'm fairly good at Biblical passages. It's part of the job. But this one was not immediately familiar to me. I knew enough to assume it had something to do with King Saul or David, but that was all. I wondered what this was really about. I also wondered if I knew this person. The voice wasn't familiar, but he or she might be disguising it.

"Then you heard my sermon on that last month?" I hadn't preached any such sermon, but I might be able to find out if this was one of my parishioners.

Again, the laugh. "Nice try, Father. You're trying to find out if I go to church there. Maybe, but maybe not. But this is my confession, so you can't tell the cops about me."

This person was not stupid. I'd been too obvious. "I won't tell anyone. But what's to tell? You haven't said anything yet.

What is this theft you're confessing? Did you break into someone's home?"

"Good. We're getting down to the facts. I didn't take anyone's jewelry or money. I stole something far more valuable, but you'll have to figure it out."

"So you stole something very valuable and aren't telling me what. Is this just a practical joke? How do I know this is the truth?"

"Truth? 'What is truth?'" A snicker. "Do you know who said that?"

"Pontius Pilate. But he didn't know Truth when he stared Him in the face."

"And neither do you. You're not as smart as you think you are. Here's a riddle to help: You won't find it in your stories by your father if you take a gander, but he was royally shattered from rhyming at all."

Then the caller hung up.

I stared at the dead phone. A nutcase. It could be someone who attended St. Nicholas, but a reasonably intelligent person could find all that the caller said online. Even so, I decided to look up the Bible passage to see if that would shed any light.

2 Samuel 1:25 was about the death of Jonathan, son of King Saul and friend of David of slaying Goliath fame. It said, "How the mighty have fallen in battle! Jonathan lies slain on your heights." It spoke of death in battle and, as far as I remembered, the closest thing to a battle in Buggy Springs lately was last Memorial Day between some Civil War re-enactors. All the deaths had been faked. Still, there was something about the call that bothered me, a sense that there might be more to it than a prank.

After a quick check, I found that 2 Samuel 1:1 and 1:23-27 had been readings last June, so it might be a church member. The church didn't have caller I.D. or call-back, so I had no way of tracing who had called. But the police did. I pulled out the phone book and started to look up the number of the Buggy Springs police department. Then I stopped. I could imagine the conversation.

"Buggy Springs Police Department," some voice would answer.

"Yes, this is Father Robert Bruce of St. Nicholas Church. I need to have a call traced," I would say.

"You need a call traced? Father, have you been threatened? Has someone been kidnapped?" the voice would ask.

"No, I think someone killed someone," I would answer.

"Why?" the voice would ask.

"He quoted a Bible verse about a killing," I would answer.

"Who made the call?" the voice would ask.

"I can't say. His voice was disguised," I would answer.

"Let me get this straight, Father. You want us to trace a call because some unkown person quoted a Bible verse?" the voice would ask.

"Yes," I would answer.

"Call us when you haven't been sampling the Communion wine," the voice would say.

Click.

Now, the police department's receptionist wouldn't be so rude as to use that last line, but I'm sure he or she would be thinking it. No, that wouldn't work. Especially since I doubted the legitimacy of the call myself.

I sat there for a moment, thinking. The caller either was an Episcopalian or knew we used the *Book of Common Prayer*. He also knew Scripture, or knew how to find Biblical quotes on the Internet. That would include a lot of people, not even necessarily church-goers. But calling to do the rite of Reconciliation, commonly called Confession? Still, people do like to tell me their worst sins. And I listen. As a rector, it's part of the job. Sometimes they want forgiveness, absolution. Sometimes it's counseling or advice. At times it's just bragging about conquests, sexual or financial. I'm not here to judge, but to give God's forgiveness. If it seems a valid confession. The braggers can go to . . . . Well, God bless their little hearts. Even if I don't.

But this had to be a crank call. If not, what could I do? Good old Samuel gave me nothing concrete to go on, even in his second book. I thought about writing the bishop to let him know about the uncontrite confession in case anything came of it, but the whole thing sounded like a crank call to me. And he already thought of me as a bit of a pain in the rear.

So I went back to my Kirkin' homily. Since my name is Robert

Bruce you would think I had been raised with stories of my famous namesake, King Robert the Bruce, and how he had led Scotland to regain its independence from the English. But I didn't have any idea of this until I saw the movie *Braveheart* with some friends in 1995, when I was in middle school. Afterwards, I asked my father if that was why I had been named Robert. I found that I had been named after my mother's grandfather. As far as our Scottish heritage, my father said he wouldn't be caught dead in a kilt, which he called a skirt. So much for respect of our history by my family.

For about an hour I sat staring at a computer screen that only said, "On this occasion when we remember Scots who . . . ." I finally gave up and called Don Frampton, the church junior warden, challenging him to a game of racquetball. If I couldn't accomplish anything else that day, at least I would kick his overweight butt all over the court.

Chapter 2

Later that morning, I was sitting in Mocha Arabesque, sipping my non-fat latte with a triple shot and paying the price for arrogance and pride: humility. Jim had whupped me good. I deserved it, but it still hurt. So did my right shoulder after I crashed into the wall as I missed a shot. Considering I was just under 30 years old, stand 6' 2" and in good condition, I should have won. But I was no athlete and it showed. After my devastating loss, I had dropped into the funkiest place in town, Buggy Springs' unique take on a coffeehouse, to nurse my wounds with caffeine.

Mocha, as it was known around town, was a cavernous affair filled with old, odd overstuffed and wooden chairs and mismatched tables. The walls were mostly covered with red wallpaper flocked with gold designs like from a bordello. Well, at least the bordellos in movies. I can't say from actual experience. Avant garde movie posters as well as local artists' creations in oil, watercolor and pencil of some unusual subjects dotted the walls, some even in frames. The menu was painted in white, yellow and orange on an old blackboard mounted in a gilt frame on the wall. Like I said, funky.

However, Mocha had the best lattes in the State of California. And that's saying a lot. It also provided its patrons with copies of *The Constitution*, the *San Francisco Chronicle*, *High Times* and various alternative newspapers that had a problem discerning fact from fiction. I have a morning routine of doing Morning Prayer from The *Book of Common Prayer* as well as a little prayer and quiet time, followed by my *New York Times* crossword puzzle in the local rag, *The Constitution*. I'd missed doing the puzzle, so I did it then, followed by reading the latest Buggy Springs news. What caught my eye was an article about Jonathan Franks, a local contractor, who had been killed in a freak accident at one of his properties. There wasn't much information except that he had been alone and his death wasn't suspicious.

Jon was, or had been, one of my parishioners, albeit normally only on Christmas Eve and Easter Sunday. But I hate finding out about something happening to someone in my church that way. He had been a big man, in his fifties, with a belly that crept over his belt. His black hair had looked dyed to me and he had worn it a little long, so that it framed a rugged chiseled face and steely eyes that many women find appealing. I hadn't known him, just greeting him and his wife on the rare occasions he attended. I made a note to make a call to his wife, Lisa.

Lisa, who attended on a semi-regular basis without Jon, was sexy, in a '60's Playboy bunny way (I'd seen my father's old magazines in my youth), with long, wavy blond hair and a curvy body with a prominent bustline that always seemed to be invading my comfort zone when I greeted her as she left church on Sundays. I may be a man of the cloth, but I am still a man, with eyes and a libido. I often found myself stepping back and finding someone else to greet.

Immediately, I was stricken with guilt for even thinking about the newly-widowed Mrs. Franks' body. Best to keep my mind focused on what I should do as her pastor and leave the lust to someone else. I would phone her to find out if the church could be of help, whether in conducting services, bringing food or having one of our women stop by to offer a shoulder to cry on. I would definitely not be making a house call myself. I would also spend some time praying about keeping my thoughts pure. Far easier said than done, but that's true of much of the Scriptures. A tough Book to follow.

I finished my latte and went back to my office after stopping by my house for a quick bite of lunch. Once ensconced in my inner sanctum, I sat at my keyboard and went back to my homily for the Kirkin'. Unfortunately, the warm weather, morning exercise and after-lunch doldrums hit me and I kept nodding off. It was times like this I wished I had a large couch in my office so I could take a short afternoon nap. But a couch in a bachelor-priest's office might be misconstrued as having other, more carnal uses. You can't be too careful about appearances, especially as a small town priest, even if you are doing nothing wrong. As it is, almost thirty and never married, I am sure tongues are already wagging.

"What's his orientation?" Hetero. "Is he leaning towards Roman Catholicism, taken a vow of life-long chastity?" No. And one I did not want to ever hear, "What goes on behind a closed door on his office couch?" Nothing, except verbal counseling. I even had a glass door to make sure my actions were transparent.

After taking a break to wash my face with cold water and grabbing a glass of iced tea from the fridge, I was able to finish my homily. I'd written my sermon notes earlier in the week, so I could relax. And call Lisa Franks to offer the church's help in her time of grief.

I found the phone number on the member database in my computer. While people who attend two times a year might not make the membership rolls in some churches, it is enough if that person also is baptized and drops a check in the plate, or is "known to the treasurer," to be a voting member at St. Nicholas. I punched in the number on my phone. After three rings, I got an answering machine, a man's voice.

"Sorry we missed your call. Leave a message and we'll get back atchya."

After the beep, I said, "Hi. This is Father Robert at St Nicholas Church. I heard the tragic news and just wanted to say that if you need anything, give the church a call. I know that it's a terrible time for you and want you to know we are here for you. God bless."

After leaving the church's number, I hung up. I would have the church secretary send a condolence note with another offer of help on Monday. I shut down my computer and went home. I should have a Netflix shipment in my mailbox to watch, the next installments of *Poldark*, plus I had some new Earl Grey tea to test, so I wouldn't be bored.

After the second service on Sunday, I stood in front of our white, wood-frame Gold Rush era church with its attached bell tower and greeted the congregation as they left. I loved that church building as much as I loved my little town. The average age of attendees was steadily climbing as many of the young people left town after high school, dying to get out of Buggy Springs.

William Bugge had set up a general store next to a spring of cool, clear water to supply '49ers with food, shovels, picks and pans for their too-often vain efforts to find gold. He got rich and built a town with a saloon, hotel and brothel to service the various needs of the miners. St. Nicholas Church was founded not long after to give the miners a place to repent the next day. The town was originally named Bugge Springs after him, but some state clerk recorded it as Buggy

Springs and the name stuck. I occasionally wonder how William felt about that.

Each and every parishioner smiled and shook my hand with some conversation that varied from a word or two to several minutes. Some, amazingly enough, even complimented my sermon. I saw Elvira Murdoch at the top of the concrete stairs, grabbing the pipe railing as she started to descend. I ran up the stairs and offered my arm.

At ninety-two years old, she was a remarkable woman. Maybe a hundred pounds soaking wet and not much over five feet tall, she was not physically imposing. Having outlived three husbands, she was still driving herself to church each Sunday, weather permitting. Having seen her drive, however, I did fear for others on the road. I had not been able to persuade her to hire a driver, though she did have enough money to do so if she wished. Fortunately, she would do little damage in a collision, since I'd never seen her go faster than about twenty-five miles per hour in her thirty-year-old Olds sedan. As she took my arm with her claw-like, arthritic hand, she eyed me a moment before speaking in her shaky voice.

"You're wasting your time with an old bird like me. I'm past the dating age."

I chuckled. "Well, if you change your mind, let me know. I'll be there with candy and flowers."

"Humph. I'm diabetic, you know, and flowers just wilt in a few days. No, look for a hottie more your age." She patted my arm. "From the way you've been eyeing that Franks woman, you'd like to get her into bed and she'd be happy to oblige."

"Elvira, don't say that," I admonished her with a slight scowl. "It's not true. Plus, the poor woman has just lost her husband and is grieving."

"Oh, tish. She's been around the block more times than my Olds. Besides, Jon was always running around on her and drinking at Higgins Digging's with loose women in the middle of the day." She held up a finger to stop me from speaking. "I know. I was his teacher and he never could keep a secret from me. Told me everything, more than I asked even. Did it right up until he fell off that ladder and died. He's gone and a healthy young man like you needs a sex life. All that libido needs a release, even if it's just with a friend with benefits. Go comfort her." She grinned mischievously. "After all, that's what a rector is supposed to do. Get close to his parishioners"

"That's not what I do . . . . I mean, I don't get close in that way . . . . I mean, that's not right for a priest. Please stop talking that way about Mrs. Franks and me." Especially since it might be overheard by others and start gossip. I was often taken aback at how this silver-blue haired lady in her pink flowered dress could say such things.

She shook her head slowly. "I can tell you a lot about their relationship, but not now. Later. You'll just sit around until some guy gets her into bed. With a face and body like hers, it won't be that long."

We had reached the base of the stairs and she pulled my head down so that she could whisper in my ear. "She has great boobs, too. And don't pretend you haven't noticed."

I felt the warmth as my face reddened. "Elvira, please stop this. If someone hears, they might misunderstand."

"Tish. Now help me to my car."

Her faded-red Olds was parked in the handicapped spot in front of the church. I walked her to the door and helped her in.

She reached up and tousled my hair as she sat in her car. "Even with your dark, wavy, sexy locks, faint heart never won fair maiden, you know. Well, she's not any maiden, so bedded a lusty wench." Her hand dropped to my cheek. "But get rid of the scruffy beard. It's not sexy."

I closed her door and shook my head as she drove erratically down the street. Some people thought of her as nothing but a crusty old gossip. They didn't know of the many times she had pressed several folded hundred-dollar bills in my hand and told me which parishioner needed it. She always did it anonymously, not even letting me tell the church secretary or treasurer. I loved the old lady, even though I did wish she'd keep out of my personal business.

A thought hit me after I closed up the church and walked toward my little Victorian house for lunch. My mystery caller had referenced the mighty falling, slain on a great height. Buggy Springs is in the foothills, at about 4500 elevation. Jon Franks had died from a fall. This was beginning to be more than a coincidence. When my mystery person had called, it had been the day after the accident. Sure, it wasn't a battle, but I hadn't read anything else in the local paper that

11

could fit.

Then I remembered the riddle, something about not hearing the story from my father if I took a gander and someone being royally shattered. It wasn't that difficult. In Mother Goose tales, Humpty Dumpty had a great fall from a wall, which rhymes with all. He was shattered and all the king's horses and men, the representatives of royalty, couldn't put him back together. The riddle described Jon's fall from the ladder.

I decided to call the chief of police on Monday and have an informal chat. He could tell me if I should call the sheriff's department. Since Jon Franks had died outside of the city limits, it would be their case. But I needed to get to know him, anyway. Lee Garcia was pretty new to the area. He'd come here from Colton in Southern California a little less than a year ago, after retiring from the police department there. It was only because he had another income that we could afford him. I only knew him well enough to say, "Hi." Time to remedy that.

With the matter resolved in my mind, I tried to get myself psyched up about wearing eight yards of Scottish wool in mid-seventies degree weather. I was sweating by the time I walked the half mile home. I'd take my red '69 SS396 convertible Camaro back for the Kirkin'.

Chapter 3

A problem confronted me as I arrived at the church: how to get out of a Camaro in a kilt without undue exposure of my assets. Fortunately, I had not gone "regimental," but had worn my boxers under my kilt. Still, there were people milling around, including a few children. How on earth, I wondered, do women get out of sports cars in short skirts?

After I awkwardly maneuvered myself out of my car, I was sure I heard muffled giggles at my dilemma. I marched into the church with as much dignity as I could manage. George MacDonald, ruddy-faced, scruffy bearded, white shirt tightly stretched across his beer belly as it hung over his kilt and his tartan tie ending about a foot above his belt, met me. He offered a small, pewter flask.

"Father, how about some really good whisky to fortify you before the service?"

I do enjoy a single malt scotch on occasion, but in the afternoon just before I was going to conduct a service was not such an occasion. I smiled and held up my hand.

"I need to keep my wits about me. Think what would happen if I announced your clan as Campbell when you brought up your tartan swatch for blessing."

He laughed, obviously knowing about the centuries-old animosity of the Campbell and the MacDonald clans.

Although this would not be a standard Anglican liturgy, I did not want to mess up my homily or incorrectly announce the clan names as representatives brought up a token to the altar rail for blessing at the end of the service. The Kirkin' of the Tartan had been created here in the States by the Scottish Presbyterian minister Peter Marshall in the 1940's. It had become one of the premier Scottish events in America. St. Nicholas had been hosting one for twelve years and I did not want to blow this one by indulging in a few drams of whisky.

At that point the bagpiper started wailing "Scotland the Brave" to announce the "gathering of the clans" and I hurried inside. It's been

13

said that a bad bagpiper sounds like he's strangling a cat and a good bagpiper sounds like he's strangling a cat, but skillfully.   I admit that I actually enjoy hearing a good piper, so maybe I am a bit prejudiced. But then again I'm more of a dog person, so maybe I wasn't as sympathetic to cats.   I miss my Aussie, Sheila, I'd lost a few years ago.

The service was short and was going off without a hitch.   At least until I was giving my homily.   That's when Lisa Franks slipped into the back of the church.   She was wearing the appropriately-black dress of a woman in mourning with a red Royal Stewart tartan sash draped over one shoulder.   However, the dress itself was not completely appropriate.   Although it was past her knees and did cover her shoulders, it showed way too much of her impressive cleavage.   I was, unfortunately, reminded of what Elvira had whispered in my ear and lost my train of thought.

"And so, my Scottish friends, I am reminded of the fullness of the breast . . . uh, I mean breadth of our Scottish community."

As the British would say, a titter ran through some of the small crowd of attendees.   Fortunately, most were not alert enough to catch my faux pas.   I hurriedly finished, omitting most of my notes.   Then I called the clans' representatives who brought some tokens of their clan, whether it be a piece of tartan cloth, a clan badge or some other creative bit, to be blessed and laid them on the altar rail.   The most unusual was a garter with a Campbell crest placed there by one of our local Goth young women in a Utilikilt, combat boots and a black T-shirt sporting a skull.   When Lisa came to the altar rail, leaned far forward and laid her sash on the rail, I focused on the list of clans in my hand so that I would not see any deeper into her cleavage.

After the service, we all met in the church's social hall for refreshments, where the Society had laid out a veritable feast.   There were platters of bread, cheese and cold cuts, small meat pies, sliced fruit, cookies, shortbread and various other desserts.   I groaned as I took a couple of pieces of shortbread.   They meant a lot more time on walking the trail to burn off the calories.

As I turned from the buffet line, I was dangerously close to the widow Franks.   She had a plate of fruit in her hand.   No desserts.   She smiled.

"Thanks so much, Father, for the phone call.   I do want to talk to you about a lot of things.   I'm very much into my Scottish heritage and have read a lot of history. I almost majored in that in college. I've wanted to join the Celtic Society meeting for years, but Jon wouldn't hear of it. Now I will. Don't you think I need to get out some and find new friends?"

"I, uh . . . think it would be great."

"I have really enjoyed this." She looked around the room. "I tried to get Jon to wear a kilt in the Stewart tartan, but he said he was German and not his thing. Personally, I think a guy looks a lot sexier in a kilt than in lederhosen, don't you?"

She laid her hand on my forearm. I was sure she could feel me shiver when she did, dumbstruck as I was. Then she suddenly seemed to be aware her hand was on my arm. "I hope that doesn't bother you."

I withdrew my arm. "It doesn't look quite proper, don't you think?"

"If you say so." Her eyes narrowed. "Maybe I'd better go."

Before I regained my composure, she was gone. I saw George close by and went to him.

"George, do you have anything left in your flask?"

He seemed surprised. "Sure, Father. Plenty."

"I think I'll have a wee dram after all."

He handed me his opened flask. I took a small swig and started coughing. It was not a fine single malt. It was Old Rotgut at its worst.

George smiled. "Too strong for ya, Father? Better stick to the communion wine."

I mutely nodded.

Chapter 4

Monday morning, after my breakfast, Morning Prayer and crossword puzzle, I called our chief of police. Doris, our church secretary doubles as a part-time operator there. She was a grey-haired, grandmotherly woman who loved knowing what was going on in Buggy Springs.

"Buggy Springs City Hall. How may I direct your call."

"Hi Doris, it's Robert. Is the Chief in?"

"Sure. What's the problem? Did someone break into the church? I bet it was those Goth kids that hang around Mocha Arabesque. You know, the ones with nose rings, black t-shirts and weird hair."

I shook my head. "No, nothing like that. I just want to get to know the Chief. After all, it's been almost a year since he came here."

"That's a good idea. You might even get him to come to church." She dropped her voice, speaking in a conspiratorial whisper. "He's Catholic, you know. Goes to St. Columba's, but not often. Sort of a C and E Christian."

"Now, Doris, God loves Catholics as much as Episcopalians. And many of our members only come on Christmas and Easter. Let's not be judgmental. Just put me through to the Chief."

Her voice was whiny, defensive. "I wasn't being judgmental. I was just . . . ." She sniffed. "Very well. I'll put you through."

After a short hold, I was connected.

"Chief Garcia here. How can I help you?"

"Chief, this is Father Robert Bruce from St. Nicholas. If you have time I would like to get together with you."

"Well, let's see what's free on my calendar." There was a pause. "I do have 11:15 on Monday morning, the twelfth of next month, if that would work."

I had hoped for something a little sooner. "I suppose that will work."

"Or we could just meet in about a half hour at the Buggy Springs

Diner. I'm going for breakfast."

"Half hour? Sure."

"See you there."

After I hung up, I laughed. The twelfth of next month. The Chief must be quite a kidder.

After finishing up a few things, I got to the Diner a few minutes early. It was only a few blocks from the church. What in Buggy Springs isn't?

Nestled in the middle of town, in a storefront on Main St., the Diner was one of three places that were open for breakfast. Mocha Arabesque served toasted bagels with a variety of toppings, going from lox and cream cheese to hummus and eggplant. Side Street Bistro had an eclectic variety of offerings, from a Hangtown fry with the usual bacon and oysters to a dirty rice and tofu wrap. Finally, there was the Diner with its truck-stop fare of greasy fried eggs, sausage and soggy home fries. You could also get stale biscuits and lumpy gravy. My least favorite place. Or most hated. Same thing. But I wanted to talk to the Chief and Paris is worth a Mass.

I walked in and looked around. The Chief was not there yet, so I took a table. Using the paper napkin from my place setting, I finished cleaning the chipped white, Formica top. The Diner looked as if it had been decorated in the 60's and hadn't been cleaned since.

The waitress stood over me like a prison matron: beefy and stern. In one hand she held a metal coffee pot. "Know what you want or need a menu?"

"Just coffee, please."

Her glare was an unspoken, "Cheapskate!" She turned over a mug sitting on the table and slopped some coffee into it. Brushing back a few strands of stray bleached-blond hair, she turned and left. At least she hadn't kicked me out.

I sipped my hot coffee. Then I dumped in some sugar and cream. I wouldn't be asking for a refill.

A few minutes later, the Chief walked in. He was a few inches shorter than I, but more solidly built. His thick, black-grey hair was combed in a pompadour and a Pancho Villa mustache curled around his mouth. The waitress met him with a smile. When he indicated that he was joining me, I saw a momentary frown cross her face. Obviously,

18

she thought me not worthy of his company, priest or not.

I stood and extended my hand. "Thanks for meeting me, Chief Garcia."

He took my hand with a firm grip. "Lee. Unless you're one of my patrol officers or dispatchers or on the city council, I'm Lee. But you can call me Chief if it makes you happy."

I liked him. And I liked his title. "Chief, I'm Robert."

We sat and the waitress came back to our table.

The Chief gave her a winning smile. "I'll have my usual, Judy."

Judy returned the smile, filled his mug with coffee and left.

The Chief turned to me as he picked up his mug. "So, now that we've met. What's the real reason you wanted to see me."

I started to protest my innocence, but decided not to. No reason to keep being deceptive. It had not been a valid confession. So I went directly to the point.

"I think someone killed Jon Franks. The killer called me the day it happened and bragged about it."

The Chief set down his mug. "Someone called you and said he had killed Jon Franks?"

I shifted in my chair. "Not exactly. The person said that he had stolen someone's life. He cited a Bible verse that describes Jonathan dying at a high place, then gave a riddle that was about Humpty Dumpty. When I found out that Jon Franks had died that day, it made sense. He was a parishioner. Well, nominally a parishioner."

The Chief sipped his coffee and leaned back in his hard, wooden chair. "So, who's your favorite author? Agatha Christie?"

I raised my hands in surrender. "I know this sounds farfetched. That's why I wanted this to be a casual conversation instead of a formal report. You're just too smart for me."

He chuckled. "After ten years on Homicide, I hope I could see through that subterfuge. Okay, Father . . . I mean Robert, what makes you think this was not some prank call? From what I heard, Franks' death was accidental."

"About the call's legitimacy, nothing but a gut feeling after years as a priest. Also my caller may have disguised his voice, which may or may not indicate I know him." I leaned forward. "Tell me about his death."

19

"Okay. Here's what I heard. Franks was on a job and got a call. Some kids were climbing all over a rental house he owned and was reroofing. He told his crew he was afraid they would climb up on the roof, get hurt and sue him, so he was going over there. A few hours later, one of the crew went over to check on him and found him lying on the driveway. His extension ladder was there too. Must have fallen over while he was climbing it. Died from blunt force trauma to the head. The driveway did it. The house was unoccupied and he had a loaded gun in his jean's pocket. No evidence of foul play."

I drummed my fingers on the table as I thought about this information. Judy brought a big plate of eggs, sausage, biscuits and gravy for the Chief and refilled our cups. Mine didn't need much and she glared at me again. Sorry, Judy.

"Okay, but what about the kids? And who made the call?"

"Good points. This isn't my case, so I wasn't really worried about it. I'll pass your information on to the sheriff's detective in charge. I'll get back to you about what he says. I don't suppose you have caller I.D. on your phone and the caller was stupid enough to not block the number?"

"No, on the first and I have no idea on the second." I paused. "Do you really like the food here?"

He shrugged. "It reminds me of my time back when I was on the force in Colton P.D. If you've ever eaten breakfast there, you'd know this is a definite step above."

I decided I would never eat breakfast in Colton.

Chapter 5

I got a call the next day.

"Morning, Father Bruce. I'm Detective Wright, Pike County Sheriff's Office. I understand from Chief Garcia that you have some information on the Franks' accident."

"Or murder."

Long pause.

"Right. Or murder. But why are you sure it's a murder?"

He had me there. I wasn't sure.

"Well, Detective Wright, there are three problems. The first is who made the call to Jon Franks about the kids on his roof? The second is where did they come from and where were they after he fell? The last is the call I received about his death."

"The call came from a throw-away cell phone. Since Jon's rental was in Santa Maria Ridge, the pot-growing center of the county, that's hardly a surprise. It's the standard phone for growers. As for the kids, if they were there when he fell, I'm sure they ran. Nobody loves the cops up there and they sure wouldn't have called us or stuck around until we showed."

He'd punched holes in my first two points. The ol' one-two. I could almost feel his smug grin as he prepared for the knockout punch.

"And, correct me if I'm wrong, Father Bruce, but you had an anonymous call that quoted some stuff out of the Bible and never even mentioned Jon Franks."

I sighed. "It was a quote about the death of Jonathan, the son of King Saul. There was also a riddle about Humpty Dumpty. I admit that it sounds a bit flimsy when you put it that way, but did you do an autopsy?"

"Since there were no witnesses, we did a basic one. It was an obvious accident and the results proved it. When he fell off the ladder, he broke his right shoulder and cracked his skull. Those aren't the medical terms, but that's close enough. He fell off the ladder and died. It was an accident."

21

I tapped my fingers on my desk. I just couldn't let it go. That phone call was a challenge, a puzzle. Jon Franks was the solution. "Did you check for any foreign substance in his head wound or look for anything in the area with blood on it, like maybe a rock?"

Detective Wright chuckled. "No, CSI Pike County was out on one of our many serial murder cases and was not available. We did, however, check his B.A.C. It was .07. Not legally drunk, but not safe on a ladder."

"Hmm. Is there any possibility of doing another autopsy, one that checks out the wound more carefully and with a full tox screen? If his wife agrees to it, of course."

"No. He's dust. Literally. He was cremated."

I was taken aback. Already cremated? I hated to ask my next question, but I had to. "Did Lisa Franks have any reason to kill him?"

"If she did, she did it from San Francisco. We did check her alibi, even though there was no sign Jon's death was anything but an accident, and she was at some pricey spa all day, evidently even got something called a Brazilian wax. You familiar with that?"

"No. I mean, I know what it is, but I'm not really familiar . . . ."

He chuckled. "We're not total incompetents, Father. I thank you for your help, but we'll take it from here. Good-bye."

I exhaled slowly. Being made to look like a paranoid old lady, a Miss Marple, was not pleasant. But she had always been right.

I clicked my pen as I pondered what I should do. Wisdom said to drop it. Cut my losses. Still, I had this gut feeling Detective Wright was wrong. But maybe that was from the salsa on the chicken and brown rice burrito I had for lunch at Carlotta's earlier. Like Scrooge's gruel. A source of phantasms.

In detective novels, the wife is the one to suspect. Often it's for some big life insurance policy. The Lord knew she had ample reason to kill him, even if Jon had no life insurance. That did not mean she did it. What if it were someone else? Someone I had never even heard of? I needed to talk to someone who would know about Jon's private life. The best source of gossip for men is a job site.

I picked up the phone, checked the directory and punched in the number.

"Hello?"

"Mrs. Franks, this is Father Bruce." Best keep it a little formal.

"Father, so good of you to call."

"I just had a quick question. I know that Jon had a job going and wondered if I could get the address."

Long pause. I had blown it. I should have asked how she was doing, what were her plans, et cetera. Jon had already been cremated, but I was doing a memorial service on the next day. Stupid. Unfeeling and stupid. I rushed to rectify my error.

"I need to get a feeling for Jon and his work for my eulogy. Talking to his employees might help. If they're still working on the job, I mean." God forgive me for this deceit. But I would do as I said and include what they said in the eulogy.

"Of course." A short laugh. "I'm afraid his workers won't give you a pretty picture of him. But go for it. He was working on a house on Ridge Court. I think it's 14795. Somewhere around there anyway. I never got involved in his business."

"Thanks. I'll see you at the service."

"Right. I, uh . . . ." She hesitated. "Bye, Father."

I studied the dead phone for a moment. Should I call her back? But it was getting late and if I wanted to catch Jon's employees, I'd better hightail it to Ridge Court.

I did find it. But it was 14579 Ridge Court. Same numbers, just a little different order. Fortunately, it was the only house under construction that I could see from the street. When I pulled up, I saw that work was still under way. A couple of beefy guys in T-shirts and jeans, tool belts hung on their hips like gun slingers, were carrying a sheet of plywood into the framed doorway of a skeleton that would someday be a house, while a country singer and a power saw vied for attention. One had a shaved head with a black goatee and the other a 49er ball cap.

I followed the workers inside and found the sources of the cacophony: a portable radio and a bushy-bearded, heavy-set man in overalls with no shirt cutting a two-by-twelve with a Skilsaw. His long red hair was pulled back in a ponytail. The man finished his job and the whine of his saw stopped, but the music played on. Loudly. The man glanced over at me, then turned away and stacked the cut timber on top of a pile of them.

"Hello?" I called.

He shook his head, but turned to me.

"What?"

"I'm Father Robert.   I'm looking for someone who can tell me about Jon Franks."

The man in the overalls went over to the radio and turned it off. He turned to me and smiled.   There was no smile in his eyes.

"That would be me."   He wiped his right hand on his sawdust-covered overalls and offered it to me.   "I'm Todd, the asshole's son."

Chapter 6

I was momentarily at a loss for words. I had forgotten that Jon had a son, much less one who had both worked for him and disliked him. He looked almost as old as Lisa, who was obviously his step-mother. There was a lot about Jon Franks that I didn't know.

I shook his hand. "I, uh . . . . Nice to meet you."

His son was a big man. Not as tall as I was, but stocky, with a big chest, waistline and arms. He grinned. He was missing his right canine. "Sorry to shock you, Padre. I just call 'em as I see 'em. What can I do for you?"

"Call me Robert. I'm neither Roman Catholic or a chaplain. I'm doing your father's funeral service and I wanted some background from people who knew him. I thought I would try here first."

"Everyone calls me Red, 'cause of my hair. And with the women, my middle name is Hot," he said with a wink. "You, know, Red Hot Franks. Like my wiener."

I didn't smile at his lame double entendre. In light of his father's recent death, it was more than inappropriate. "What can you tell me about your father?"

"He was a bastard." He held up a forefinger, as if suddenly struck by a thought. "No, wait. That's me. I'm the bastard. He was the asshole who never married my mother and then found some slut my age to bang."

I sighed. "I'm sorry you didn't get along with your father, but I'm looking for information I can use for his eulogy. Something other than . . . derogatory words. About his work here, maybe something on the last day when he got a phone call and left."

Red slowly stroked his beard. "Let's see. He showed up for work on time with a can of Coors in his hand. 'Breakfast of champions,' he used to say. Started riding me. Did a little work. Had me open him another Coors. Kept riding me. Did a little work. Had me open another Coors. Got a phone call. Yelled that some punks were messing with one of his rentals and he was going to kick

25

their butts, hopped in his truck and left. End of his day here. End of him."

"Okay. I get the idea. Can you say anything positive about him?"

He shrugged. "He was my sperm donor. When's the service? I might go for laughs."

"Tomorrow at one in the afternoon."

"Do I have to wear a shirt?"

"If you would. And maybe not a T-shirt."

"I'll see if I have a clean T-shirt. The words on it, I mean." He laughed. "I've got to get back to work. Someone's got to keep these jerks in line."

He picked up a two-by-twelve, put it across a couple of sawhorses and started at it with his Skilsaw, ending our conversation.

As I walked back to my car, I pondered what I would say about Jon Franks. Something other than he was a sperm donor for a crude son. He drank beer well?

A tap on my shoulder interrupted my thoughts. I turned to see one of the plywood carriers. He was the one with a shaved head and black goatee.

"Father, I heard you talking with Red and thought you might want to hear about what Jon was really like."

Maybe something positive? "I would love it."

"Well, Red's mom died of breast cancer about ten years ago and Jon was there with her when she died. Red went into the Army and was an MP at Fort Rucker, but got kicked out for puffing weed while on guard duty. He bummed around for a while until Jon brought him up here. Now he bums around here."

"He acts like he's the boss."

Shaved head shrugged. "I don't know. Our pay checks have 'Jon Franks Construction, Inc.' on them. No one else seems to be in charge. I need the money, so I'll keep working as long as I get a check." He spat on the ground. "Or until I deck that asshole. Sorry, that bastard."

"I get the idea you don't like Red, but what about Jon? Anything good about him?"

"Yeah. A lot. I've worked for Jon since he came here, about eight years ago. He builds a quality house. I've worked for guys who

26

took shortcuts to save a buck, but not Jon."

I needed something more personal. "How was he as a boss?"

"Cool. I mean, he expected you to show up for work and to do your job right, but the guy was really cool." He looked off into the distance, blinking. "My kid got hit by a car a couple of years ago. Hit and run. She was in the hospital, intensive care, for five days before she . . . ."

He took a breath. A tear rolled down his cheek. He didn't wipe it away. "I didn't have any medical. The hospital wanted their blood money. Threatened to take my house. Jon talked to them. Paid them something. A lot, I think. I wanted to pay him back, but he wouldn't even talk about it. That was Jon."

I wanted to put a comforting arm around his shoulder, but could see that this was the kind of guy who would take offense. All I could do was say, "I'm sorry for your losses. Both of your daughter and of Jon."

He shook his head. "Yeah, well . . . . I just hate hearing that pot-smoking punk say those things about his own father."

"I appreciate your telling me this. Can you add anything about the day Jon died?"

"Naw. It was pretty much like Red said. But all the screw ups he made was why Jon was riding his ass." He paused, shifting uneasily on his feet. "Jon did drink. I used to tell him that if he ever got stopped by the cops he would be busted. I don't think he cared. Like nothing mattered anymore."

"What about Lisa? How did they get together?"

"She's one hot piece of ass." He winced. "Sorry, Father. Anyway, they married about a year ago. Met at Higgins Diggins Saloon and drove over to Reno for a quickie wedding the next day. Must have been one hell of a night for Jon to do that. He was single when we left work on a Friday and he was married when we started on Monday."

"Did you get to know her?"

"Not really. Looked cheap, to me. She'd come around here with her tits half out and jeans so tight you could see her . . . ." He cleared his throat. "Anyway, Jon didn't seem to mind it at first. But then she stopped coming by. He said it wasn't good to have her hanging around the jobsite. Too much of a distraction."

27

"Everything seem okay between them?"

He shrugged. "Guess so. Jon didn't talk a lot. Never about him and Lisa."

How to put this? No easy way. "Do you know . . . if there was any violence?"

"Violence?" He looked quizzical for a moment, then angry. "Is she saying he beat her? She's a lying bitch. He loved her."

"I've never talked to Mrs. Franks about her relationship with Jon. It was just a rumor and–"

He grabbed my arm and shook me. Fire flashed in his eyes. "Lies! Nothing but lies. Tell me who said that crap and I'll set 'em straight. I'll kick the shi--"

"Stop. No one is going to kick anything out of anyone."

He glared at me, but I stared him down. He released my arm and backed away. I was sure his grip had left permanent indentations on my biceps.

"You've given me some good information for my eulogy, about how great Jon was to you. I promise that I'll use it."

He was calmer and back in control of himself, embarrassed at his outburst.

"Sure. Thanks. Sorry about the, you know, grabbing you like that."

I smiled. "No problem. All part of my job. The eulogy and forgiveness."

He started to turn away.

"Wait. I never got your name."

"Tony. Tony Mazzoni."

"Tony, I have one last question. The phone call Jon got. Any idea if it was really about his rental?"

Tony nodded. "He was pretty mad, yelling in his cell. He said something like, 'Those fu . . . . ,' I mean, 'Those freaking kids are messing with my property? I'll teach them.' Then he hopped in his truck and hauled ass out of here."

"So you know where he was headed?"

He shrugged. "Sorta. Jon has . . . had a bunch of rentals. Shacks he picked up for pretty cheap." He paused. "Maybe they weren't nothin' fancy, but he wasn't renting to any rich guys, ya know."

"Thanks. Will I see you at Jon's service?"

28

He nodded. "But the church roof will probably fall in when I walk through the door. I'm not a 'church' kind of guy, you know."

"No problem. Churches are for guys like you. And I can pretty much guarantee the roof will stay up. We just redid all the rafters last year with heavy-duty timbers."

He laughed, gave a dismissive wave and walked back to the job.

I noticed Red was watching us, but he quickly turned away when our eyes met.

Chapter 7

Self doubt settled on me as I drove away. Lisa had been out of town and had no proven motive. Well, he may have been a wife abuser, but maybe not. Red didn't like Jon, but that didn't mean he killed him. Every kid wasn't an Oedipus, no matter what Freud said. There were no other major suspects. Then there was the call to Jon's cell that let everyone off the hook. Maybe it was just an accident. My anonymous phone call had me tilting at windmills. Time to get back to doing the job the congregation hired me for and God had called me to do. Quit playing Sam Spade.

I stopped by the Golden Sunset Convalescent Hospital to visit a couple of my parishioners. One was George Miller, who was recovering from hip surgery and would soon be going home. The other one was Imogene Casper. Or at least that's how we all knew her. It had been her stage name.

I can't pretend I like going to these places. My mother had died in one similar. She'd died of cancer, but she'd also had Alzheimer's. It had been in a very highly-rated facility, but there always seemed to be the stench of disease and death in them, even in the best ones. And Golden Sunset was not the best. As I walked down the corridor of worn linoleum and chipped light green enamel, I saw trays of unwashed dishes and banana skins piled on a couple of carts.

After a quick chat with George, I looked for Imogene. I found her in the activities room, where the only activity I had ever seen was watching TV. She was sitting in a wheelchair, staring out of an unwashed window, her hands folded across a greyish-pink blanket in her lap. There was a tiredness in her eyes, lit by the flickering light from some reality show on the TV.

I pulled up a rickety wooden chair and sat next to her. She turned and smiled. Resting one talon-like hand on mine, she coyly batted her eyes as she primped her black, page-boy wig.

"Why, Father Bobbie, you should have warned me you were coming. I look a mess."

31

I smiled. I came every Wednesday at about this time. "I was just in the neighborhood and thought I would stop by to see Pike County's famous movie star."

"You charmer." She blushed. Or at least I thought she did. Hard to tell with so much white make-up. "Those days are long past."

"But you still look ravishing."

She twirled the end of her hair with an arthritic finger. "You're such a schmoozer." She paused, dropping her hand to the red silk scarf draped around her neck. "Did I ever tell you about when Claude Rains kissed me? I was an extra on the set of *Casablanca*, a girl in Rick's place, and the director had a scene in mind where Louie would make a pass at one of the waitresses. Me."

I rubbed my chin thoughtfully. "I can't say that I remember that one." Can't, because it would hurt her feelings. "Why don't you tell me?"

"I was young and pretty then." She squeezed my hand. "Now don't go saying that I still am. I may be forgetting things, but I'm not senile."

She settled back in her wheelchair, stroking her stained white blouse. "He may have been short, but that man could kiss." She giggled like a little girl. "And his mustache tickled, too."

I smiled and she continued to revel in her tale of her Hollywood glory days. Even if she had never been more than a bit actor.

Imogene had not quite finished her story before she was dozing in her chair, a little drool gathering at the side of her slack, lower lip. I dabbed it with my handkerchief. I glanced at my watch. I had just about enough time to make an appointment with Don, my junior warden, to talk about repairing the lights in the chancel. They had been flickering of late and I did not want some New Ager thinking Jon was "visiting" us during his funeral service.

I dropped by the front desk on my way out. Two women in blue nurse's scrubs, one tall, angular-faced, bleached blond with a ponytail and one short and fat with curly, gray-black hair, were chatting too much to notice me. I recognized them from my previous visits, but both were fairly new. The few times I'd seen them they always seemed to find a way of disappearing before I could talk to them.

"Excuse me, ladies. I just left Imogene Casper in the activities room and she's fallen asleep. Would one of you be so kind as to take her to her room?"

They both looked at me blankly. Then the tall one rolled her eyes and turned to her co-worker. "He means Irina Kaspersky. That old bag who thinks she's an actress." She glanced at me. "Who're you? Her grandkid or something? Why don't you take her?"

"No, I'm her pastor." I caught her name tag. "Julie, she may need personal attention and that is not the type of thing a pastor should be doing."

She shrugged. "I'll check on her after I have a cig break. If I get time." Her friend snickered.

I gritted my teeth. Lord, give me patience.

"Look," I said, keeping my voice calm even if I weren't, "I can go to your manager and complain. Mrs. Gertz, isn't it? If that doesn't work, I can call the State Ombudsman and register a formal complaint. I know Golden Sunset is already on thin ice after Mrs. Watkins died in her wheelchair in the activities room just last week. So let's do it the easy way and have your 'cig break' after you take care of Imogene."

Julie rolled her eyes, but started to mosey towards the activities room.

I turned and started to leave, but looked back to see Julie giving me the finger. I stared at her coldly. She dropped her gaze and her hand.

"One last thing about Imogene. She still has a good memory, so she will tell me how she was treated and it had better be nicely. Don't make me angry. You won't like me when I'm angry."

As I strode through the reception area with its fraying, stained gray carpet and out the door to the parking lot, I wanted to scream in frustration. Where was common human kindness? Concern for one's fellow man? I shook my head. Anyone who thinks society is progressing doesn't read the newspaper, watch TV or deal with people.

I stood by my car. Had I over-reacted? Perhaps. Maybe I would take in some candy for the caregivers' station next time I was there. Many were kind and hard working. But those like Julie and her friend made my blood boil. In my mind I could see them leaving my mother to soak in her own urine while they discussed the latest episode of *Real Housewives* of somewhere.

When I got to the church, Doris had already left. Among my telephone messages was one that said, "Don cancelled." Another said,

33

"Call your sister."

I braced myself as I picked up the phone in my office. It was never good when I called Janet. She was twelve years my senior, more like an aunt than a sister. There were just the two of us kids, but she was off to college when I was in first grade. Let's just say we were never close.

Janet picked up the phone on the first ring.

"Hello, Accident."

Obviously she had caller ID. She called me Accident because that was what Pop called me. He had thought he was safe from further fatherhood when I came along.

"Hello, Sister Dearest. To what do I owe the honor of your call?"

"We've got to do something about Pops."

"What about him?"

"You know what I mean," she spat out.

Ever since our mother died, Pops had changed. He retired and started spending money wildly, but he probably had far more from his real estate ventures than he could spend in two lifetimes. Since he loved music from the late '60's and early '70's and was a frustrated musician, his latest escapade had been buying a small recording studio, forming a rock band and recording his favorite music. The band had been pretty good, with Pops on bass guitar and back-up vocals, and sold well on Amazon and iTunes. Unfortunately, the band named themselves the Great-full Dead and the Grateful Dead rightly objected. The judge saw it their way and Pops was lucky to escape with only ceasing to market as Great-full Dead. Typically for the new Pops, he broke up the band and sold the studio rather than just change the band's name. Every so often, one of the CD's will crop up on eBay and sell for way more than it did new.

"Has he started a new band?"

She snorted. "I wish. It's what he's doing with his newest slut, Nadine."

I leaned back in my chair. "How much can an eighty-year old man be doing? And be careful what you say. She might be our stepmother someday."

"I sure as hell hope not, but she's spending his money like she is. He just bought her a new Lexus."

I sighed. "Let it go. He'll do what he wants no matter what anyone says. Especially me. And we both have more than enough from Mom's trust to keep us from starving."

"You're worthless. I'm stuck down here watching Pop throw away our inheritance and you don't give a rat's ass."

"I love Pops, but it's best I'm far away from him. You know that. But if you think it would do any good for me to come down to Pacific Palisades, I will."

She was silent for a moment. I could hear her breathing. "It'd be a waste. I don't know why I even called you."

"To hear my charming voice. Or maybe just to vent. Do it anytime you want. I'm here for you and am ready to go down if you want." I paused. "By the way, remember how you used to say, 'Don't make me angry. You won't like me when I'm angry?'"

"Yeah. What about it?

"Why did you say that?"

"It's from a TV show, *The Hulk*. I meant if you made me mad I'd go postal on you."

"Oh. Thanks. Glad I never made you mad."

"Right." A pause. "Bye, Accident."

"Bye, Sister Dearest."

I wondered if the caregiver had ever watched *The Hulk*.

My phone rang.

"St. Nicholas Church, Father Robert speaking."

A man's voice. "Don't you return your damn calls?"

"Sorry. I don't know what call you're talking about. I just got in and I'm going through my messages now."

"It's Red. I've got some dope for you on the old man's death."

I leaned forward. "I'm listening."

"Not now. I'm on the job. Meet me at Higgins Diggins at six."

I gave a short laugh. "I'm not really into the bar scene."

"Meet me."

The line went dead. It looked like I was going to Higgins Diggins.

Chapter 8

I remember a scene in the movie *Silverado* where Kevin Kline pushes through the swinging doors of a saloon and takes a deep breath before saying, "I love the smell of a saloon." As I entered Higgins Diggins, I could not relate to Kevin's comment in any way. Although smoking inside bars had been outlawed years ago, the stench of tobacco clung to the unvarnished pine walls like a dead skunk's spray. Combined with the aroma of stale beer and the sweaty bodies lined up at the long bar, it was nauseating. Holding my breath as much as I could, I surveyed the crowd, looking for Red.

Patrons were jammed together along the 19th century mahogany bar. From what I could see of it, it had once been a work of art, but now it had chipped ornate carving and a gilt-framed, beveled-glass mirror with peeling silver behind it. A classy lady with fading beauty. It seemed oddly out of place in the long, narrow room, but I knew from my reading that it had been saved from the old Empire Hotel when it burned down in the 1940's and just left there.

It was an interesting cast of characters in the room. Tattoos abounded, some even on the men. Maybe half of the men looked like construction workers with three-day beards and T-shirts, others like mountain men with full beards and plaid flannels with the sleeves rolled up. The women varied from young with long, black hair to old with bleached blond locks. Everyone was frantically laughing and drinking. There were plenty of rednecks and red necks, but no Red.

I saw a small table that appeared abandoned, with just a few empty beer glasses left by the previous occupants. I sat down, careful not to rest my arms on the amber puddles on the peeling-varnished table top. I glanced at my watch– 6:03. I wondered how long I should wait before considering this a waste of time.

A waitress wandered over with a tray, removed the glasses and gave a swipe across the table with a stained, wet bar towel. She stood in front of me, holding the tray against her hip with a sleeve-tattooed arm. Her tattoo had the wicked stepmother from "Snow White" interlaced with the red demon from "Fantasia" and Malificent from "Sleeping Beauty." Obviously, a Disney fan. Thin to the point of emaciation, her black tank top hung on her like it belonged to a Raiders' defensive tackle.

She studied me for a moment through dead eyes, blackened with heavy mascara. With my polo shirt and khaki trousers, no doubt she thought I had wandered in the wrong door.

"Whatcha want?"

"Umm." I hesitated, not wanting to order, but knowing I could not stay if I did not. "How about a Diet Coke. Very little ice."

A smile crept up one side her mouth and she turned and shouted to the bar. "Bart, ya got any 'Diet Coke' back there?"

She made it sound like an obscenity and several people turned and glanced my way with a smirk. Fortunately, I didn't know any of them. Unusual in our small community, but I didn't normally hang with this crowd.

Bart, the goateed bartender, shook his shaved head. "Ya know we do, Carly. Cut the crap and just do yer job."

Carly shrugged and sauntered away. The bar crowd soon lost interest. I glanced at my watch. 6:05.

By the time my watch read 6:31, I had nursed my ice-cube laden Diet Coke about as long as I could. I was ready to drop my four bucks for the Coke and a tip for great service on the table and leave, when Red walked through the door. Or should I say staggered.

He saw me and lurched to my table, plopping heavily in the captain's chair across from me. He grinned stupidly at me and said nothing.

Our waitress came over and gave him a half smile. "Same-old, same-old?"

He nodded.

She looked at me with a mocking grin. "A refill, Preacher-man? Or maybe some booze? It'd be live if you got turnt up."

Busted. How many others recognized me? It was a small town.

"No, I'm fine, thanks."

With a careless shrug, she turned and left.

I sat for a moment, wondering if it was worth asking Red

anything while he swayed in his chair. But I had already wasted half an hour waiting, so I would try.

"Red, why did you want to meet me?"

His eyes narrowed with suspicion. "I did?"

"Yes, you did. You called me from your jobsite and wanted to meet me here at six."

He cocked his head, puzzled.

"Red, you said it was about your dad."

A light flickered dimly in his eyes. "Ah. My dad. He's dead."

"Yes, he's dead." I dug in my pocket for my money clip. This was going nowhere fast. I had skipped dinner. Time to cut this short.

"And you wanna know who killed him." He smiled smugly.

I stopped digging. "Yes, I'd like to know who did."

Carly appeared with a glass of beer and a shot glass of amber liquor. A boilermaker, no doubt. Red dropped the shot glass into the beer and a sudsy overflow sloshed on the table. Carly rolled her eyes and left.

Red bent over and sipped his beer with the glass still on the table, then leaned back and sighed.

"Red, do you know who killed your father?"

He grinned and nodded.

"Who?"

He leaned forward and waved me to come close. Reluctantly, I complied. His breath could have wilted an oak tree.

"Follow the money," he said in a stage whisper. Then he leaned back and picked up his beer, dripping it all over his shirt.

"Follow the money? What money? His business? Life insurance?"

He took a noisy swig, burped, then laughed. "Ya don't know? Daddy was a loan shirk . . . loan shark."

"Loan shark. You mean like The Mob?"

"Nooooo." He laughed again, slapping his hand on the table. Faces turned to us. "Small time stuff. Loaned money to other builders. Hard money loans. Lotsa juice. If they were slow on paying, things happened. Baaad things."

"How bad?"

He shrugged. "A wall'd fall down. Maybe roof'd fall in.

39

Somebody might get hurt." He eyed me as he took another swig, then set his glass down. "Maybe even die."

I was stunned. "You're saying that Jon was a loan shark who even killed people?"

He spread out his hands in front of him. "Ya never know 'bout some people, do ya?"

"Why should I believe you?"

He cast his eyes heavenward. "Forgive me, Father, for I have shinned." He dropped his gaze and met mine with a cold stare. "I may have helped a floor jerst . . . joist or a rafter to go boom a time or three. It was the only O.T. that cheap ash . . . asshole ever paid."

I was silent for a moment, considering how oddly coherent Red was for a drunk.

Carly moseyed over.

"You dudes want anything else?"

I shook my head. "I'm fine."

I reached into my pocket for my money. I had to get away from this place, this person who could do such evil things without remorse. He reached across and clamped my arm with a grip like the jaws of a pit bull.

"Thish one's on me. Your money's no good here. Right, Carly?"

She shrugged. "Whatever."

He released my arm and, with a grin, turned to the waitress. "I'll have another, ya sexy bitch. I've finished givin' the Father my confeshon."

I rose from my hard, uncomfortable chair, feeling dirty. "Thanks for the Coke."

Still grinning, he turned to me with a quick wave. "See ya round."

When I got to the door, I glanced back. Carly was standing close to Red, looking a bit bored as he stroked her skinny, jean-clad buttocks while he finished his beer. He must be a good tipper.

I walked home, seething with righteous anger. I'd been used and I knew it. A little phony slurring and swaying did not a drunk make. He was no more drunk than I was. He'd given me information he knew I'd follow up on. But why the charade? Had he been my mystery caller? Had he'd used the "confession" routine to try to keep me from turning him in for his admitted crimes, but with no intent of actual confession and penance?

There was no seal of confession. I'd send a letter about this to the bishop to put in his "red file" of potential problems. I had no qualms about turning Red in. But if I told the police, he'd say he'd been drunk and didn't remember saying anything like that. Besides, I doubted that the cops would be interested in an uncorroborated story like he'd told me. No names, places or dates. I had nothing but the loan shark angle as a motive for Franks' "murder."

As much as I hated to admit it, Red had succeeded. Like some detective in a cliché-ridden movie, I'd "follow the money."

Chapter 9

Saturday, the day for Jon Franks' memorial service, was memorable. It started with a series of mini-disasters and didn't get better.

Weather.com had predicted a possibility of a cold rain, but not very likely. Any snow in Buggy Springs in November is unusual. The odds of an eight-inch storm before Thanksgiving is about as good as having a christening in a Southern Baptist church. So when I woke up with a thick blanket of white on my front porch, I was dumbfounded. At least we hadn't lost power. Yet. Outages often happened after a snowstorm. Snow so early that the trees hadn't had a chance to have their leaves fall did not bode well for our town's electrical grid. So I started the coffee brewing while the current was still flowing, pulled on my boots and down coat and fired up my snow blower to clear my steep driveway.

While I trudged behind the blower as it struggled through the wet snow, I grumbled to myself about the unfairness of it all. Then I glanced around at the beauty surrounding me; I was mentally chastened. I had moved here because I loved the trees and the change of seasons, so stop complaining. I looked skyward. Thanks, God, for reminding me.

Once the driveway was reasonably cleared, I went inside, shed my heavy gear and poured a mug of tea. There had been no paper delivery, so I had no crossword puzzle to do. As I turned on my computer to check emails after my Morning Prayer, the phone rang.

"The rectory. Father Robert speaking."

"Father Robert, I want you to do something for me." It was Lisa.

"Anything I can. What is it?"

"Don't say anything about Jon. Just do the stuff out of the Prayer Book."

I was taken aback.

"Don't you want a time for people who knew Jon to share their memories?"

"No. Just the service from the Prayer Book."

"If you want that, Lisa, it's not a problem. I, uh . . . I assume you have your reasons."

"I do."

I waited, expecting some further explanation, but all I got was silence. I finally broke it.

"Well, I'm digging out of the snow, like you probably are, so I'd better get back at it. I'll see you at the service."

"Yes, I'll see you about one." There was a long pause. "Thanks, Father Robert."

The line went dead. Really dead. I could not get a dial tone. Thanks, snow.

I stood a moment, holding the phone, thinking. I had already prepared a short eulogy, based mainly upon what Tony Mazzoni had said, but dropping that was not a problem. I'd spent more time researching than writing anyway. Having the "grieving widow" nix any eulogy or remembrances was very strange, though. What was going on?

I sipped my tea as I sat down at my computer. I'm on cable, which is very fast when it's working. When it's working is the key phrase. It wasn't. Snow, again.

That was a problem. We had recently put the heater at church on a new thermostat that was very high tech. You could access it from any computer if you had the code. It was a gift from a parishioner who loved gadgets. But this sudden storm had come on a cold front that turned out far worse than forecasted and the thermostat setting was programmed low on Saturdays. I glanced at the clock. It was ten o'clock and the service was set for one in the afternoon. Barely enough time to knock the chill off the nave if I got down there quickly.

After a quick shower and shave, I hopped into my old Ford pickup. During the good weather, I drove my Camaro, but my '83 Ford Ranger four-wheeler was my foul-weather friend. While the once-dark-blue paint was faded and scratched, it was always ready with its rugged, off-road tires to carry me through the roughest weather. Except when it wouldn't start. And it decided that morning it was staying in the warm garage. The starter turned the engine over until it died, but the engine never fired.

44

I'm no mechanic. I can change the oil (when I feel like getting greasy), air up the tires and keep it full of gas, but that's about it. I needed to get a ride or at least get someone to turn on the heat at church. I pulled out my cell to call Don, the junior warden, but it wasn't working. No doubt the tower was out of service because of the water-heavy snow.

I sighed and set off through the snow on foot. I was just up the road from the church, off on a narrow side street, and often enjoy walking the half mile to it. On a cool spring or autumn day, it is quite relaxing, but slogging there through eight inches of wet snow is like jogging in twenty pound boots. Before I got to the church, I was soaked from sweat and from clumps of snow falling from the trees. I was wearing a narrow-brimmed wool fedora that protected the top of my head, but my wool pea jacket was sopping wet. Stupid. I knew better than to wear a wool coat in a wet snow. As soon as I got in the church, I'd crank up the heat and put the coat over a vent to dry.

As I started to cross the street to the church, I heard a loud crack, like a high-powered rifle. A huge, leafy, snow-encrusted branch from an oak tree crashed down not thirty feet in front of me. As it did, it took down some power lines, sending sparks flying as they were pulled from an overhead transformer. I said a silent prayer of thanks that I had not been walking any faster.

My hand was shaking as I opened the front door. I flicked up the light switch. Nothing. No electricity. So much for heat in the church. Or drying my jacket. It was going to be one cold service. Probably in more ways than one.

Not long before one, a crowd of mourners began to fill the church. If you consider eight people a crowd, that is. I had lighted all the oil-filled "candles" in sconces along the wall and candlesticks behind the altar, but they did little to help the dim light filtering through the stained-glass windows on both sides of the nave and in the back of the chancel. I stood by the door in my vestments that hid the holey flannel shirt (or holy, in this instance) I had scrounged from our help-the-homeless donations. My black chasuble added a little warmth, but not much.

The first to arrive was Lisa, escorted by Red. Under her arm she carried a miniature coffin of dark wood and brass. After she shook my hand, she pointed to the coffin.

"I brought Jon. Red made this for him out of walnut."

God forgive me, I almost said, "Jon always looked so much taller when he was alive." But I didn't. I just nodded, smiled sadly and asked, "His ashes?"

Red laughed. "Yeah, he was always wanting Lisa to haul his ashes."

She glared at him and went inside. Red grinned at me and followed, without taking off his black ballcap.

Next came a red-headed woman, maybe forty, in a black coat and snow boots. When she opened her coat, she revealed that she was stuffed into a short, black dress like a sausage. It wasn't that she was fat, but any extra pounds were accentuated by her clothes. In the dim light, it was hard to see her face that well, except that she had heavy makeup. Her eyes were red and she had a wad of kleenex clutched in her hand. She hurried past me, head down, avoiding my outstretched hand.

Then came Tony, who pulled off his snow-crusted ball cap as he walked in with a petite young woman with short brown hair and a spider web tattooed on her cheek.

"Father, this is my wife, Brandy."

"Nice to meet you, Brandy. Thanks for coming in this weather. I'm sure Lisa appreciates it, too."

She looked at me with eyes smoldering with rage. "Tony'd have come if it was twenty feet out there. Jon wasn't any saint, but he helped us out when we really needed it. But all this church crap doesn't matter to me. And I don't give a damn about that slut he married."

I took a breath. "I'm glad you're here, though. I'm sure Jon would be too."

Next came three men together. One of them was older, maybe mid-sixties. He wasn't tall, but broad-shouldered and tough-looking. He glared at me from under gray, bushy eyebrows and limped inside with his soggy, straw cowboy hat still on his head. He was followed by two beefy young men in down coats and matching Raiders ball caps who never glanced my way.

I looked upward. "Lord, what have you gotten me into?"

Then I walked up to a small table in front of the altar, where Jon's Lilliputian casket rested.

46

I surveyed the pews. Those I knew were in the front pews, those I did not were in the back.

"First, I would like to apologize for the lack of lighting and heat, but this storm has taken out our power."

"Hah," said the old man in the back. "I always said it'd be a cold day in hell when I was in church with that crook Jon Franks."

I saw Tony start to move, but his wife held him back. I had to take control or this could become the scene of the next Ultimate Fighter.

"Sir, this is the house of the Lord." I used my best schoolmaster tone. "If you cannot respect Jonathan Franks and his widow, then I ask that you respect this place of worship." I paused. "And kindly remove your hats."

Red rolled his eyes, but he took off his Raiders ballcap. The old man in the back glared at me but the unknown redhead went over and pulled his hat off his head. His companions slowly removed their caps, whether out of respect for the church or fear of the redhead didn't really matter.

I opened my prayer book to The Burial of the Dead on page 469.

"I am the resurrection and the life," I began.

After I finished the rite, the mourners could pay "last respects" to the deceased. First Lisa kissed her hand and touched the casket. Red walked by without a glance. Tony and Brandy stood a moment at the altar, his arm around her shoulders. Then he gently rested his free hand on the casket for a moment and went back to his pew. The redhead, dabbing her eyes with one hand, gently touched the casket with the other. I was standing close enough to smell the alcohol on her breath. Next came the old guy, long gray hair and bald spot now exposed. He stood for a moment, giving the casket a glare colder than the one he had given me. He grabbed the casket, opened it and spat inside.

I was momentarily too stunned to do anything.

He turned and walked toward the door.

Red laughed loudly.

Tony let out an anguished roar and started out of his pew, Brandy clinging to him to hold him back.

I recovered my senses and rushed down the aisle, just ahead of Tony. The two beefy men blocked my way while the old guy grinned at me from behind their protection.

"I don't cotton to any of this religion stuff, so feel free to kick the crap out of him," he said with a smirk.

"You have defiled the house of God and made a mockery of this service." My hands were clenched tightly at my side. "Leave now and do not come back unless it is to repent."

"And who's going to make us?" He sneered as he spoke.

I leaned forward. "I will."

When Jesus drove the moneychangers out of the temple, he never considered the odds. At that point, I didn't either. I'm no small guy and did some boxing years ago, but I was outweighed and outnumbered. I didn't care. Righteous anger.

"And I will." It was Tony, who had walked up behind me.

"And me." It was the redhead, her voice slurring.

The beefy guys looked at each other and then back at the old guy. He shrugged.

"Aw, hell. I've done what I meant to do, boys. Let's get outta here."

After they left, I was shaking. Rage, adrenaline, maybe even a little latent fear. I was hardly aware of the mourners as they left. The redhead ducked out without a word. Red grinned at me. Tony and Brandy mumbled something appreciative before they left. Lisa took my hand, holding it tightly as she said how wonderful the service had been, while Jon was tucked under her other arm.

After I put on my still-wet coat and locked up the church, I trudged home. Of course, there was no power there either. I was chilled to the bone. After putting on dry clothes and a warm sweater, I fired up the wood stove. As I sat close to it warming my hands, I sneezed. Great. I was getting a cold. My last mini-disaster for the day.

Chapter 10

Sunday morning, the sky was blue. The snow clouds were gone, but the ground was still white out my window. My indoor-outdoor thermometer said that it was twenty-eight outside and fifty-five inside. My trusty stove had struggled to keep the old Victorian warm, but, just like buying a back-up generator, I had delayed putting in new insulation and double-pane windows. I hated messing with hundred-plus year-old craftsmanship and was paying the price. Sometimes keeping things original was just plain stupid.

I sipped my hot cup of tea and mopped my runny nose. With my heavy cardigan pulled close around my neck, I was still cold. Even if it hadn't been so frigid outside, my sweater wouldn't have kept me warm. I had the chills. I should not go to church and infect the congregation, but could not leave them standing out in the cold either.

My phone was still dead but my cell phone worked. Thank God for small favors. Unfortunately, the wardens' and church secretary's home phones must still be out and they weren't answering. I knew Doris and Jim both lived in those mysterious black holes we had in the area where there's no cell phone reception, but Willy Sutton, my senior warden, didn't answer either. I left messages on everyone's cell phone about my plight, then made another cup of tea to drink as I dressed for my trek to church.

We have two morning services, one at 8:30 and the other at 10:00. I was tempted to wait and see if I got a call back, but I could not leave the early service attenders out in the cold. So at 7:30, I stoked the fire in the stove to try to keep the house warm and set out.

I was wearing my warmest clothes: a heavy down coat, Sorel boots and my wide-brimmed Tilley to keep my head dry. The steep drive was a sheet of ice, so I carefully crunched through the snow alongside it. The icy crust gave me a firm footing, but I was starting to feel weak and tired before I even got to the road. It was going to be a long walk.

About halfway to church, my cell rang. Well, it played

"Scotland the Brave," my ringtone. I pulled off my thick glove with my teeth and dropped it to the ground, tugging my phone out of my pocket.

"Hello. Robert speaking."

"Father? This is Willy. I just turned on my cell when I got to church and got your message. Are you okay?"

I coughed. "I've been better. Just a cold, so I'll live."

"Where are you?"

"About halfway to church."

"You're not on foot, are you?"

"Yes. It was easier than walking on my hands." I started to laugh, but coughed instead.

"What about your truck?"

"Battery's dead."

"Why not jumpstart it from your Camaro?"

Good question. Where did I have cables for that? Somewhere in the garage, if I remembered right.

"I, uh . . . guess I'm not thinking right. Besides, I figured the road was still blocked."

I could hear Willy talking to someone. "Father, wait where you are. The cavalry is on the way to take you home. There's only four of us, so we'll just do Morning Prayer."

I started to argue. Robert the martyr would be there. But who was I fooling? It would be better for me to stay away even if I could actually stand long enough to do a Communion service.

"I'll be waiting."

I ended the call, stumbled over to a tree and leaned against it.

A few minutes later, I heard the roar of an engine before I saw the truck. It was a new Chevy four-by-four, jacked up on tires so big they looked as tall as I am. With no chains, the driver had it revved high to keep moving, shooting rooster tails of snow behind it. It stopped in front of me and the passenger door popped open. Tony Mazzoni, the late Jon Franks' employee, grinned at me from behind the wheel.

"Hey, Father, need a lift?"

I sighed in relief as I settled into the leather bucket seat with the heater blasting on my feet. "More than you know. So the road is open?"

He shrugged. "Sorta. If you don't mind driving over a few lawns. But they're covered with snow anyway."

I shook my head. "Looks like I will have a few fences to mend after this. Or lawns to replant."

He waved his calloused hand. "No worries. I'll handle it."

When we got to my house, he tried to get up the icy drive a couple of times, but finally agreed with me to park on the street and walk up. He took my arm and helped me stagger up the hill like I was an old man. I was too weak to protest. I persuaded him to come inside for a cup of tea.

The first thing he did was restock my wood pile by the stove. While he stoked the fire in the stove, I made the tea. As I handed him a hot mug of English Breakfast, I asked, "How did you happen by the church when I called?"

He looked uncomfortable. "I didn't just happen by. I went there on purpose."

I was stunned, happily so. "You came to church?"

"Yeah, well, the roof didn't fall in or nothing yesterday. And you seemed pretty cool. For a preacher, I mean. So I thought I would see what all this church stuff is about."

"And I wimped out."

"Man, you sure as hell didn't wimp out. If I hadn't got to you, they might have found your bones when the snow thawed. That's loyalty to your people."

I started to laugh, but coughing took over again. I finally got control. "That's a pretty big exaggeration. However, speaking of loyalty, I do have a couple of questions about Jon. Will you help me?"

He looked away. "I'm not saying nothing bad about Jon."

"I wouldn't ask you to. But others have and his memorial service makes me wonder. Will you help me?"

He met my eyes. "Yeah, sure. If I can."

I settled in my rocking chair by the stove, wrapped again in my cardigan and mug of tea in hand, and motioned for Tony to sit in the chair next to me.

"Tell me, Tony, do you know any of the three men or the woman who came to Jon's service and sat in the back?"

"Sure. The three guys were the Zachary's. Ben and his two sons, Choke and Chewy. The woman was Cindy. Cindy Wolfe."

51

"Okay, I now know their names. How about what they do and why they reacted the way they did at the service? Loved him or hated him."

He shifted uneasily in his chair. "Well, before Lisa, Jon was . . . ya know . . . . He and Cindy were going at it. She still had the hots for him, I guess. Ben owns Beezer's Bar a few miles down Forty-nine. He's got sorta a saying, 'If you wanna get blitzed, go to Beezer's.' It's that kinda place, ya know."

I sneezed into my handkerchief and wiped my nose. "I know. I've heard of Beezer's. What I don't know is why he hated Jon."

Tony shrugged. "You'd have to ask him."

"One thing that bothers me, Tony. The way Cindy acted was not like a jilted lover. More like a current lover."

"You don't have to worry about that stuff, being a priest, but a guy needs to have his woman, ya know, do it for him. After they got married, Lisa wouldn't hardly spread her legs. Jon didn't talk about it much, but he loosened up one night when we had a few beers after work. Cindy still loved him. So what?" He stood. "That all?"

"One last thing. I heard something about Jon making loans to people, usurious loans. Do you know anything about that?"

He looked to the floor, not meeting my eyes. "I don't know what that 'user-whatever' crap means, but he just helped people out. Maybe they didn't like that he wanted his money back after a while, but that wasn't Jon's fault. I gotta go."

I pulled myself to my feet. "Look, I'm not trying to defame Jon's memory. I just want to understand him. You've been a great help. And I really appreciate you saving me on the road." I put out my hand. "Thanks."

Tony shook my hand and slowly smiled. "No problem, Father. I get a little, ya know, protective of Jon. He was good to me."

I walked him to the door, stopping only for a coughing spasm.

Tony paused at the door. "Ya got enough food to last a couple of days?"

"Plenty of canned soup and chili. Not a gourmet menu, but easy to heat on the stove."

He studied me with a concerned look. "Look, Father, my wife's a nurse. I'm going to have her stop by tomorrow."

I started to say, "That's okay, I'll be fine," but the coughing hit again.   By the time I recovered, he was gone.   I was left with a number of unanswered questions.   Like what kind of person names his kids Choke and Chewy?

Chapter 11

It was six o'clock on a cold, clear morning. I had spent the rest of the day before shivering. I had gone to bed under a warm down comforter, but it was soaked by midnight. Night sweats. I finally got up about four, made some tea and tried to read Tim Blanning's *The Pursuit of Glory* by a kerosene lamp. Concentrating on the French Revolution was impossible, though, so I just sat in misery as I awaited the dawn.

I had phone service again, but still no power. I huddled in my rocker near the wood stove, wrapped in my heaviest cardigan and a tartan wool blanket. As I sipped from a spoon of hot chicken soup, an image flashed in my mind of Scrooge eating reheated gruel in *A Christmas Carol*. Odd how quickly we can go from hale and hearty to feeling like death would be an improvement. I was trying to keep my teeth from chattering long enough to eat when I heard a noise, the sound of a small gasoline engine.

I got up and went to look out the kitchen window, where the noise seemed to be originating. I saw a shape of a man, dimly outlined by a flashlight he was holding, at the door for the house's heater, hovering over what looked like a generator. There was a knock at the door and I went to it, carrying my lamp. When I opened the door, I was hit by the freezing air.

Brandy, Tony's wife, stood on my doorstep, holding a large pot.

"I'm freezing my butt off out here, so step aside before I drop this soup all over your porch."

She brushed past me before I had a chance to respond and set the pot on my stove. She pulled back the hood of her parka and looked me up and down.

"You look like hell. Sit down before you fall down and let me check you out."

I obeyed, mainly because I was about to fall down. I forced a smile. "This is a surprise. If I'd known you were coming--"

"You'd have baked me a cake."

I looked at her in surprise. I had that song on an old Eileen Barton record I'd inherited from my grandmother and hadn't listened to it for years.

"So you're into old music?" She didn't look the type.

She looked at me oddly. "Old? The Maxes only recorded it a few years ago."

"Ah." The Maxes, of course. Whoever they were.

She pulled off her snow gloves and dug into a satchel slung across her shoulder, bringing out a tongue depressor and small flashlight. "Say that again."

"So you're not into old music?"

"No. Ahhhh."

"Ahhhh." Then I coughed.

She checked out my throat, then my heartbeat and breathing with quick efficiency before sticking an electronic thermometer under my tongue. Only then did she drape her stethoscope across the back of her neck, slip off the satchel and remove her coat. The forced-air heater had come on, thanks to the generator.

"What's the prognosis, Doc?" I managed to mumble.

She pulled the thermometer out, studied it, then gave me a quick smile. "You'll live. At least for a while. But you'll never sing opera."

Her voice was low, almost masculine. It was incongruous to her petite form. Dressed in a black turtleneck, black jeans and black boots, she looked like a Goth elf. She took the mug of soup I had been eating, sniffed it and poured it down the garbage disposal.

"Do you have a ladle?"

"Uh, yeah. Second drawer down on the right of the sink."

She ladled soup from the pot she had put on the stove and handed it to me.

"Your prescription for now is chicken soup."

I looked over at the sink. "That's what was already in my mug."

She sneered. "That canned crap? The sodium alone will kill ya."

I took her soup and began to eat. It was really good.

"Great soup." I was feeling a little better already. "But isn't it illegal for nurses to prescribe."

56

"I'm a nurse practitioner, so no. Anything else? I have to get to work soon."

"I do appreciate this. You and Tony are great."

She shrugged, "That's Tony. Once he likes you, he's there for you any time. Just don't get on his bad side."

"Like Red. But he sure seems to have liked Jon."

She shrugged again, but looked down and said nothing.

"How did you feel about Jon? He helped you two a lot, didn't he?"

Brandy took a deep breath. "He did that. When Jody got sick, he did everything he could to help. Money, paid time off for Tony. You name it."

"But?"

"He was a dirty old man. He seemed to always brush my tits or my ass when he got close. Always forgetting to look up at my face. Really great when we needed help, but he wasn't the saint Tony thinks."

"So Tony never knew."

Fear crept in her eyes. "Don't ever tell him. It'd kill him."

"Don't worry. But did Jon ever try to . . . go further?"

"I was on the streets when I was fourteen. You name it, I probably did it. So if he'd wanted me to go to bed with him for helping Jody, it'd been no biggie to me. It'd kill Tony if he found out, though. We got together when I was seventeen and he's the reason I'm a nurse. I owed Jon a lot for his help, but I owe Tony my life. I'll protect him any way I can."

She turned away, but I thought I saw tears in her eyes.

A knock at the door. It must be Tony.

I stood as she grabbed her coat and gloves. As soon as she had them on, she picked up her satchel.

"Look, stay warm and inside, eat your soup and take ibuprofen for the fever. I've got to get to work. I'll check on you later."

Without another word, she hurried out the door.

Tony stuck his head inside. "Hey, Father Robert, I put a new battery in your truck and brought an old generator I had for your heater. The road's open and PG&E says you'll have power by this afternoon. I've got to get Brandy to work now, but call me if you need anything."

"I'm fine. Thanks so much for everything." I waved to him. "And thank Brandy."

"Sure will."

He closed the door. I settled back into my chair and picked up my mug of homemade soup.

Just after eight that morning, the phone began to ring off the hook. I had a phone hard-wired at the rectory for emergencies like this. The first call was from Doris, the church secretary.

"Oh, Father Robert, I just heard how bad you are. Can I do anything to help? Call an ambulance or something?"

"I'm not that sick, Doris. Just the flu. I'll be fine."

"Are you sure? I really want to help if I can."

"I'm sure."

After a number of much-the-same calls from several parishioners, I got a very different one.

"Hello?"

Long pause.

"Hello?"

No response. I was almost ready to hang up.

"Father Bruce, look up Exodus, chapter thirty-four, verses six and seven."

It was the same raspy voice again. What was in Exodus 34? Old Testament law, if I remembered correctly. Was it about Moses and the new stone tablets of the law? Fortunately, I had a Bible close at hand and grabbed it, trying to kill time while I looked it up.

"So, you're into the law? If you are passing judgment on others, don't forget about removing the log from your own eye before worrying about the speck in someone else's."

"God judges. I execute."

Frantically, I flipped the pages. Chapter 34. I was right. The second set of tablets that replaced the ones Moses destroyed when he saw his people worshiping an idol.

"Are you tracing this call, Father?"

"No. I have no way to trace this call. I'm just reading the verses you gave me. By the way, I solved your first riddle about Humpty Dumpty." The caller seemed rather arrogant. Maybe I could get a rise out of him. "Pretty easy, you know."

"Then riddle me this: It ain't a child's toy that gives that kin of a polecat its demise. At least you know what the change will revise."

58

The caller hung up.

I read the passage.

"And he passed in front of Moses, proclaiming, 'The Lord, the Lord, the compassionate and gracious God, slow to anger, abounding in love and faithfulness, maintaining love to thousands, and forgiving wickedness, rebellion and sin. Yet he does not leave the guilty unpunished; he punishes the children and their children for the sin of the parents to the third and fourth generation."

Talk about out of context and a bad translation, that was it. I checked the lectionary and found Exodus 34:1-8 was the Old Testament reading for the Feast of the Holy Name, January 1st. Was it just luck, or was the caller taunting me with readings of the Episcopal lectionary?

The riddle made no sense until I looked up polecat. Then the lights came on, literally and figuratively. A pop gun is a child's toy and the kin of the polecat is a weasel and a son is also kin. The change is money and also revise is change, as in Jon's will. Nursery rhymes, again.

I grabbed the phone and punched in the Chief's number. When I got him on the line, I said, "Chief, you need to find Todd Franks. I think his life is in danger. He's going to be shot for his inheritance."

59

Chapter 12

The Chief didn't answer me for a moment.

"Don't tell me. You got another phone call from your guardian angel."

"More like my personal demon. But, yes, I did."

"And he said he was going to kill Red Franks."

I paused. "Well, in so many words."

"What words?"

"Umm. It had to do with children paying for the sins of their fathers and *Pop Goes the Weasel*."

I could almost sense him roll his eyes.

"Great. Another Bible quote and nursery rhyme. And I don't suppose you now have caller I.D.?"

"I've never needed it before this." I rubbed my burning forehead. It hurt to think. "Look, can't you check on who just called me through the phone company?"

"Not without a court order or your written permission. I'll see everyone who called you recently, though. Is that okay?"

"Sure." But who all had called me that morning? Oh, heck. Scott Williams, Mr. Conspiracy Theory himself. He thought the CIA arranged to have the Twin Towers collapse. Don't even mention the Grassy Knoll. If he found out I'd given his name and unlisted number to "the authorities" .... "No, I can't do that."

"Then we're done. Have a nice day."

"No, wait." There must be a way to get the number to the Chief without violating any trusts. "Tell you what, let's meet at the phone company. Have them get my records on their computer screen. Then I can look at who called and give you the number of our mystery man."

"When?"

"I'll be there in fifteen."

"It's a date."

We met at the sterile, concrete-block building that housed our local AT&T office. After some urging by both the Chief and myself, the rep finally called up the screen with recent calls to my number. I had the St. Nicholas member directory, but I didn't need it. I knew the time of the call and there was one number I didn't recognize.

The Chief wrote it down. "I'll get it checked out. I'll let you know what happens."

"Can't you get it right now? Red might be dead if it takes too long."

The Chief sighed. "You must watch a lot of police shows on TV. This is a cell phone. Not a local one, either. It'll take a while."

"Wait." I was getting desperate. "I don't have Red's home number and it's not in the phone book, but you can get it. Can't you at least call him?"

"I'm way ahead of you. I did that right after we talked and I even had a patrolman go by his place and he isn't there."

"How about his job site? Have you tried that?"

"How could I when I don't know where it is?"

"I do. 14579 Ridge Court."

The Chief raised an eyebrow. "And why didn't you say this before? I could have had one of my guys check it out already. Now they're all busy. I'll have to check it out myself."

"Uh, sorry I, uh . . . I've been sick." I managed a sickly grin. Where was a coughing fit when I needed it? No cough, just a bad sore throat. "Really. I'm not running on all cylinders right now."

"Okay, I'll let it go." He grinned. "This time."

After giving the phone company a quick thanks, we went out into the cold. The Chief started to get into his patrol car.

"Wait," I said. "You'll never get there in that. Doesn't the department have four-wheelers? Like those guys in *Law and Order: SUV*?"

"That's *Law and Order: SVU*. Special Vic–" He stopped when he saw my smile. "Smart ass."

"Let's take my truck. Old Blue won't have a problem."

After a bumpy, wheel-spinning trip up the muddy driveway, we got to Red's job site. Tony and a couple of other guys were clearing snow off the plywood floors. Tony stopped and came over to us as we got out of the truck.

"Father, you should be home in bed. What gives?"

"We're looking for Red. Doesn't look like he's here."

"Nope. He hopped into his truck and split about an hour ago, as soon as he'd bossed everyone around like he was God. Must have thought he might have to do some work."

"Any idea where he went?"

He shrugged. "Any bars open yet?"

The Chief pulled out his cell phone. "I'll need the info on what he drives. I'll have my guys keep an eye out for his truck."

I was feeling pretty tired and decided to go back to my truck and sit down while the Chief got his information. I was almost there when a wave of weakness washed over me. Or maybe I should say hit me in the face. I reached out for a nearby tree and missed. Next thing I knew I was lying in the slush looking up at Tony's worried face.

"You okay, Father?"

I tried to think. How did I get on the ground? "I'm, uh . . . fine. Great."

The Chief knelt beside me, checked my pulse and felt my forehead. "You're burning up."

"Look, I'm just a little dizzy. I'll be fine."

"I'm taking you to emergency."

"No you're not. I'm going home. I just need some rest."

"You need—"

"I want to go home," I interrupted. "I'll call my doctor when I get there. No hospital."

I sat up, but got dizzy again. "I would appreciate a hand, though."

Tony picked me up like I was a baby and carried me to my truck. No mean feat, in light of my six-two, one eighty-five pound size. He put me in the passenger side and the Chief got in the driver's. Tony fastened my seat belt like I was a helpless child and gave me an admonishing look.

"You should go to the emergency room."

I shook my head and managed a smile. "That's for sick people."

When I got home, the Chief made sure I was bundled up and had a hot cup of tea before he left, promising to return my truck as soon as he could. Sitting in my rocker in front of the wood stove, I was dozing when my door flew open and hell's fury stormed in.

Actually, it was Brandy, but she was doing a good imitation.

63

She stomped over and stood, arms akimbo, in front of me.

"What the hell do you think you're doing?"

I looked down at the half-full cup on the table next to me. "Having a cup of tea?"

"Tony called me, so I know." She brandished a tongue depressor like a sword. "Open."

I obeyed and she stuck in the depressor.

"Damn," she muttered.

"Whaaa?" I asked around the wooden stick.

"Looks like strep. I'll take a culture. I'm starting you on Amoxicillin. You're not allergic to it, are you?"

"Naaa."

She took a swab of my throat, then stuck a thermometer under my tongue just as the phone rang. She walked over and picked up the receiver.

"Father Robert Bruce's residence."

A pause.

"I'm his nurse. Who the hell are you?"

I struggled to my feet to grab the phone, but she motioned me down and brought it to me.

"It's the chief of police," she said, as she handed me the phone.

I grabbed it. "Chief? Sorry about that. My nurse can be a little . . . brusque."

"That's not what I'd call it. Hope she's a better nurse than receptionist. I called to let you know the cell phone is a throw away. But we found Red."

Were we too late? "And he's dead?"

"If he doesn't practice safe sex, he may be soon. One of my guys spotted his car by a duplex on Orion Court. He was busy with some girl. He came to the door in just a T-shirt. Red's fine, but my guy may never recover."

Home of skinny Carly from Higgins Diggins, perhaps? Poor girl.

"Maybe the killer hasn't acted yet." I offered lamely.

"Or maybe all these calls are just a hoax. Anyway, your truck is on its way,"

"Thanks, Chief. Sorry about all this."

"Yeah, well, next time you think of calling about some

64

anonymous tip, don't.   This department is too small to chase geese."

"Yeah.   Sorry, and thanks again."

As I hung up, Brandy stood in front of me, looking official in her blue scrubs, and handed me a glass of water and a pill.

"Take your medicine."

I sighed.   "I just did."

Chapter 13

By 10:00 the next morning, I was feeling much better. I had answered my emails (except for offers to invest in Nigerian get-rich-quick schemes), already said Morning Prayer, done my crossword puzzle and was relaxing with a cup of tea with honey and lemon as I watched a streaming video of BBC's *Inspector Lewis*. I heard a tap on the door.

"It's open," I called. It hurt my still-sore throat.

The Chief came in and gave me a hard look.

"You always leave your door unlocked?"

I shrugged. "Never had a problem."

"You never lived in Colton." He glanced over at the TV. "English cops, huh? Have you solved the case?"

"You watch these shows?"

He shook his head. "Not my cup of coffee. My wife likes them, though. I'd never be a cop where I couldn't carry a gun. Anyway, I'm sorry I ran you through the wringer about Red. I was P.O.'ed about wasting so much time on such a scumbag."

"I'm sorry I wasted your time. If Red were in danger, I had to act. He may be no saint, but we're all sinners and equal in the eyes of God. His life is worth me making a fool of myself."

"You did." He smiled. "Didn't someone say something about being a fool for God?"

I was impressed. "St. Francis of Assisi. Anyway, I would appreciate it if you could keep an eye out for Red. I'm not sure this was a hoax."

"Right. I'll assign my best detectives to do that."

"I'm not kidding, Chief."

"I am. I have three men and no detectives. Red's a big boy and can take care of himself."

Could I blame him for thinking this was a big joke? "Well, thanks for what you've done. But ask your guys to keep watch. As a personal favor."

"You're about out of those." He paused. "Okay, I'll tell them to watch out for anyone trying to whack Red. Good enough?"

"Yeah." Best I could hope for, under the circumstances.

He walked to the door. "Well, I've got a town to keep safe. Take care."

"Thanks, Chief. You've been great. I mean it."

As he went out, he turned back. "You mean I've been grate. Like on your nerves."

I smiled. "No, I mean great."

After The Chief left, I had a little quiet time to start on my next sermon. But about 11:30, there were a couple of quick taps on the door. Then Brandy walked right in, dressed in her usual scrubs, with a fleecy coat and satchel.

"Okay, Father Bob, let's see how you're doing. My shift is starting, soon, so let's cut the small talk."

Before I could reply, she stuck a thermometer under my tongue and grabbed my wrist to take my pulse. After a couple of minutes, she dropped my hand and pulled out the thermometer.

"Good. Temperature's down to 101.6. Let's see your throat. Open."

I obeyed.

She peered in by the light of a small flashlight and grunted.

"Still white, but not any worse." She clicked off the light. "Have you had any lunch? Any soup left?"

"Lots. It's in the fridge, but–"

"No 'buts.' It's good for you. Doctors haven't figured it out yet, but that's no surprise. If you want the real scoop, ask a nurse."

I was just going to wait until noon. Instead I just sat back and watched her ladle some soup in a large mug she scrounged out of a cabinet and nuke it. It was like having a bossy pixie in the house. She plopped the mug and a spoon on my computer desk in front of me. "Eat that while it's hot. I've got to get to the hospital. Anything else I can do for you?"

"Don't call me Bob."

"Huh?"

"I hate Bob. It's a float on a fishing line. Call me Robert or Rob. And thanks for everything you've done."

She laughed. Suddenly, she was no longer just cute. She was

68

beautiful. "You're welcome Father Rob. Catch you later."

As she turned and opened the door to leave, she came face-to-face with Lisa Franks. The sparks between them would have ignited any flammable liquids in the room. Lisa spoke first.

"What are you doing here? Does your husband know?"

Brandy clenched her fists.

"Unlike some people who are glad to get rid of theirs, I'm happy with the husband I've got. I'm here as Father Rob's nurse, not to get him in bed with me." She paused. "Oh, wait, is that a Victoria's Secret bag?"

Lisa glanced down at the bag she was carrying. "It's from Trader Joe's." She looked up. "You can see that."

"You can see Rob's been sick, so go easy on him if you get him in the sack." Brandy checked her watch. "I have to get to work."

She pushed past Lisa and left.

For a moment, I wondered if Lisa would leave. She hesitated, but came inside and closed the door. For a grieving widow, she looked predatory. Her jeans looked painted on. When she slipped out of her fur-lined parka, her black sweater hugged her like a glove. It was tight and she filled it out well. Very well, indeed.

She smiled at me and set her bag on the kitchen table. "I brought you a few things to get you back on your feet. Hummus, pita chips and a box of Irish tea bags."

I quickly realized this was no mere social call. Especially when she came behind my chair and began to massage my shoulders and cooed in my ear.

"Robert, you are so tense. You need to relax."

Yeah, right. Especially since she leaned over as she gave me a massage, nestling my head between her breasts. I grabbed the arms of my chair and pulled myself up.

Turning to her, I said, "I'm sure you're only trying to help me, but this is not appropriate. You are a recently widowed woman and I am your pastor."

She stood for a moment, eyebrows raised and arms still extended over where I had been seated. Then she lowered her arms and her eyes narrowed momentarily. A grudging smile slowly crept along her mouth.

"I'm sorry if I offended you, Father. I was just trying to be

69

nice."

"You didn't offend me, Lisa. It's just that . . . ." You seem to be trying to seduce me? "We both have to make sure there is no appearance of . . . well, wrongdoing."

She gave a short laugh. "Wrongdoing? You sound like some Puritan from the 1600's."

I had handled that poorly. "Look, it's just that we live in a small town and people talk. We don't want to give them any fodder for the rumor mill."

"Well, we wouldn't want to do that, would we?"

She grabbed her coat and headed toward the door. As she opened it, she paused and turned.

"I'm not some dumb blond, you know. You're afraid of me, that I might actually pull some human emotion out of you. Heaven forbid, that you might even feel sexual desire."

Before I could respond, she was out the door, slamming it as she went.

I reflected on what she had said. Yes, she exuded a sensuality that I did feel. I am a man, after all. But I also have enough self-restraint and commitment to my God-given calling as a priest to say, "No." We are not merely rutting animals, whatever Hollywood might think.

First I ate my soup and then did a little more email correspondence. Next I started work on the following Sunday's sermon. My mind did not seem to be working, so I leaned back in my high-backed computer chair, closed my eyes and tried to think. I must have dozed because the next thing I knew the front door was open and Tony was carrying a load of firewood inside.

"Tony? What are you doing here instead of at work?" I shook my head, trying to clear the fog from my mind.

He grinned. "Pretty obvious, Father. Carrying firewood. And it's about a quarter after five, so work's over."

It was starting to get dark outside. I must have slept about four hours. With some effort, I stood. "I appreciate it. I suppose Brandy sent you."

"You figured her out, didn't you? She's sorta adopted you. Like a stray dog." He laughed. "She keeps picking them up, too."

Well, I like dogs, having lost my treasured Aussie a couple of

70

years ago, so I wasn't offended. Still, I'm not a stray. Before I could think of a reply, Tony dropped his load of oak next to the wood stove and turned to me, rubbing his gloved hands together.

"Brandy thought you'd want to know what happened at the job site this afternoon. Lisa comes bombing up in that Lexus LX she drives. She looks really pi-, uh, mad. Sees Red sitting on his ass, drinking a beer, and lays into him, telling him to watch his step. They're yelling and screaming, and the rest of us are trying not to laugh. Man, she's got a mouth on her. Worse'n Red's. Anyway, he tells her to clear out, that it's his business now. She's yelling that he's gonna be sorry, that if he messes with her, she'd cut off his, uh, you-know-whats."

"I-know-whats." I shook my head in wonder. "So she left?"

Tony shrugged. "Sorta. She drove outta there so fast I thought she was going to fly off the side of the hill. Then she's back, jumping out of her car and back in Red's face. You'll never guess what happened then."

"Probably not."

"They went off to the side and talked all quiet-like. Then they had another argument and she takes off again. Wild, huh?"

"Wild." What was going on?

Tony finished restocking my firewood box and stoked the wood stove before leaving. I mulled over this latest news. Who had inherited the construction business? Red had said to follow the money. But had that been a red herring, pardon the pun, or a real clue?

Chapter 14

Since my real job is concerned with the Lord rather than the law, the Jon Franks' case went on the back burner for a while. After all, he wasn't going anywhere and Red seemed to be in no immediate danger. From a murderer, at least. Having twice made a fool of myself, I would have to be sure of a threat before raising the alarm again.

About ten, I got a call from Doris.

"Father Robert, Elvira fell on some ice a couple of days ago and went to the hospital. She didn't break any bones, but is pretty bruised and can't walk, so she's in Golden Sunset for a few days. I thought you'd want to know."

"Elvira had a fall? Why didn't you tell me?"

"We were worried that you'd go visit and get sicker." She paused. "Besides, if you were contagious, it wouldn't be good for you to go there."

"I should have been told right away." I stopped and took a deep breath to calm myself. Doris had just been trying to watch out for me. Still, it wasn't her call. "Look, Doris, I appreciate your concern for me, but I must know immediately when someone in the parish might need me. If nothing else, so I can pray for them."

She sniffed. "I prayed for her, Father. Aren't my prayers any good?"

"Of course they are." Offending Doris had not been my intent. "No doubt you have God's ear more than I. In the future, though, please let me know right away just in case there is something I need to do. Okay?"

"Okay, Father. You know I'm only trying to be efficient."

"And you are."

After she hung up, I ordered flowers for her on line. Never hurts to go the extra mile.

Since George had healed enough to escape, Imogene and Elvira were the only parishioners from St. Nicholas Church at Golden Sunset. The odors had not improved. Julie, the finger-flipping care giver, was behind the counter and jumped to her feet.

"You shouldn't be here." She paused, her eyes nervously darting. "Are you here to see Irina?"

I shouldn't be here? Ah. It was Tuesday morning, not Wednesday afternoon, my day for visiting the sick. But why the reaction? I decided to play along.

"Who else would I be here to see?"

"Well, she's . . . ." She paused. "She's in the middle of her bath."

"Then I'll see Elvira Murdoch while I'm waiting."

"But . . . but you said you were here to see Irina."

"No, you assumed that. I'm going to see her next, though. I'm sure she will be finished with her bath by then. Now, where do I find Elvira?"

"You can't see her now, either." Her chin jutted out defiantly. "Come back tomorrow afternoon."

I took out my cell and started poking numbers.

Julie eyed me suspiciously. "Who are you calling?"

"Lee. I mean Chief Garcia. I'm sure he can drop by and sort this out."

"Wait." She forced a smile. "No need for that. Elvira is in room 7, corridor C."

"I will be back," I said, and returned her smile. "And I will see Imogene then."

Finding the room was easy. Seeing Elvira was not. She was asleep, looking pale, small and fragile in the white-sheeted bed. I pulled up a chair and sat in it. After a few minutes, she awoke and drowsily looked around. She saw me and smiled, then reached out with her hand.

"Father, how are you?"

I gently took her hand and smiled back. "I'm fine, Elvira. What's this about you going ice skating without any skates? Are you going into extreme sports?"

"You think I'm going to let the young punks have a monopoly on all that fun?" She chuckled briefly, but winced and stopped.

"What's wrong?"

She shrugged. "Oh, the doctor says I broke a few ribs. They don't wrap them anymore, so all I get is oxy-something and a pat on the hand from the doc.   No problem, though.   I had it worse when I crash-landed a B-29 at Hickam Field in '45."

"Oxycodone?"   I paused.   "You flew bombers?"   Elvira never ceased to surprise me.

"Only to Hawaii.   I was a WAAF.   A better pilot than most men, but a woman was only good enough to ferry planes, not fight in them.   Anyway, I'll be okay."   She paused, her eyelids drooping. "There was something I was going to tell you about that Franks' thing. Something Jon told me.   I taught him when he was in fifth grade, you know, and he's always told me what was happening in his life.   He's quite something with the girls, you know.   But sometimes, he isn't wise.   I'll think of it in a minute."

"It'll wait.   Just get better."

I don't know if she heard me.   She was already asleep.   I gently laid her hand at her side and slipped out of the room.

When I returned to the front desk, Julie was not there.   Instead, a Hispanic woman, short and a little overweight, was seated at reception.   She looked up as I approached.   Her name tag said Juanita.

"You want I help you?"

"I'm here to see Imogene."

"*Si*.   You that Padre Julie say was here to see her.   She ready now."

"But she wasn't ready before?   Never mind.   Where is she?"

"Activities room."   Juanita smiled.   "Nice lady.   Movie star, you know."

"Yes, she was."   I returned her smile.   "Thank you, Juanita."

Imogene was in her wheelchair in the activities room with the perpetual soaps blaring in the background.   I'm sure they are always on in hell, too.   I pulled up a chair and sat by her.

"How are you this morning, Imogene?"

Her face lit up with joy.   "Why, Bobbie, it's good to see you."

"It's good to see you too.   Have they been treating you okay?"

"Fine.   I just had a bath.   First one this year."

"First one this year?   Are you sure?"

"Of course, Bobbie.   It was right before the last time you came to see me."

I rested my hand on hers.   "Wasn't that last week?"

Her brow wrinkled.   "Was it?"   She shrugged.   "I guess I

forgot. But it is good to see you."

We chatted a while, mainly about her days of acting glory. When I left, Juanita was still at reception and I stopped there.

"Juanita, do you talk to Imogene often?"

"Oh, yes. She very nice lady. Like my *abuela*."

"Abuela?"

"Oh, sorry. My English not so good. Grandmother."

"Your English is very good. I was wondering if you noticed any changes in Imogene."

"She forget sometimes." Juanita cocked her head. "She not finish her word puzzles. Get angry."

"Thanks, Juanita." Crossword puzzles, no doubt. We had talked about how we both loved them months ago. "Keep an eye on her for me."

"Yes, Padre."

"And on Elvira, if you would."

"Yes, Padre."

"*Gracias.* That's about the limit of my Spanish, so we'll speak in English, if that's okay."

She nodded with a grin.

My next stop was the church. Don met me there and we looked over the old, wooden structure. The storm had caused no serious damage, although we should repaint in spring and a couple of trees would need to be trimmed. We had been fortunate. I asked Don to join me for lunch, but he had errands to run.

After a bagel with lox and cream cheese at Mocha Arabesque, I headed home. When I got there, Brandy was waiting on my doorstep with her satchel in hand.

She glared at me. "I hope you haven't made yourself worse by running around."

"I'm doing great."

"We'll see."

After we went inside, she gave me a quick checkup. As she packed her satchel, she shook her head.

"Well, it looks like you're getting better, in spite of yourself."

"Thanks, Doc."

"Nurse practitioner and you know it." She paused. "I, uh . . . . Are you going to be at church Sunday?"

76

"I don't know. I thought I might go skiing instead. I hear the runs are great at Squaw Valley right now."

She snorted. "Okay, dumb question and dumber answer."

"Sorry. Once a smart alec, always a smart alec. Yes, I will be there. Why?"

"Me and Tony are thinking of coming. Maybe bring a friend. That's all."

"Great. I'll be glad to see you there."

Without another word, she was out the door.

As I brewed a pot of Earl Grey tea and built a fire in the wood stove, I considered the day. I was concerned about Elvira and Imogene. I had rushed out and forgotten my oleum infirmorum. Next time I would take the holy oil to anoint them when I prayed for them. They were both ailing, one of body and one of mind. And then there was Brandy. Like Russia, "a riddle wrapped in a mystery inside an enigma."

Tea was much simpler than people. I poured myself a full mug and sat by the fire.

Chapter 15

My mind was wandering as I sat in my office, sipping a mug of Irish Breakfast tea. Different mug, different tea. It was just after nine in the morning and I was already on my third mug as I finished my crossword puzzle. Maybe I'm a tea addict.

Doris burst in without knocking.

"Oh, Father, I can't believe it," she choked out between sobs. "She's dead."

"Who's dead?" Had someone else been murdered?

"Elvira. I called to see how she was doing and they said she died during the night."

It was a moment before I could speak with a steady voice. A pastor is not supposed to have favorites in the congregation, but Elvira was definitely one of mine. And I had forgotten my oleum infirmorum. holy oil for anointing the sick, when I last saw her.

"Thanks for letting me know, Doris. I'll go right over to Golden Sunset."

I took my stole and my oleum infirmorum as I left.

Julie was at the desk and greeted me in her normal cheery fashion.

"Weren't you here just yesterday? We have better things to do than get Irina ready to see you any time you drop by."

"I'm here to see Elvira Murdoch. Is she still in her room?"

Julie looked confused. "She's dead."

"I'm glad you noticed. Is she still in her room?"

"Yeah. We're trying to get hold of her grandson to see what to do with her."

Good luck. Artemis Jr. was probably on his sailboat in Hawaii. Actually, just Artemis, since his dad died of cirrhosis of the liver a few years ago. Both of them had bled poor Elvira's bank accounts dry and never even showed up for Christmas.

"If you ever reach him, tell him I'll be glad to handle all the arrangements."

"And send him the bills?"

Did I detect a smirk?

"If he agrees. If not, I'll handle them." I smiled. "And I will stop by to see Imogene before I leave."

What a difference a few hours make. Elvira had been talking of flying B-29's and now she looked like a wax museum figure. A sheet was drawn up to her chin and her face was limp, with her mouth slightly open. I put on my stole and made the sign of the Cross on her forehead with the oleum infirmorum.

"Deliver your servant, Elvira, Oh Sovereign Lord Christ, from all evil, and set her free from every bond; that she may rest with all your saints in the eternal habitations; where with the Father and the Holy Spirit you live and reign, one God, for ever and ever. Amen."

The prayer was really for me. Elvira had already gone to Him. I stayed a moment, my hand on her forehead. Dear Lord, I loved that woman.

When I returned to the desk, Julie smiled at me. It was as sincere as a politician's handshake.

"Irina is ready for you."

"She likes to be called Imogene."

Julie's eyes flashed defiantly. "Her name is Irina."

I studied her. "Is Julie the name you were given at birth?"

"I, uh . . . ." She looked down, suddenly finding some paper on her desk very interesting.

"Then have the sense of charity to call her the name she wishes. She is a real person with feelings, you know."

Julie nodded, but did not look up. "She's in the activities room."

As I walked down the corridor, I wondered why I had asked Julie that question. Something about her just didn't seem right. I couldn't put my finger on it, though.

When I got to the activities room, the infernal TV was blaring in the background, some morning show with a young woman laughing with a guest old enough to be her grandfather. Maybe soaps aren't the worst thing on TV. Juanita was combing Imogene's hair. I took Imogene's hand.

"Good morning, Imogene. You look lovely, as usual."

For a moment she seemed confused, not recognizing me. Then

80

she smiled.

"It's good to see you, Father. This is my hairdresser. The studio sent her to get me ready for my next scene."

Juanita shrugged and smiled sadly. "Almost done. She a beautiful lady."

"That she is, Juanita. So, what have you been up to, Imogene?"

"Well, I had visitors here last night. One of them was a real sexpot. It was Marilyn Monroe. I've met her before. It's a great story."

I patted her hand. "Yes, you had a part in *The Seven Year Itch.*"

"Oh." She looked down. "I guess I already told you."

"That's okay." Stupid. That was just plain stupid of me. "I'd love hearing about it again."

"No, I won't bore you." She glanced up coyly. "But my other visitor was not a movie star. She was a nurse. I bet you didn't know that."

"No, I didn't. Was she one of the nurses here?"

"No." She shook her head. "But she was wearing a nurse's uniform. Not the white dresses like they used to wear, but a blue pants suit. But you know what was strange?"

"No, tell me."

"She had a spider web on her cheek."

Brandy. What had she been doing here? She and Marilyn. Okay, Imogene was not exactly a great witness, but a spider web on her cheek?

I leaned forward. "Are you sure you saw the nurse with a spider web last night?"

"Of course I am. I have a great memory."

There must be a way to verify this. "Was anyone else here?"

"No." She shrugged. "The other people here are really old and go to bed early."

"Okay, you were alone." I paused. "Was the TV on? Were you watching anything?"

"Oh, yes. I was watching Claude. *Casablanca* was on."

I wouldn't bet on that. I turned to Juanita. "Were you here?"

She shook her head. "I go home to my children. I no watch the TV."

"Can you check with whoever was here to see if Imogene had

81

any visitors?"   What if it weren't about Imogene?   "Or if Elvira Murdoch had any visitors?"

She shook her head.   "I try.   We no have a . . . a . . . sign-up book?"

"A sign-in register.   Just do what you can.   Ask around."

"I try."   She stood.   "I must go now.   People need me."

I hated having her nose around.   If Julie and her friend thought she was helping me, they might find a way of getting her fired.   But I had to be sure that Elvira had not been helped to die.

I went back to her room.   Nothing had changed.   I took Elvira's cold hand.

"What happened?   Did someone kill you?"

She did not answer.

After several hours working at the church, counseling those who were still alive and much troubled, looking over the schedule for the upcoming Advent services and performing various other rector duties, I went home.   My phone was ringing as I opened the door.

"Father?   It's Doris.   An Artemis Murdoch has been calling for you.   Is he related to Elvira?"

"Her grandson and only living relative."

"Do you want his number?"

"Just a sec."   With a bit of rummaging for a pen and paper, I was ready.   "Shoot."

I called him.

"Hello?"

"This is Father Robert at St. Nicholas in Buggy Springs.   I am sorry about your grandmother."

"Yeah.   Well, she was old.   You said you'd handle everything for a fee?"

"No fee."

"Uh huh."   He sounded suspicious.   "Tell you what, I'll give you five grand to handle it all: funeral plot, the whole bit.   I don't do anything.   Do we have a deal?"

"Maybe.   As long as I have power of attorney to handle all her affairs."

"You mean her money?   No way."

"I don't care about her money.   I want control over her remains. Nothing more."

He hesitated. "Okay, but I'll only go to ten grand and no more. That means, anything else you spend on her is out of your pocket, right?"

"As long as you agree to the rest."

"I'll have my lawyer FedEx the paperwork."

I couldn't resist. "Will you be here for her service?"

"I, uh . . ." He cleared his throat. "I'll be away on business."

"Right."

He hung up. Obviously, it did not matter when the service was, he would be "away on business" no matter what.

I called Golden Sunset to let them know that I would be handling everything. Then I made another call.

Doris answered. "Buggy Springs Police Department."

"That was quick. I thought you just called me from the church."

She chuckled. "I came here right after I called you. What can I do for you, Father?"

"Is the Chief in?"

"I'll connect you."

After a moment, he answered.

"Chief Garcia."

"Chief, it's Robert."

He sighed. "So who's going to be murdered now?"

"Maybe it's already happened. I want you to do an autopsy on Elvira Murdoch."

"Who's Elvira Murdoch? I haven't heard anything about her death, so why do an autopsy?"

"She died in Golden Sunset. I think she may have been killed."

"Why?" He paused. "Golden Sunset is a convalescent home and people die at places like that all the time without being murdered. Plus, you're not the next of kin, so unless you have hard evidence, why should I do an autopsy?"

"Call it a hunch. I'm going to have power of attorney for her affairs, so humor me. If it comes out that it was 'natural causes,' I'll personally pay the bill for the autopsy."

"How old is this Elvira?"

I cringed. "Just a little over ninety."

"A little over ninety?" He laughed. "Okay, Robert. I like you, so I'll see you your autopsy and raise you. If you lose, you pay and drop this whole 'murder in Buggy Springs' bit. If it's murder, Buggy Springs will pay. Agreed?"

I paused. I used to play penny-ante poker with my sister and my hunches never seemed to lose. When I was in elementary school, I got some of my sister's slumber-party sorority sisters to play strip poker with me when she had gone to get ice cream. They couldn't believe that Janet's cute kid brother was a card shark. That and a couple of books from my father's library were my early sex education. "You're on."

After he hung up, I opened a bottle and poured myself an Oban single malt scotch. With stakes this high, tea just didn't seem appropriate.

Chapter 16

On Friday I met the Chief at Mocha Arabesque to get the coroner's report. Since Artemis, Elvira's loving grandson, had promptly sent the papers for the power of attorney, I had a legal right to read the coroner's report. The Chief had called and set up an appointment to give me the report. I wasn't sure what that meant, whether there was something interesting in it or he just wanted to gloat that he had been right. I was sitting at a battle-scarred table that had once been varnished, sipping my non-fat, triple-shot latte, when he walked through the coffee house door with a manila envelope in hand.

"Well, Robert, you started without me. Did you buy me one too?"

"Sorry, Chief," I said as I rose from my chair. "What would you like?"

"Coffee. Strong and black." He gave a short chuckle. "I figure you can pay for the coffee, since you won the bet and my department got stuck with the bill for the autopsy."

I stopped in mid-rise. "Then she was murdered."

"So it would seem. Smothered, probably with a pillow. There were cotton fibers in her front teeth that matched her pillow case." He shook his head. "Hard to believe it, but she still had her real teeth."

I settled back down in my seat. "Where do we go from here?"

"You go to the counter and get my coffee." He paused. "And an onion bagel with butter, too. Then I'll show you the report."

When I returned with the coffee and bagel, the Chief handed me the envelope.

"Nothing much more than I told you. No evidence of a struggle. Since she was old and heavily sedated, it's no surprise."

I pulled the report out of the envelope and leafed through it. Much of it might as well as have been in Greek. Well, Greek might have been better because at least I am semi-literate in that. When I got to "cause of death," I saw "suffocation." She also had a high reading for something called eszopiclone, evidently the sedative.

I looked up at the Chief. "So, you never answered me about how we're going to find her killer."

"What do you mean we, white man?"

"Huh?"

The Chief smiled. "Sorry. It's an old joke about the Lone Ranger and Tonto surrounded by hostile Indians. I mean Native Americans. Anyway, that's Tonto's line when the Lone Ranger asks, 'What are we going to do?' Helps if you're over sixty."

"I'll take your word for it, but you're avoiding my question."

The Chief sipped his coffee. "Damn. It's cold. We should have gone to Buggy Springs Diner." He sighed. "Not really. There's no 'we' in investigation, but there are a few 'I's.' I will be going to Golden Sunset and check it out. I will be questioning anyone who might have seen or heard anything. Unfortunately, the crime scene has been scoured. And I don't have any leads. Not even a hint of a motive."

He paused, looking me in the eye. "I don't suppose you have any information. Like someone who had a grudge against her or would inherit a lot of money."

"Well, I think her estate goes to her grandson. He's on his boat in Hawaii, so you can rule him out. As far as I know, Elvira didn't have any enemies. She was a bit forthright in her opinions, but there'd be a lot more killings if that were a reason to murder." I thought about Julie and her friend. "She might have offended some of the staff at Golden Sunset. But I doubt if any of them would kill her for that."

The Chief pushed away the cup of cold coffee and stood, bagel in hand. "I've got to get back to work, mercilessly tracking down wrong-doers."

I stood, too. "Thanks, Chief. Please keep me informed."

He winked. "I'll let you know when I go to make my arrest. I'll loan you a vest when we bust down the door and go in shooting."

He was laughing as he left.

Why did I think Elvira's murder was connected to Jon Franks' death? There was something pricking the back of my mind, something about Elvira that I should remember. Well, there may not be any "we" in investigation, but it has more than one "I." And this "I" was not finished yet.

With the autopsy out of the way, Elvira could be laid to rest. Her funeral service was held the next Tuesday. Her fellow parishioners packed the nave, even more than the added folding chairs could hold. The weather had turned cold, harbinger of the Advent season, and everyone was bundled warmly as they came into the church. Everyone except Elvira, who I had arranged to be in her favorite pastel-flowered, silken summer dress, hidden in the closed mahogany casket.

Intellectually, I knew that it didn't matter to her now, but I wanted to please her. Or her memory. Since her family had been in Buggy Springs from the Gold Rush days, she had a place in the family mausoleum in Pioneer Cemetery. Considering Artemis' indifference to her, I was glad she had a prepaid place of rest for her mortal remains.

Since she had always preferred Rite One, I performed her service in that King James-type English that she had loved. I opened my *Book of Common Prayer* and began.

"I am the resurrection and the life, saith the Lord."

After the service, six pallbearers whom I had chosen from the many who had volunteered carried Elvira out the door. Two somber men in black (but no sunglasses) from New Forest Funeral Home loaded her like so much cargo into the back of the hearse. The sky was overcast and a chill wind wormed its way under my vestments. I shivered, but not just from the cold. Why hadn't I told everyone to dress in pastels, like Elvira would have wanted?

We drove to the cemetery and parked near her mausoleum. The granite was weather-stained and eroding. A weeping angel at the peak of the roof had lost its facial features to time and weather. The rusty iron doors stood open and a musty smell almost gagged me as I walked inside. I turned in the doorway as the two men from New Forest rolled Elvira up on a metal cart. I started The Committal.

> "In the midst of life we are in death;
> of whom may we seek for succor,
> but of thee, O Lord,
> who for our sins art justly displeased?"

Way too dark. Why had I used this part of Rite One? Funerals are for those that are left behind, not for those who are with the Lord. Too late now, but I would make sure that the wake afterwards would remember Elvira as she should be remembered: lively, witty and a bit mischievous.

When I finished, people hurried to their cars to get out of the cold. The wake, a reception in Elvira's memory, would be held at the parish hall, so we would drive back from whence we came. I was even starting to think in Rite One. As I walked to my truck, Lisa came alongside me. She was wearing a black coat that came mid-calf that looked like real mink. Non-PC, if it were. She linked her arm around mine. She seemed to have forgiven me my previous rebuff.

"Father Robert, it was a beautiful service. You have such a way with words."

"The credit goes to Thomas Cranmer."

"Who?"

"The guy who wrote most of the original *Book of Common Prayer*."

She giggled. "Silly me. I thought Shakespeare wrote it. It sounds like him."

I decided to be kind. "The language is similar, but Cranmer was an archbishop."

"Of course, I remember that." She said with a wave of her hand. "So, are you going to the potluck?"

"You mean the celebration of Elvira's life?"

"Yeah, that. I'm going."

"I'll be there. I didn't even know you knew her."

"Oh, sure. We talked together a lot."

We had reached my truck, so she released my arm and started to walk away, calling back, "See ya there."

Lovely Lisa was becoming a pain. I got in my truck and headed to the church.

I had used what was left of Artemis' ten grand to pay for a great spread of food and drink at the celebration. The hall was sultry from gas heat and packed, warm bodies. The fire marshal would probably have objected at how many were packed in the room, if it weren't for the fact that he was there. After allowing people time to mingle and charge their glasses, I stepped up to the mic for the church's portable sound system.

"We're going to have a time for you to talk about what Elvira meant to you. There are many who want to share, so be brief, please. Since I already have the mic, I'll start."

I took a sip from my plastic glass of local cab.

"When I first got here, Elvira wasn't very friendly. She didn't like change. I think the only reason she tolerated me at all was that Father Reeve had died, so St. Nicholas had to have a new rector. Then I gave the sermon on when Jesus turned the water into wine. I told about when I first heard the story at the age of six and tried to duplicate it. I raided my father's wine cellar and grabbed a bottle of Château Pétrus Bordeaux. I poured it out and filled it with water, then gave it to my dad to see if it was better than the wine that had been in it. He demonstrated that he did not believe in 'spare the rod.'

"After church, she told me, 'I guess you'll do. Just don't die before I do. I hate breaking in new rectors and I've had to do a lot of that in my lifetime.' Then, as she was starting down the steps, she yelled, 'And stay the hell away from my wine.'"

While everyone was laughing, I handed the mic to the next person. I was too choked up to say anything more. I was taught that men never cry in public and that is sometimes a hard rule to keep. I dearly love the women like Elvira and Imogene. Maybe that's why I'm not married. I haven't found any women my age like them.

After a couple more people spoke, Brandy stepped up and grabbed the mic from Ann Wills, a middle-aged woman who was a regular at the eight o'clock service. Brandy was dressed in black jeans and turtleneck, reminding me of pictures of the 1950's Beatniks.

"Sorry if that was rude, but I've got to go to work and wanted to say how much Elvira meant to me. I was her nurse when she went to the hospital for her broken leg a couple of years ago and she hired me to stop by her house a couple of times a day when she got out."

She stopped, wiping her eyes with the back of her hand. After a moment she continued.

"A lot of people treat me like sh-- . . . uh, dirt 'cause I've got this tat and I don't dress fancy. Elvira made me feel like . . . like her equal. And I know I wasn't. Tony, my husband, and I were having problems, mainly 'cause our Jody died, and I was going to leave him. She told me, 'He's not perfect, Hon, but neither are you. He doesn't beat you or

89

run around on you.   He's not a drinker or gambler.   He lets you be yourself.   And you know he didn't cause your child to die.   He's a damn sight better than most, so stick it out.   Besides, you'll probably outlive him anyway, so you can try to do better second time around.'   Because of her, Tony and I are still together and I'm grateful to her.   When I saw her lying helpless in that bed at Golden Sunset, it tore my guts out and--"

Her voice caught and she shoved the mic at the next person in line, disappearing in the crowd.   I tried to follow, but the press of people made it impossible.   She was gone.

I managed to avoid Lisa until the wake was breaking up.   She had her coat on, but open to reveal her short, tight, black dress.   The same one she wore to her husband's funeral.   Maybe she bought it especially for such happy occasions.   She took my hand in hers.

"I didn't get to talk to you at all.   I'll be at church Sunday, so maybe we can have a chance to chat afterwards."

Before I could reply, she was out the door.

That night I nursed a mug of Earl Grey tea as I mulled over the day.   Imogene had seen Brandy at Golden Sunset the night Elvira died.   She had probably seen Lisa, too.   It bore investigating.   And I would be the "I" in that investigation.

Chapter 17

TV cops always say the first few hours after a murder are the critical time to question witnesses. I was well past that time, but later is better than never. First, I had to stop by the church office for a meeting with Don, the junior warden. As the man in charge of the church structure, he was hassling with the latest problem of a hundred and fifty year-old wooden building. The new, high-tech heater for the church didn't work as well as the old one and the company who installed it was as clueless as a Luddite as to why. Three thermostats and several head-scratching sessions later, we were no closer to a resolution than when we had started. Don was there when I arrived.

"Well, what do you think?" I asked, as I settled into my desk chair.

Don ran his hand though his thinning, blond hair. "I hate to say it, but I think we got a lemon. Tear it out and start again."

I shuddered at the thought. First, I hoped it would all be done before the rapidly-approaching Christmas services. Second, I knew the owner of Buggy Springs Heating and he would balk at eating the cost of a replacement. I'm not into confrontations.

Don smiled, as if sensing my discomfort. "Don't worry, Robert. I'll handle it. I was in business for twenty years and I can be the bad guy when I need to be."

No wonder he beat me in racquetball in spite of lacking six inches on me and weighing probably twenty pounds more. Gutsy determination.

I grinned. "Just be nicer to him than you are to me on the court."

He laughed. "I'll keep the velvet glove on my iron fist."

I planned to leave right after the meeting, but it seemed everyone knew I had dropped by the office and called me there. It was almost noon before I had a break.

As I sorted papers and prepared to leave, I called Doris into my office.

"Doris, what do you know about Lisa Franks and Brandy Mazzoni."

"Lisa is a parishioner at St. Nicholas and Brandy doesn't attend."

I stared at her in wonder. All I got was bare-bones facts that I already knew?

"Uh, anything more personal? Like who they see, what they do when they're not at church? Rumors, maybe?"

She reddened. "That would be gossip. That's a sin. I was reading sermons online and there's one about gossip being the eighth deadly sin. From Proverbs."

Just my luck. All my preaching on that topic made no impression, but Doris has an epiphany from some website preacher. And at this moment.

"Doris, I'm not asking for personal reasons or so that I can tell anyone else. I am a priest, so consider this like confession."

"Confession? So I can tell you and it won't be gossip?"

I nodded, trying to look pontifical.

She settled into the chair next to my desk. "Well, then I've got some stories to tell you. Brandy's a local, you know. Went to Bullsheeps."

"Bullsheeps? Is that an agricultural school?"

She laughed. "Before it was renamed Ansel Adams High, the school was Buggy Springs High School and the kids, well, the polite ones called it bullsheeps and the others called it a worse name." She winked. "You know what I mean. It's from B. S. H. S. But she got kicked out when she pulled a knife on her algebra teacher. Maybe stabbed him. That wasn't long after she stabbed her stepfather." She leaned closer and whispered, "But the charges were dropped. I never did find out why. She left for several years and came back with that Tony guy."

"Her husband, you mean."

"Well . . . ." She glanced around, as if someone were eavesdropping in the church office. "He may be her husband, but he must not be enough for her. I hear she's been seen with at least one other guy. And I don't mean shaking hands."

I sighed. I hated rumors because most were lies or at least distortions. If it weren't for Elvira's murder, I would have stopped

92

Doris immediately. But she wasn't finished.

"Now, that Lisa isn't from around here. I hear she's from Texas. A Bible-Belt Baptist and you know what that means."

"What does that mean?"

Doris shifted uneasily in her chair. "Well, she's not a cradle-to-grave Episcopalian. I don't even know why she started coming. I hear she was married twice before and didn't even divorce the last one before marrying Jon Franks. And she's a lot smarter than she acts. I heard she's gone to college and has a degree in something. Zoology? Or is it geography?"

"Maybe it's in zoo-ography." I tried not to smile when I said it.

Doris wrinkled her brow and paused a moment.

"No, I don't think that was it. Anyway, she's got something going with a younger guy on the side. You know, her 'bad boy.'"

"I think you mean 'toy boy.'"

Doris rolled her eyes. "Come on, Father. Toy boy? Like Barbie's Ken? You're pulling my leg."

"I guess I am." I rubbed my forehead, feeling a headache coming on. Too much information. "Has anyone actually seen her with this . . . bad boy?"

She raised an eyebrow. "She's sneaky, but look at the way she dresses. Way too . . . you know. But Angela thinks she saw a hunk doing her yard work one day."

Not exactly evidence. "Anything else important?"

"There's a lot more, but . . . ." She reddened. "It's mainly gossip about their, you know, sex lives. Do you want to hear it? I mean, since this is a confession and all."

I leaned back in my chair. "No, Doris, you've told me everything I need to know and more. Never tell anyone else any of this . . . this . . . this stuff. Just try to wipe it from your memory."

She seemed stunned. "But Father, what if I need to testify in court or something?"

Testify in court? About gossip that was probably half-truths or lies?

"Trust me, you won't. Let all this . . . information die here. Otherwise it *will* be gossip."

She sighed. "I'll try, Father."

After a quick bagel with lox and cream cheese at Mocha

Arabesque, I headed to Golden Sunset, thinking about what had happened there. Both Brandy and Lisa had visited Elvira before she ever went into Golden Sunset, so Imogene seeing them visiting Elvira there was not unusual. Who else might have stopped by to do a little killing? Or did she rub one of the staff the wrong way? That was unlikely. Although it would be easy to smother a helpless, sedated old woman, only a perverted mind would do it. Maybe a sociopath.

Ask me if I believe evil is real, I would point to people like Elvira's killer.

After taking a last gulp of clean air, I opened the door to Golden Sunset. Julie was at the front desk and seemed to find it very important to study some papers on a clipboard she was holding.

"Good afternoon, Julie."

For a few moments she continued to look down, then finally glanced up at me with a frown. "Come to make more trouble?"

Honey rather than vinegar, I told myself.

"No, I need your help." I smiled. "I'm sure you've heard that Elvira was murdered."

She shrugged. "Yeah, some cop came by and asked me a bunch of questions. Like I killed her or something. You tell them I was mean to her?"

"Not at all." I paused, thinking. "Did you get to talk to her before she, uh . . . died?"

"Yeah." She glanced down at her papers again. "She was okay. Not a whiner, like some of them." She looked up at me. "Not that I would hurt any of them. The whiners, I mean."

"Let's step back a few days, Julie." Time for some honey. "Pretend we're on the same side. Because we are. You're trying to do a difficult job and help people. So am I. Often they don't appreciate it. Get mad at us for no reason. We have bad days when it seems that everyone is dumping on us. I know I do. But we both are concerned about those who are under our care. Elvira was under both your care and my care. Now she's dead. So will you help me?"

She studied me for a second, then nodded.

"Good, Julie. There's a chair next to you. Is it okay if I sit down?"

She shrugged. "No one is supposed to come behind the counter, but I don't give a damn. Come on around."

94

I went around the front desk and sat in the threadbare swivel chair next to her.

"So, who was on duty the night Elvira died?"

Her chin went up. "I was. That's why that cop made it like I was to blame. And now you."

"No, no, no." I shook my head. "You didn't kill her." I hoped I was right. "But maybe we can find who did. Then you can shove that in the cop's face."

She sighed. "Honestly, I can't tell you much. Me, Becky, and Wendy were on duty, but Becky was . . . . Well, don't tell anyone, but she was stoned and fell asleep in the lounge. She's the short one you met with me that one time . . . . Anyway, Wendy was cleaning up looney 102, uh, Mrs. Bates, 'cause she had a big BM all over her bed. She'd pulled off her Depends. Makes you sick. I was busy on the phone a lot and don't remember the visitors, 'cept that nurse with the spider web tat and some blond. I know Elvira was alive after they left because I gave her pain meds. Had a hard time getting her awake enough to take them. Then the east door alarm kept going off and I had to run over to check it."

"Door alarm?" North was towards the front door, so East . . . . "The East door is near Elvira's room. Did you find anyone when you checked it out?"

She shook her head. "Nothing. I thought it might be one of the inma . . . residents having some fun with me. Some of them are tricky, you know. But the last time it went off I ran over to the door to catch 'em. There's no way one of these old farts could have hobbled away before I got there. No one was there."

"How many times did the alarm go off?"

Julie frowned in concentration. "Four? No, it was three. Yeah. I'm sure it was three. Well, maybe four."

"So someone could have come in through that door and killed Elvira."

She shook her head. "Nope. It's locked. Only opens from the inside."

I mulled this over. "But someone could have opened the door for the killer."

She stood, slamming her clipboard on the desk. "So now you're saying I let this killer in?" She sniffed. "So much for being on

95

the same side."

I looked in her eyes. "No, I just showed that you had nothing to do with it. If you had let the killer in, why tell me about the door alarm?"

She collapsed back into her chair. "Yeah, that's for sure. This has been a nightmare. I mean, people here croak, but we've never had anyone murdered. Makes you think." She looked at me. "Father, do you think I'm a bad person?"

I took a breath. More honey. "All of us have both good and bad in us. Human nature. We make choices every day and those choices are either good or evil. God wants us to do good. I hope you remember that every time one of your 'inmates' needs you."

"I will, Father." She reached out and rested her hand on mine. "And thanks."

"No need to thank me. It's part of the job."

Julie looked down, blushing. "No, thanks for not saying anything to anyone about . . . you know, the change."

The change? I was puzzled. Did she mean about her name? Why did that matter so much? Then, seeing Julie from the side, I noticed it. A distinct Adam's apple.

Okay, I was surprised, but I didn't react. I've been blessed with a poker face, which is often good for counseling situations. But I admit that I did pull my hand out from under Julie's.

I smiled. "Well, Julie, I am far more concerned with how you treat the people under your care than who you once were. If I felt you were being cruel or neglectful, I would report that and that alone. You understand?"

Julie nodded. "When you said that about changing my name, I almost died. I used to be Julian. How did you know?"

Had I subconsciously noticed her neck before? His neck . . . whatever. Perhaps I had. I wasn't sure. I shrugged. "It's not important."

"I do appreciate it. I'm fully a woman now, but some people wouldn't understand. Thanks for not judging me."

"'Judge not that ye be not judged.' Jesus' words from the Gospel of Matthew. Who am I to go against Him?"

"Well, thanks." She paused. "When is your church service on Sunday?"

"We have two, no music at 8:30 and a sung mass at 10:00. You'd be welcome to come."

"I might."   She smiled.   "I just might."

As I walked out the door, I considered how I felt about Julian becoming Julie.   If I were to be honest, I was rather uncomfortable about it.   But the passage I had quoted was Gospel truth.   Judge not. A wise rule to follow.

Before I left, I checked out the alarmed door.   It looked fine, except there was a sticky substance, like tape adhesive, by the latch.   If tape had been used on it, that would explain how someone could get inside unseen and why the alarm kept going off.

.

Chapter 18

I was no sooner out the door than my cell began to play "Scotland the Brave." I glanced down to the caller I.D. Janet. I sighed and answered.

"Hello, Sister Dearest."

"Get down here. We've got to get Pop declared mentally incompetent."

"Nice to hear your voice, too. How are you?"

Long pause.

"I feel like hell, Accident. Pop's gone off the deep end. How are you?"

"Just heavenly." I sighed. "What's the problem with Pop now? Did he buy Nadine a new Porsche?"

"No, he bought that slut a boat."

"That's nice. Maybe he'll get outside more. He used to like fishing."

She snorted. "I doubt that. It's over seventy feet long. He has to hire a guy to run it. It's as big as a house inside. He paid almost a million for it. Claims he got a deal."

"Maybe he did. What's the builder's name?"

"What makes you think I know that?" She was screaming.

"Because I know you. Who built the boat? How much did he pay?"

"It's a Queenship Barretta Pilothouse and he paid almost eight hundred thou." She sounded calmer. "But he put about two hundred more into upgrades and stuff."

"And was it a good deal?"

"I suppose. But that's not the point. He's throwing money around like crazy. And it's all because of that slut."

"I trust you don't call Nadine that to Pop. He might just disinherit you."

"I know how to keep my mouth shut."

Couldn't tell by me.

"Besides," she continued, "Richard would tell me if Pop were making changes in his will."

I'd never trusted Pops' lawyer, just too slimey. "Nice that you have such a close relationship with Tricky Dickie. Especially since he doesn't worry much about client confidentiality. Ever wonder why he's doing this?"

"Richard is a good lawyer and he's just keeping an eye on my interests."

I shook my head. I'd bet he had more planned than just watching out for her interests. I hoped Bradley was there if ever he stopped by for a chat, but Bradley seemed to never be home. "Pop bought a boat that he can well afford at a good price and has been going with a woman forty years younger than he is. Any other cause for declaring him insane?"

"Isn't that enough? There's more, though. He's really losing it. You'll see when you come down."

"I can't come down right now. I can't get away until after Christmas."

She was silent for a moment. "Well, if that's the best you can do. Just don't wait too long or all our inheritance will be invested in Pop's toys. Including the two-legged one."

She hung up.

It started to snow, wet and sleety, as I drove over to St. Nicholas. Doris gave me a cup of coffee as I went in. To be honest, I don't really like coffee in its American version, especially the bitter liquid Doris brews, but I thanked her. At least it was hot. After spending the afternoon doing a little of God's work like working on my sermon, answering emails, and preparing the agenda for the evening's vestry meeting, I reflected on my conversation with my sister. Somehow, my family ended up worshiping different gods. My dear-departed mother had been a life-long Episcopalian and I had followed in her footsteps as a Christian. My father was an agnostic. Or, especially since Mom had gone, a hedonist. Then came Janet. She worshiped Mammon. Wealth. Hers or anyone else's that might become hers. She had even made a profit in her two divorces. But she was never satisfied with her gains, never had enough. We had never been close, but we seemed to get farther away every year. She was desperately unhappy and I wished I knew some way to reach her. We were divided by a chasm of sarcasm. Any time I tried to cross it, she burned my bridge.

It was dusk when I left the church. The vestry meeting wasn't for a few hours, so I decided to find out why Ben Zachary hated Jon Franks so much he spit in his ashes. Did that also mean he hated him enough to kill him? And if he did, why kill Elvira? So I headed out to Beezer's Bar to see if I could get some answers.

Although I had seen the bar when I drove out of town on Highway 49, it wasn't exactly my kind of place. As I pulled in the pot-holed, gravel parking lot, its false front almost hid the fact that it was an old Quonset hut. Almost, and that was because it was almost dark. There were a couple of pickups parked by the door. I pulled around the side and parked in front of a railroad-tie retaining wall so none of my parishioners would see my truck if they drove by. If they came in the bar, they would have to explain to me why they were in a place that's motto was "Get blitzed at Beezer's." I had a different reason for being there.

White paint was peeling on the wood false-front and the door stuck so badly that I had to jerk it open. Clouds of smoke greeted me. A poorly-vented open-pit barbeque in the center of the room and a couple of guys smoking at one of the tables in open defiance of state law mixed the pungent smell of charred beef with tobacco. A long, dark bar stretched along one side wall with the requisite dirty mirror behind, reflecting liquor bottles lined up along it. An arched, smoke-stained, acoustic-tile ceiling gave the feel of entering a dimly-lit tunnel.

Ben was the bartender, with his long, grey hair pulled back in a ponytail. He had on a greasy, white shirt with the sleeves rolled up that displayed muscled forearms. One son was at the barbeque, wearing a Raiders ball cap just like he had on at Jon Franks' memorial service. His black T-shirt was stretched tight across his arms and chest. And his belly.

I walked over to the bar and sat on one of the cracked-Naugahyde stools. The chipped, varnished pine bar was covered with glass ring stains. Ben came over and eyed me suspiciously.

"Yer that preacher from Franks' funeral, ain'tcha?" His voice was not friendly.

I smiled in what I hoped was a disarming fashion. "Guilty as charged."

"Whatcha want?"

"How about a Diet Coke."

He sneered. "We don't have no diet crap here."

I shrugged. "Then how about a Coke?"

He grabbed a glass from behind him, scooped up some ice, and shot it full of Coke from the soda dispenser gun.

I took a sip. The mix was off and the glass looked dirty. I set it on the bar.

"That'll be five bucks," Ben said with a smug grin. Obviously, he had no love of the toothbrush.

Okay, I knew I was being taken, but I paid him plus a dollar tip. I needed to get on Ben's good side, assuming that he had one.

At that point, his son strolled over from the barbeque. He was almost as tall as I, with at least fifty pounds on me. He leaned on the bar, close enough for me to know he was not into deodorant.

He looked over at Ben. "Hey, old man, ya need help?"

"With preacher-man?" Ben spat on the ground and glared at me. "Naw. He's just leavin'. Right?"

"Wrong." What was that phrase I learned in my Latin class? *Fortes fortuna adiuva.* Fortune favors the brave. "I overpaid you for this Coke and even tipped you for lousy service, so you can at least answer a few questions about Jon Franks."

Ben and his son were not smiling. For a moment I thought I might end my days in a smelly, greasy bar. But then Ben shrugged his shoulders.

"Ya got balls, if not brains. Okay, whatcha wanna know?"

I gave an inaudible sigh of relief. "Why did you hate Jon Franks?"

"I was doin' okay here. Then my boy, Choke, had a little run in with the man. They got him on growing. I needed to bail him out and get a lawyer, but we was low on cash. Franks was a regular here and said he'd help." Ben spat again. Definitely not a floor clean enough to eat off of. "I was stupid. We ended up with a big-interest loan that'd give him the land and half the business if we miss a coupla payments. Been bleeding me dry ever since. Asshole."

I glanced up at Ben's son. "But it came out okay for you? I

mean, bail and a lawyer?"

He leaned closer. Obviously, he must feel the same about dental care and mouthwash as his father. "I ain't Choke. I'm Chewy."

"Got it. Chew, don't choke." I turned to Ben. "So now that Jon Franks is dead, your troubles are over."

"I signed papers. Now I got a new asshole on my ass."

"Lisa Franks," I said.

"That bitch?" Ben laughed. "Naw. Franks' kid, Red. Just came in today to tell me things ain't gonna be any better."

That was a surprise. He'd told me to "follow the money." And it led to him. Without thinking, I sipped my Coke. A mistake. I set it down and stood up.

"Thanks for your help."

Ben smirked. "Will it get me ta heaven?"

"Faith, not works."

"Huh?"

I tossed another five on the bar. "Come to church and I'll explain."

He studied me. "If all you churchgoers got the balls you do, I jus' might. No promises, though. I still think it's a load of crap."

"If you give it a chance, you might change your mind. I'd be glad to see you there."

I opened the door and headed back into the cold.

Snow flurries swirled around me. There was about an inch down and more coming. I buttoned my pea coat and pulled a watch cap out of my pocket, looking like some marooned sailor as I slogged through the snow to my Ranger. I climbed inside, noticing that there was no interior light. I turned the key. Nothing. I checked the headlight switch to see if I had left it on. Nope.

I fished my flashlight from under the seat and got out. Like I've said before, I'm no mechanic. Still, I had to check to see if I could figure out what was wrong. I opened the hood and shone my light in the engine compartment.

A battery cable was hanging down, unattached. That didn't happen by accident. As I reached down for the cable, I heard the roar of an engine. Through the gap between the bottom of the hood and the cowl I could see through the windshield the dark form of a large vehicle with no lights on charging the rear of my truck. I was going to be squashed like a bug between the front of my truck and the retaining wall. I had no time to get around to either side, so I dropped to the slushy ground below my front bumper.

I heard a crash, pain shot through my head and all went black.

Chapter 19

A voice. "Is he dead?"

Was that God?

A blinding light, so bright that I could feel it through my closed eyelids. But no tunnel.

Another voice. "How the hell should I know?"

That definitely wasn't Jesus.

It was Choke.

I opened my eyes and tried to raise my hand to block the light. Pain shot through my wrist and I yelped.

"What'd he say?" Choke's voice.

"Turn off the light," I managed to gasp.

The light clicked off and soothing darkness covered me.

"Thanks," I mumbled. "What happened?"

"What'd he say?" Choke again.

"He wants to know what happened," Ben said.

How could I have mistaken Ben for God?

"Oh. You was hit by a truck. Well yer truck was hit by a truck. I don't think it were no accident."

"Hell, boy, we know it weren't no accident. Whatcha using fer brains?"

I was spared further backwoods dialog when a siren, followed by flashing red and blue lights, arrived.

The Chief knelt at my side. "Robert? Can you hear me?"

"Yeah. My ears are working fine." I winced as a twinge of pain reminded me my arm wasn't. "I may have a broken arm, though."

"At least you're alive. An ambulance is on its way. What the hell happened?"

"I think I was hit by a truck."

"A truck?"

"My truck. Somebody rammed it while I was under the hood, trying to put my battery cable back on. It was a set up."

"Did you see who it was?"

105

"Yeah, someone driving a big vehicle with no lights." I groaned. "Sorry, that's the best I can do."

The Chief glanced around. "How about you guys?"

By the headlights of the Chief's car, I could see Ben hold out his empty hands. He shrugged. "Me and the boy had nothin' to do with this. The preacher came here was asking questions about Jon Franks and we heard a big crash right after he left. We pulled him out from under his truck to see if he was still alive."

"Pulled him out?" The Chief shook his head. "You never move an accident victim, you dumb-fu–"

He was thankfully cut short as the ambulance rolled in, red lights flashing and siren blaring.

After a wild ride in the ambulance on the curvy, snowy road, I found myself under the care of the ER nurse, Brandy Mazzoni, in Foothills Community Hospital.

Taking my swollen wrist in hand, she poked it a bit. "Does this hurt?"

"Ow!"

"Can you move it?"

I tried. "Sure, if I'm into pain."

"Can't you keep out of trouble?" she said, with a shake of her head.

"Sorry. I forgot to duck."

She frowned. "I thought you were hit by a truck at Beezer's."

"I was quoting President Reagan. That's what he said when John Hinkley shot him."

"Oh." She cocked her head. "But he didn't die, did he?"

"He did, but a long time later and it had nothing to do with being shot."

"Whatever. You have a sprained or a broken wrist. I'm sending you to X-ray." She paused. "And I've got someone I want you to meet after we get you squared away."

As my gurney headed toward X-ray, I hoped whoever she wanted me to meet had a better sense of humor.

About an hour later, I was back in ER and Brandy was studying my X-rays. The advantage of a small hospital is that normally you're treated a lot faster than in the big-city ones.

106

She turned off the light behind my X-rays and turned to me.

"You've got a sprain. Doesn't seem like a bad one, maybe grade 1. The doctor will be in here soon. Since it's Doc Walters, he'll have me put your arm in a sling so that you don't use it for a couple of days. He'll have you put an ice pack on it for twenty minutes every three hours for the next couple of days and take Aleve for the swelling. He'll have you get it checked in about a week. In forty-eight hours, you can take off the sling and do some simple exercises to keep it limber. I've got a sheet that will show you how to do them. Stop if they hurt too much. Any questions?"

I shook my head.

She held out her hand toward the door behind me. "Good. I'd like to introduce you to Helen, my cousin. She dropped by to visit me here. Tony's out of town tonight, so I asked her to take you home after we patch you up."

I turned. I was at a loss for words. A tall, dark-haired vision of beauty stood there. Long, wavy hair framed a face that could have launched a thousand ships as easily as her Greek namesake. She reminded me of someone. An actress. A young Catherine Zeta-Jones. Not a dead ringer, but a lot of similarities.

She smiled and walked up to me, putting out her hand. "Hi. It's nice to meet you. Brandy has told me so much about you, Father Bruce."

She looked even better close up. I managed to find my voice and shake her hand. "Call me Robert."

"Call me Hel. Only one 'L,' though. That's the nickname Brandy gave me."

"Like the Norse goddess?" I almost bit my tongue after I said it. Hel was the goddess of the dead. But in her tan coat with a thick fur trim, she looked like she came from a colder clime.

She laughed. "I hope not. My father wasn't Loki and I don't reign in Hell."

I grimaced. "I really didn't mean it that way. I often speak before thinking. Open mouth, insert foot."

She shrugged. "We've all done it."

"Yeah, but I've done it so often I have Nike imprinted on my tongue."

She laughed again, a melodious sound in the alto range. "I'm going to get a cup of coffee and clear out the front seat of my car so you'll have room to sit. See you in a while."

"Uh, great." Say something cool, idiot. "I'll enjoy that." Not cool.

After she left, Brandy eyed me.

I shifted uncomfortably. "Did I do something wrong? This was your idea, wasn't it?"

She nodded. "It was. She needs to be with a man who's not a bastard. Just be very nice to her. She's not like me. She's smart, but not wise. A few years ago, she was in a relationship with a jerk who was brutal, mentally and physically. I had to rescue her."

"Rescue her?" The little pixie beat up the bad guy?

"I drove over to her place, threw her stuff in my truck and was leaving when he tried to stop us." She hesitated. "I shot him."

Shot him? "Is he . . . ."

Brandy looked away. "He's dead. He had a knife." She turned back to me. "She's doing okay now, but go easy on her. Don't try to get her into bed right away."

"Whoa." I started to put my hands up in surrender, but stopped when the pain hit my wrist. "I'm really not that kind of guy. I actually try to practice what I preach."

She shrugged. "I thought you would. But I just wanted to give you a heads up."

Brandy left to see to another patient and I had a little time to reflect on what she'd said before the doctor arrived. I had dismissed Doris' gossip as just that. But what if she had not only killed Hel's abusive manfriend, but had also stabbed the two men Doris described? Would it be possible that she had tired of Jon Franks' advances (or worse) and had gotten rid of him as well? However, I knew she had not tried to kill me at Beezer's. After all, she seemed to like me and had even set me up with her cousin. Right?

After a couple of hours of having the doctor do exactly as Brandy had said he would and finally finishing all the paperwork to get released, Hel met me at the exit as Brandy rolled me out in a wheel chair, at her insistence.

As soon as I got out the door, I stood and turned back to her. "I can take it from here. It's my arm in a sling, not my legs."

"Whatever," she said with a touch of disgust in her voice.

"I am grateful to you for all you've done for me, but I can walk."

Hel opened the passenger side door for me. "Don't worry, Booze. I'll make sure he gets home safe."

I raised an eyebrow. "Boos?"

Hel chuckled. "Not like booing the umpire. Booze, like Brandy."

I turned to Brandy and laughed. "Booze is your nickname?"

Her eyebrows lowered ominously. "Only for my closest friends and relatives, Bobbie-boy. So don't go spreading it around."

"No worries. I wouldn't want to get on your bad side."

"Yeah, well . . . ." She flashed a wry smile. "Take him the hell home, Hel. And don't do anything I would do."

As we headed out of the parking lot in Hel's Ford Edge, I pondered Brandy's sense of humor, what little of it there seemed to be.

Hel and I didn't talk much on the way home. She seemed uncomfortable driving in the snow, which was still falling heavily, and gave mainly monosyllabic answers to my questions.

"So, where are you from?"

"Huh?" she said as she peered out of the windshield.

"Are you from California?"

"Oh. Yes."

"Northern California?"

She leaned forward in her seat, hunching over the steering wheel. "Uh-huh."

"Take the next left."

"What?"

"Turn left at the next opportunity."

"Oh. Right." She shook her head. "I mean left."

"Would you rather I didn't say anything except where to turn?"

She sighed. "I really would. This weather is freaking me out. I'm from Malibu and we don't get any snow there."

"No problem." If she were so distracted that she'd say Malibu was in Northern California, she was definitely freaking out.

When we got to my house, she pulled in the drive and stopped. Her hands had the wheel in a death grip. When I reached across with my unslung left hand to open the door, she suddenly noticed me and hurried around the car to my door. I climbed out.

"I appreciate your chauffeuring me home," I said. "Would you

109

like to come in for a cup of tea or coffee?" I paused. "I'd offer you a glass of wine, but this doesn't look like the night for it."

"Thanks. I could use a shot of tequila right now, but I'll take a rain check." She glanced up at the flakes coming down, covering everything with a blanket of white. "Or a snow check."

I was worried about her in this weather. "Are you sure you'll be all right? You could stay here until Brandy or Tony could pick you up. I'd offer to drive you home in my truck, but it's in worse shape than I am."

"I'll be fine. There's only, what, about a foot of snow so far?"

I glanced down at my feet. "Maybe three inches, at most. Look, I have a spare room and promise to behave like a gentleman if you would like to stay."

She laughed. "I can't imagine you acting any other way. I have all-wheel drive and snow tires. I'll be fine. But I'd better get rolling while I still can."

"Be sure and call me when you get home. Or wherever you're staying."

"I will. I'm staying with Brandy and Tony and I'm sure they have your number." She leaned over and kissed me on the cheek. "Now get inside, Bobbie-boy."

I watched as she slowly drove away. I hated to be called Bob, Bobbie or anything like that. Unless it was by some of the elderly ladies in the church. Or Hel.

Then I went inside and stood looking out the window. My wrist ached and I should ice it. I should also turn on the lights. Instead I just wanted to savor the moment.

Chapter 20

I finally turned and went to the kitchen for an ice pack. As I opened the freezer, I heard a car drive up my driveway. Then there was a knock at the door. Hel must have forgotten something. I hurried to the door and flipped on the outside lights.

"Is that you, Hel?

I opened the door to the Chief, standing with a puzzled look. "Don't you mean, 'Hell, is that you?'"

I reddened. "Sorry, Chief. I thought it was Booze's cousin, Hel. She just left."

"Okay, I don't even know if I want to know what you're talking about. But since you're not even going to ask me in out of the cold . . . ." He pushed past me and stepped inside. He held out a gun, a stainless automatic with the slide open. "I come bearing a gift. A loan really, but that doesn't sound as good."

I didn't take it. "What's that for?"

"In case the nut in the truck comes back to finish the job. Officially, I'm not doing this." He cocked his head. "Have you ever fired a gun?"

I sighed and took the gun with my left hand. I popped out the clip, which was full, and pulled back the slide to kick the round in the chamber out, wincing as I did. Then I flipped the safety, which uncocked it. "A Smith & Wesson model 639. Never fired this particular model, but my dad has a 5906 that I can keep within a 3" pattern at 25'. I'd prefer the Glock 27, if I were wanting a handgun. It's .40 caliber and much easier to conceal. But since I'm not looking for a handgun . . . ." I handed the gun, the clip and the extra round back to him.

The Chief shook his head and took the proffered gun. "Are you a pacifist, one of those guys who'd rather die than protect yourself?"

"Not really." I reached behind the door and picked up my aluminum softball bat. "I'd use this without a qualm. It's just that handguns have such a bad rep in this state that any priest shooting someone would get raked over the coals as a hypocrite in the press, locally, regionally and nationally, even if it were self defense."

"Show me how you'd protect yourself with that."

I went to a batter's stance, bat held high. I grimaced as pain shot through my right wrist, almost dropping the bat. The Chief stepped back one step, out of my reach, and lifted the empty gun, finger off the trigger. "Bang, you're dead."

"Point made." I lowered my bat. "I'll make sure my attacker is in the strike zone."

He snickered. "Yeah, I bet you will." He handed me a business card. "My cell's on it. Call me if you wise up. Or if you're shot while swinging for the bleachers."

After he stomped out the door, I studied his card. He had a point. Considering my lousy batting average when I played on the church softball team, maybe I should reconsider. After my first season, the St. Nicholas Nighthawks (our team) would have benched me if we'd had enough players. I'd have retired voluntarily, but it would have meant the end of our undermanned team. So we endured each other and the trials and travails of having a priest who looked like a jock and hit like a wimp. I stashed the bat behind the door and went for my shotgun.

I'd inherited a Holland & Holland Royal Deluxe 12 gauge side-by-side shotgun from my mother. She had been quite a woman. No wimpy 28 gauge for her. It was in excellent condition and, last time I'd checked, was worth over fifty grand. I'd thought of selling it and donating the money to her Tri-Delt Sorority to give to St. Jude's Children's Research Hospital in her name, but just couldn't get rid of her cherished shotgun. Instead, I kept it locked in my bedroom closet safe. I punched in the combination and pulled it out.

It was a beautiful piece of ballistic workmanship, with engraved silver receiver and impeccable walnut stock. I cracked it open and dropped in a couple of birdshot shells. It hurt my wrist even to do that. After snapping it shut, I set the safety and went back into my living room. Birdshot is not likely to kill anyone, especially at any distance, but will crimp their style. Just in case, I also stuffed a couple of double-ought buckshot shells in my pocket.

I set the shotgun next to my baseball bat and went into the living room. It was getting late, but I was too wired to go to bed and my wrist was aching. The hospital had given me a bottle of oxycodone, however I avoid pills as much as possible. I don't even take aspirin. Although I am not much of a drinker, I decided that, under the circumstances, a wee dram of Macallan 18 year-old scotch would be okay. I poured a shot into an Edinburgh crystal whisky glass, dripped in a little water, and wandered over to look out my front window. I took a sip. I've read this whisky described as tasting like "stewed apples, dusted with cinnamon, that finishes with cloves and a hint of orange peel." It just tasted like great whisky to me.

In order to watch the snow fall, I flipped on the outside lights. There is something strangely calming about watching snow drift down, quieting the night and the soul. The tire tracks left by Hel and the Chief were slowly filling, lost in the sea of white. I glanced down at my glass, considering whether or not to stay awake and finish my drink when the crystal flashed red. Then it stopped as a red dot moved across my chest.

Although I only own the shotgun, my dad had a veritable arsenal, of which I had fired many in my younger days. One of his rifles had an Aimpoint scope that put just such a red dot on a target. Without a second thought, I dropped to the floor, landing on my sore wrist. I gritted my teeth and stifled a yelp. Sharp cracks of what seemed like a hundred gunshots echoed through the room as my window shattered. Crawling on my belly, I headed for my shotgun in the entry. Staying on the floor, I opened it, replaced the birdshot with double-ought buckshot and closed it. Then I clicked off the safety. Whoever took those potshots at me was playing for keeps.

My heart pounded like a kettle drum as I considered my options. I needed to get to a phone. I headed for the kitchen, crawling with the shotgun cradled in the crooks of my elbows. Before I got there, I heard the roar of a barely-muffled engine that faded into the distance. Most likely, my assailant was gone. I wasn't ready to take that chance and stayed low. Once I got into the kitchen, I got to my knees and grabbed the phone, dialing the number on the Chief's card.

I heard him yawn. "Yeah? You ready to come to your senses and take the gun?"

With great effort, I kept my voice calm, even if I weren't. "Someone just tried to kill me. I think he's gone now, but would you come over?"

113

"What the . . . . Hell, yes. I'll be right there."

"When you get here, give a 'shave and a haircut' knock before you open the door so I don't unload both barrels of my shotgun on you."

"Shave and a haircut? Oh, that Roger Rabbit thing." He paused. "You have a shotgun?"

"Just get over here."

"On my way."

I crawled back into the entry and sat on the floor with my shotgun resting in my lap. I looked down at my hand. Blood from a glass cut dripped on my jeans and it was shaking. I had never been so close to dying as two times this night.

A car roared up my street within minutes. It stopped in front of my house and there was a pounding on my door. Rat-tat-a-tat-tat.

Relief washed over me. I clicked on the safety. "It's unlocked."

The door slowly opened and the Chief peeked around it. "Don't shoot. I come in peace."

"I haven't shot anyone in weeks, so you're probably safe." I stood and rested the shotgun in a corner after I set the safety.

The Chief sniffed. "Is that booze I smell?" He eyed me as he unzipped his parka. "Have you been drinking? Your clothes are a mess. And did you leave a window open? It's cold in here."

"I did have one sip of scotch, then crawled through the rest of my drink. I guess that didn't help." I gestured to the living room. "And I now have plenty of fresh air."

The Chief glanced into the living room. "Holy . . . . What did you do to your window?"

There were glass pebbles all over the carpet with snow drifting through the opening where my window had been. My jeans and shirt had holes and scotch stains from my trip out on my belly. And it was getting very cold. I shivered.

"If you check out the wall, you'll find a bullet hole or two." I grabbed a coat off the hall rack and put it on.

The Chief went over to the wall and studied it. "There must be dozens of holes. That's twice in one day someone came after you. Did you say something offensive in your last sermon?"

I shrugged. "No more than usual. Not anything that merited a machine gun attack."

He traced a bullet hole with his fingernail. "Looks like about a .30 caliber. Judging from the rate of fire, maybe from an AK-47. Cheap and nasty. I'll get a couple of bullets dug out tomorrow and run them through ballistics."

"Great. Maybe the North Koreans are after me." I walked into the living room. My original, mint-condition Hogarth engraving of Lord Lovat had three holes in it. My insurance company wasn't going to be happy. "Would you give me a hand putting some plywood I have in the garage over the window? I'm wasting energy."

"Someone empties a magazine at you and you're worried about your heating bill?"

"Under similar circumstances, when someone missed a shot at him, Winston Churchill said, 'When my time is due, it will come.' It's a worthy concept."

He shook his head. "You're one cool cucumber."

"That's me. Joe Cool." I hid my shaking hands as I said it.

Chapter 21

When I finally got to bed, I didn't sleep much. With my mom's shotgun as my bed mate, I kept jolting awake at the slightest noise. I never realized how much houses creaked before that. About five, I brewed a pot of strong tea and headed for my favorite rocker. I pulled my thick, terrycloth robe tightly around me and sipped my tea, cradling the shotgun between my legs. I sat in the darkness of my violated living room, trying to make some sense out of what had happened.

I must have dozed because the next thing I knew my grandfather clock was chiming eight and I was shivering from the cold breeze slipping past the makeshift plywood window covering. I turned up the thermostat, nuked a refill of my mug of tea and went to my computer to find a glass shop. Gold Rush Glaziers had a nice ring to the name, so I called them.

"Gold Rush Glaziers, Rod speaking. Need a new window, Father?"

For a moment I was taken aback, but I remembered caller I.D. "Yes, I do . . . . But how did you know that?"

"My sister's a waitress at the Buggy Springs Diner. Everybody's talkin' 'bout you gettin' shot up. You get patched up already?"

I rubbed my forehead. Great. The gossip mill was working overtime. "I'm fine. The only casualties were a window and a wall. I just need a new picture window."

"You got the size?"

"Uh, not yet. It's about five feet tall by maybe seven wide. Do you have one in stock?"

He laughed. "We don't carry anything like that anymore. All special order. Get me the exact measurements and I'll order it for you."

Order it? "How long will that take?"

"Well normally two-three weeks." He paused and I hoped he was going to say he could put a rush on it. "But it's the holidays, you know. Probably more like four."

I closed my eyes. Four weeks of a freezing cave instead of my beloved living room.

"You there, Father?"

"Yeah. I'm not an ice cube yet. I'll call you back after I measure the opening."

"You do that."

I hung up. Not only did everyone in town know that my window had been shot out, but I would have to live without it for a month in the middle of winter. Lord, was this meant to be a trial of my patience?

A pounding on my front door brought me out of my reverie. I was still in my robe and shearling slippers, and my shotgun was propped up in the corner. Since I doubted that last night's sniper had returned, I cinched my robe's belt, brushed back my hair with my hand and went to the door. As I opened it, Brandy, like a militant Munchkin, shoved me aside and stomped in.

"What are you doing, getting shot at?" She glared at my right wrist. "And where's your sling?"

I closed the door with my left hand, slipping my right behind my back like a guilty child. "It's hard to crawl out of the line of fire with one hand, you know."

She unzipped her parka and slowly pulled a stainless steel handgun almost as big as she was out of her shoulder holster. She offered it to me.

I shook my head. "Why is everyone trying to arm me? I have a twelve gauge that is more than enough." I studied the gun. I recognized it as one like my dad had in his collection: a Desert Eagle autoloader with a ten-inch barrel. "What is that, a 44 Magnum?"

"No, a 50 AE."

Whoa! "And you can shoot that without knocking yourself into the next county."

She shrugged. "Ask Hel. It saved her life." She reholstered her hand cannon and glanced over at my boarded-up window. "When are you going to get that fixed?"

"According to Gold Rush Glaziers, in about four weeks."

"Go get dressed in something less ridiculous." She pulled out her cell phone. "I'll get you a window."

I started to protest that, under the circumstances, a terrycloth robe wasn't ridiculous, but she was already talking on her cell. I went into my bedroom and pulled on a pair of cords and a warm sweater. Brandy was talking on her phone. Or rather yelling on her phone. As I came back into the living room, she was already off the phone and zipping up her coat.

"Leaving so soon?" I said with a grin. "I was going to offer you a cup of microwaved tea."

"As tempting as that sounds, I have a job." She grinned back. "Besides, I'd rather eat grasshoppers than drink leftover tea."

Just before she closed the door, she said, "Tony'll be here in a few to check out your window."

"Thanks."

I hoped for a few minutes alone. I like doing Morning Prayer every day and really needed it at that point. I'd almost been killed last night and I was fighting to keep in control. Some quiet time with God wouldn't hurt. But my phone was ringing, so I grabbed it.

"Rectory, Father Robert speaking."

"Father Robert? This is Lisa, Lisa Franks. Are you okay? I called the hospital, but they said you weren't there."

"I'm fine. I suppose you're calling about what happened last night."

"I sure am. I heard someone rammed your truck at Beezer's, tried to kill you, that you almost died."

I sighed. At least she didn't know about my window being shot out. "I'm fine. Just a sprained wrist, nothing more." I just wanted to get off the phone and have breakfast.

"I'll be right over to help you. I can cook for you, help you take care of things."

"No." That was the last thing I wanted. "I can still use both hands. I don't need any help. Really. I'll see you Sunday at church."

"Well . . ." She hesitated. "If you're sure you're okay–"

"I'm fine. Thanks for calling."

After I hung up, I made a fresh pot of tea and started some oatmeal, Scot's porridge, breakfast of champions. Just as I got it in the bowl, there was a loud knocking at the door. I grabbed a hot mug of freshly-brewed tea and, after casting a wistful glance at my hot oatmeal,

119

answered the door.

Tony stood there, glaring at me. He had on a heavy, canvas coat and a black watchcap covering his shaved head. "Brandy says I have to find you a window."

"Uh, I don't expect that. She told me she could get one for me, but I don't want to cause a problem."

"If I don't find one, I'll have the problem, so let me get to it."

He pushed past me and went into the living room. I stood for a moment, trying to think of a response. I had none, so I followed him. He had a tape measure out, checking the dimensions of my window.

Tony turned and glared at me. "You know this is not a standard window."

Like my irregular window size was my fault? "I wasn't aware. I haven't had to replace it before."

He grunted and pulled out a small notebook, writing in it.

I stood there, waiting for him to say something. Finally, I broke the silence.

"Can you help me?"

He gave me a hard look. "I'll get your damned window and block in the sides so it will fit. We've got a job that's hung up, so I'll steal it from there and replace it before it's a problem. But understand this, you stop getting Brandy involved with this dangerous crap."

I was stunned. "I never got Brandy involved in this. She appeared on my doorstep this morning and called you. I didn't ask her to do anything."

He stepped close, pugnaciously staring in my eyes. "I'm very protective of Brandy. I mean what I say. If I feel someone's a threat to my Brandy, he's gonna be in a serious hurt. Got it?"

Enough of this. I may be a cleric, but I keep in shape and had four inches on him. I matched him, glare for glare. "I did nothing here. I've been shot at and now threatened when all I've done is ask a few questions."

"Maybe some questions are best left unanswered," he muttered. "I don't want her hurt and now she's running around with her gun again, saying she's gotta protect you. I don't like it."

Before I could respond, he turned away and headed to the door. "I'll be back with the window later. If you leave, don't lock up."

"Thanks, but--" I called just before he closed the door.

I pondered what Tony had said.   Although he had claimed Jon was a good guy, Jon had put the make on Brandy.   Could that "loyal friend" bit have all been an act?   I needed to check on his whereabouts when Jon had died and when some truck tried to kill me.   I also wished I knew if he had a full-auto assault rifle.

Chapter 22

With almost being killed two times in less than six hours and getting almost no sleep last night, I felt I needed a little R & R. I called the church office and Doris answered.

"St. Nicholas Church. Good morning and God bless."

That was a new greeting. I rather liked it.

"It's Father Robert, Doris. I was thinking of taking the day off."

"Oh, Father, you should. Were you hurt bad?"

"No, I wasn't hurt bad, or even badly. I wasn't hurt at all. Obviously, the gossip has reached you. I just lost one window. That's all."

"Don't worry about a thing. I cleared your calendar. Do you want me to reschedule Dean or just tell him to call you in a week or two?"

Dean Watkins was a young man of twenty-two who had lost both his parents in a car accident. Now he was having anger issues, including with God. He'd been getting into bar fights, striking out at anyone because God wasn't in his fist's range. The court had given me the task of counseling him for anger management. Hearing his name gave me a jolt of reality. I hadn't suffered anything but a minor inconvenience and I was shirking my duties. Time to get back to work.

"I changed my mind, Doris." I checked my watch. I was supposed to meet with Dean in less than twenty minutes. "I'll be right there. If Dean shows up before I get there, have him wait."

"After what happened to you? I don't think–"

"Then don't try." Had I actually said that? I rubbed my temples with my thumb and forefinger, then slowly exhaled. "Sorry, Doris. That was a horrid thing to say and I apologize. I'm a little on edge."

"Well, considering you were almost killed, I accept your apology." She sniffed. "But I do have feelings, you know."

"I know and I'm so sorry for being such a . . . jerk. I'll be in as soon as I can."

After a quick shower and shave, I was headed out when the Chief pulled up in my drive.

"Where ya heading, Robert? Before I left last night, I found a couple of shell casings in the snow. Looks like for an AK-47. I wanted to dig a couple of slugs out of your wall for a ballistics check."

"Have at it. The door's unlocked."

"Unlocked?" He shook his head. "Are you crazy? Someone just tried to kill you."

"It's Buggy Springs, Chief. I often forget to lock my door. Besides, whoever's been trying to kill me doesn't seem to want to look me in the eye when he does it."

"Or she."

"What?"

The Chief shrugged. "Don't rule out a woman. Maybe it's some lonely old lady who thinks you haven't paid her enough attention."

"Some--" I rolled my eyes. "Whatever. I have more important things to do than this."

"I'll lock up when I finish."

"You do and I won't get my window fixed."

He snorted with disgust. "Okay, okay. You didn't live in Colton, that's for sure. Don't blame me if everything's ripped off when you get back."

I made the sign of the Cross. "I absolve you of all responsibility."

He headed for my front door, saying, "I absolve you from having no common sense."

When I got to the church, Dean was already there. I took him in my office and we talked for almost an hour. I wasn't sure I was getting through, but we prayed together before he left. At least that was something new.

I returned a number of phone calls, mainly from parishioners seeing if I were still alive. It tried my patience not to just yell, "I'm fine, so leave me alone." But I was the rector and I had to thank each and every one for their concern. It was almost noon before I finished.

124

I sat at my desk, making notes on the hard facts I knew. It wasn't much.

1. I had a call from an unknown caller who quoted scripture about the mighty falling and made a riddle about Humpty Dumpty.
2. Jon Franks died in a fall from a ladder, a suspicious accident.
3. Elvira had been murdered in her bed.
4. I had a call from an unknown caller who quoted scripture about the sins of the fathers going down to the sons and made a riddle about Pop Goes the Weasel.
5. Someone tried to smash me with a truck.
6. Someone tried to shoot me with a fully automatic weapon.

However, there were a number of questions that arose from the case. Case? I was beginning to sound like a detective. Maybe it was time I thought like one. I started a new sheet.

1. Why had the killer called and taunted me in the first place?
2. Did the killer actually know the Scriptures or had merely googled them?
3. What was the motive for killing Jon Franks?
4. What was the motive for killing Elvira Murdoch?
5. What did the deaths of Jon Franks and Elvira Murdoch have in common?
6. Why had two attempts been made on my life in about six hours?
7. Who owns a big truck and a full-auto weapon?

I leaned back in my chair, propped my feet on my desk and studied my notes. I started listing suspects. Since a woman could knock over a ladder, hold a pillow on an old woman's face, drive a truck into another or shoot a gun as well as a man, I had to be gender-blind in my listing. In my gut, the brutal violence of the acts pointed to a man, but I could not be sure. I had to be systematic, so I considered each one as I listed his or her name. I started with the immediate family, often the best suspects.

Son Todd Franks hated his dad. But did he have anything to gain by killing him if Lisa got everything? Then again, money wasn't the only motivator. Hate was a strong motive for murder. Still, he had taken over the note on Beezer's Bar, so maybe he had received some of Jon's money as an inheritance.

Then there was the sexy, or over-sexed, Lisa Franks, who had much to gain when Jon died. But she was safely away when Jon was killed. She didn't appear to have any real allies to do the deed for her. No one seemed to really like her. But she could have brought someone in from out of the area, someone from her past life, to do the dirty work. However, did Todd taking over the Beezer's Bar note mean she had not inherited Jon's estate? I needed to find out.

The Zachary's were next. Ben had hated Jon and had good reason to kill him. But it had not erased his debt. Or at least according to him. What if he had made a deal with whoever did take up the note for a big reduction or better terms? Choke would have helped. He seemed to do what his daddy said. And Chewy was no saint. A family trio had a lot of appeal. Were all of them in the bar when I left or was one out waiting in a truck for a chance to play ram-the-rector?

I hesitated before putting the next names down. I didn't want it to be either or both of them, but I had to consider the possibility. I picked up a half-empty bottle of water that had been sitting on my desk for a couple of days and took a swig. I almost wished it were scotch, but I don't drink often in the daytime and never in my office. Bad habits. As a pastor, I wanted to always think the best of people, even if it weren't true. As a detective, I had to consider what was the worst they could do. I preferred being a pastor. But I wrote down the names.

Tony Mazzoni had almost given a veiled threat about asking too many questions and might have taken care of Jon for making advances on Brandy. Had Brandy told him? Was his appreciation for what Jon had done for them overshadowed by what he had tried to do to Brandy? Was his fondness for his dead boss only an act? If so, I should see if he were in any school plays when he was younger since he had seemed sincere.

Brandy Mazzoni had previously shown how she handled men who were a danger to women. She also did not seem to have the same fondness for Jon that Tony had.   And she was smart enough to engineer the whole thing.   But why have Tony try to kill me, then patch me up? Maybe he had been trying to scare me instead of kill me.   But how could he have known I would have dropped under my truck instead of becoming road kill on my front bumper?   Or maybe Tony was acting on his own when he went after me, trying to protect his wife.

I sighed.   I'd listed everyone, no matter how little I wanted to, and no suspect was standing out.   So I added another one.   Unknown person or persons.

That last one bothered me.   Who hadn't I considered?   I needed to check on anyone who might have had a problem with Jon Franks, no matter how seemingly minor and I knew exactly who could help me with the names of any of Jon's enemies I might have overlooked.   I went out of my office to chat with Doris.

Chapter 23

Doris was hard at work, talking on the telephone while she typed up the church newsletter on the computer. Since she was turned away from the door between our offices, she didn't see me enter.

". . . and the bullets missed his head by less than an inch. I understand he hid in the kitchen all night, waiting until dawn to call the Chief for help. Not only that—"

She must have sensed me behind her. I could see the muscles in her shoulders tense.

"Uh, Kathy, can I call you back? I need to see if Father Robert needs any coffee." As soon as she hung up, she turned around, feigning surprise at seeing me. She pressed her right hand to her ample bosom. "Oh, Father Robert, you startled me. You must be part Indian to sneak up on me so quietly."

I stifled a smile. Time to lay it on thick and see if she could help me. "Actually, I am about 1/32 Blackfoot Sioux, on my mother's side. Some cavalry officer fell head-over-heels in love with a Sioux woman and scandalized his Boston family by marrying her. My nose is my inheritance from her. You are very observant."

"Well, I try to keep my eyes open. I had noticed your nose." She blushed. "I never mentioned it because some people might be, well, offended if I pointed it out."

"I'm not that sort. Since you do keep a keen eye on what's happening in town, maybe you could help me on something that, quite frankly, has me baffled. I'm compiling a list of suspects in Jon Franks' murder, but I only have a few. Could you write up a list of anyone who might have had a problem with Jon, no matter how small?"

"It really was murder then?" She shook her head. "I don't know what's happening in our town. First Jon is murdered and then someone tries to kill you, a man of the cloth. The whole place is going to hell in a handbasket."

"There are still many good people here, but we need to find who isn't as quickly as possible. Will you help?"

She straightened up in her swivel chair, puffing out her chest. "You can count on me, Father. I'm not one to gossip, but this is important. I'll have you a list in a couple of hours."

"Thanks, Doris. I'm going back to the rectory for a bite of lunch."

As I started for the door, I remembered that I had walked to church. My truck was probably D.O.A. "Uh, Doris, do you know anyone who might have a four-wheel drive for sale? I can't drive my Camaro in the snow."

"Oh, of course, Father." She reached for her old-fashioned Rolodex. "Jimmy Bee is always buying and selling cars and trucks. I'll call him."

"Can you have him contact me at home? I'll walk there."

She started to rise from her chair. "I'll drive you home, Father."

"No, that's alright. I need the exercise." Plus I had once ridden with Doris and did not want to relive that harrowing experience, even the short distance to my house. "Just call Jimmy for me and make the list of people who had a problem with Jon."

She settled back in her chair. "Consider it done, Father."

As I walked to the door, I glanced at my reflection in the window. I hadn't lied about my Blackfoot blood, but I had exaggerated about inheriting my nose from my great-great-great-grandmother. Then again, my nose was long and straight, so maybe I hadn't exaggerated that much.

Chapter 24

Although the road had been plowed, the footing was rather icy and treacherous, so I was relieved to make it back home without a slip. When I went inside, I was glad to see that I had a new window to give me a view and keep me warm. I needed a cup of tea, so I headed for the kitchen. There was a bill on the counter that said "Window- $1200, Install- $800, Discount- $1500, Total- $500, Paint is wet so hands off. Same for Brandy." It was dirt cheap and I knew it. I wished Tony were here so I could thank him, but his latest attitude made me reluctant to call him.

After brewing a pot of Earl Grey, I went in the living room to check out my new window. I had lost an inch or two on each side with new wood trim to cover the shrinkage. The workmanship was good and the paint looked dry. I touched it with the tip of my finger. It wasn't dry and I left fingerprint proof of my infraction for any future CSI investigator. I wiped my finger on my handkerchief.

A blue and white Ford truck I didn't recognize pulled up in front as I was looking out the window. It had large, chrome wheels and an extended cab, plus a chrome bumper protruding about a foot and a half in front with a winch. It was big. The man who climbed out of the cab and headed toward my front door was not, at least in stature. He was maybe five feet, six inches, with a belly that pushed past his open leather coat. He had a thick, brown beard and a fringe of long hair around his bald pate. As he walked, he hitched up his jeans, that immediately fell back below his belly. He saw me watching and grinned. His smile was missing a tooth or three.

As I opened the door, he stuck out a hand with grease under the fingernails. "Jimmy Bee, Rev. Doris says ya need a truck."

With a sling on my right arm, I took it with my left hand and he shook it with a firm grip. Not one of those show-off power squeezes, but the strength of hard work. "Nice to meet you, Mr. Bee. Just call me Robert."

He bent over laughing, then coughing. I was about to pat him on the back when he straightened and pulled a wrinkled blue bandanna from his pocket and wiped his eyes and runny nose. "Naw, just Jimmy. Last name's Banaszewski, but nobody can pronounce it, so I go by Jimmy Bee." He nodded toward the truck in my driveway. "So, whatcha think? It was owned by an old guy out in Sierra City since it was new. Only 89,000 original miles. Ready for a test drive?"

I looked down at his grubby jeans and his torn coat. I feared what the truck would look like inside, but he had driven out to me and I owed it to him to be polite. "Sure. Let's go. I'll get my coat."

As I grabbed my pea coat off the rack by the door, Jimmy cocked his head as he studied my living room wall. The bullet holes were all still there and the Chief had enlarged several to take out the bullets. "Ya make someone mad?"

"Must have. Know anyone in the area with a truck, a full-auto weapon and didn't like Jon Franks?"

He shrugged. "Maybe a third of all the men 'round here, including me, and almost as many women."

Jimmy walked out the door and climbed in the passenger side of the truck before I could ask more. I followed, looking over the exterior of the big vehicle as I did. The paint was in great condition, with no dents. My guess was the truck was maybe twenty years old, but well maintained. Gritting my teeth for what was in store for me after seeing Jimmy's clothes, I opened the door.

I have a saying I try to live by: never assume. I should have heeded my own advice. The interior was immaculate. It had cloth, high-back bucket seats that were covered by old beach towels. I pulled the one off the driver's seat and the cloth looked almost new. The carpet was clean and had floor mats. I climbed inside, sinking into the comfortable seat, and turned to Jimmy.

"How old is this truck, anyway?"

"It's an '86." He grinned again. His teeth showed he liked tobacco. "Nice, huh? She's an F250, a four-wheel drive with a 460 engine. Fire her up."

I turned the key and the engine roared to life. It idled smoothly.

Jimmy patted the dash. "I changed all the fluids, tuned her up and detailed her. She's got air, power windows and locks, and cruise. Changed the radio so's you can use an iPod, if you want. Take her out."

I put the truck in reverse and carefully backed down my drive. My old truck had been a Plain Jane, simple vinyl bench seat, standard transmission and no extras. This one had an auto trans and every extra. It was also much bigger than my short-bed Ranger. It would take some getting used to.

As I maneuvered along the icy road, the truck felt easy to control. I settled back in my seat and glanced over at Jimmy.

"So, besides you, who would want to kill Jon and shoot up my house?"

He raised an eyebrow. "I don't have no tears for Jon Franks, but I don't have enough cause to kill him. He used me to find a buyer for his Lexus, then stiffed me on the commission. But if I kicked the ladder out from under every S.O.B. that gypped me out of a few bucks, there'd be a lot more corpses 'round here." He chuckled. "And I wouldn't miss if I'd opened up on ya."

I didn't doubt him and shuddered. I eased the big truck onto the main highway and kicked it up a bit. The big engine responded quickly. "So, who would be your first choice for who would kick out the ladder and barely miss me?"

He stroked his beard. "Got a few ideas. Know the Zachary clan?"

"We've met."

"Snakes, every one of 'em. Then there's the brat, Jon's kid. Don't know that he's got the baguettes. And Jon's wife has good cause."

"His wife?" Except for money, I wasn't aware of any "good cause."

"Sure, Jon'd been bird-dogging half the pu–" He reddened and cleared his throat. Interesting how often that happens when people talk to me. "The purty women 'round these parts. I heard he'd got one put up in one of his houses. Made regular visits."

I slowed and made a U-turn, heading back home. From what I'd heard so far, any woman seemed Jon's type. "You know who the woman is?"

"More like a kid. Carly, the waitress at Higgins Diggins."

Surprise, surprise. The Goth young woman Red had been pawing at the bar when we met was involved with his father. The

133

threads were getting twisted, becoming a rope that might hold things together. And maybe hang the killer, if I could only figure out where the rope ended.

"So, Jon provided a love nest for Carly. Did he do that for any other women?"

Jimmy brayed so loudly I almost lost my hearing. When he regained control, he pulled out a bandanna and blew his nose, then wiped his eyes. "Yer funny, Robert. 'Love nest.' Ya sound like one of them there old movies." He wiped a little spittle from the side of his mouth, then wadded his bandanna back in his pocket. "He shacked up with a lot of 'em before he got hitched, some fer years, and a few of 'em shared him, too. Far's I know, Carly's the only one got a place to live after Lisa got her hooks inta ol' Jon. Course he and Cindy Wolfe was gettin' it on and he picked up a lotta . . . uh, loose women at the bars 'round here."

"Would any of them want to kill Jon?"

Jimmy cocked his head and stared out the window for a few moments.

"Naw, he paid 'em purty good when he dumped 'em. Some of their men might not have been so forgiving, though."

"Like?" Like Tony, I almost said.

"Like Tony Mazzoni. Ol' Jon paid off a big hospital bill when their kid died so's I figure he was paying off Brandy for keeping him happy. Tat for tit, if ya get my meaning. Then there's Dagwood. He'd be plenty p--" Jimmy cleared his throat. "Perturbed if he'd found out about Jon and Blondie. But I never heared that he did."

I was surprised that Jimmy knew the word "perturbed." How much of his red-necked hick routine was just that: a routine. "Uh, Dagwood? I don't think I know him."

Jimmy howled with laughter again and, again, out came the bandanna to absorb bodily fluids. "We call him Dagwood 'cause he's thick as a brick and loves big sandwiches, and his blond wife is built like a brick sh–" He winced. "Shrine. Like Blondie in the comics, ya know."

I stifled a laugh. Being a priest makes some people react in such an amusing way. "So, what's this Dagwood's real name and where can I find him?"

"Dwayne Bell. He works for Jon. I mean, he worked for Jon.

134

Too stupid to get a job anywhere else, so I guess Jon put him to work to pay off Blondie for her services in the sack."

Worked for Jon Franks? Could it be the big man I'd seen carrying a sheet of plywood with Tony? What did he look like? All I could remember was a black 49er ball cap.

I took a chance. "He a sports fan?"

Jimmy cocked his head, giving me a quizzical look. "Total nut for the 49ers. Why?"

I shrugged. "I guess I met him."

I pulled into my drive, put the truck in park and turned off the engine. "Well, Jimmy, what do you want for this beast?"

He eyed me. "Cash?"

"Sure."

"Three large."

It took me a moment. Who was I dealing with? "You mean three thousand dollars?"

He nodded his head. "Yeah. I sure don't mean three bills." He stuck out his right hand. "Deal?"

I shook his hand. "Deal."

Chapter 25

After I'd dug three thousand dollars out of my safe, paid Jimmy for the truck and dropped him at the Buggy Springs Diner, I went home and nuked a mug of Earl Grey tea. Mug in hand, I settled back in my chair with my new picture window to think. Something was bothering me about what Jimmy had said. Actually, a couple of things. The first was what Jimmy had said about Tony and Brandy. Had Brandy lied about rejecting Jon's advances? If so, Tony's claimed feelings for Jon could have been an act. Under the right circumstance, I'd see the pair of them committing murder and I didn't like that vision.

The second bother was a niggling in the back of my mind. As I sipped my tea, it came to the front. Jimmy had said something about kicking the ladder out from under Jon. How did he know that? I went to my computer and called up the website for *The Constitution*, our local rag. Although we may be small town in some ways, everyone has a website, including our newspaper. I called up the article about Jon Franks' death. It only said he'd died in a tragic accident, nothing about a ladder. I leaned back in my desk chair. It looked liked James Banaszewski, a.k.a. Jimmy Bee, had just joined my suspect list. Then there was Dwayne Bell, a.k.a. Dagwood, who I had never even heard of before Jimmy named him. The list was growing, not shrinking.

My phone started ringing, breaking my reverie, and I answered it.

"Father Robert. May I help you?"

"Hey, Robert, I've got the ballistic's report back." It was the Chief. "It was an AK-47. So far, no match on the bullets to any known gun."

I pondered the information. "Any idea who might own an AK-47 around here?"

"Well, they're cheap and efficient weapons, so growers love them. But they're usually shooting at each other. None of the ones we've confiscated came back to yours."

"Great. So it wasn't a cop with a confiscated gun, but it could

137

be an unknown local pot cultivator who's never been busted. If it were, my life could be up in smoke."

"Up in smoke? Is that a joke?"

I sighed. "A bad one, obviously. It was the title of a Cheech and Chong movie about smoking pot made decades ago. However, I do have a couple of names to check out. They're only based on rumors, but I guess that's all we've got."

"Shoot. I mean, give me the names."

"James Banaszewski and Dwayne Bell."

"Jimmy Bee and Dagwood? Dumb and dumber." The Chief chuckled. "See? I know movies, too."

I groaned. "Very funny. I'll recommend you to *Saturday Night Live*. But there's something about Jimmy Bee. He's not dumb, believe me."

"I'll check them out. Funny thing is that Dwayne's the one who found Jon's body, but there was no reason to suspect him of anything. You know if he or Jimmy had a motive?"

"Well, Jon gypped Jimmy on a car deal and Jimmy knew that someone knocked Jon off a ladder." I hesitated before I said that Jon had rewarded Dagwood because he'd had an affair with Blondie. I remembered that Jimmy had implied the same happened with Brandy and Tony. I wasn't ready to incriminate them. "Then Todd said something that made me wonder. To quote another movie, 'Follow the money.'"

"*Jerry Maguire?*"

I laughed. "Close, but no cigar. Deep Throat said it in *All the President's Men*."

"Deep Throat? Wasn't that a movie, too?"

"Not one I've seen, but you may have." Silence. "Anyway, that just might be the key to solving this case. The money, not the movie."

"I got that. I'm not stupid." The Chief paused. "Until we find out who's taking potshots at you, I could loan you a Kevlar vest."

"Thanks, but I'll stick to cloth vestments."

"Not exactly body armor. Don't forget that the Bible says God helps those who help themselves, you know."

"Sorry, that's like 'cleanliness is next to godliness': a nice adage, but not Biblical. It came from Algernon Sidney, a

138

Parliamentarian during the English Civil War of the 1600's, not that you'll care. Just let me know if you find out anything interesting on those guys."

"Will do. Just keep your head down until I find this wack-job."

"Hard to do when you're six-two."

He laughed. "Yeah, that's why I'm glad I'm five-nine. Catch ya."

Chapter 26

After I hung up, I went into my kitchen and made a turkey-on-rye sandwich. I poured myself another mug of tea. I needed to find out more on the backgrounds of my suspects. I considered calling the Chief and asking him to do background checks on the whole group, but decided it was too early, since all of them might be innocent. I'd be very embarrassed if no one on my list was the killer and this were all a time-waster for him. No, this was up to me. I'd seen websites listed in Google that were for investigating people, so I took my lunch to my computer and starting searching.

I found a site called InstantChecker.com that claimed it could give me the lowdown on anyone's past history, including "court records, address history, bankruptcies, property records, contact info, real estate info, judgments, liens, and so much more!" For a nominal fee, of course. I paid $23.95 for a one-month membership with unlimited searches and began digging.

The site overstated its investigative power. I got the birth dates, addresses and astrological signs of everyone I checked out, plus advice on which signs were compatible with the person I was checking out. There were a few arrest records, rated from "Possible" to "Least Possible." Most of them were from far out of state and for people that obviously weren't the ones I was checking out, like there was a Dwayne Bell who had been convicted of murder and was now out of prison, but he was black, looked about sixty and lived in Mississippi. But the local Dwayne Bell, a.k.a Dagwood, had a DUI on his record here and an assault conviction in Oklahoma. He was also married to Starburst, possibly named after the candy, not Blondie or Tinker. Todd Franks had two assault arrests, but no convictions. The whole Zachary clan had records for disorderly conduct, assault and such, which was no surprise. The rest of the info for everyone, including social media sites, were all incorrect and/or worthless.

However, the site offered their Gold Check for $18.95 per person, which *might* include "civil judgments, corporate affiliations, properties owned, old phone numbers, email addresses, tax liens, weapons permits, foreclosures, SSN issuance date/location, business associates and much more!" "Might" was the operative word and there was no guarantee I'd get better information. I'd been stung once and I wasn't going to plop down almost twenty bucks a person to check everyone out, especially when it *might* only be more astrological data.

After going through several sites that gave ratings to other sites, I decided to try eCertify.com. This one cost $2.95 for a special 5-day offer, then you would be charged $21.95 per month if you didn't cancel. It was worse than the first site, with incorrect emails and no results for some on my list. It also didn't have astrological signs. Oh, well, I'd just have to figure those out myself.

After about two hours of messing around with these worthless sites, I cancelled my "memberships." Basically, I paid over $25 and got nothing that I probably couldn't have found by digging online for a few minutes. Like showman and circus owner P.T. Barnum never actually said (but was attributed to him by a competitor), "There's a sucker born every minute."

Since I am a subscriber to *The Constitution*, I went to their website and started a search of the names. Although it's a small-town rag, it is very up to date, even digitalizing all of the archives back to April 16, 1865, when it had been founded. Their first headline was that Lincoln had died the day before, at the hand of a "Confederate cur." But I was looking for much later curs. And I found them.

Brandy Quillon had shot Helen Anderson's abusive boyfriend, Drudge Drury. Drudge Drury? With a name like that, he was born to be bad. But then, a quillon is part of a sword. Names can be very enlightening. The case had been thrown out because of an illegal search that found the gun, plus Drudge had just left Helen almost dead when Brandy shot him. Not exactly what she had told me, but close enough. Whatever happened when she was in high school with her teacher had stayed in high school because she was a juvenile, so I found nothing about it in the paper. She wasn't newsworthy after the series of articles about her shooting Drudge.

I tried all the other names. James Banaszewski was mentioned a number of times, but mainly because of hassles with the county over a "village" of Old West-style mini-buildings he'd built on his acreage. He tried to make sure they were under the square footage that required a permit, but had erred a couple of times. Instead of going through the legal requirements for a permit, he'd bulldozed them down in front of the building inspectors. After meeting Jimmy Bee, it didn't surprise me. The only interesting news item was when his house had been searched after a neighbor claimed he'd threatened him. Because they didn't have a search warrant and the neighbor had been proved a liar, the case had been thrown out. However, Jimmy had agreed to let an AK-47 with a folding stock they'd found be destroyed in exchange for having no charges filed. But Jimmy was also the type to have a spare stashed somewhere.

I found the wedding announcement for Jonathan and Lisa Franks. Listing Jon as a "noted local builder and investor," Lisa was described as "Lisa Williams, a retired professional from Lawton, Oklahoma." Except for Jon being involved in several lawsuits over the houses he built, there was not much else in the paper's files. I made note of the names on the lawsuits. He'd also had a building site closed down because of safety issues twice. Plus he'd had a run in with the Atsugewi Indians when he'd tried to hide ancestral burial grounds he'd dug up on one of his construction projects. One of them, George Watson, had threatened to kill Jon for desecrating their tribal burial site. Jon was coming through as a less-than-upstanding citizen. I added George Watson's name to my suspect list. Who hadn't wanted to kill Jon?

As I sat, pondering what I'd found, there was a knock on my door. I considered getting my shotgun out of the safe, but opted for trusting my fellow man. Maybe not always the best choice, but it was the Chief and meeting him with a gun in my hand wouldn't have been the best approach.

He looked around. "No new bullet holes or broken windows?"

I shrugged. "The day's not over yet."

"Yeah, well . . . ." He looked down at a folder in his hand. "This won't make it much better. A friend of mine in the FBI ran the bullets we recovered here through NIBIN and I got the ballistics report back. The bullets were from an AK-47 that was used in a bank robbery in Lodi. Two guys pulled it off. A guard was wounded."

I sat down. "So we've got a bank robber after me."

"I don't know. The Feds killed a guy whose prints matched the

143

shell casings recovered at the bank and got back most of the money." The Chief settled into a chair across from me. "The problem is they never found the gun or the rest of the money."

"And now this bank robber is gunning for me." I reached over and picked up my mug of tea. I took a sip. It was cold, just like my investigation. I got up and went to my computer, taking my list of suspects off the desk. I handed it to the Chief. "You might want to check them out."

He studied it. "The usual suspects?"

I laughed. "Just like in *Casablanca*. And maybe just as helpful. I'm not getting anywhere with them."

He folded the list and put it in his coat pocket before rising. "Well, I'll check them out." He went to the door. "The Feds are wanting in, but I'd rather work this myself, okay? We're still a small town and I can get more done without them around."

"It's your call. You're the Chief."

He grinned. "Yeah, I am, aren't I?"

After the Chief went out, I cleaned up my dishes and put on my coat to leave. Then the doorbell rang. Maybe I should install a revolving door. I answered it and Lisa Franks rushed in.

She wrapped her arms around me, pushing her ample breasts tight against me. "Oh, Father, are you okay? I just heard about the shooting."

I carefully extricated myself from her embrace and held her at arm's length. It hurt my still-sprained wrist and I winced.

"Oh, Father, you're hurt. I heard you were wounded in three places. One of them was a little . . ." She glanced down at my crotch. "Well, embarrassing."

"Whatever you heard, the rumors are wrong. Like I told you, I sprained my wrist when my truck was hit, but that's all. The only things wounded here were my window, my wall and my pride. He got away before I could get him."

She put her hand to my cheek. "But you're a man of peace. What could you have done if you caught him?"

I gently removed her hand. "Too much, maybe. I haven't felt very peaceful lately. But you're right. I'll let the police handle this. I need to keep my perspective. I'm here as a pastor of my congregation, not an avenging angel." I glanced at my watch. "And now I need to get back to St. Nicholas. I've taken too long of a lunch."

"Of course, Father. You go back to the church and take care of things. Let others handle this problem. You have far more important concerns to worry about." She cocked her head and leaned forward, like for a kiss.

With a quick step back, I leaned away. "Uh, thanks, Lisa. I appreciate your support."

I edged around her and opened the door. "I've got to go. I'll see you Sunday?"

She brushed past me, glancing over her shoulder. "Of course, Father. You just want to be rid of me."

"I, uh . . . ." But she was out the door.

Chapter 27

Just as Lisa was getting in her car, another car pulled up. It was Hel in her Ford Edge. As she got out of her car, Lisa slowed for a moment. I thought she made a quick gesture at my window with her middle finger before speeding off, but I couldn't be sure.

Hel was dressed in a beige hooded parka with form-fitting beige pants and some wooly snow boots. She looked stunning. She smiled at me and I returned the smile. She came close, giving me a hug and I didn't pull away.

"Hey, Robert, you look pretty good for a dead man."

"The rumors of my demise have been greatly exaggerated."

She stepped back and cocked her head. "Huh?"

"It's a popular misquote of Mark Twain."

"I don't get it. I'd heard you were dead. What's that got to do with Mark Twain?"

"Nothing, really." I shrugged. "It was a little joke. Not worth explaining."

Hel's face turned into a scowl. "Look, I can tell when I'm being talked down to. I came over because I was concerned, but I think I'd better go."

As she turned toward her car, I caught her arm. "I wasn't talking down to you. It's just easier to take things like being shot at with a bit of levity." I grinned sheepishly. "Sorry, it's my weird sense of humor, okay?"

She hesitated. "I just don't like being treated like some dumb blond."

"But you're not blond." Oops! That hadn't come out right. Maybe she wouldn't catch my faux pas.

"I know I'm not blond. I meant . . . ." She gave me a suspicious look and pulled back. "Are you saying I'm–"

"A beautiful and intelligent person, with lovely black hair." I was tempted to brush back a lock of her shimmering hair from her face, but resisted.

Hel rolled her eyes. "Way too smooth, Bobbie. You sound like you're in a pick-up bar."

I stifled a grimace when she called me Bobbie. However, considering her mood, I wasn't about to correct her. "It really wasn't meant as a pick-up line, just a compliment. I'm not even familiar with the bar dating scene."

She placed her hands on her hips. "Are you implying that I am?"

I held up my hands in front of me, in surrender. "Look, this isn't going the way I'd planned. Can we back it up to 'hello' and start over?"

"You won't have me at 'hello.' In case you aren't familiar with it, that's a movie quote from, um . . . ."

"*Jerry Maguire.*"

She stomped her foot. "I know that, if you'd given me a chance to say it." She turned to the door. "I can't take any more of your smart-ass remarks. I'd better go before I say what I'm thinking."

I was stunned. Smart-ass remarks? "Sorry, if I–"

She held up her hand. "Don't. I'm glad you're okay, but I need to leave."

Then she was gone, closing the door none too softly.

"Well, that went well," I muttered. "Hell hath no fury like a woman named Hel."

I needed to go back to the church office, even if I didn't feel very pastoral right then. The word could mean serene and calm as well as my rector's duties, but neither fit me at that point. With a sigh, I went out and climbed into my monster truck, the Beast.

As I sat at my desk in my office, lost in thought as I tried to figure out what had gone wrong with Hel, Doris knocked on my door.

"That Brandy woman is on the phone for you," she said with a disapproving scowl.

The day was going from bad to worse. Brandy had already told me what she'd do to me if I hurt her friend and I had no doubt she would do it. I took a deep breath before I picked up my phone.

"Before you say anything, I'm really sorry if I offended Hel. I tried to tell her that–"

"Forget it, Bobbie. She weirds out over nothing sometimes.

148

She told me all about it, but that's not why I called."

I exhaled, slowly. Again with the Bobbie. "I really am sorry if I offended her." I paused. "Why did you call?"

"Me and Tony were talking about who might've killed Jon and he said a couple of things I thought you'd want to know. You know Dagwood?"

"Dwayne Bell." At least I knew his real name.

"Yeah. Todd fired him today. Said something about him stealing his business, but Tony doesn't know what he meant. Maybe he's giving inside info to other contractors. If Jon had found out, it wouldn't have been pretty." She chuckled softly. "But if Dagwood had found out about Jon and Blondie, it would've been worse."

Interesting. "You said a couple of things."

"Yeah. Did you know Dwayne's from Oklahoma?"

I played dumb. "So he's a Sooner. Is that a problem?"

"Huh?"

"Sooner is slang for someone from Oklahoma," I explained. "Like a Prune Picker is someone born in California."

"Prune Picker? You're kidding me."

I chuckled. "No, it's pretty much forgotten now, but that was the nickname during the Depression. So what does Dwayne's home state have to do with anything?"

"Guess who else is from Oklahoma."

I didn't have to guess. I remembered the announcement in *The Constitution*: Lisa Franks was also from Oklahoma. Was it just a coincidence?

"Lisa Franks."

"Good one, Bobbie. You're not that dumb after all. Did you know that he showed up just a few days after she married Jon and started working for him?"

Coincidence was looking less likely. "No, I didn't."

"Now you do. Thought you'd like to know, especially since he might be trying to kill you."

I didn't say anything for a moment as I processed this new information. Then I realized the line was silent as she waited for my response.

"Uh, thanks, Brandy."

"Nada."

She hung up and I mulled over her words. I needed to find out more about the Bell family. I called the Chief.

"Whatcha want, Robert?"

Caller I.D., of course.

"Chief, I just got some information about Dwayne Bell. Did you know that he and Lisa Franks are both from Oklahoma and came to Buggy Springs about the same time?"

He snorted. "Yeah, I already found that out. Well, not about getting here about the same time, but it figures. Them being half brother and sister, you know."

I wasn't ready for that. "But I saw her marriage announcement in the archives of *The Constitution*. Her last name was Williams when she got married."

"Second marriage. She married some guy when she was sixteen, a Harley Williams. Didn't last long. I checked her out. Besides, she had a different father than Dwayne."

"What is this place? Some soap opera or sleezy reality show? Is Brandy really the illegitimate daughter of Jon Franks' long-lost sister?"

The Chief laughed. "Maybe. I haven't finished checking out your list. Stay tuned for the next episode of *As the Stomach Turns*."

"Is that show still on? I mean the real one, not your joke one."

"No idea. If not, we're doing a revival in Buggy Springs. I'll let you know what I dig up for a new show."

"I can't wait."

Chapter 28

After fielding a few more calls about my health, including one from the bishop (How had he found out?), I was ready to go home. Still, I needed to see how close Lisa and brother Dwayne were. Could they have conspired together to kill Jon and then Elvira? I now seemed to be wearing a bull's-eye target on my chest and needed to get more information on them. No better place to check out local gossip than the Buggy Springs Diner. I dug in my lower-right desk drawer for my emergency medical supplies and found some Pepcid. Taking a prophylactic pill, I headed out to my truck and the Diner.

It was snowing heavily and I was glad for four-wheel drive as I drove up Main St. I had a little trouble finding a parking place big enough for the Beast. The street was surprisingly busy for the weather, with no parking available in front of the Diner. No doubt the locals were stocking up on fat and grease in their systems to help them survive if they were snowed in, their version of eating whale blubber. I ended up having to trudge a couple of blocks from where I parked to the Diner.

As I opened the door, the smell of sweat and an over-heated deep fryer hit me like a punch in the gut. The place was crowded with guys in flannel shirts and women with sweatshirts. Everyone was talking loudly and the noise reverberated off the walls. I looked for a friendly face.

A grey-haired, pony-tailed guy with a shaggy mustache was strumming on an acoustic guitar, singing something I couldn't hear over the din of loud conversations. He had a small amp with a mic, but it wasn't big enough to compete with a gang of vocal people in a small, hard-surfaced room. Judy, my bleached-blond waitress from when I'd last been there with the Chief, saw me and rolled her eyes. She pointed to a table for two stuffed in a corner that was empty. I smiled and nodded, then headed for my assigned spot, checking out the crowd as I did.

Small towns are small, which is why so many of the "usual suspects" were there. Todd Franks was sitting with his step-mother,

Lisa, and another woman about Lisa's age with bright red hair. She was the woman who had wept at Jon's memorial, but was no longer squeezed into a black dress. Instead, she was squeezed into a red sweater that clashed nicely with her hair, but accentuated her bustline. Todd grinned at me and Lisa gave a weak wave with an embarrassed smile, but the other woman ignored me. I returned Lisa's wave. Interesting. I thought the son and the widow didn't get along and now they're having a drink together.

Julie from Golden Sunset was sitting with a man I vaguely remembered from when I'd been at Higgins Diggins, and he had his hand on hers. Julie saw me, smiled and waved. I waved back, continuing toward my table in the back.

Then I saw the guy who'd been carrying plywood at Jon Franks' construction site, the one known as Dagwood. The busty blond he was with must be his wife, Blondie. While they sat at the same table, they both looked like they'd rather be somewhere else. Dagwood was just who I'd hoped to find there, so I detoured to their table.

Dagwood looked up at me. "How's it going, Father?"

"Can't complain . . . ." I almost said Dagwood. It took me a moment to recover. "Dwayne. How are you doing?"

"Hanging in." He cocked his head. "I don't remember telling you my name, Father. How'd you know it?"

Because I've been checking up on you? No, not wise. Think quickly. "It's a small community and people are my business. I try to learn as many of our townfolks' names as I can." I turned to the blond who was wearing way too much makeup. "For instance, this must be your lovely wife, Starlight?"

"Starburst," Dwayne growled. "Her name's Starburst."

Oops. I should have brought cue cards. At least I hadn't said Blondie.

Starburst gave a coy tilt of her head. "Starlight is fine when you put in that 'lovely wife' stuff." She glared at Dwayne. "It'd be nice if you called me 'lovely wife' sometimes."

This was not going in a productive direction. Their table had two settings, knives and forks wrapped in paper napkins, so they obviously hadn't eaten yet. "Look, I'm making a mess of things. How about if I buy you two a beer or a glass of wine for your dinner as an apology?"

152

Dwayne shook his head. "I don't drink. I was raised in the Pentecostal Bible Church."

But Starburst beamed. "I'd love a glass of wine."

After several attempts, I caught Judy's eye. I kept motioning to her until finally she gave me a disgusted look and moseyed over.

"Yeah, what?" She glared at me. "This isn't your table, ya know."

"Judy, I would like to buy this young couple a round of drinks."

"We only got beer and wine."

Dwayne wasn't shy. "I'll have a Coke," he said, then nodded toward Starburst. "She'll have wine."

Judy made a note on a pad with a stub of a pencil. "What kinda wine?"

Starburst looked unsure. "Uh, what kind do you have?"

"Red and white."

I lifted my eyes to the grimy ceiling. Judy was a veritable font of information. "Judy, what kind of white and red?"

She gave a disgusted sigh. "I'll check."

While she was gone, I took the opportunity to question my suspect. Or pry, depending on your point of view.

"So, Dwayne, I hear you moved here from out of state. Texas, was it?

He eyed me. "No, from Oklahoma."

"Oklahoma?" I acted surprised. "Did you know we have another Sooner in our little town?"

"Yeah, Millie. She's my sister. Well, half-sister. Didn't have the same Pa. So what?"

At that point, Judy reappeared at the table.

"Charles Shaw."

It took me a moment to realize she was announcing what wine they had. Two-buck Chuck. If that's what it still cost. When in Rome, or the Buggy Springs Diner . . . .

"Uh, Judy, what varietal?" I asked.

"Huh?"

"What kind of white and red wine? Are they a chardonnay and a cabernet sauvignon?"

"I'll have to check." With a sniff, she left.

I turned back to Dwayne. "Who's Millie? I thought you're

153

Lisa's brother."

"Yeah, now she's Lisa." He snorted in disgust. "She always hated her name 'cause it sounded down home, thought Lisa sounded more high falutin.'"

"So, did Lisa have Jon hire you when you moved here?"

"No way." He glared at me. "She's never done anything to help me. I'm a damn good rough carpenter and that's why Jon hired me. Or maybe to get at Lisa, since he knew I was her half-brother and she resented me." He turned his glare to Lisa's table. "She probably told Jon not to hire me. I haven't talked to her since I got here and she's ignored me. She's too high class for me, finishing college and all. Called herself a 'professional,' even after she lost her license. I went to college, too, but Starburst and I got married, so I dropped out. But Lisa'll get hers. Like our Ma used to say, 'Pride goeth before a fall.' That's in the Bible, you know, book of Proverbs." He smiled proudly. "I did go to Oral Roberts University for almost a year. That's a school for real Christians, not like you Episcopalians."

I ignored the insult, but grimaced at the misquote. "Pride goes before destruction. It's a haughty spirit that goes before a fall."

"Huh?"

Before I had to explain, Judy came to the table and made her announcement. "We got mer-lot and chee-nan blank."

I winced inside, but didn't correct her. Instead I turned to Starburst. "Which would you prefer, merlot or chenin blanc?"

"Uh . . . ." She looked uneasy. "What do you think?"

"Merlot. It's safer." I turned to Judy. "Charge it to my table."

"What table? You lost your table while you were shootin' the bull."

I glanced over and saw Willy, my senior warden, and his wife at my table. He waved and I waved back. He didn't know I'd lost my table to him and I wasn't going to tell him. Judging from my last experience here, it was no loss.

"Okay, Judy, what do I owe you for the drinks?"

"Two-fifty for the Coke and four bucks for the wine."

Nice profit. Four bucks for a glass of Two-buck Chuck. I gave her a ten. "Keep the change."

I finally got a smile from Judy. I turned back to Dwayne.

154

"What did you think of Jon?"

"He was okay, but a bit too much into the lusts of the flesh for me. But he did give me something in his will."

Judy returned with the drinks and plopped them on the table. "Ready to order?"

"Could you give us a couple of minutes?" I asked.

She rolled her eyes and went away.

I turned back to Dwayne. "So, Dwayne, why did he do that?"

He shrugged. "Dunno. Guess it was 'cause we were kin. In-laws, ya know."

I glanced at Starburst, but she was intently studying her glass of wine. If he only knew.

"What do you think of Todd?"

He finished his Coke and set it on the table a little too hard. "We don't always see eye to eye. He can be a real jerk."

Nothing about being fired. Why? Pride?

As I stood, I looked over at Lisa's table. "By the way, is that redhead with Todd and Lisa, Cindy?"

Dwayne didn't even turn to look. "That's Cindy alright. Cindy Wolfe."

As I walked out I wondered why Franks' widow and his mistress were meeting with his son.

Chapter 29

I drove home through the falling snow, thankful for the Beast's four-wheel drive. I trudged through the deepening snow on the drive, into the rectory. Having lived alone for so long, I normally enjoyed my solitude. However, going into the dark, cold house that night was depressing. I had thought that Hel and I might have had a chance together, but her explosion for no reason gave me pause. She was attractive . . . no, stunning, and had a great personality when she wasn't on a rant, yet also had a lot of baggage that I wasn't sure I could handle. Still, I wasn't a kid just out of college with a bevy of desirable, available women in the wings and maybe I needed to be a little less picky. No one was perfect, least of all me. Just as I was going to call her, my phone rang. Maybe it was she.

"Hello?"

"Father Bruce? It's Lisa."

I stifled a sigh of disappointment. "How are you? I hope you had a good dinner at the Diner?"

She spat out a laugh. "Not really. It's a dive, but that's where Todd wanted to meet. His tastes are, well, so . . . plebeian."

In spite of being no fan of the Diner, I remembered Dwayne's description of Lisa: prideful. It fit. "What can I do for you, Lisa?"

"I just wanted to explain."

"Explain what? You were out to dinner with your stepson and . . ." What should I call Cindy? Your late husband's mistress sounded a little odd. "A friend."

She snorted. "Don't play dumb. Cindy was Jon's old bedmate. And I do mean old in both senses of the word. But she gets an inheritance from Jon's estate. Todd gets some, too. Jon was very generous to people who didn't deserve it, but life's full of surprises."

Interesting. "So you didn't know what was in your husband's will?"

She hesitated. "Everything is in a trust. I'm named in the trust, but so are a lot of others."

Hmm. Motive for murder? I'd like to see the trust. "Did he have insurance?"

"If you're hinting I killed Jon for life insurance, he didn't have any. Instead, I actually have less spending money than when Jon was alive."

"So, if you don't mind my asking, how did the estate divvy up?"

"I got the house and some stocks and annuities, Todd got the paper for a couple of loans Jon had made and two-thirds of the construction business, Cindy Wolfe got the rest of the annuities, Dwayne Bell got one third of the business, no doubt because his wife slept with Jon, and the little slut from the bar got the house she's living in and the rest of the stocks."

"You mean Carly, the cocktail waitress at Higgins Diggins? But she wasn't at your meeting."

"Yeah, the rest of us have to work out some details, but she gets her house for screwing Jon, free and clear. I asked her if she wanted to talk about things, but she just flipped me off. I wanted to kick her skinny butt." She paused. "Sorry, Father. That wasn't very Christian, was it?"

I sighed. "No, it wasn't. You need to try to forgive everyone, even those who sin against you. Remember the Lord's prayer asks God to forgive our sins as we forgive those who have sinned against me."

"Yeah, well, that's easy for you to say. You haven't been screwed like I have."

Fortunately, the line went dead before I could reply. I was not feeling very Christian at that point. I closed my eyes, thinking about what she had said and all the other information I'd recently unearthed. The pool of suspects had grown rather than shrunk. Not good.

There is a saying that you should never take a drink if you think you need one. I didn't need one, but that last conversation made me want one. My last tumbler of scotch had ended up on the carpet, so I again poured myself a Macallan. Fortunately, my Edinburgh crystal glass had survived the attempt on my life and I used it. This time I did not stand in front of the window. I settled into my chair and watched the snow fall as I tried to make some sense of it all. I was reminded of a novel from the 1950's that later became a soap opera, *Peyton Place*. I'd never read it myself, but understood it was about a small town that was full of dark secrets and hypocrisy. Was that Buggy Springs? Lately, it seemed to be. I set my empty glass on the side table and slowly stood.

I wandered into the kitchen. One hard thing about being single is "dinner for one." Although I am not a bad cook, taking the time to make a decent dinner often seems not worth the effort. It was one of those nights, so I scanned my options in the freezer. While the term "TV dinner" has been supplanted by euphemisms like "prepackaged meal" and "prepared dinner," it still means substandard fare. I pulled out a Szechuan shrimp stir fry that, from experience, looked far bigger and more appetizing on the cover than its contents actually were and popped it into the microwave.

While my dinner was being zapped, there was a knock at the door. I answered it to find Hel. She was dressed in her hooded teal parka and matching skin-tight ski pants, looking fantastic. She smiled.

"Hi, Bobbie. How are you?"

It was like nothing had happened before, no past problems.

"Uh, fine. You?"

"Never better. Mind if I come in?"

I stepped back, letting her past. The buzzer on my microwave went off. I ignored it.

Once inside, Hel slowly took off her coat, revealing a thin, ribbed sweater that showed off her great body, and handed her coat to me. Every motion looked planned, carefully planned for effect. I took her coat and hung it on a hook by the door.

Hel lifted an eyebrow. "I heard a buzzer. Was that your microwave?"

"Yes." I was heating my sad, pathetic solo frozen dinner, which makes me sound like a real loser. "I often reheat my tea in it."

Not a lie. A deception, yes, but not an out-and-out lie.

"I thought you might be heating your dinner." She cocked her head, looking very desirable. "Then you wouldn't want to take me out."

"Let me get my coat," I said as I opened my hall closet.

159

Chapter 30

A short time later, we were seated at Solstice, the classiest and most expensive restaurant within seventy miles. The only reason we got in with no notice on a Friday night was the snow.

The owner, Charles, seated us and handed us our menus. He was trim, clean-shaven, with neatly cut grey-black hair. As usual, he was dressed impeccably, wearing camel-colored trousers, a navy blue blazer and light blue shirt, with a tastefully-chosen silk tie and complementary pocket square. "So nice to see you, Robert. It's been a while."

I grimaced. Solstice was worth the price, but not a place to go alone. "I know. I've been a little busy lately, Charles."

"I understand." Charles gave me a half smile. "Would you like to know the specials?"

"Hit us, dude," Hel said with a shake of her head.

I gulped, but Charles seemed unfazed.

"Besides our menu items, tonight we have a halibut steak topped with crab legs in a butter, caper and kalamata olive sauce, served with jasmine rice. We also have a rack of lamb with garlic and herbs over smashed red potatoes."

Hel rested her chin on her interlaced fingers, staring at me. "No oysters? Bobbie needs oysters tonight."

I glanced over at Charles, giving him a wan smile and a slight shake of my head. But he was giving her his attention and, except for slightly raising an eyebrow, did not react.

"I'm sorry, Chef Paul does not have oysters on this evening's menu. We do have a starter of fresh mussels, which is also a mollusk, with saffron-brandy cream. Would you like an order of them?"

She frowned. "Not the same stuff. How 'bout wine?"

Charles pointed to a wine list on the table. "We have a fine selection. If you know what you are ordering for your main course, I would be pleased to make a couple of recommendations."

She rolled her eyes. "Just bring us a bottle of your house red."

I had to intercede before this got ugly. "Charles, how about the Sangiovese I had the last time I was here?"

"Nice choice, Father." He smiled, but it seemed more out of pity than amusement. "I'll get a bottle from our cellar. In the meantime, Amanda will bring you some bread and tapenade while you peruse the menu."

As Charles walked away, Hel sneered. "Snotty little fag, isn't he?"

No matter what my personal feelings about a person's life style, I abhor bigotry. I frowned. "Charles is a friend of mine. Please do not use such derogatory terms about him or anyone else in my presence."

"You mean snotty? No, I know what you mean." She slapped one of her hands with the other. "My bad. Won't happen again." She gave me a wry smile. "We okay now? I can apologize to your little buddy, too, if you want."

I could picture how that would go. "No, that's not necessary. You only said that to me." I paused. "Besides, I know of a number of women in town who would attest to his heterosexual orientation."

She leaned forward, eyes wide. "Ooh, they talk about this in Confession? Tell me more."

I spoke through gritted teeth. "Not a chance, so please drop it."

"Whatever." Hel picked up her menu and studied it. "What's good here? Steak?"

I wondered if the Buggy Springs Diner would have been a wiser choice. "The rib eye is very good. I'm going for the lamb tonight."

"I hate killing little babies for my food." She kept her eyes on the menu. "I never eat lamb or veal."

So it's better to kill them when their adults? "Then I suggest the rib eye. Would you like a salad or starter?"

"No starter." She winked. "Unless you want to duck into the rest room together for a quickie before dinner."

I was saved from stumbling through a reply by Amanda arriving with sourdough bread and tapenade, followed by Charles with the wine. He uncorked it and poured a taste for me. It was excellent and I nodded my approval. He poured some into Hel's glass, then mine.

Hel studied her glass. "Is this a taste or are you going to give me a real glass of wine?"

162

Casting a surprised glance at me, Charles poured more into her glass. As he did, she put a finger on the neck of the bottle and made sure her glass was filled nearly to the top.

The dinner was not enjoyable. The food, as always, was wonderful. The company was not so wonderful. I was reminded of an old movie, *The Three Faces of Eve*. The first Hel I'd met was, well, normal. Then there was the second one, the Hel who took everything I said as an insult. The last one, the one I took to my favorite restaurant and who embarrassed me many times, was Hel on wheels. She was wild and uncontrollable, with a bawdy sexuality and an unbridled tongue. After my one glass of wine, she finished off the bottle. Thankfully, she did not want dessert. Well, her innuendo was that she wanted more of an erotic than an epicurean finale. I paid the bill with a generous tip that, hopefully, would dull Charles' bad memory of the evening.

On our way back to the rectory, she tightly held my arm and it was only by using my greater physical strength that I kept her from pressing it to improper regions. I was in a quandary. She had obviously had too much wine and it was not safe to let her on the road. But what would happen if I let her in my house? When we pulled up to the rectory, she saved me the trouble of deciding by hopping out of the Beast and running up to my front door.

"Could you open up? That wine you gave me ran right through me." She giggled. "I need to pee like a geyser."

I opened the door and followed her inside. "Second door on the right, down the hall."

As she ran toward relief, I took out my cell and called Brandy. "Hello?"

"Your cousin's out of control. I need you here now!"

She slowly exhaled. "I was afraid of this when you called the last time. She must be off her meds. Did you give her any alcohol?"

"We went to Solstice. I had a glass of wine and she polished off the bottle."

She paused. "Has she been flirty or–"

"Amorous? Oh, yes. That's an understatement."

"Damn. She's a nympho after two glasses. I'll be there in five to ten."

163

"Make it five. Or less."

As I disconnected, Hel walked into the room.

"Who were you talking to?"

"A parishioner who has a sick relative." No lie, there.

"Well." She glanced around. "You have anything to drink around here?"

"Let me get you something." I headed into the kitchen and turned on the Keurig. I don't drink much coffee, but it's great for guests.

Hel followed me. "Don't you have anything with more kick than coffee?"

"I'm not much of a drinker. I get sleepy if I have too many." True.

Hel unzipped her coat and dropped it on the floor. Her sweater was tight and thin. I'd taken off my coat already and she pushed close to me.

"Who needs coffee? I'll keep you awake," she said, breathlessly.

"I need coffee." I gently pushed her away. I had to take control. "You are a very attractive woman, but this is not right. Let's have a cup of coffee and get to know each other better." Get to know each other better? I inwardly grimaced at my own cliché.

She looked down at my crotch. "I know all I want to know already."

Jesus said that "the spirit is willing, but the flesh is weak." As Hel had noticed, my flesh was definitely weak. I turned away and put a cartridge in my Keurig. After I pushed the brew button, it gurgled and coffee dribbled into a mug I put under the machine.

"Is French roast okay?" I said over my shoulder.

"I like to French," she said, as she moved up behind me and wrapped her arms around me.

Where was Brandy? I surreptitiously checked my watch. It had only been three minutes.

With a quick twist, I pulled away from Hel. "Do you want low-fat milk or non-alcoholic Irish creamer in your coffee?"

She gave me a lopsided grin. "Are you Irish?"

I was saved by the bell, or rather the roar of a vehicle pulling into my drive. Within a few seconds, my door flew open and Brandy

164

rushed in. Dressed in snow boots, ski parka and what looked like pajama pants, she had obviously not taken time to worry about her attire before coming to my aid.

Brandy wrapped her arm around Hel's waist. "Honey, you okay?"

Hel shook her head, as if to clear her thoughts. "I'm fine. Bobbie and I were just getting better acquainted."

Brandy glanced over at me. "Well, that's fine, but you've had a little too much to drink and you know what happens then."

Suddenly, I felt like a villain who had been taking advantage of Hel's diminished capacities. "Uh, thanks for coming, Brandy. Could you drive Helen home?"

"Sure." She looked to Hel. "Give me your keys and wait in my truck."

"I can drive." Hel stuck out her lower lip like a petulant child.

"Remember the DUI you got last year? You hated jail. Give me your keys and we'll pick up your car tomorrow."

Hel dug her keys out of her purse, handed them to Brandy and stomped out of the front door. It was obvious who was the alpha in their friendship.

After Hel left, I turned to Brandy. "I'm no expert, but is Hel manic-depressive?"

She didn't meet my eye. "She has some mood swings. Her doctor says she's a little bipolar. No big deal. She takes Symbyax and it helps, but she says it makes her fat and stupid."

A *little* bipolar? "I'm sorry about what happened, but I had no idea."

She shrugged. "I know. We're cool. I'll take Hel home. Pour yourself a stiff one and be proud that you didn't take advantage of her, Bobbie." She flashed me a grin as she glanced at my crotch. "After you take a cold shower."

165

Chapter 31

I took Brandy's advice. For my "stiff drink," I put the kettle on and got out some Earl Grey tea. I hopped in the shower while the water for my tea was heating, keeping the temperature cold. It was not something I normally did on a winter night, but I needed it. Hel had tempted me. If not for her crazy actions, would I have resisted? I hoped so, but couldn't be sure. She was a very attractive woman with a great personality, at least the first time we met. While the Apostle Paul wrote that all Christians were saints, none of us were perfect. And I felt neither saintly nor perfect after my close encounter with Hel.

After a night like this, I needed to spend some time alone in prayer and meditation. It was after ten, but I didn't plan to get up until six the next morning. I wanted to get to church early and catch up on neglected business. Dressed in my warm robe, I poured the boiling water over the tea. As I watched the timer for three minutes, my cell phone rang. Caller I.D. said it was my sister. I answered it anyway.

"Hello?"

"Do you know what he's done now?"

"Hello, Sister Dearest. It's nice to hear from you."

"He's bought a damn plane."

"Wait a sec. I'm going to pour myself a mug of tea before we get into this."

I set the phone on the counter and strained the tea into my mug. Taking the phone, I settled into my favorite easy chair with my favorite tea for a long, unfavorite conversation.

I put the phone to my ear. "Now, tell me about Pop's latest escapade."

"Weren't you listening, Accident? He bought a plane!"

"Did he buy it for Nadine?"

"Nadine?" She paused. "He dumped her yesterday. Then he bought himself a twin-engine Tecnam. He spent four hundred grand on it."

"A least he won't marry it."

"What?"

"You were worried he'd marry Nadine and you'd lose some inheritance."

"Funny." She wasn't laughing.

Then my cell buzzed, showing me I had a call waiting. Caller I.D. said "Greg Katz," a member of St. Nicholas I very seldom saw in church.

"Sorry, Sister Dearest, I need to take a call. I'm putting you on hold."

"You're wha–"

I cut her off as I took the call.

"Yes, Greg, what can I do for you?"

"It's Emma, Father. Greg was in an accident. I'm at the hospital with him. It looks bad. Can you come?"

"I'll be right there."

I went back to my sister. "I've got to go. One of my parishioners is in the hospital."

"You can't leave now. This is import–"

I disconnected and went to get dressed. Although I was sorry that Greg was injured, it felt good to be doing what I was called to do. Maybe God was giving me a wake-up call about how I had been prioritizing my life of late. After all, I was a priest, not a detective.

When I got to the hospital, I hurried into the emergency room entrance. Ours is a small hospital with maybe 50 beds, but modern and with a decent ER and OR. We even have a full lab and an MRI machine, thanks to the generous donations of a few wealthy patrons. But the ER is small, with only three beds. I found Emma sitting in the otherwise-empty waiting room outside the ER.

A small, attractive woman, Emma was huddled inside a red ski jacket that was probably Greg's and dwarfed her. Her gray-streaked brown hair was pulled back in a ponytail that made her look both older than her actual mid-thirties age and vulnerably youthful. Worry lines creased her face and she massaged her bare hands together, whether from the cold or worry I did not know. I sat next to her and took one of her hands. It was ice cold. She seemed to suddenly become aware I had come into the room.

"Thanks for coming, Father. Sorry to bother you, but I didn't

168

know who else to call." She hesitated. "We don't have many close friends any more."

It stung that I was a last resort, but at least she did call. "You can always call me. I'm here for you. What happened?"

"He hit a tree. He was driving home and slid off the road." She blinked back a tear. "He wasn't wearing his seatbelt."

"Where was he coming from?"

"Beezer's Bar." She stared at her hands, chapped and red from her job washing dishes at Buggy Springs Diner. "The cops are getting a blood test on him. If he gets another DUI, he'll go to jail. It's all Jon Franks' fault for firing Greg 'cause of his drinking."

I sighed and squeezed Emma's hand. "I understand how you feel, but Greg had a problem with drinking long before Jon fired him. And he did have that DUI a while before Jon let him go."

She nodded, now in full tear mode. I admit, I always feel rather helpless when a woman cries. I released her hand and dug my clean handkerchief out of my pocket. She took it, wiped her eyes and blew her nose, then handed it back to me. I motioned for her to keep it. I'd get a clean one when I got home. She stuffed it into her coat pocket.

She looked at me, her eyes still full of tears. "But Greg's a good carpenter. He deserved another chance."

I knew that Greg's DUI had been on the way home from work. Using power tools and climbing ladders while drunk was an accident waiting to happen, but I didn't say that. It was surprising that Jon had kept Greg on as long as he had.

I stayed on relatively safer ground. "Has he found any work since?"

She shook her head. "Just an odd job here and there. Greg thought he'd get hired back on after Jon fell off that ladder, but Todd keeps putting him off."

"Well, don't you think that's to be expected, considering the drinking issue?"

She snorted angrily, then wiped her nose on her worn and faded flannel shirt sleeve that poked past her jacket. She must have forgotten the handkerchief I'd donated. "Todd used to get drunk on his ass on the job. He just didn't get caught. And Jon walked around holding a can of Bud a lot. Greg got fired 'cause . . . ."

She hesitated for a moment, looking down at her hands, then

169

continued. "At first, Jon said he'd let the DUI go 'cause I'm so sexy, so I know he canned Greg 'cause I wouldn't put out."

I was taken aback. Jon was turning out to be the scum of the Earth. I wished I'd had no part of his funeral. "Why didn't Greg go to the Labor Board."

She sighed, still keeping her eyes down. "No proof. I was going to record Jon on my cell the next time he talked to me about how horny he was and that his wife wasn't making him happy, but he fired Greg first. Todd promised he'd set things straight when he got the business."

Interesting. "So, was Todd expecting to get the business from Jon any time soon? It doesn't seem that Jon was the kind of guy just to hand it over and he was fairly healthy."

Emma shrugged. "No idea. All I know is that Todd owns it now and, after everything Greg did for him, treats him like he's a piece of . . ." She glanced at me. "Dog-do. That's what got Greg drinking so much."

Nice rationalization, but I chose not to say so. "Tell me about the accident."

She wiped her eyes. "He'd had a beer and was driving home when he slid off the road. His old Chevy truck isn't a four-by-four, you know. We can't afford one. He's got a couple of bags of sand in the back for traction, but they weren't enough."

"How bad are his injuries?"

"Bad. The doctor said he has broken ribs, a punctured lung and he didn't know what else. They took him to surgery about . . ." She checked her watch. "About a half hour ago."

"Maybe we'll hear something soon." I managed a weak smile. "Let's pray for Greg and his surgeons."

She nodded and bowed her head.

I said a prayer aloud for Greg and the skill of those helping him as Emma fought back her sobs. Then we waited.

It wasn't much more than ten minutes before the doctor came out in his green scrubs. He walked over to us and stood, looking down from a position of authority.

"I've finished with the operation on your husband, Mrs. Katz. How are you doing?"

I almost said, "How do you think she's doing? Her husband

170

has been in surgery and you haven't told her anything." But I didn't.

Emma glanced nervously at me. "I, uh . . . I'm okay, I guess. How's Greg?"

"Greg is in the Post Anesthesia Care Unit." No smile. "He broke three ribs, punctured a lung and just missed putting a rib through his heart, but was very lucky. I expect him to make a full recovery, in time. He won't be able to work for a few months, which is to be expected. As soon as he's in his room, the nurse will let you know and you can visit him."

Without another word, he turned and walked out.

Chapter 32

Emma took my hand. "Thanks for coming, Father Robert. You really helped me a lot. I was so alone."

"Glad to be here for you. I'll wait and go in with you to see Greg."

"It's okay. I feel a bunch better knowing Greg's not going to die." Her smile brightened her face. "Nothing's gonna go wrong for us now."

I gave a quick prayer that the Blood Alcohol Content test wouldn't change that.

After about an hour, a nurse let us know that Greg was in his room and we could visit him. He was not awake, so I was more there for Emma than him. However, I put my stole on and pulled out my oil stock, anointing his forehead with oleum infirmorum in the Sign of the Cross before giving the prayer of Laying on of Hands and Anointing.

"O Lord, holy Father, giver of health and salvation, send your Holy Spirit to sanctify this oil, that, as your holy apostles anointed many that were sick and healed them," I began.

When I finished, Emma looked uncomfortable. "I know we haven't been to church much lately. Everything sorta got us down, Greg out of a job and all. It's like the whole world's sitting on top of us."

I smiled at her in my most benevolent-priest manner. "I'm not keeping count of how often anyone comes to church. That's between you and God. As for feeling oppressed, remember Jesus' words. 'Come unto me, all ye that labor and are heavy laden, and I will give you rest.'"

She grabbed my hand. "Thanks, Father. You're great. We're gonna start coming to church again as soon as Greg gets out, okay?"

"That'll be wonderful." I glanced at my watch. "If you're okay, I'd better get going."

"I'm a bunch better." She smiled, a thankful smile making it

173

all worthwhile. "See you on Sunday."

As I headed out of the hospital, I started to wonder what Greg had done for Todd. Kicked a ladder out from under the man who'd ruined his life, Jon Franks? I hoped not. When Greg was feeling better, I needed to ask him a few questions.

The Chief was walking in the door as I was walking out.

"You're working late, Chief."

He checked his watch. "Nope. Early. What about you?"

"Here to see a parishioner who was in an accident."

"Greg Katz? Same guy I'm here to see."

I shifted uneasily. Had he come to arrest Greg? The BAC test normally takes weeks to get back. "Why?"

"I wanted to let him know that there were a lot of witnesses who say he only had one beer, so he's probably okay on the DUI charge."

"You came over here after midnight just to tell him that?"

He held up his hands. "Hey, we're a small town. 'To protect and serve,' you know."

I eyed him suspiciously. "That's just covering B.S. with air freshener and hoping no one smells the stink. Spill."

He sighed. "Okay, okay. Just don't blab what I'm going to tell you to anyone."

I made the sign of the Cross. "I'll consider it your Confession, at least in how I treat it."

"I guess that'll do." He pulled his coat collar up. We were standing in the doorway with the automatic door open. "Let's go inside and talk. It's freezing here and I'm from Southern California, ya know."

"Me, too, as you also know." I stepped inside and let the doors close behind us. "I always say it's a great place to be from."

He chuckled. "Yeah, me too. Well, here's the problem. The guys at the bar said Greg was on his cell with someone right before he left. Got a little hot with whoever he was talking to. They didn't hear most of it, 'cause the bar's noisy, but they heard him yell, 'If it weren't for me, you wouldn't even own the business. Now make good.' He was talking to Todd Franks."

That didn't sound good. Then it hit me. "How did you know he was talking to Todd?"

174

He looked like he'd eaten a bad oyster. "I, uh . . . I checked the records."

I thoughtfully stroked my chin. "Hmm, I'm no lawyer, but don't you need a search warrant for that? Did you get a judge out of bed for this?"

He glared at me. "You said this was like Confession."

I raised my hands in surrender. "It is. But I can't let you commit a crime. Greg's still under from his operation and Emma knows nothing, so let it go for tonight." I remembered the time. "Or this morning. You can't arrest him on this, no matter what. He didn't say he'd killed anyone. Let me be there when you question Greg tomorrow. I mean later today. Okay?"

He rolled his eyes. "Whatever you say Father Shylock."

"You mean Father Sherlock."

He grinned. "Do I? You're taking a pound of my flesh here."

Great. A literate cop with a weird sense of humor. I couldn't resist a dig back. "You can afford to lose it. Too many donuts."

He scrunched his eyes. "Ouch, not nice."

It wasn't and I felt badly about it. "Sorry, knee-jerk reaction. Make that a jerk reaction."

He solemnly raised his hand. "Father, I forgive you."

"Good. Now give Emma Greg's cell and we'll talk after we've both had a little sleep."

"What makes you think I have his cell? Maybe I contacted the phone company and did a trace on all the cell calls at the bar."

I groaned. "You got it from his truck after the wreck and illegally checked to see who he'd spoken with last. Occam's Razor."

"Huh?" He looked puzzled. "What's this got to do with shaving?"

"Occam said that the simplest solution is normally the right one. Slice through the crap with a razor and you get the truth. Give Emma the cell."

"Okay, okay." He shook his head. "We'll talk later."

"Later is right." I was exhausted

When I got home, I checked my messages and listened to my sister rant about our father until my answer machine cut her off. I deleted it.

I was concerned about Greg, but I was also concerned that I

175

couldn't seem to get away from this case. Father Sherlock, indeed. I chuckled. But maybe God was giving me a message. And who was I to question God?

I groaned when my alarm went off at seven. I normally got up at six, but slept in since I hadn't gotten to bed until after one. I rolled out of bed, brushed my teeth, and hopped on my treadmill.

Recent studies have shown that walking in the woods for an hour is good for the mind as well as the body. I'd rather do my walk that way than on a rubber belt, but snow made it difficult. After an hour on an artificial incline, I took a shower and made breakfast. I was just getting into my oatmeal, tea and morning crossword puzzle after Morning Prayer when my cell rang. Caller I.D. said it was the Chief. I was beginning to think that I should give him his own ring tone. I checked my watch. 8:18 a.m. Since we had talked not that many hours ago, I had a gut feeling it was not good news. I sighed. Doing my *New York Times* crossword puzzle was probably out now.

"Good morning, Chief, how can I help you?"

"You can't unless you know what killed Greg Katz."

Greg was dead? I was at a loss for words. But the Chief wasn't.

"Did you hear me? Katz is dead."

I took a breath. "I heard you. His injuries didn't seem that serious. The doctor said everything went fine with the surgery. What happened?"

"At this point, I don't know. I've ordered an autopsy. My guess is murder."

"Wait, you said murder? Why guess that? No autopsy yet, so was there any evidence of it?"

"Your Adkin's Shaver. After his operation, Katz was doing great. He'd been telling Todd on the phone earlier that he was calling in his debt. Now Katz's dead."

I pondered this. "That's a pretty wild leap, even if it makes some sense. But Greg was safe in the hospital."

"And Todd paid him a visit. At least, he was seen in the hospital in the wee hours of the morning."

I was trying to grab a bite of oatmeal in the pauses and stopped mid-bite. "Whoa. How does he explain that?"

176

"I haven't asked yet. Give me time. I plan to go to his place with a search warrant in hand, but the judges around here don't get up this early on a weekend. In the meantime, I've got a murder to investigate."

I downed my tea in one gulp. "Okay, I'll meet you at the hospital."

"I'm already here, working the case. I only called 'cause his wife keeps asking for you."

Poor Emma. The roller coaster of her life just came off the tracks. "How's she doing?"

"A basket case. She's been here all night to be near Katz. A nurse let her sleep in an empty room. Then they found Katz dead and woke her up. Got her on some meds to calm her down."

"I'm on my way."

"Yeah, and pick me up a couple of donuts on the way."

Obviously, he was still bugged by my too-many-donuts remark. He disconnected before I could come up with a witty reply.

Chapter 33

As I drove to the hospital, I had trouble concentrating on the icy road. When I started this mess, investigating Jon Franks' death, it had been a bit of a lark. After all, I barely knew Jon and it was more like solving a movie mystery. I hadn't taken his death as seriously as I should have and now Elvira and probably Greg had been murdered as well. It wasn't fun anymore. Guilt washed over me as I wondered if Elvira and Greg would still be alive if I'd just kept my nose out of it and done the job I was called to do: be a pastor to my congregation. Maybe it was time to do just that.

As I pulled up in the hospital parking lot, I resolved to stick to the business I had been called to do. I saw Emma through the glass doors to the waiting room, standing with her coat on in spite of the well-heated room, arms wrapped tightly across her chest. She was facing away from the doors, but turned around when I opened one.

She rushed up to me and hugged me. "Thanks for coming here again, Father. You're gonna find out who killed my Greg."

It wasn't a question.

I gently freed myself from her grip. "I think I need to step back from all this. You see . . . ." I wasn't sure how to put it. "You see, I may have been responsible for Greg's death."

She stepped back, looking at me with horror. "You? How?"

I turned away, unable to look her in the eye. "All this started when I began to look into Jon Franks' death. If I'd left well enough alone . . . ."

"No." She grabbed my arms, clinging tightly to them with an air of desperation. Her meds must not be working. "Todd did it. I heard the cops talking. He was here."

"Okay, that may be true." Loose lips and all that. I looked into her sad eyes. "If he had anything to do with Greg's death, I'm sure they will find out."

Her grip tightened. "If you poking around had anything to do with Greg's death, then you owe me. Find who did it and make sure he

179

pays."

Before I could reply, the glass doors flew open and a tall, lean woman with long, gray-black hair flying behind her stormed in. She shoved me aside and pulled Emma to her breast, hugging her tightly and glaring at me.

"Are you okay, *A Stóirín*? What have these Nazis done to you?"

With her long nose, weathered face, Navaho blanket coat, and moccasin boots, I might have thought she was a native American, but I had learned enough Gaelic to know she had referred to Emma as 'my darling,' so I doubted it. Plus she had striking blue eyes.

Emma pulled back enough to speak. "Father, this is Rainbow, my aunt. She lives up on the Ridge. Rainbow, Father Bruce was here for me when Greg got in his accident and . . . ."

Her voice choked with tears, she stopped.

The Ridge is also known as "Area Code 420." While there is no 420 area code in the U.S., although it is the country code of the Czech Republic, the meaning was obvious. Not everyone who lived there grew pot, but it's said that any brush fire in the area attracted all the local stoners to inhale the smoke.

I smiled at Emma's aunt. "Nice to meet you, Rainbow. I wish it were under better circumstances."

She frowned. "There's no good time to meet a tool of fascist oppression."

"I thought I was a Nazi. How did I go from German to Italian?" I instantly regretted my smart-alec remark. "Sorry, sometimes I get hung up on etymology. What I mean is, I'm not really into politics. I have enough to do being there for my parishioners without worrying about tax rates and trade deficits."

She sneered. "Marx said that religion is the opiate of the masses. The state created it to keep them oppressed and you're their tool."

"I believe that you mean the 'opium of the people.' That's what Marx wrote." I grimaced inside. Bad move. Rainbow was getting under my skin, but correcting her quote would win no friends. Or converts. "Look, I'm just glad you're here for Emma. We both care about her and want to help. That's the important thing, isn't it?"

"Of course," Rainbow sniffed, her arm still across Emma's

shoulders. "I'm just protecting her from bad auras. Like yours. I'm taking her home with me."

As Rainbow guided Emma to the door, the young widow looked back at me. I had to ask.

"Emma, are you sure you have no idea what Greg did for Todd?"

Emma looked away. "He never told me."

Rainbow fixed me with a look that could kill. "Will you leave her alone? She's grieving and now you're accusing her of . . . what? Being a part of his murder? You're a real ass, you know."

Stunned, it took me a moment to react. "I wasn't accusing her of--"

But it was too late. The doors had closed behind them.

I considered running out after them. Emma's eyes had betrayed she knew something, even if not everything. But with Rainbow acting as a cross between mother hen and a harpy, it most likely wouldn't accomplish much if I did. I was saved from having to decide when the Chief came into the lobby from one of the corridors. He was wearing jeans and a navy blue sweatshirt with white lettering that said, "IF YOU HATE COPS, NEXT TIME YOU'RE BEING ROBBED CALL YOUR LAWYER." He stopped in front of me.

"Well, Robert, where're my donuts?"

"Donuts?"

He let out an exasperated sigh. "I asked you to bring a couple of donuts when you came. I've been here all morning and the only food I can get here is out of a machine. Wasn't I clear?"

"I thought it was a joke. You know, after my comment about . . . ." I felt like an idiot. "I can run get some. It won't take long."

He waved his hand in disgust. "Just forget it. I'll take you back to the body and you can do your bit." He glanced around. "Where's Emma?"

"Her aunt came and picked her up." I paused. "She lives on the Ridge."

He grunted.

I followed him until we got to a room with crime-scene tape across it. The Chief lifted it and we went in. Greg was on the bed with no covers, just his hospital gown. Black dust showed that

181

fingerprints had already been taken.

The Chief walked around the bed. "Do your last rites quick-like, 'cause the county medical examiner is going to be here soon and take him away."

"There's no such thing as last rites," I said, as I took out my stole and put it on.

"You sure? That's what I always heard you guys did when someone died."

"I'm sure." I suppressed a smile. "After all, I'm in the business. 'Anointing of the sick' is often mistaken for it, but that's a last prayer for healing. Greg is past that."

He rolled his eyes. "Whatever. Just do your church stuff before the M.E. gets here."

"I'll use the Litany at the Time of Death, even though it's a little late." I took out my oil stock and opened it. Dipping my thumb in it, I made the sign of the Cross on Greg's forehead.

"Into your hands, O merciful Savior, we commend your servant, Greg." I began. I finished the Commendatory Prayer with, "May his soul and the souls of all the departed, through the mercy of God, rest in peace. Amen."

I heard The Chief mumble an "amen" right after mine and follow my sign of the Cross. Maybe a few of his Roman Catholic roots were sprouting. But he quickly shrugged them off. "You done?"

"Yes," I said, as I took off my stole. "So tell me about what happened? You said Todd was here?"

"Here, as in this hospital: yes. Here, as in this room, a good bet. We've bagged and tagged Greg's cell and I'll bet Todd's prints are all over it. Might even be all over this room. We've got them on file, so it won't take long to check."

"Why was he here? I mean, killing Greg is the obvious answer, but the way he did it seems a little heavy-handed. And why would he touch Greg's cell?"

The Chief gave me a sly grin. "Because Todd's number was in the 'calls made' listing when I brought it here and it's gone now. All calls were erased. Heavy-handed is Todd's middle name."

"I thought it was Red Hot," I muttered.

"Huh?"

"Nothing. So a nurse told you Todd was here?"

The Chief got a pained look on his face. "Sorta. We got an anonymous call from one of the nurses who said she saw Todd here."

"Anonymous? Did you ask all the nurses who were here if it were one of them?"

"Not all." He nervously rubbed his cheek. "There was a shift change and we haven't been able to talk to all of them."

"So, an anonymous tip that Todd was here is all you have? That and possible incriminating prints on Greg's cell that Todd somehow forgot to wipe off when he was deleting an incriminating phone number. Sounds like you've got this all wrapped up."

The Chief gave me a sour look. "You sound like you're going to be Todd's defense attorney. You have a better theory?"

"Only that even if Todd's prints are on the cell phone, someone else could have killed Greg. I'd like to see the autopsy report when it's done."

He hesitated. "I don't know. It's against procedure."

"In Buggy Springs?" I gave my best *Treasure of the Sierra Madre* bandito sneer. "We ain't got no stinkin' procedures."

He laughed. "I'll consider your request."

"How about if I bribe you with a donut and a cup of coffee?"

"Make it a cinnamon roll and you're on."

"Done. Let's go get your bribe."

Chapter 34

My expenses increased when the Chief ordered two cinnamon rolls at Deadly Donuts, while I went with a jalapeno bagel. Deadly Donuts was owned and operated by a hard-working Vietnamese family and I was glad to support them. When I walk in the door, Trang always gave me a grin and started my non-fat latte. He was the head of his clan and his friendly attitude, along with great donuts, had made the business a success.

I once asked him why he called the shop Deadly Donuts. He made a pretend gun with his finger and aimed at a non-existent target. "Deadly. You know, like perfect shot. Our donuts are perfect." I didn't have the heart to tell him that it might have a negative connotation to many people. Since his business had thrived, I must have been wrong.

Most people were buying donuts to take home and we were lucky enough to score one of the white, plastic tables and a couple of chairs. As the Chief scarfed down a cinnamon roll, I pushed for more information.

"So, did this nurse make a 9-1-1 call about seeing Todd?"

He swallowed his mouthful of cholesterol and took a swig of coffee before replying. "Not exactly. It was a call into KMUK. They called us."

KMUK, also known as K-MUCK by locals, was our community exposé radio station. Volunteers took shifts as DJ's and commentators. Some of the DJ's were very good, playing moldie oldies, Celtic, New Age, world, bluegrass and other, often eclectic, music. However, some of the commentators seemed to relish expounding upon every conspiracy theory that floated around the Net. I hadn't realized that the NSA was really run by the KKK in alliance with the remnants of the KGB until I heard it on K-MUCK.

"KMUK called you about a call they got. Did they record it?"

The Chief shook his head, mouth stuffed with his second roll.

"I'm assuming it was a woman who called."

He slurped some coffee, then cleared his throat. "That's a sexist thing to say. You're assuming all nurses are women. You also think all doctors are men?"

"So KMUK didn't know if it was a woman or a man."

He sighed. "It came from one of their DJ's. I was lucky Sunshine Superman even called an agent of the repressive regime who persecutes honest pot farmers. He reported it and claimed he had no idea. You know how he is."

Sunshine made no bones about hating the police, broadcasting every complaint against them, true or not. "Got it. Smart move if this nurse was the killer."

The Chief leaned back in his plastic chair, studiously folding the rim of his empty cup. "I know Todd's dirty. My cop gut tells me that and I've never been wrong."

"Maybe it's a reaction to too much sugar."

"Funny." He shook his head as he studied his mutilated coffee cup. "Trust me, Todd's at least involved, if nothing else."

After I went home, the Chief called me.

"Well, I got the autopsy report back on Greg."

"And?"

He snorted. "And nothing. The M.E. doesn't know what killed Greg. He should still be alive."

"But he isn't. He didn't die a natural death."

"Whatever the hell that means. Everyone dies from something, even old people. I told the M.E. to keep digging." He paused. "He didn't think that was funny."

"It's better if he were a mortician."

After I hung up, I sat down to work on my sermon. I'd been obsessed with murder and mystery, spinning my wheels while neglecting my duty. It was Friday and I was running out of time. As I tried to study the readings for Sunday, my mind kept ruminating over all my suspicions. I would like to have talked to Sunshine Superman, but his program had finished a couple of hours ago and he had often talked about a plot between the Vatican and the CIA. As an Anglican, I had no tie to Rome, but I doubted it would matter to him.

Getting back to writing my sermon, I read the Old Testament passage for Sunday, from the book of Isaiah. "The wolf shall live with the lamb, the leopard shall lie down with the kid." But this passage was about a time that had not yet come. The wolf and the leopard were raging through Buggy Springs and God seemed to be telling me to stop them. I would learn nothing about the predator, or predators, who killed people in my town by writing a sermon. I grabbed the keys to my truck and headed out the door.

As I drove into town, I saw Todd heading the other way in his pickup. Sitting next to him was Cindy, Jon's widowed mistress. Was that the right term for a mistress of a dead man? I had no idea, but a lot of strange ideas came to me when I saw them together. I'd seen Todd paw Carly, the waitress at Higgins Diggins who'd been given a house by Jon Franks and probably had been one of his many flings. Now Todd was with Cindy. Did he figure that by sleeping with the women his father had that he would take on his mantle; become the true heir of a besmirched heritage, like Absalom sleeping with the concubines of his father, King David? I shook my head. This was beyond my psychological expertise.

Since some of the snow had melted, I was able to find a parking place in front of the Buggy Springs Diner big enough for The Beast. I was welcomed by Judy as I went inside. Well, welcomed may not describe how I was received. She pointed at a table and walked away. I needed to tap into this source of local gossip, so I sat and patiently waited until she returned.

Hand on hip, she looked down at me. "So, just coffee again?"

"I'll have a cup of your wonderful coffee and a turkey sandwich on sourdough with no mayo and sliced tomatoes instead of fries."

She rolled her eyes. "Sure. We can do that."

I gave her my most charming smile. "I really appreciate your accommodating my special dietary needs. Health issues can be so problematic."

"Oh, uh . . . ." Her face changed from judgmental to sympathetic. "We're glad to help. I'll be right back with the coffee."

"Thanks, Judy."

After she left, I had a mild pang of guilt. I had no health issues. But, then again, it was a mild deceit for a good cause. Any sympathy Judy had for me would make it easier to garner information, information that could catch a killer.

187

When she returned with my coffee, I asked her, "So, was that Todd Franks I saw coming out of here?" It was a good guess, since I knew he ate here often.

"You mean Red Hot. Yeah, the jerk." She snorted. "He's a piece of work. He and that slut Cindy were whispering together like a couple of teenagers. She's a lot older than him and was Jon's . . . ." She blushed. "Well, it ain't right."

I nodded non-committally. "I wonder what it was all about?"

"Well, I never eavesdrop, but . . . ." She glanced around, then turned back to me. "I heard something about Red sayin' Lisa was gettin' too uppity. He told Cindy that the two of them had to do somethin' about it. Then our idiot busboy dropped a plate, so I didn't hear what she said to him. When Red saw me lookin' at him, he dropped a twenty on the table and they left." She sniffed. "That made my tip a buck twenty-seven."

I tried to look shocked. "That's horrible. Don't worry. I'll try to make up for him."

She smiled. "Thanks, Father. You're good people."

I returned her smile. I couldn't help but notice that she needed some dental care and resolved to make my tip help the cause. "Thanks, Judy."

After Judy left, I mulled over what she'd overheard. The Chief must be right. Todd was up to his neck in all this. But how? And he'd been the one who said, "Follow the money." But what better way to throw off an investigation than to pretend to be an informant? And what better way to do that than just quote a character in a movie? I needed to find out more about Todd, a.k.a. Red Hot Franks. And I knew the next person to talk to. Carly, the cocktail waitress.

188

Chapter 35

It was just after one when I went through the door of Higgins Diggins. In the words of the old song, the regular crowd was there. Well, not really a crowd, but just the usual suspects again, few though they were. I love old movies as much as I love old music. Most of them wore flannel shirts or sweaters, even though the thermostat was up far too high for me. It was more of a miner and carpenter gathering than Goth and grunge, but there were a few of the alternative dressers. Funny how some fads cling to life when they should die. And Carly was there to keep Goth alive.

She looked at me without expression when I entered, the only guy in corduroy slacks and an Irish fisherman's sweater. I sat at a table, only noticing that it hadn't been wiped down after I was seated. I didn't rest my elbows on it. Carly sauntered over, a study in black. With the heat cranked up, she got away with a sleeveless black Tee that showed off her emaciated arms and colorful tats. Her black jeans hung low on her hips, revealing a little skin between her jeans and Tee.

She looked down at me, the whites of her eyes showing through her black mascara. "Diet Coke, of course."

I hesitated. I did want a diet Coke, but needed to somehow get her to open up to me and that didn't seem to do the trick. I could order a beer, but I don't like beer. Wine would sound pretentious. It was way too early for the hard stuff, but . . . .

"Do you have Johnny Walker Black Label?"

Her eyes widened a little. "Yeah. How do ya want it?"

"Uh, with ice and a little water."

She turned to the bartender. "Bart, Preacher-man wants a Johnny Black, rocks and a splash." She paused. "Make it a Carly."

He laughed.

I almost asked what a "Carly" was, but didn't want to sound ignorant. She sashayed over to the bar, looking like a skinny, middle-school kid who wanted to look sexy. Except for Malificent glaring back at me from her shoulder. After picking up the drink, she

189

brought it to my table and set it down with a flourish. She cocked her head and smiled, the most animated I'd ever seen her.

"Here ya go, Preacher-man. Cheers."

"Thank you, Carly. Would you join me? My treat."

She looked around and shrugged. "Why the hell not?"

While she went to the bar, I pulled off my sweater and sighed. I had on a short-sleeve chambray shirt and felt instant relief. Carly returned with a beer, sat across from me and took a sip. It left a line of foam across her upper lip, hiding her black lipstick.

"First you order a real drink, then you make a pass at me. What's next? Invite me up to your place for a quickie?"

Maybe the scotch was a bad idea. From its amber color, it was a stiff one, too. I took a small sip. It was stiffer than stiff.

I shook my head. "Look, this was probably a stupid way to go about it, but I wanted to talk to you about Jon and Todd Franks. You seem to know Todd and, well, I heard that you were Franks'--"

"That I was his bitch?" She slammed her glass down, sloshing her beer on the table with all the other stains. "I thought you might be different, not drag me to the ground like all the uncool in this crappy town." She sneered. "But you're just like all the rest, Preacher-man."

I held up my hands in surrender. "I'm only trying to find out who's murdering people in our town. Sure, I heard rumors about you and Jon, but I'm coming to you to learn the truth."

"What is truth?" She laughed mirthlessly. "Surprised I know that one? When my mom got religion, she made me read the Bible with her every night. Pilate said that to Jesus. Too bad more of you religious types don't practice what you preach."

Ouch. Her mother "got religion" and I'm "Preacher-man" who doesn't practice what I preach. Obviously, she did not have a very high opinion of Christians. "We Christians do fail in following Christ's teachings at times, but we're just regular people who try. I admit that I often fail myself, but I also keep trying to do better. That is the truth about me." I sipped my drink. It was even stronger than I remembered and I set it down. She had used the quote made by my mystery caller who got me into all this. Coincidence or a slip? "So why don't you tell me the truth about you?"

"Okay. I'm no slut. You believe me?" Her eyes narrowed as she watched me.

"I do believe you. But you do know it's normal for people to make judgemnts based on what they see?"

"Screw 'em." She swigged her beer. "Why am I a slut when Jon's widow runs around showing off her tits and sleeping with scumbags?"

I sat back. "So, Lisa is, uh . . . having affairs?"

She laughed again. "Are you for real?" Then she gave me a curious look. "You *are* for real, aren't you? This place is Sodom and Gomorrah and you don't see it." She sighed. "First, I never slept with Jon or Todd, not that 'Red Hot' Todd didn't try. Second, the house Jon gave me was for my mother, but she died before he got around to giving it to her. Jon was okay, but Todd's a real fu–"

I held up my hand to stop her. "I get it. It was just that I saw him in here the other night with his hand on your, uh . . . ."

She rolled her eyes. "My ass, Preacher-man, my ass. I curve him because I'm chillin' 'til Jon's estate closes. Gives me the house I'm in. Maybe a bit more, too. I figure be cool so Todd doesn't go and mess things up. After it's over . . . ."

She reached in her jeans pocket and pulled out a knife. The blade shot out. "Deadass, if he grabs me again, he'll be a soprano."

I leaned back in my chair. "Okay, I understand how you feel about Todd, but there are better ways to handle him than that. Like a restraining order."

"You don't know Todd. He's sus. He'd crap on a restraining order." She paused, sipping her beer. Then she held my eyes in her stare. "I'll bet he 187'd Jon. He was always telling me 'bout how Jon dissed him and he couldn't wait until the old man croaked and he got everything. The day Jon checked out, Todd comes in and tells me he got bank. Maybe he didn't wait."

"Carly!" It was Bart the bartender. "Get your skinny ass over here and serve the customers."

She stood, grinning and winked at Bart. "All the kinky dudes think my skinny ass is snatched."

As she turned to leave, I asked, "What's the bill?"

She waved her hand as she walked away. "Don't worry 'bout it. I'll get Bart to forget it."

I left a twenty as a tip. I also left most of my drink. If I'd finished it, I'd probably be over the legal limit. All I needed was to be

191

known as the potted priest.   Or plastered Preacher-man.

Back home, I mulled over what I'd heard in town.   The more I
looked into this, the more Todd came to the fore of the suspects.   I
needed to find out more about his background.   I could call the Chief
since he was of the same mind, but I was afraid it would take longer
than I wanted to wait and he might not share everything with me.   So I
made a call to someone I had met about two years ago, a private
investigator from Southern California named Morg Mahoney.

Morg had a tough edge to her, but she seemed to have a good
heart.   I'd met her briefly in Incline and she'd come to St. Nicholas one
time.   We'd hit it off very well and found some common interests,
including old movies.   It was too bad she lived in Long Beach and I
lived in Buggy Springs.   It killed any real chance of getting better
acquainted.   When she'd left that Sunday here, she gave me her card
and said if I ever needed any help on investigations to give her a call.
She was probably joking, but I needed help.   Plus I got the feeling
she'd bend a few more rules than the Chief would to get the info I
wanted.   I flipped open my card file and found hers.

Her phone rang twice before she answered.

"Mahoney Investigations, Morg speaking."

I decided to play a prank.   "Yes, is the boss there?   The man
who actually does the investigating?   I don't want to talk to the
secretary."

"Very funny.   But, Robert, I have caller I.D. and your number's
not blocked, so you're busted.   Anyway, long time no see.   Or hear,
should I say.   How are things in Boondocks Springs?"

Boondocks, huh?   "Busy and exciting.   We've all been talking
about Jeb Hatfield's new pig litter.   His sow had seven and one looks
like it'll be a prize winner at the next county fair.   He's taking bets on
it.   Martha McCoy made up a batch of moonshine she's been selling at
the church socials.   Made the whole congregation Holy Rollers.   How
are things in Lucre Beach?"

She laughed.   "Evidently not as lively as up there. And if
there's any lucre here, I haven't seen it.   I'm barely making rent.
What can I do for you?"

"I need a favor."   I remembered her rent statement.   "I would
like to hire you for a problem up here.   Well, three actually.   Three

people have been murdered and I need information on my prime suspect."

"You're a bit out of my area of operation--"

"No, I don't need you to come up here. I would like to have you research a name for me. I tried, but I didn't get much."

"Give me what you have."

I gave her a rundown from the worthless investigation sites I'd paid for, including his address and phone number.

She said nothing for a moment. "That's all? No Social Security or driver's license number?"

"Sorry."

"Any other info at all?"

"Well, his father was Jon Franks. I don't know who his mother was. I can try to find out, but it'll take time and I'm in a hurry." Then I remembered my conversation with Dwayne. He could well have been my mystery caller, especially having attended a Bible-based college. He also got a third of Jon's business. "Could you also check on a Dwayne Bell from Oklahoma who went to Oral Roberts University about a year and married a woman named Starburst?"

"You're kidding." She chuckled. "What, was Kit Kat already married?"

"Funny. I know it's not much to go on, but how soon can you check them out?"

"How soon do you need it?"

"Yesterday?"

She chuckled. "You sound like all my clients. I'll get back with you if I can get anything. Or if I can't."

After we disconnected, I brewed a pot of tea and sat down at my computer to work on my pesky sermon. My phone rang and I answered it. It was my sister.

"Do you know what he's done now?"

I did not have time to hear my father's latest escapade. "No, and I don't care. Goodbye, Sister Dearest."

I hung up. I pulled out my lectionary and read the lessons for Sunday. Then I read Luke 1:49-51: For the Mighty One has done great things for me, and holy is His name. His mercy is for those who fear him from generation to generation. He has shown strength with his arm; he has scattered the proud in the thoughts of their hearts.

193

Was I being proud, reveling in my role as a priest and looking down on my own sister? I needed to set my heart right. With a sigh, I refilled my mug of tea and made the call.

"Okay, Sister Dearest, tell me what he's done now."

Chapter 36

After enduring a familial haranguing, where I learned that my father was taking up scuba diving from his new boat under the tutelage of a young, attractive, blond dive instructor, I finally was able to hang up and finish my sermon. It was almost midnight and I was exhausted. Then my phone rang. With a groan, I answered, fearing who it might be.

"Hello Robert, did I call you too late?"

It was Morg. "No, I was just finishing some writing. Besides, sleep is highly overrated."

She laughed. "Only at night. Just never call me early in the morning. You might find a bullet can travel over the phone. But I've got a couple of questions on this Todd guy. First, does this guy go by 'Red Hot'? And, second, is his name really Jonathan Todd Franks, Jr.?"

"The answer to the first question is yes, he does. Hard to believe, but if you met him, you wouldn't wonder. As to his real name, his dad was Jonathan, so it makes sense. Why?"

"I have some info. It's funny how people post personal stuff on the Net. Red Hot Franks has a Facebook page. He posted a photo of his dog tags, saying that the Army was a bunch of Nazis and he was glad to get out. I blew it up and enhanced the photo. They had his name, social security, religious preference and blood type." She chuckled. "I didn't know that 'Kama Sutra' was a religious preference."

"It sounds like Todd, but I'll bet he doesn't know that a sutra is a Hindu or Buddhist book of religious aphorisms. So, now that you have that information, what's next?"

"Since I know I've got the right guy, I'm on the mainline now. I just wanted to be sure I had the right Todd before I went any further."

"What about Dwayne?"

She slowly exhaled. "There are more than a few Dwayne Bells from Oklahoma. I'm working the Oral Roberts U side, but I can tell you that Starburst Bell has a Facebook page that lets it all hang out. I mean her pictures seem to always show her leaning over with a low neckline. Anyway, I'll call you when I get more info."

"Uh, next time could you make it a little earlier? I'm not normally up this late."

She laughed again. "No problem. I'd hate to ruin your beauty sleep."

After I hung up, I thought about going to bed, but my mind was still in high gear. Dwayne could well be my mystery caller, but why? He didn't seem to like the Episcopal Church, but was that a motive? Also, I needed to ask Carly a couple more questions, ones I'd been a little hesitant to ask before. I checked my watch and it was officially Sunday and I had an 8:30 service in a few hours, but Higgins Diggins was still open. It was snowing lightly, so I bundled up in a heavy coat and gloves before hopping into the Beast and firing it up.

When I walked into the bar, it was like déjà vu. The same characters seemed to be working on the same drinks. Maybe there was a dress code, or even an appearance code, for the bar that I wasn't aware of. I would hardly call it a dress code, since it was still jeans and flannel shirts or ragged sweaters. This time the thermostat had been lowered, so I was glad for the wool Pendleton I was wearing. Carly came over, this time wearing a too-large black sweatshirt that had a white skull with a knife diagonally piercing it on the front.

"So, Preacher-man, a handle of Johnny Black?" she asked with a smirk.

"I'll go with a Diet Coke." I shrugged. "I'm too much of a lightweight for the drinks you serve here."

"I'm straight with that. I had to finish your last one, anyway." She started to turn, but stopped. "I'm a hell of a lot lighter than you, but I keep in practice."

Before I could think of a reply that wasn't critical, she was at the bar. Shortly, she returned with my drink and plopped it on the table.

"Here ya go. Don't drink it in one shot, now."

I chuckled. "Thanks, Carly. Would you join me for a moment? My treat for whatever you want."

She silently studied me until I had to speak.

"Look, I have a couple more questions. I would very much appreciate it if you would sit here a few minutes and talk to me."

196

She dramatically rolled her eyes. "Whatever. First, I'm getting my drink."

After a trip to the bar, she sat across from me with a glass of amber liquid. A few ice cubes floated in it. After a long sip, she sighed and set it on the table. "A triple Gentleman Jack ain't no gentleman. Whatcha wanna know?"

Carly did not seem the type who would appreciate subtlety, so I barged in. "Are you Jon's daughter?"

She took a big swig of her drink and shook her head. "On fleek. Who spilled that tea?"

"Okay, I have no idea what you just said, but I'm guessing that means yes."

She looked up at me. "Yah."

"So Jon gave you the house because you're his daughter."

"Yah. So?"

"I'm just putting pieces together." I sipped my Coke. "I take it Todd doesn't know you're half-siblings."

She leaned forward, chin jutting belligerently. "Ya gonna tell him?"

"Why would I do that? Unless it was to get him to stop touching you improperly."

Carly leaned back in her chair and roared.

Bart the bartender glared at her. "Carly! You gonna sit on your ass or do your job?"

I looked around and didn't see anyone needing attention. I glanced at my watch. It was almost two in the morning. I pulled out a twenty and waved it.

"Bart, this is your tip for being understanding. I just have a couple of questions and it's almost closing time. Is it okay?"

He shrugged. "Hell, why not?"

I turned back to Carly and saw her drink was almost empty. And I'd bought it for her. I was an enabler.

Carly smirked. "Well, Preacher-man, you don't have to worry about Red Hot grabbing my ass any more. He was in here and copped a feel. I punched him, but Bart saw it all. He tossed Red Hot out on his ass." She laughed until she started hiccupping. She finished her drink. "Not on his ass, on his face. Its imprint's still in the snow on the sidewalk."

197

"Time!" Bart yelled.

I stood and dropped a fifty on the table. "Will that cover our drinks?"

"Hell, I'd go home with you for that." She laughed loudly again. "Ya wanna?"

I leaned over. "Carly, you're a wonderful young lady, so don't act like a . . . slut. We've all got some problems in our lives, but sometimes it helps to talk about them. We have a woman in the church who is a very good listener. If you want her number, I can get it for you."

She turned away. "Don't preach at me. I like who I am."

"Just call me if you ever want to talk." I stood and walked toward the bar.

"Hey, Preacher-man!"

I stopped and turned.

"You're okay. For a Preacher-man."

As before, I understood enough of what she had said to get the gist. I motioned to Bart, who came over to me. "Is she driving?"

"Naw. She just lives a couple blocks up the street."

I gave him the twenty I'd waved.

"Will you make sure she gets there safely?"

He grinned as he took my money. His teeth were yellow. "I'd a done it anyway, but I'll take yer Jackson."

I shrugged. "As long as you make sure she gets home safely, it's well spent."

He laughed as I went to the door.

When I got back home, I collapsed into my bed. Sleep did not come quickly. I was far too involved with finding a murderer to turn off my brain. It was sometime after three before I surrendered to the arms of Morpheus.

Chapter 37

When my 6:30 alarm heralded the new day, it was still dark. One thing about living at the higher latitudes is that the days get very short in the winter. I rolled out of bed, grabbed a quick shower, ate a bowl of oatmeal with a mug of tea, and rushed through Morning Prayer and my crossword puzzle before heading to the 8:30 church service.

I made it through the service without dozing off. Wearing vestments and saying the liturgy does help. Then again, having the Chief there caught my attention. He was a Roman Catholic. After the service, I stood outside the door to shake the hands of all who had attended. In spite of my heavy vestments, my hand was not all that was shaking in the freezing weather.

Lisa Franks came out and took my hand in both of her gloved ones. Her gray, quilted coat open, showing off a tight, black sweater that accentuated her upper curves and yoga pants that did the same below. Her hot breath formed a fog in the frigid air around us as she spoke.

"Oh, Father, I'm so worried about you. After those attacks on your life, I just want to be sure you're okay."

"I'm fine, Lisa. Really." I patted her hands as I pulled mine away. "But thanks for your concern."

She rested her hand on my arm and looked into my eyes. "If you'd like to have dinner some night and talk about theology, I'm available."

I smiled and slipped my arm from her grasp. "That's so kind of you. Have a wonderful Sunday."

She hesitated, as if she wanted to say more, then half-way returned my smile and walked away.

The Chief walked up the sidewalk from his police car parked at the curb. He raised an eyebrow as he watched Lisa sashay off, but thankfully didn't comment. His gaze returned to me as he shook my hand. "You busy?"

I held back my sarcastic comment that a priest was only busy on

Sunday (what some people think) and said, "Why?"

"I met Judge Wilkins at the Elks dance last night and he decided to be nice. I guess Jack Daniels gave him a weak moment. You won't believe it, but I got a search warrant for Todd Franks' place. "

"You mean Jonathan Todd Franks, Jr.'s place."

The Chief cocked his head. "So he's really Jon Boy Junior? How'd you find that out?"

"A friend of mine found it on his Facebook page." I neglected to mention his social security number was there, too. I didn't want him to know I had Morg checking on Todd in case she found something he'd need a warrant to get and didn't have one. Deniability and all that.

"Huh." He shook his head. "I can't understand people wasting their time on that stuff. My wife got me to watch some videos of cats and stuff people taped and put on the internet. A couple were funny, but it got old quick. Anyway, you ready to make a visit to Todd's place?"

I grimaced. My face almost froze in the cold. "Can it wait a couple of hours? I've got a 10:00 service, but I'm free after that."

He shrugged. "Sure. I'll go to the Diner for a cup of joe. Meet you there."

"Great. See you in a couple."

As I hurried inside to try and thaw out before the next service, I wondered who else in Buggy Springs called coffee "joe." Or in the whole state of California, for that matter. It fit the Chief's image: a guy who liked life to be plain and simple. Like his coffee.

Once the next service was over, I pulled on my heavy, wool duffle coat and warm gloves before heading to the Buggy Springs Diner to meet the Chief. Judy was there, pouring coffee at a nearby table, and gave me a smile. Funny how a little friendliness will change a person's attitude. That and a generous tip.

The Chief finished his coffee in a gulp and dropped a ten on the table. "Let's go."

We climbed in his SUV and headed to Todd's place. It wasn't quite off the grid, but it was in rough country, up a gravel road on the Ridge. Since technically this was county rather than city, the Chief had no authority there and the sheriff's department was meeting us. Fortunately, interagency disputes had not reached Buggy Springs.

Fresh snow had fallen and our SUV bumped and spun its way up the road.

I grabbed the armrest to steady myself. "Looks like we're the first ones here."

The Chief grinned as he fought the wheel to keep us on the road. "I may have given the wrong time to meet to our buddies in green."

My, interagency rivalry was just more subtle in Buggy Springs, I mused.

We reached a plateau on our climb and the Chief parked the SUV near a large, snow-covered flatbed truck. We climbed out and started toward a small A-frame house when I noticed something and stopped.

"Uh, Chief, I think you should see this."

He spun around. "What?"

I pointed at the left front of the truck. There was no wheel on it, but something was holding the truck up. It looked like a snow-covered body.

"Crap." He sighed. "If that's Todd, I'm not going to be happy."

"I imagine he won't be either," I muttered. Then I crossed myself and reached into my pocket for my stole.

Since there was a fresh, two or three inch layer of snow, there were no prints or tire tracks to worry about as we slogged over to the truck. The Chief brushed the snow off the body. The removed wheel was leaning on the truck's fender and the brake drum rested on the body's chest. It was Todd, his beard crusted with ice and his eyes closed. The sharp rim of the brake drum had sliced into his chest. The Chief dug into a mound of snow in front of the truck and brought out a large, old-style bumper jack.

"It looks like Todd here was as stupid as he looked. Jacked up the truck to work on the suspension or the brakes or something without using jack stands and it fell on him."

Before we got any further with our investigation, a sheriff's SUV roared up the road and skidded to a stop next to ours. A man in a brown uniform and parka with the Pike County Sheriff's logo hopped out and stomped over to us. He was as tall as I was and skinny, but had a bit of a pot belly.

"What the hell, Chief?" His Southern accent made it almost sound like "hail." "I thought this was a joint operation."

The Chief looked sheepish. "I texted you, Bob, that we'd be coming in earlier."

He glared from under his cowboy hat with a plastic rain cover, his face flushed and his thick, red mustache quivering. "You knew I couldn't get here that fast." Then he noticed Todd and the jack in the Chief's hand. "What the hell?" It seemed to be his favorite question.

The Chief shrugged. "It doesn't seem to matter now who was here first."

Bob stepped back. "Now you're screwing up my accident scene?"

"I think the snow did that," I said in the Chief's defense.

"Yeah, well . . . ." Bob finally seemed to realize I was there. "Who the hell are you?"

"Bob, this is Father Bruce," the Chief said with a slight smile.

"What the . . . hey?" He glanced at the stole I had over the back of my neck. "Sorry 'bout the language, Father. I, uh . . . ."

I held up a placating hand. "No problem. I've heard a lot worse. So, is this your crime scene or the Chief's?"

"Crime scene?" Bob and the Chief said almost in unison.

Bob grinned. "So is this your Father Brown who comes in and makes us look like idiots by catching the clues we missed?" He turned to me. "Well, I'm not going to state unequivocally that there was no foul play, but it's not obvious that there was. I'd say that the truck fell on him and killed him when the jack slipped. But we'll dig around in the snow and let you know what we find." He paused dramatically. "Wait, you're a civilian, aren't you? I guess we don't have to let you know. But, if Lee asks nicely, I might let him know."

I gave him a small smile. "Just don't mess your crime scene up too much when you dig Todd out. Never know what you might find buried. And I'd suggest an autopsy with a tox screen."

Bob laughed. "So now you're Buggy Springs CSI? And why would I order that?"

"If the truck fell on Todd and killed him immediately, his eyes should have been open. But they were closed. If he were drugged and unconscious when the truck was dropped on him, his eyes would be closed. Not only that, the brake drum cut into his chest, but there was no bleeding. It could be because it was so cold, but I think he was actually dead when he was put under the truck." I shrugged. "Then again, I'm only a civilian."

Bob bent over the body, studying it. "What the hell?" He looked up at me. "You might be right Father . . . ."

"Brown," the Chief said with a grin.

I knelt in the snow and recited the Litany at the Time of Death from the *Book of Common Prayer*. While Todd had not shown any signs of faith, in the BCP we pray to God for those "Whose faith is known to you alone." We are not to judge and there's always hope.

Chapter 38

I had wanted to go into Todd's house with the Chief and Sheriff Bob, maybe get a little more info on that poor human popsicle, but the Sheriff refused. "You may be Father Brown, but I'm Inspector Lestrade," he said with a smirk. "This is my crime scene and I don't need Buggy Springs CSI."

I smiled instead of advising him on his confused detective stories. I might need his goodwill in the future and did not want to get off on the wrong foot. Thankfully, he did have one of his men who arrived not long after give me a ride home, so I didn't have to wait in the freezing weather for the Chief to finish there and take me.

Once home, I lighted a fire and brewed a pot of strong English Breakfast tea. As I wrapped my hands around the hot cup, they were shaking. It had been a bone-chilling experience in more ways than one. Although a priest does see dead bodies, I had now seen three people who I was sure had been murdered. That was more than enough for a lifetime.

Although my mystery caller had foretold Todd's death, it hadn't happened right afterwards and Todd hadn't been shot. Perhaps the caller hadn't been in on his death. Perhaps that had been a prank call and Todd's actual death had been coincidence. Still, on *NCIS*, Gibbs' Rule 39 was "There are no coincidences." I smiled. Since when had TV shows become a source of wisdom?

I sat at my desk and logged in on my computer. There was a message from Morg to call her. I did.

"Mahoney."

"Bruce, here. Report."

There was a moment of silence and I wondered if she realized I was parodying her terse style. If so, would she think it amusing or insulting? I was about to apologize when she chuckled.

"Okay, Robert, I'll stop being so wordy and cut to the chase. I'm sending you a rundown on Red Hot. Let me know if you've got any questions."

"I, uh . . . ." How should I word it? "Red's not so hot anymore. In fact, he's below room temperature."

"Red's dead?"

I couldn't resist. "You might say he was iced. We found him under several inches of snow."

Morg started laughing.

Guilt for using such dark humor about someone's demise made me grimace. Why was I such a lover of bad puns? "Look, Morg, that was crass. I meant to say that Todd died under suspicious circumstances."

"Crass?" She laughed again. "You're a rank amateur compared to me. Anyway, the late, great Red Hot is dead. He was a red-hot suspect, in my book. He was kicked out of the Army for insubordination, but a little checking showed that was only the last on a long list of issues with the Army. He had been a medic and suspected of selling drugs, but a court martial didn't convict him. He'd had a lot of problems with the law, including drug arrests and assaults, though those were bar fights. He was on parole so many times the revolving door must have hit him in the ass a few times."

"Okay, he was not a nice person." I sipped my tea. "But why start killing people, even his own father."

"Money? He was in debt up to his eyeballs. His credit cards were maxed out and he had no real assets. Did he get an inheritance?"

"Funny you should ask. He got his dad's business and some promissory notes." I leaned back in my chair. "But if he killed the other three, who killed him?"

"Well, I'm sure that if I were there, I could tell you," Morg said. I could almost see her smirk. "But maybe if he killed for money, maybe someone did the same to him. But then again, it could be revenge by a relative of someone he killed. Or it could be his past caught up with him. Then again–"

"I get the idea. Who knows?" I sighed. "Thanks for all you did."

"No problemo. My best friend is out of the country this Christmas and I was getting bored with checking out cheating spouses anyway. I'm sending you an email with all I found. If nothing else, it's a study in our failed justice system."

"Yeah. Well, thanks again."

206

After we disconnected, I mulled over the new information. Todd had said, "Follow the money." It seemed like the time to do just that. I called the Chief's cell. He answered on the third ring.

"What now, Robert?" He didn't sound happy.

"Sorry to bother you, Chief. Are you still at the crime scene?"

"Hell, no. Sheriff Bob told me to take a hike. Said he'd email me a report." He snorted. "So much for interagency cooperation."

I hesitated.

"So, why'd you call me, Robert?"

"I need information. I'd hoped you'd have access to Todd's house."

"Well, I don't. Why?"

"There might be some documents that could help."

"Sheriff Bob and his crew have taken over." He paused. I could almost hear the gears running in his mind. He'd love to show up the sheriff. "But I get the idea that Bob's only going to be looking at the physical evidence. We should be able to sneak in there later tomorrow. What're we looking for exactly?"

"I wondered if Todd had a will. I also was curious about his financial situation and . . . Holy cow!" I'd been scrolling down the info from Morg and hit a stopper.

"What?"

"Did you know Todd was married to Cindy Wolfe?"

"Who's Cindy Wolfe? . . . . Wait, wasn't she Jon's mistress? You mean she's his son's wife? That's sick. Really sick."

I continued reading. "Actually, ex-wife. They were only married a few weeks, right after Todd went into the Army."

"It's still sick. I got a gut feeling that this is going to get a lot weirder. That Jon was some Don Juan." He chuckled. "Or maybe I should say Don Jon."

"Yeah, he sure was." I didn't tell him about Carly. "Look, if we can check out Todd's place, it might help. And I'd really like to know about the tox screen on Todd."

"Sure. I'll give you a call tomorrow about getting into Todd's house. No promises on the tox screen. Not my call."

After we disconnected, I sighed as I leaned back and sipped my tea. It was cold. As were my leads. My computer screen told me it was after five. As my father would often say, the sun was over the

207

yardarm. I decided to pour a little single-malt scotch.

I went to my liquor cabinet and selected a bottle of Oban. My dad liked the Islays, but they're too peaty for me, like scotch gone bad. He said it was because I was a wimp and was never an athlete. Maybe he was right, but I still didn't like Islays. I poured a reasonable amount in my Edinburgh crystal glass and added a splash of water before settling back in front of my computer to finish Morg's email. I took a sip and read.

All she had told me about Todd was true, and then some. His military record was a disgrace. He'd enlisted right after sexual assault charges against him had been dropped. I noted the name of the woman. She was in my parish, a woman now in her 50's who was still attractive. However, she was a modest woman who didn't dress in an overly sexy manner, not one I'd put with Todd, literally or figuratively. I wondered if she finally got revenge.

The next items of interest were the bar fights. I'd expected them to be at Higgins Diggins. Two of them weren't. They'd been at Beezer's Bar. All three times he'd been fighting Choke, the last was at Higgins Diggins and Todd had ended up with a broken jaw. In the end, no charges had been filed. Only the police reports of the incidents remained. Why had they been fighting? As Alice would have said, curiouser and curiouser.

Getting only more questions from my research, I took a sip of whisky and rubbed my eyes. Maybe a trip to Todd's place would help. In the meantime, I was neglecting other duties. I'd left a drunken Carly in the care of Bart the bartender the night before. Her inebriated condition was my fault. I should make sure she was okay. I called Higgins Diggins.

"Higgins Diggins. Whatcha want?"

It was Bart. "This is Father Robert. Is Carly there?'

"She didn't come in today. Said she had 'personal business,' whatever the hell that is."

Probably a hangover. My fault. "Did you make sure she got home okay last night?'

He laughed. "Hell, she didn't need any help. Walked outta here right after you did."

"Wait, I saw her. That drink I bought her put her over the top."

"Ya kidding? She can drink us both under the table at the same

208

time." He paused. "I guess you want the money back ya gave me to make sure she got home."

"Keep it. Just tell me how to make sure she's alright."

"I, uh . . . ." He took a breath. "Well, I'm not supposed to give this out, but I trust you."

He gave me her cell number and address, then hung up.

I called the cell and got the message, "Hey, leave a message or don't. Who the hell cares?"

I left a message to call me, then went outside, hopped in the Beast and headed to town. Her house was a small Victorian, white with a turret. Although it was hard to see much at night, the house looked to be in good repair. It didn't fit my image of Carly's home. There were no lights on and no one answered my knocking.

I went to my truck and dug out a notepad. I wrote, "Carly, please let me know that you are okay. Thanks, Preacher-man."

I slipped it under her door and I headed back to the rectory. As I drove home, her words about what she'd do if Todd bothered her came to my mind. He had bothered her. And now Todd was dead.

Chapter 39

After my late night the night before, I got to bed early. I spent a couple of hours staring into the dark as I tried to put the pieces of the puzzle together. Everything had pointed to Todd as the killer. He easily could have followed his father and killed him. Although no one had seen him at Golden Sunset the night Elvira had been murdered, the alarm for the exit door had gone off a few times, so he could have gone in and out. I was willing to bet that his truck was the one that tried to ram me and that he owned an AK-47. He had been seen in the hospital the night Greg was killed and his prints were on Greg's cell. Now Todd had been killed. Most of them had been members of my parish, even if only nominally. If I didn't figure this out soon, I might not have a parish. I finally dozed off into a fitful sleep.

When I awoke, it was still dark. I glanced over at the clock. 5:27. One thing about digital clocks is that they give you the exact time. The heater hadn't come on yet, but I threw off the covers and shivered my way into the bathroom for a hot shower. I had a lot to do that day and I needed to get started.

As I ate my oatmeal and sipped my tea, I went over my to-do list in my mind. First, I'd call the Chief and see when we could get into Todd's house. I doubted the sheriff would be searching Todd's papers for what I was looking for: his will, if he had one. If I didn't find what I was after there, I would see if Jon's lawyer would help me. I would see if Lisa could help me with that. Then I'd drive out to Beezer's Bar to find out what Todd's problem with Choke had been. Finally, I would have to brave Rainbow's wrath and talk to Emma. I was sure she knew more than she was saying.

As I finished my second mug of tea, I settled back in my chair. I had a plan of action. God help me, I had to find this killer before I lost another parishioner. I picked up the phone to call the Chief, but fortunately noticed that it was wasn't even 6:00 before I did. So I did Morning Prayer and my crossword puzzle before sitting down at my computer and starting working on my next sermon, the one for Christmas Eve. It was hard to believe that it was almost Christmas and I hadn't done much to prepare. I'd been so focused on the grim murders that I hadn't given proper thought to the joyous season. But my mind wouldn't focus.

Frustrated, I pulled on a heavy coat and warm gloves, stuffed a pair of latex gloves in my pocket and drove the Beast to Todd's place. It still wasn't light when I got there and my headlights eerily danced around his snow-shrouded truck and some overhanging branches as I drove up the driveway. It hadn't snowed since we'd discovered the body, so my tire tracks blended in with all the ones from police vehicles. I dug out my five-cell Maglite and climbed out of my pickup. The early-morning quiet was surreal, oddly out of place at a death scene. There was a yellow crime scene tape around the truck, stretched to some nearby trees. I avoided the area and slogged through the crisp, icy snow to the house, careful to stay in some footprints already there. Luckily, the house had no tape around the door. However, I had no keys and no lock-picking tools. Even if I'd had some, I wouldn't have known how to use them. I muttered a short prayer as I tried the knob. It was unlocked.

Once inside, I considered turning on the lights. Todd had no close neighbors, but someone might see the glow from the road below, so I stayed with my flashlight. The little A-frame was a lot like Todd: dirty, messy and unorganized. Empty beer cans littered the floor, take-out Chinese food cartons were piled on the coffee table and porn magazines almost covered the tattered, plaid sofa. Although I'm certainly no expert in the field, in this day of free Internet sex material, I was surprised so much printed material was even available. But then, Todd had not struck me as a techie, so he might have stayed with the old-school smut. There was a layer of fingerprint dust over hard surfaces and I carefully avoided disturbing it. The bright light of my Maglite illuminated the disgusting, one-room house. The bed was, of course, unmade and dishes were piled in the sink and on the counter. A half-full bottle of gin and a grapefruit juice carton were sitting near the edge. The smell was of stale beer and rotting food, with a trace of urine. There was one interior door, which I guessed led to the bathroom. I chose to leave it at that, since my stomach might not take it if I went inside. Best to leave no DNA behind.

212

What I wanted were any files that might give me information about Todd's finances, but there was no desk in the room. Although there was an old printer on the floor by a ragged, stained sofa, there wasn't any computer. I checked everyplace I thought Todd might keep personal papers, including the night stand by his bed. I didn't know anyone collected used condoms. Thankfully, I was wearing gloves. I found unpaid bills, but no other paperwork. Then, as my light shone across a copy of *Variations* that obviously had nothing to do with Goldberg or Bach lying on the floor, I spied a small stack of manila file folders under it. They were the only things in the place that might be helpful. As I squatted and pulled them from under the magazine, I heard the sound of an engine and headlights flickered across the front window.

There was no way the sheriff was returning at this time of the morning to resume his search. But what if the killer had missed something after eliminating Todd and decided to come back to get it? What if the files I had in my hand were what he wanted? I quickly turned off my flashlight and ducked behind the sofa. There was little cover in the room, so my options were limited. Whoever drove up the drive would see my truck. My Maglite was over a foot long and made out of stout aluminum. I gripped it tightly, ready to use it as a club. If I went down, I'd go down swinging. I wasn't a violent man, but I also wasn't a pacifist.

I heard the crunch of the snow as someone approached the house. The door swung open and a stocky figure was outlined in the doorway. Should I charge him or wait until he got closer? He clicked on a flashlight and ran its beam across the room. I ducked as the light went over the sofa. Then it swung back and stopped just above me.

"Come out, come out, wherever you are."

I sighed. It was the Chief. I slowly stood, hands in the air, still clutching my Maglite and the file folders. "Don't shoot."

He laughed. "Put your hands down, Robert. I knew it was you when I saw your truck." His light went up to my hands. "What's in those?"

"I have no idea. I just found them," I said as I lowered my hands.

"Let's head to the station and find out. That way, they're in police custody and you didn't tamper with evidence."

213

"How did you know I was here?"

"I didn't. I couldn't sleep and wanted to see if forensics missed anything."

"You mean Sheriff John's team?"

He cocked his head. "I think you mean Sheriff Bob."

"Right. Slip of the tongue. There was a TV show for kids with Sheriff John who showed cartoons a while back. Before your time." I paused. "Mine, too, but my father told me about it."

"I think I heard about him somewhere. Let's get a cup of coffee and hope remembering the stink of this place doesn't ruin it."

When we got to the station, the Chief parked in the red zone in front. I opted for a legal spot a few spaces down. He pulled out his key and opened the front door, turning off the alarm as we entered.

I looked around at the semi-dark city hall. "Who answers the phones?"

"We turn 'em over to sheriff's dispatch from midnight until 8 in the morning. If anything happens, they call whoever's on rotation, then me, if it's important." He chuckled. "I don't often get that call. Not like Colton."

We went into a back room, where there was a Keurig. The Chief caught my look and grinned. "We're state of the art here. All the latest equipment. Just no people."

As we sipped our hot coffee, I opened the files. The Chief took some and I started going through the others. We had spent about an hour going through them when the Chief said, "Well, I'll be a son of a b . . . beehive."

I looked up. "Something interesting?'

"I'll say." He leaned back in his chair. "Ol' Jon Boy Senior, put all his assets in a trust. That's what this is, a copy of his trust. He set it up so Todd, Lisa, Carly, Dwayne and Cindy got any profits off their parts as long as they were alive, but it goes back in the trust if they die or get disqualified."

"Disqualified?" Sounded like a race rather than a trust.

"Yeah, like Lisa would be disqualified if she got married again, so everything she got would go back in the trust for the others."

"So the money's not really theirs?"

He shook his head. "Jon really wanted to control his money

214

from the grave. His trust's got more conditions and clauses than the Obamacare bill and his lawyer's the trustee."

"So all the others in the trust now get a share of Todd's portion?"

"That's where it gets real interesting. What happens is different for each person." He sipped his coffee, prolonging the suspense. "For Todd, Ben Zachary gets half his loan wiped out. Then Dwayne gets enough ownership of the business to have 51%. And . . ."

I was losing my patience. "And what?"

"Then Lisa Franks and Cindy Wolfe each get an eighth of what's left. And that bar waitress, Carly, gets the rest."

My heart sank. Carly had two reasons to kill Todd. He'd assaulted her and she would profit from his death. It was not good. Still, Ben and his boys had a reason to kill Todd, too. So did Dwayne, going from fired to majority owner of the business. Not only that, I couldn't imagine skinny Carly dragging Todd's probably 250 lb. body out of his shack, jacking up the truck, taking off the wheel and dropping it on him. Not unless she had a big, red "S" under her black T-shirt. But she might have had help.

"What's our next step, Chief?"

"How about I take care of police business and see what breaks," he said with a raised eyebrow. "And you do your church stuff?"

216

Chapter 40

It was before eight, so I got to St Nicholas before Doris arrived. It was quiet and peaceful as I made a pot of tea in the compact kitchen. I had just settled into my desk chair with a steaming mug to go through copies of the files from Todd's place the Chief had made for me when my cell rang, or rather played "Scotland the Brave." It was my sister. I let out a sigh before I answered it.

"What has he done now, Sister Dearest?"

She was silent for a moment. Then she spoke so softly that I could barely hear her. "He's in the hospital."

"Who's in–" I knew. Pops of course. "What happened."

"He won't tell me. I found out because a friend of mine saw him there when she went to visit another patient. You have to call him."

"Of course." We may not have been the closest family, but we were family. Blood was thicker than water and all that. "Where is he?"

"Cedars-Sinai, of course. Nothing but the best for him." She sobbed. "How could I say that? I'm just mean."

"No, you aren't, Jannie. You're just upset. It's okay."

"Jannie?" She was crying. "You haven't called me that . . . since we were kids."

"I know. I'm sorry for that." I was trying to keep it together.

"He's got orders at the hospital that no visitors are allowed. I called and they said they wouldn't let me in." Another sob. "Call him, Robbie. He'll talk to you. He always liked you better."

Liked me better? Liked Accident better? I doubted that, but I'd try. "I'll call him."

"Thanks." She paused. "You know, Bradley's parents are in Australia, so the four of us could come up to your house for Christmas dinner."

I shook my head. She'd hate it. My 1800 square-foot place had two spare bedrooms with a total of two bathrooms and her 7800

217

square-foot mansion had separate bedrooms for Todd and Tyler, my nephews from hell, and had five bathrooms, probably one extra, just in case one of Jannie's little demons destroyed one. Besides, Janet and I did best when not too close. "Thanks, but you have your life down there and I've got services to officiate up here."

"That's probably for the best, since we're not into that church stuff." She sounded relieved that I'd declined her offer. "Just let me know what's going on with Pops."

"I will. Take care, Jannie."

"Yeah. Thanks, Robbie."

She hung up.

I leaned back in my chair and closed my eyes. Was there a prayer in the *Book of Common Prayer* for messed up families? I didn't know of one, but there should be. I knew mine wasn't the only one. I sipped my tea. It was cold. I went back to the kitchen and popped it in the microwave. I knew I was delaying, but I dreaded calling Pops. He'd never been in a hospital in his life before as far as I knew, so it must be serious. But why hadn't he called? Because you don't do that in the Bruce family. My mom had been different, but she'd only been a Bruce by marriage. After she died, the rest of us had spun off, like planets with no sun to keep them together.

I settled back at my desk, got the number online and called the hospital. After wading through the answering system, I finally was connected to Pops's room.

"Hello?"

He sounded tired.

"Hello, Pops."

"Accident. I suppose your sister told you."

"Only that you're there. She has no idea what's wrong." I paused. "Same as I."

"Couldn't you say, 'Same as me,' like a regular guy?" He chuckled. "Of course not. No one in our family is regular. Except in our bathroom habits."

"Are you going to tell me why you're there?"

His was silent.

I waited.

He sighed. "Okay, but only if you don't tell that nosy sister of yours."

218

"Only if it's not serious. She deserves to know if it is."

"She deserves a swift kick in the butt if she doesn't butt out of my life." He waited, evidently hoping I'd appreciate his play on words.

I wasn't amused.

After a moment, he sighed. "Okay Accident, here's the story. After you were born, I got snipped. One accident was enough for me. Now, Ashley wanted kids if we got married and I checked in to get things reconnected."

"Wait. Married? Who's Ashley?"

"Lauren's twin sister. You dated Lauren, didn't you?"

I had dated Lauren Colter briefly in high school. She was a year younger than I, but far more experienced. Her idea of a fun date was to go to a party and get high. Not my scene. Now my father was dating a woman not even my age. It was a shock.

"I, uh . . . . You're marrying Ashley?"

He gave a short chuckle. "Not now. They couldn't reconnect things. Doc Samuelson messed things up too much when he made the snip and Ashley won't marry me unless we have kids. I'd sue Samuelson, 'cept I'd have to dig him up to do it. Well, reconstruct his atoms from carbon, since he was cremated."

My head was spinning. I realized I was gripping the edge of my desk with my free hand. "This is all too much. What's going to happen now?"

"I'm out of here in a few hours and I'm taking my boat on a long cruise. Just me and the crew. Ashley's history."

"What do I tell Janet?"

"Nothing." He hesitated. "Tell her I had 'a medical procedure' and I'm fine. That's all. I've got to go now, Accident. A pretty nurse is here to check me out."

With that he hung up.

I sat, staring at my phone. Finally, I sipped my again-cold tea and wondered how I got such a weird family. That reminded me I needed to call Janet.

She answered on the first ring. "Is he dying? Oh, Robbie, I'm driving over right now to be with him as long as I can."

"Uh, I don't think that's a good idea, Jannie."

"Oh, no. He's already dead, isn't he?" She sobbed. "I'm too

219

late to tell him I love him."

I gritted my teeth. My cowardly father had left me with this mess. "No, he might already be released. He just had a medical procedure and everything's fine."

"Procedure? What kind of procedure?"

"It was, uh . . . just a minor one." I wished I could lie and say I didn't know, but I couldn't. "He's doing so well that he's going to take his boat out for a while."

"He told you and you won't tell me?" her voice had a hard edge. "After I'm the one who called you? Thanks a lot, Accident."

The line went dead. So much for getting close again. Maybe our blood wasn't all that thick after all. I closed my eyes and rubbed my temples. If this were how the day was going to be, I ought to go back to bed and hide under the covers.

After Doris arrived, I spent the morning making calls, writing letters and finishing my article on Christmas for the church's e-newsletter. The article was about Christmas as a family time and that we were all part of the family of God. After my conversation with my sister, it rang a little hollow.

Just before noon, I got a call from the Chief.

"You sitting down, Robert?"

"That's all I've done this morning after I left you."

He chuckled. "Yeah, well, it's a tough life. I, on the other hand, have been busy. I got the preliminary report from the coroner. He says you were right about him being used as a jack stand. It crushed his chest, but it wasn't Todd's cause of death. He was stabbed too, but that didn't kill him."

He paused dramatically.

Stabbed? Carly? I had no patience with this. "Don't play games with me. It's not a good day for it. What killed him?"

"He had a high content of alcohol and ketamine in his system. THC, too, but that just means he's smoked pot in the near past. The medical examiner said it could have been a heart attack from the alcohol and ketamine. But the kicker is that the coroner also found an injection mark on his neck. Since it had looked like Todd had been crushed, we probably wouldn't have found it if we hadn't been suspicious."

"What's ketamine?"

220

"It's an anesthetic that started being used during 'Nam. Nowadays, it's still used as a battlefield anesthetic, but also it's used to treat asthma and veterinarians use it for small animals. In a sane world, only dogs and cats would experience it, but people are crazy. Since it's a tranquilizer, it's also used as a date-rape drug."

I remembered the gin and grapefruit juice. "Did the sheriff check for ketamine in the glasses? Or did Todd inject himself."

"I don't know. No word from the sheriff on what was in the glasses yet, but no one injects drugs in his neck. There were tracks on his arms, but they were old. No drugs in the house except for weed. Lots of it. Well, bongs and honey oil, too. The M.E.'s been looking for anything else in his blood, but none of the tox screens have come up with anything so far."

I was doodling on a pad by my computer, thinking about what the Chief had said. Todd had been stabbed, drugged, injected with something, possibly an unknown poison, and crushed under his truck. Somebody wanted to be sure he was dead.

I chuckled. "Reminds me of Rasputin possibly being poisoned, stabbed, shot and drowned."

"Ras-who?"

"A Russian mystic who the Russian Tsarina–"

"Not my jurisdiction," the Chief interrupted. "I'm more concerned with Buggy Springs, U.S.A."

"Got it." I was properly chastised for my wandering. "Have you talked to all your 'usual suspects'?"

The Chief chuckled. "Yeah, and none of them have a decent alibi. Well, I don't know about one of them. Carly's missing. So's Todd's old Bronco. Suspicious, huh?"

I stopped doodling, realizing I'd been writing her name. "I suppose it is."

Chapter 41

Since I was sure that Emma Katz had more to tell me about Greg that morning in the hospital, I would need to brave Rainbow's hostility to find out. No doubt she would attack with a fury. But, as Shakespeare wrote, "once more into the breach." I would go see Emma at Rainbow's, if necessary. On the way, I stopped by Golden Sunset to see how Imogene Casper was doing.

Julie was on duty at the desk when I went inside. The smell was still as nauseating, but Julie was much warmer than when I had first met her.

"Hi, Father Robert," she purred. "Here to see Imogene or is there someone else from your church here?" Did she bat her lashes?

"Only Imogene, as far as I know. Is she in her room?"

"No, she in the activities room. I think she has a new man-friend." She grinned. "Do you feel it? There's romance in the air."

"Uh, okay." I edged away. "I'll go see Imogene."

Imogene was seated on a small couch next to a white-haired man who was holding her hand. An expensive-looking walker was at his knee. She was in a red-flowered dress with pearls that were no doubt imitation. Her hair looked like it had been recently permed. Her companion was wearing a bright red sport coat with a black pocket square, a red pinstriped shirt, black bow tie and a big smile. When she saw me, Imogene excitedly waved me over to them.

She beamed at the man next to her. "Father Bobbie, this is my good friend, William Powell."

He proffered his free hand. "So nice to meet you, Father Bruce. I feel I already know you from what Imogene has told me about you."

I shook his hand. "I feel I know you, Mr. Powell. I've seen so many of your movies. I loved you in *The Thin Man*."

Imogene laughed. "He's not that William Powell, silly. William was in stationery."

He grinned, showing teeth too perfect to be original. "Now I'm

223

just stationary." He looked over at Imogene like a kid on his first date. "As long as Imogene is by my side, I'll remain stationary."

I fought to suppress my laugh. "Well, I'm happy for you both. You are looking very well." I winked. "Just don't do anything I wouldn't do."

"Oh, Father, that's pretty limiting." Imogene blushed. "After all, you're a priest."

I let my laugh out, then patted her withered hand. "You give me too much credit. I'm not perfect." Then a thought hit me. She had told me Marilyn Monroe had visited her the night Elvira had been killed, yet she knew that her William Powell was not the dead movie star. Maybe she wasn't delusional. "Imogene, do you remember the night Elvira . . . passed away?"

"You mean when she was whacked? I heard all the juicy details through the grapevine. Some of the inmates here think it was a mob hit. But you already asked me about when Elvira was whacked." She gave me a hard stare. "Do you think I'm senile?"

"Of course not." I lied. "But you said Marilyn Monroe visited you that night. And she's, uh–"

"Dead. I know that." She rolled her eyes. "I didn't mean the real one. She had blond hair, sorta pretty and big bosoms. Lots of makeup, but she's not as young as she acts. Know who she is?"

"I think I do." It fit Lisa to a T. I smiled down at Imogene. "I'd better be going."

"Well, it was nice seeing you, Father. Be sure and say 'Hi' to Father Luke."

I started. "Uh, I will." Father Luke had been the priest at St. Nicholas before me. He had a heart attack and died, collapsing over the altar while serving the Eucharist. Imogene had been there. Maybe she had seen the real Marilyn.

As I walked out, Julie was on the phone. She raised her eyebrows, gave me a wiggly-fingered wave and mouthed, "Bye-bye." I managed a smile and nodded.

I had Emma's cell number from when she'd called me from the hospital when Greg was murdered, so I called her.

"Hello?"

"Emma, it's Father Robert. I'd like to meet with you."

A long pause. "When?"

"Are you free now? I could drive out to you."

Another pause. "No, I'll meet you in town. How about the Diner?"

My favorite place. "Great. When?"

"Give me thirty minutes, okay?"

"No problem. See you in thirty."

She disconnected.

The good thing was she would see me and soon. The bad thing was thirty minutes was too long to do nothing and not long enough to do anything. I drove to the church to check in with Doris. She was studying her computer screen and didn't even look up when I walked in.

"Anything I should know?"

She kept her eyes on her screen. "How would I know? I'm just your minion."

I sighed. "You are not my servant. You are a valued employee. There is a difference." I didn't add that "minion" implied faithful. No doubt she got the term from the movies.

She spun around and glared at me. "Then why don't you tell me what's going on? I hear from everyone else that you've found a body and are trying to solve the case, but nothing from you. I'm just a stupid minion."

I closed my eyes and rubbed my temples. When I opened them, she was still glaring. "Okay, here's the lowdown." For the next twenty minutes, I gave Doris the for-publication version of all that had happened since I last saw her. Everything was going well until I told her I had to leave.

"Where to?" she demanded. "To find another parishioner's body?"

"I certainly hope not. I'm meeting with Emma Katz. Her husband was murdered, you know, and she might need some counseling and consoling." Not a lie, but not all the truth. But anything I told Doris would soon be all over the Buggy Springs Gossip Network, BSGN. It was far quicker at getting the news out than CNN.

She seemed slightly mollified. "Well, tell her she's in my prayers."

"I will," I said as I hastily exited.

225

When I got to the Buggy Springs Diner, Judy was there. I wondered if she lived there. But my generous tips must have helped since she smiled and motioned me to an empty table. After I was seated, she pulled out her order pad.

"Whatcha want, Father?"

"Just coffee."

"Hear you found Red Hot's body." She leaned in conspiratorially. "Was it gruesome?"

I gritted my teeth. I'd made progress with her, so no need to say what I was thinking. "It's never pleasant to see a dead body. It's not something I really want to remember or talk about."

"Yeah, I understand." She nodded solemnly. "I found my ex after he blew his brains out."

I didn't know what to say. So sorry for your loss? It must have been horrible? I understand why he did it? Oops! Instead, I nodded and said nothing.

Emma arrived at the same time as my coffee. Unfortunately, so did Rainbow, wearing a poncho and woven headband. They sat down at my table.

Rainbow leaned forward and glared. "Won't you just leave her alone?"

I sipped my coffee. I understood why it's sometimes called mud. I slowly set my cup down and met her gaze. "I want to find who killed Greg and three other people in this town. Why don't you ask Emma if that's bothering her or not?"

Rainbow half stood. "You self-righteous–"

"Stop!" Emma slammed her hand on the table. "I'm here because I want to be." She pointed at Rainbow. "Sit down."

If looks could kill, I'd have been in need of a mortician. But Rainbow sat.

Judy showed up, eyes opened widely.

I smiled at her. "Whatever they want, put it on my bill."

Rainbow gave me an impish grin. "I'll have an omelet with everything on it, a side of fries, fruit, orange juice and a latte."

Judy gave her the evil eye. She had a new person not to like. "We don't got lattes. You too good for coffee?"

Rainbow shrugged. "Fine. Coffee."

Judy turned to Emma. "What can I get you, honey?"

Emma was staring at the table. "Just coffee."

After Judy left, Emma looked at me, fear in her eyes. She grabbed my hand. "I think I'm in trouble."

"Why?"

"If I tell you, will you tell the cops?"

"If you are truly sorry and confess, I cannot break the sacrament of Confession and the law can't force me to." I glanced over at Rainbow. "But she is under no such legal protection."

She sneered at me. "I wouldn't give the pigs the snot in my kleenex."

Emma grabbed my hand. "Then I want to do a Confession right now."

I looked around. "I don't think–"

"Now. I mean it."

I pulled my stole out of my pocket and put it around my neck.

Emma started to cry. "Father, forgive me for I have sinned. I know who killed Jon and why."

Chapter 42

I noticed our table was getting some suspicious stares from the patrons. And from Judy. It sounded like there might be some legal issues with what Emma said, things that shouldn't get into the local gossip mill. I put a twenty on the table and nodded at Judy.

Then I rose. "My office would be more private." I smiled at Emma. "Shall we go over to St. Nicholas?"

Emma nodded and stood.

Rainbow grabbed Emma's hand. "Stop right there, Father Perv. You think you'll get her in some private room and–"

"Don't!" Emma shouted at Rainbow, as she freed her hand. "I need to get this off my chest."

Rainbow glared at me. "That's not all he wants off your chest, honey. I know his type." She stood. "I'm staying with you the whole time."

I held up my hands in surrender. "Look, my office has a glass door and my secretary's desk is right outside, she can see if anything inappropriate happens. And she's not the most tight-lipped person I know. Plus you can sit with her and watch, too."

She shook her head emphatically. "Not good enough. I'm going to be right next to Emma the whole time."

I met her eyes. "That is fine by me, but it's completely up to Emma."

Emma started for the door and mumbled just loud enough for Rainbow and I to hear, "Whatever."

As we were walking out, Lisa was walking in, holding onto the arm of a man I'd never seen in town. He was maybe 50 years old, about 5'9", stocky, with a reddish-brown, trim beard and a fringe of hair the same color creeping out from under a black cowboy hat. His long, black, leather coat was open, showing a beer-belly that hung over his silver, oval belt buckle. He looked like a Johnnie Cash wanna-be, down to the black jeans, Western shirt and lizard-skin boots.

Lisa beamed. "Father Bruce, I want you to meet Walt Durham.

He's going to reopen the old Bet-'Em-All gold mine."

Walt grinned, displaying a gold incisor, and put out his hand. "Glad to meetcha, Bruce."

I took his hand. "It's Robert. Bruce is my last name. So, you're planning on reopening the mine? Do you expect any problems with pumping out tens of thousands of gallons of arsenic-contaminated water to do it?"

His eyes narrowed. "You ain't one of those eco-freaks, are ya?"

I shook my head. While I am not an "eco-freak," I do believe in not destroying the environment. "Just curious."

His smile was cold. "Well, curiosity killed the cat, ya know."

"Oh, Father Bruce," Lisa interrupted. "Don't start an argument. Don't you want to do the wedding for Walt and me?"

A little quick? I forced a smile. "I would be glad to, Lisa."

She leaned forward, letting her coat fall open to reveal a very tight, white sweater. "It might be the last time you see me before we move to Texas."

I edged toward the door. "We will all miss you, I'm sure."

It looked like Elvira had been right about some man connecting with Lisa quickly after Jon's death.

When we got to the church, Doris looked up at the three of us from her desk chair and started to say something, but I held up my index finger to stop her. "Hold all calls. I'll talk to you later."

Emma was still crying as Rainbow held her close to herself and alternated giving Doris and me the evil eye. Emma and Rainbow sat on the small sofa in my office and I closed the door before dropping into my desk chair. I put on my stole and pulled a couple of copies of *The Book of Common Prayer* from the bookshelf by my desk and handed one to Emma. Rainbow leaned away as though it was infected with Ebola.

"Let's turn to page 449." I waited until Emma found it. "Now let's say the first part together:

> "Have mercy on me, O God, according to your loving-kindness;
>   in your great compassion blot out my offenses.
> Wash me through and through from my wickedness,

and cleanse me from my sin.
    For I know my transgressions only too well,
    and my sin is ever before me.
Holy God, Holy and Mighty, Holy Immortal One,
    have mercy upon us."
Then Emma read, "Pray for me, a sinner."

We continued the rite until it got to the part about enumerating her own sins and she began to cry again. After using half my box of kleenex, she got enough control over herself to talk.

"I could have stopped it. I was working as a temp for Jon's lawyer. I'm real good at organizing files. I took classes on Word, Excel, Powerpoint, all of that Microsoft Office stuff. We could afford them before Jon canned Greg. Then we had to sell the four-wheeler and buy that junker Greg was driving 'cause my jobs didn't bring in enough steady money, you know. Jon was an ass . . . ." She sniffed, but didn't break down. "So when I saw that email from Jon to his lawyer I made a copy. That's what started it all. It's all my fault."

I waited for her to elaborate, but she stared at her clasped hands and stayed silent. I've read that the secret of investigative interviews is to wait until the other person breaks, but I was not in that business. Besides, I'm not that patient. I broke first.

"What did the email say?"

"Jon found out that Todd was hitting on Carly. He was real mad and was going to cut him out of his will. I didn't get it. Jon f–" She hesitated, glancing up at me. "Fooled around with any woman who'd have him, so what was the big deal?" She shrugged. "Anyway, Greg said Todd should know. After Greg told Todd, he said it wasn't going to matter. That he'd have the business real soon. Like, that week. And he did. But Greg got nothing and now he's dead. Todd killed Jon, then Greg, so he wouldn't rat him out."

I sat there, silently pondering this information. I'd already figured that Todd had very likely done the dirty deed, but it didn't explain who made the phone call to Jon that got him up on a ladder in the first place. Maybe Greg?

"Do you know if Greg called Jon about vandalism at one of his rentals on the day Jon died?"

"Not that I know of. When was that?"

I thought back. "November 15th. No, make that the 16th."

"No way I can remember that far back. Didn't the cops check Greg's phone?"

"Someone erased the call history. Most likely, Todd."

She blinked her eyes, losing a fight with tears. "He was the devil himself. I hope he rots in hell."

I didn't point out that the devil wouldn't rot in hell since it's his home. Instead, we finished the Liturgy of Penance. It ended with me making the sign of the Cross and saying, "Our Lord Jesus Christ, who offered himself to be sacrificed for us to the Father, forgives your sins by the grace of the Holy Spirit. Amen."

Rainbow bolted out of the sofa. "Are we done here? Or are you going to shove her down to poke home your misogynistic crap into her? Isn't that what you do to all the stupid women who come to you for help?

I sighed. "Rainbow, Christianity is not your enemy. It's a message of God's love."

"The hell it is." She snorted. "Haven't you heard of the Salem Witch Hunt? What, about a hundred women were burned at the stake by you misogynistic Christians?"

I could make a witty retort, like about a quarter of those hanged as witches were men and two were dogs, with no burnings at the stake, and it was young women that did the accusing, so it wasn't really about men persecuting women. But it would do no good. "What happened then was not what God wanted. Twenty-one people were executed because of mob hysteria and that was evil. However, the civil authorities did the condemning and Cotton Mather, a minister, is the one who did the most to stop it. But that was a long time ago with a lot of background history and this is now. So let's work together to help Emma, okay?"

Her eyes narrowed. "Go to hell."

She grabbed Emma's hand, flung open the door, and pulled her out. Emma mouthed a silent "Sorry" as she followed.

As Rainbow dragged Emma past Doris, she snarled at my secretary. "You fat cow, you're nothing but a pawn of the establishment. Go to hell."

Before the stunned Doris could respond, they were gone.

Doris looked at me. "What was that about?"

232

I shrugged. "Just being my charming self."

She rolled her eyes. "Well, that worked out well. You certainly made a friend."

"Actually, we found some common ground."

"Like what?"

As I turned to go back in my office, I grinned. "We both believe in hell."

I called the Chief.

"Yo, Padre. Wassup?"

I shook my head. He sounded like an old beer commercial. "I just thought you'd like to know that I solved Jon's murder and possibly Greg's."

"Okay, spill it."

The Chief must have gone over the limit on caffeine.

"Todd found out that Jon was angry with him, maybe going to cut him out of his will, and killed him. Greg knew about the whole thing, so Todd killed him."

"Well, you've given Todd motive, means and opportunity, but no proof. And wasn't he with Jon when he got the call that sent him up the ladder?"

"That's why you need to subpoena Greg's cell phone records, because there's a good chance he made the call to Jon."

He chuckled. "I already got the records for Jon's phone. A burner cell made the call. You're losing your touch, Father Sherlock."

I mulled that over in my mind. If Greg were cautious, he'd have had a burner for the call. But, even if he had one, it was probably in the dump by now. It looked like Emma's confession had given me more good theories that I couldn't prove.

"Question, Robert. Assuming Todd was going to be cut out of the will, how'd he find out about it?"

How, indeed? Obviously, I couldn't explain how I knew. "Maybe he went to that psychic over on Main St. Had a tarot-card reading or something." Not exactly a lie, but . . . .

"You believe in that stuff."

"Of course not, but Todd's dense enough to."

"Right. You really want me to believe that you came up with this wild theory without some real information? How'd Todd know

233

about any changes to Jon's will?   And why'd you think Greg knew about Todd's plans?"

The Chief was just a little too quick.   "Okay, I've been snooping around.   I heard that Jon and Todd were not getting along from a couple of sources.   It was getting worse, so it's no great leap for Todd to suspect that he was on his way to getting cut out of the will. Todd told Greg that he was going to own the business soon.   Why would he say that?   Because he was going to kill his father.   Then he realized his mistake in telling Greg, so he killed him.   Q.E.D."   It sounded lame to me, but it was the best I could do off the cuff.

"Cue-edie?   What the hell does that mean?"

Good.   I had hoped to distract the Chief from my source of information.   "Didn't you take geometry in high school?   It's from Latin, *quod erat demonstrandum*, or 'that which has been demonstrated.'"

He grunted.   "Just when I think you're okay, you come up with geometry and Latin.   Well, you haven't 'demonstrated' anything but a wild imagination.   What a fairy tale.   Let me know if you figure out how Goldilocks did it with a glass slipper in the gingerbread house. Meanwhile, I need to do real police work."

I sighed in relief.   "Sorry, Chief.   It seemed like I had it."

"Yeah, you've got it alright.   Lack of common sense."

After I hung up, I decided to find proof of my "common sense" without breaking the sacrament of Confession.   Todd had said to follow the money.   Who profited by his death?   Carly, of course, but I did not think she would actually kill anyone.   Well, if she did, it would be in a moment of rage and not carefully planned.   Dwayne had a motive, but the Zachary clan also had good reason to kill Todd.   I wondered how big a debt had been erased when Todd died.   Time for a talk.

Chapter 43

When I climbed into the Beast, I noticed that there was a cassette tape sticking out of the stereo that the previous owner must have left and pushed it in. It took me a minute to recognize the driving guitar and brass melody that came out of the speakers. It was "Peter Gunn," a Henry Mancini theme song that I'd found on an old record album in Pop's collection as a kid. He told me it was from a TV show that he barely remembered, except for the "hot chick" who was private detective Gunn's girlfriend. Typically Pops.

The song was playing as I parked in the empty gravel lot by Beezer's Bar, making me feel a little like the cagey P.I. going in to grill a suspect. But I was a priest in a clerical collar instead of a tough guy with a gun. As I got out of my truck, I remembered the last time I had been there. It had cost me my pickup. I had been fond of that old beater. It was getting a little dark, so I grabbed my 5-cell Maglite flashlight. It had a powerful beam to light the way back to my truck, but also could crack a skull.

I glanced skyward. "Father, forgive me for my violent thoughts," I muttered, as I opened the door to the bar. "And keep me from acting on them."

It was dusk, which comes early in the winter when you're as far north as Buggy Springs. The only light came from the "Beezer's Bar" neon sign flickering above the door, which still stuck when I pushed it open. Once inside, the dense smoke from the barbeques hung over the room. Ben was sitting in a wheelchair in front of the bar, his right leg propped up. Choke was behind the long bar. Or was it Chewy? Did it matter? Other than that, the place was empty.

I went up to Ben. "You may not remember me, but I'm Father Bruce."

He shrugged. "Yeah, I remember ya. Whatcha want?"

"I'm looking into a murder. I'd like to ask you a few questions."

He laughed. "You ain't no cop. Why should I talk to ya?"

I gently pushed the wheel of his chair with my foot so that he faced me. "Because my friend, the Chief, will be asking them next, and he's not as nice as I am."

Ben spat on the floor, which seemed a habit. "I told ya. I didn't kill that bastard, Jon. I was nowheres around when it got done."

"I'm talking about his son, Todd, who held the mortgage on this establishment." I paused. "What happened to your leg?"

"Bruised my foot. Car fell on it." He shifted in his wheelchair. "Todd got hisself killed?"

"Don't tell me you didn't know. This is too small of a town for that. And now you don't have much of a mortgage anymore, do you? Very convenient."

Ben's lip lifted in a snarl. "You 'cusing me of killin' Red Hot?"

"Not yet." I leaned down. "Did a car fall on your foot or was it a truck? Todd's truck."

Ben glanced over to his son. "Chewy, kick his ass, then throw him out."

As Chewy came around the bar, I loudly slapped the palm of my hand with my Maglite. Chewy stopped in his tracks. He may have been heavier than I, but I keep in shape while he kept in fried foods. Fat is not muscle and he knew it.

"I'm leaving," I told Ben. "But I wonder if you called Todd when I left the last time I was here to tell him I was asking questions."

He looked away. "Ain't no law against it, if I did."

I backed slowly out of the bar. Chewy glared at me as I went out the door. At least I knew he wasn't Choke. Fortunately, the Zacharys had been the bullies I'd thought them to be and backed down when confronted. Getting into a bar brawl was not something I ever wanted to add to my résumé. It definitely would have done a lot of damage to my standing as a priest in the community and with the bishop.

I considered calling the Chief about Ben's foot being injured by a falling vehicle and that he'd probably called Todd about me the night my pickup was rammed, but I couldn't prove anything. I had more questions than answers. I climbed in the Beast and headed home.

As I pulled into my drive, a Ford Edge was next to me. Hel got out of her little SUV and crunched through the frozen snow towards my truck. She was a vision of blue apres-ski wonder in tight pants, a parka and fur boots.

I waved as I got out of my truck. "Hi. Nice to see you."

She brushed back a lock of hair. "I had to see you before I left."

"You're leaving?" My heart sank. In spite of her strange behavior at times, she was attractive and interesting, when she wasn't in her manic state.

"I'm dropping off my rental at Sacramento and taking a flight home. I need to get back to my comfort zone. I get antsy if I'm away too long, and you know what happens then." She shook her head, a sadness in her eyes. "Besides, I've done enough damage to my image for you to remember for years."

"But—"

She touched my lips with her forefinger, silencing me. "Take care, Father Robert. You're a keeper, but not for me. Okay?"

Before I could reply, she hopped into her car and backed down my drive. I stood in stunned silence as I watched her go. I wanted to race after her, to wave her down and ask her to stay, but I knew it would be futile. There had been a finality to her words that I had to accept.

After standing in the cold, watching the tail lights of Hel's car fade away, I went inside. I checked my watch and it was a little after five, so I poured myself a Macallan's whisky. I settled into my rocking chair and sipped the amber elixir. Then my phone rang.

I picked it up. "Rectory, Father Robert speaking."

"I didn't want to ice him."

Although the voice was soft, breathless, I recognized that it was Carly.

"Okay, Carly, where are you?"

"No, I'm not sayin'. But I didn't want to ice that moth-- . . . creep."

I took another sip. "I believe you. Tell me what happened."

"He came into the bar all turnt, talkin' like I was bae. Wanted FTF time at his crib." She choked back a sob. "Sure, what the hell. Bimho move, huh? So he drove me there, hella dump. Made salty dogs, with, like, salt on the rim. I saw him drop somethin' in mine. Figured it was a roofie or some crap. Facepalm. I mean, like I'm fam, ya know? The perv. So I swapped drinks when he wasn't lookin'. Then he comes at me, all thirsty, and I O.J.'d him."

"Well, from what I can tell, all you did was trade the drugged drink Todd gave you for his and defend yourself. That's not murder." I paused. "Now I know you're a very intelligent young woman, so would you do me the favor of speaking in normal English? Maybe I'm getting old, but I'm having trouble understanding you."

My phone was silent for a moment.

"Carly, did you hear me?"

"You checked me out on the Mensa directory, didn't you?"

"Uh, no." I'd joined Mensa when I was in college on a whim, or maybe an ego boost. I'd kept up my membership for all these years for much the same reasons, but never did anything with it. I didn't even know Mensa had a directory with my name in it. If I'd been a real detective, maybe I would have.

"I checked the website directory and saw your name. You saw mine, right? Admit it."

"Carly, saying you were intelligent was just an observation, nothing more. I had no idea you were a Mensan, although I'm not surprised. But I'm sure you can use words someone as uncool as I can understand."

"You didn't check me out? Crap." She sighed. "Okay. No F-bombs. I'll keep it clean and in the Queen's English, probably better than she speaks. Todd tried to drug me and I switched drinks. He downed his in three gulps. Then he must have realized the swap and came at me. I pulled out my knife and stabbed him. Then I took his Bronco and drove here. It was self-defense."

I mulled over what she had said. "Sounds like it. So you stabbed him and left him in his house?"

She let out a short sob. "I know I should have called 9-1-1. He was staggering when he came at me, but he was still awake when I left. I thought I'd barely poked him and he'd call for help. I was scared and ran. I guess he bled to death, huh?"

"No, he may have had a heart attack. He had tried to drug you with ketamine."

"Heart attack? How much Special K did he put in my drink anyway?"

I leaned forward in my chair. "Why?"

238

"Because if you seriously O.D. on K with a lot of booze, it can cause a heart attack." She paused. "That's why Todd made salty dogs, the grapefruit juice kicks up the potency."

I would need to talk to the Chief. But it brought a question to mind. "How do you know that?"

"One of my squad . . . uh, a friend of mine died that way when I was in college. She was into the club scene and said Special K gave her . . . uh, more pleasure in sex. Tried to get me to use, but I'm not into that. One night, she used too much K and drank too much, like a pint of vodka. O.D.'ed. Not too smart for a Jeff."

I was taken aback. "You went to Amherst?" A Jeff was someone who attended Amherst, or at least used to be. I knew that because I'd read an article not that long ago about how Amherst had removed Lord Jeffrey Amherst, the founder, as the unofficial mascot because of a letter he wrote in the 1700's espousing giving smallpox-infected blankets to Native Americans.

"For a year, on a scholarship. Dropped out 'cause it seemed everyone was more into causes than education. When my so-called friends harassed me when I didn't march in protest of Lord Jeff, I'd had it." She snorted. "That's a rich kids' thing. Just working part time and going to school was taking all my life. So I quit school."

"Carly, you need to come back and talk to Chief Garcia. You didn't kill Todd and you need to get it cleared up." I paused when a thought hit me. "Do kids shoot Ketamine into their neck?"

"No way! Why?"

"Just wondering. So, are you coming back?"

"Yeah, I guess so. I like Buggy Springs. Can I call you when I get there and have you go with me to Five-O?"

I chuckled. So much for Queen's English. "Sure, I'll go with you to meet McGarrett."

"And don't tell anyone in Buggy Springs that I went to Amherst or you'll be sorry."

Then the line went dead.

I wondered if Carly still had her knife.

Chapter 44

I called the Chief.

"I talked to Carly.   She didn't kill Todd."

"Glad to hear that.   Where can I pick her up?"

I leaned back in my chair.   "Well, I talked to her on the phone and I didn't ask where she was.   Our conversation mainly had to do with what happened the night Todd was killed."

"You're saying she didn't tell you where she is?"

I pondered that for a second.   "No, she didn't give me her address."   Not an actual lie, if a little misleading.   "But she did ask me to go with her to see you, so I don't think it matters."

"What's her phone number?"

"She called on my landline here at the rectory.   I don't have caller I.D. or any of that expensive stuff, so I really don't know what the number is on the phone she used."   Absolutely true.   "I do have a couple of questions about Todd.   Did he have enough ketamine in his bloodstream to have caused his heart attack?   How serious was the knife wound?   And did you have any luck with figuring out why he had a puncture mark on his neck?"

"Since you've been so helpful with Carly, maybe I should tell you to pound sand."   He paused, then chuckled.   "What the hell. Sheriff Bob told me to keep you out of it, so here's what I know.   The ketamine was not that high.   Based on his body weight and time of death, he'd probably taken about a gram and a half.   The knife wound was pretty superficial, not deep and no organs hit.   Still no idea about the injection since it had no drug trace around it.   Does that help?"

"A little.   It proves Carly didn't kill Todd.   I'll let her explain when she gets back in Buggy Springs."

"If she gets here."   He chuckled again.   "Thanks, you've just told me she's out of town.   Somehow, you knew that."

Oops.   I needed to remember that the Chief was not stupid. "She'll be here.   I have faith."

"We'll see.   I've been on the job too long to have faith."

241

I laughed. "Faith *is* my job."

"Right. Talk to you later."

After I hung up, I thought about who else would benefit from both Jon and Todd's deaths. The Zachary clan, Carly and Dwayne were high on the list. Jon's widow Lisa and his mistress Cindy Wolfe, who had once been married to Todd, were next. Although I knew Lisa, I'd never really met Cindy, so I went to my best source of background information. I called the head of BSGN, Doris.

After a few pleasantries, I got down to business. "So, Doris, what can you tell me about Cindy Wolfe?"

"A lot. She should have the last name of leopard instead of Wolfe." She hesitated. "This isn't gossip, is it?"

"No, it's not gossip because I won't be repeating anything that won't help save lives." I paused. "Did you say she should have a last name of leopard because she won't change her spots?"

She laughed. "That's true, but it's not what I meant. Until she started running around with Jon, she always was after guys a lot younger than her. You know, a leopard."

"You mean a cougar."

She snorted. "I guess. Same thing, really. A big cat. And that's what she is. I've known her for a long time and she's always liked to get her claws into men and money. Especially men with money."

"So there were others between Todd and Jon."

"You mean Jon and Todd. No, but there wasn't much time after Jon died before she hooked up with Todd. That's really sick, don't ya think?"

"I try not to judge, but when Absalom, son of King David, slept with his father's concubines, it was probably to show he had taken over the kingship. Maybe Todd was doing the same, but I do think it was wrong in this case as well." Obviously, Doris did not know of Todd and Cindy's marriage, which only made matters worse. "Did she go out with other men before Jon?"

"Hah." It was not a laugh. "She'd been with half the men in Buggy Springs. Maybe she should have had the last name of alley cat instead of leopard."

This was getting too much like gossip and I needed to change the subject. "I know she doesn't go to St. Nicholas, but is she a member of any other church?"

"If you call it that. She goes to that Aura Terra Center. You know about it?"

I did. Dr. Anne Siddartha was its self-proclaimed priestess, duly ordained under the authority of the Center's international headquarters in a nude ceremony at the Yuba River. Her hubris of assuming the name of the Buddha was only the beginning. Her PhD was in "Auric Psychology" from the Edgar Cayce University for Religious Fulfillment. Impressive. I'd heard of her Liberating Women program that seemed mainly to be concerned with liberating older women from their money. I sighed. I needed to talk to Cindy and could tell it was not going to be easy.

"I know about it. Thanks, Doris. I'll let you know if I need any more information."

"Oh, you can find Cindy at the Buggy Springs Diner almost every morning at ten. I don't think she wants to get up too early after her hard nights." She paused. "I only say that because I'm always ready to help, Father."

I shook my head. "I know you are. Just don't give this kind of help to anyone else."

After I hung up, I sipped the last of my whisky. I needed it. I'd be dining at the Diner in the morning.

At 9:45 a.m., I took a deep breath and went in the Diner's front door. I looked around, but Cindy wasn't there. Neither was Judy, my favorite waitress. A skinny, blond, young woman with her hair in a ponytail and a severe case of acne came up to me.

"Ya want the counter or a table?"

I smiled. "The counter will do for now. I'm hoping to meet Cindy Wolfe when she arrives."

She shrugged. "Whatever." She motioned with her right hand. "Counter's there." Then she walked away. Customer service did not seem to be a priority at the Diner.

I took a seat at the counter on a stool covered in ripped red vinyl and grabbed a grease-stained menu from a chrome stand. It was out of curiosity since I'd already had my oatmeal much earlier. The menu looked like it had been there since the Gold Rush and never been

243

cleaned. I was only going to have coffee and prayed it had improved since the last time.

The guy behind the counter came up, wiping his hands on his dirty apron. His black ponytail was longer than the waitress' and he had the same acne, but she didn't have his three-day beard. His skinny arms had tattoos that looked like they'd been done by a five-year-old with a felt-tip pen and his dead eyes stared at me.

"Yeah?"

I gingerly put down the menu, glad to be rid of it. "Just coffee."

Without a word, he turned around, grabbed a mug and filled it from a glass coffee pot and plopped it in front of me.

"Nothin' else?"

"Cream for the coffee, please?"

He snatched a small, metal pitcher from another counter patron and dropped it in front of me before turning away. I had just sipped my coffee, finding that it was worse than before, when Cindy walked in.

She was maybe forty years old, but my dad would have said she had "many miles," or, more cruelly, was "rode hard and put away wet." Once she'd probably been rather attractive, maybe beautiful, but age and hard living seemed to have taken their toll. She wore black yoga pants with a tight, pink sweater, showing through her open ski parka. Her body was voluptuous, with curves in all the right places. However, her red hair looked poorly dyed and her makeup was way overdone, with raccoon eyes and fake eyelashes that looked like spiders. When her eyes met mine, I saw a tired woman who was trying to compete with younger ones for the eligible males.

I stood. "Cindy? Can I buy you breakfast?"

She stopped and studied me. "There's always a catch if a priest wants to buy you a meal, like he expects payment in kind." She smiled, but her eyes didn't. "What the hell, why not? You're not bad to look at."

We sat at a small table near the front window. The blond waitress dropped two menus in front of us before disappearing. Suddenly, I missed Judy.

Cindy studied her menu, not looking up. "So, what's the deal here? I know you're not trying to hook up with me, so why are you here? Just so you know, you can't save me. I'm too far gone."

244

I smiled. "Just so you know, I don't save anyone. God does. And no one is too far gone." I paused and sipped my rancid coffee. Ugh. "But that's not why I'm here. I want to know about you, Todd and Jon."

She shrugged. "I was Jon's lover. So what?"

"And Todd's ex-wife."

She opened her mouth, but said nothing, eyes wide with surprise.

Our waitress inopportunely chose that moment to come for our order. She stopped chewing her gum long enough to speak. "Whatcha want?"

I looked up at her. "I'll stick with my coffee."

She rolled her eyes, then turned to Cindy. "You cheaping out, too?"

Cindy took a deep breath. "No, I'll have the fruit with yogurt. And a glass of red wine."

The waitress gave her a knowing look, then walked away. Wine at 10:00 a.m.

Cindy twisted her paper napkin, not looking at me. "So you know. Okay, I was married to Todd. Then I was Jon's mistress, but not at the same time. Is a woman whose rent gets paid still called a mistress? Anyway, you've nailed me as a slut. So what? Do you get your jollies by doing that?"

"Of course not. I'm only trying to find out who killed Jon and Todd. Someone far holier than I said judge not, lest I be judged. Will you help me?"

She met my eyes. "That was Jesus who said that, wasn't it?" She laughed. "I was raised a Methodist. Okay, how can I help?'

"Tell me your story with the Franks family."

Our waitress arrived with Cindy's food and wine. Cindy took a serious swig, then smirked. "Careful, Father. You don't know what you're asking for. You might get your ears singed."

Chapter 45

Cindy took another drink of her wine, then studied her glass. "I met Todd when he was at Buggy Springs High. He was a defensive tackle for the Claim Jumpers and I helped sell food for the school at halftime. Even then, he was pretty forward, making passes at me." She laughed. "Forward passes from a tackle and I was the receiver. I waited until he turned eighteen until I let him go for the goal line. Touchdown!"

A few of our fellow patrons looked around when her voice rose and she put her arms in the air to signify the touchdown. I nervously smiled at them before turning back to Cindy.

"I don't want to insult you, but you were a little older than Todd."

"No insult. I was a cougar on the prowl, one of the best. I was pretty hot then and he wasn't the only young stud I had. High school jocks love sexy, older women." She finished off her wine and somehow got the attention of the waitress, motioning for a refill of her glass. "Anyway, I got fond of Todd and he went crazy for me. He was Red Hot and I was his Red Hot Mama. After high school, he joined the Army and we got married. Didn't tell Jon. But he found out."

The waitress arrived with the second glass of wine and Cindy took a swig. She hadn't touched her breakfast.

"Uh, Cindy, don't you think you should eat something."

"Yeah, yeah. You sound like Jon, always tellin' me what to do." She laughed a little too loudly. "He told me and Todd that we'd be broke if we stayed together. If we divorced, he'd 'take care of me' and bring Todd into the business when his hitch was up. Todd's eyes were already wandering, so he agreed. I was sorta collateral damage. I slept with Jon and he gave me money, good money. He made his deposit and I drew out the cash. Cha-ching!"

She said it while stabbing the air with her forefinger, like ringing up a sale. Again, people turned to look and I forced a smile.

Cindy nibbled a few pieces of her fruit. It looked like what came frozen in bags at discount grocery stores. She stopped, laid down her fork and took another gulp of wine.

"I did get sorta fond of Jon after a while. I guess that happens when you have sex with someone for so many years. I even cried when he died." She took another swig of wine. "After Jon died, Todd and I hooked up again, but it wasn't the same." She paused, wine glass in hand. "Yah wanna know what's weird? I had no idea he put me in his will. If I had've, I might've killed him for it. He owed me big time. Does that make me a suspect?" Then she gave me a seductive smile. "Feel free to frisk me. Wanna do a strip search?"

After I paid the bill for my coffee plus Cindy's fruit cup and three glasses of wine (she ordered another just as I was leaving), I headed to the church office. It was December 22nd and I still had a lot to do before the Christmas Eve service.

As I came in the door, Doris greeted me with a disgusted stare. "I hear you had a fun breakfast with Cindy the slut."

I stopped. "Doris, that is evil speech. First, I met with Cindy to talk about Jon's and Todd's deaths. Second, you should never refer to anyone as a slut." I didn't add, even if Cindy called herself one.

She rolled her eyes. "Yes, Father. Forgive me for I have sinned. Now, will you actually be doing church business today or be playing Father Brown?"

"Church business. But that does include ministering to people you might not like. Our Lord was criticized for fraternizing with prostitutes and other sinners, you know."

Doris grunted and turned back to her computer screen.

I went into my office and pondered the morning. Cindy said she didn't know what was in Jon's will, but Todd had a copy. Had he told her? Had they plotted Jon's demise? While Jon was definitely no saint and sounding more and more like a demon, no one had the right to play God and end his life. And then there was Todd.

The phone rang and I could see through my glass door that Doris had left her post, so I answered. "St. Nicholas Church, Father Robert speaking."

I could barely hear the response. "It's me. I'm ready to go to Five-O."

"Carly? Where are you?"

"Sittin' outside the butt-ugly city hall. I'm scared."

In Buggy Springs, the police station and the city hall shared a modern, yellow-brick building on Main Street that stuck out from its wooden Victorian neighbors like a pimple on a beauty queen's nose.

"Hang on, I'll be right there." For Carly to say she was scared must mean she was terrified. I scribbled a quick note to Doris and ran out the door.

As I drove the Beast to city hall, I called the Chief on his cell and he answered.

"Hello, Robert. Can I call you back? I'm a little busy right now."

"Are you at the station? I'm coming in with Carly."

He was silent for a moment. "Where is she?"

Good. No one had noticed her yet. "I'll be there in a couple. We're coming in together."

Another pause. "Why are you coming in with her?"

"She's frightened and needs my moral support."

He sighed. "Okay."

Then he disconnected. I pondered his attitude. He must not have had his morning coffee yet.

As I pulled up to city hall, I saw a dirty brown Bronco about the same age as my truck, but far worse for wear. The paint was faded and patchy, with numerous scrapes and dents, and it sat on rusty chrome rims. It was also sitting in the no-parking zone right in front. I found a legal spot and parked.

As I got out of my truck, Carly hopped out of the Bronco and came to me. She was wearing a heavy black coat and a black, bushy Russian ushanka hat. She looked like a Goth Muscovite.

She wrapped her arms around herself, fear in her eyes. "I don't feel good about this."

I managed a smile. "It'll be okay. The Chief's a good guy."

"Promise it'll be okay?"

"Promise."

I opened the heavy, glass door and followed her inside. The police station is on the right and I opened the door for her. She hesitated, then went in. Behind a thick glass window, the dispatcher, Ann, smiled at me. I'd known her for years.

249

"Hi, Father Robert. What can I do for you?" There was a small grill in the glass and her voice was muffled.

"We're here to see the Chief. He's expecting us."

She punched a button on her console and spoke into her headset. When she pushed another button, there was a buzz unlatching the heavy wood door beside me and I pushed it open. The Chief was standing a little down the hallway and I followed Carly in.

As soon as we cleared the door, an officer behind it pushed it shut. The Chief walked closer.

"Carly Nelson, I'm arresting you on the charges of the murder of Todd Franks and grand theft auto for stealing his car."

I heard the sound of the officer pulling out his handcuffs and stepped between Carly and him, blocking his way and glaring at him. He was at least six inches shorter than I and looked like his only exercise was lifting a hamburger. He nervously looked to the Chief and I turned to him, too.

"What the hell is this?" My voice was trembling with anger.

The Chief's eyes didn't raise to meet mine. "Sorry, it's not my idea. Sheriff Bob issued the warrant. I'm just following orders."

"You and the Nazis. Carly didn't kill anyone and you know she couldn't have dragged Todd's body out, under his truck. Plus she just used the Bronco to get away from Todd, her attacker." I looked over at the cop who had his handcuffs out. "Don't even think about putting those on her."

The Chief gave a short wave to the side and the cop put them away. "We'll have to frisk her, though."

Carly let out a choked sob. "All I've got is this."

The cop reached for his gun and I turned to Carly. She held her knife, with the blade closed. I snatched it from her and handed it to the cop. "Here, take it and leave your gun alone. She's no threat to you." I looked back at the Chief. "Have Ann frisk her, not this Barney Fife."

The Chief nodded, then finally met my eyes. "I'm sorry about this, but I am a cop and the job requires me to do some things I wish I didn't have to."

I took a slow breath to calm down. "I'm a priest and the job requires me to do things I'm glad to do." I turned to Carly. She was shaking, tears streaming down her cheeks. Her mascara was running and she looked like a frightened child. I pulled out my handkerchief and handed it to her. "I've got to go now, but I'll handle this."

"You promised everything would be okay," she barely managed to squeak out.

"And I will keep my promise, but I need you to give me a little time, okay?"

She nodded. I wanted to pull her to me and comfort her, but I could only squeeze her hand before I left.

I glared at the Chief. "I'll be back."

After I said it, I realized I'd quoted *The Terminator* twice. Considering how I was feeling right then, it was too bad I hadn't used an Austrian accent. After I went out the door, I slammed it so hard the wall shook. Ann looked up, startled.

It wasn't her fault. I waved. "Sorry, Ann. I . . . ." I could think of nothing to say, so I quickly left.

Chapter 46

As I entered the church office, Doris looked up. "Where'd you go? Your note just said it was an emergency."

"It was. I had to play Judas."

"What?"

"No time to talk. I have to go hang myself."

Doris' eyes went wide.

I sighed as I headed into my office. "A bad joke. I have to see if I can right a wrong."

I closed the door and went online. I found the number I needed and called.

"Laura Gunn and Associates. How may I direct your call?"

I leaned back in my desk chair. "Laura Gunn, please."

"I'll connect you with her assistant. Hold, please."

After a short interlude of tuneless music, a pleasant woman's voice came on the line. "This is Jennifer. How may I help you?"

"I need to speak with Laura, please."

"I'm sorry, she's tied up in a meeting. May I help you?"

I drummed my fingers on the arm of my chair. "How long will she be tied up?"

"It's hard to say. She has a very full schedule. If you would care to leave a mess–"

"Look," I interrupted. "Go into the meeting and tell her Father Robert Bruce . . . no, tell her Rob Bruce needs to speak with her immediately."

"I'm afraid I can't do–"

"If you don't, she's not going to be happy. And, unless Gigi has changed a lot lately, she's someone you don't want to make unhappy."

"Gigi?"

"If you tell her that Rob Bruce needs to speak with Gigi right away, she'll take my call."

There was a pause, then she said, "You'd better be right. Hold, please."

I hoped I was right, too. Her name had been Greta Gunn then, Gigi to me. We'd dated in high school for a short time. She was a dead ringer for Nicole Kidman and was also one heck of a kisser. I swear she massaged my tonsils with her tongue. Fortunately for my morals, she'd transferred to another school before we went much farther. Then, when I went to Cal Berkeley for my Master's in history, we met up again. Since she'd always hated Greta, she'd legally changed it to Laura. She was in law and was known as the "Beautiful Beast." To say she was a feminist would be like saying the ACLU is a legal aid society. The Bears were short two of their best backfield players after she got them kicked out of school for sexual harassment. While they may well have been guilty, it sent shock waves through Cal.

We talked a few times over coffee, but the magic was gone. She couldn't drop the hard edge she'd become known for. The last time we got together, she said, "You're too tense when we're together. Probably because you've been sexually repressed since high school. Let's go to bed together and get that out of the way."

Actually, she used an Anglo-Saxon word, but I preferred not to think of her beautiful lips saying that, so I remembered it with a euphemism. I wondered how she remembered it, if at all, especially since I'd refused. Since I had decided to become a priest by then, I had to refuse. But it hadn't been easy.

My reverie was interrupted by Laura's silky soprano voice.

"What the hell do you think you're doing, Rob? You think you can get away with having my assistant pull me out of a meeting, just to hear you call me that hated name? I should sue you for that. What, has the sexual repression of the priesthood made you reconsider my last offer?"

Her words were harsh, but I could hear the laughter in her voice.

"Hi, Laura. I am sorry, I hope I didn't ruin an important meeting."

She chuckled. "No, but you did interrupt my nap. The meeting was that bad. Actually, I should thank you. So, did you call me just to reminisce about our past sex life, or lack thereof, or something really important?"

"I called because I got a young girl arrested. I was trying to help, but it backfired and now she's in jail, unjustly accused of murder.

I'll cover your fee."

She paused. "You can't afford me, Rob. Give me the details and I'll see if I want the case. Where are you living now, anyway?"

In about five minutes, I filled Laura in on as much as I could, including where Buggy Springs was, the murders, a description of Carly and why I needed to get her out of jail as soon as possible. I ended with, "Please do this for Carly. She needs you."

For a few moments, she said nothing and I wondered if my plea had been in vain. Then she spoke in a very matter-of-fact tone, all the levity gone from her voice. "Did they Mirandize Carly when they arrested her?"

I thought back. "Not that I remember. I was making a bit of a scene, so maybe they forgot."

"Hmm." I could almost hear the gears turning. "Is Judge Doug Bryant still on the bench up there?"

"I've seen his name mentioned in the paper, so he must be. Why?"

"He owes me big time. Unlike you, he said 'yes' to my offer. I'll make a call and get the ball rolling before I head your way."

This did not sound right. "Wait, is that ethical? I mean, wouldn't Judge Bryant recuse himself if you were involved with him then and with this case now?"

"Not if Doug-boy values his reputation. He was married at the time and, last I heard, still is." Her voice was no-nonsense, no argument. "Do you have an airport?"

"A little one, yes."

"I'll call you when I land. I've got a couple of cases I've got to address before I leave, but I'll be there A.S.A.P. Those hick cops will rue the day they arrested that girl. Gotta go."

With that, she was gone. I sat there, staring at my computer screen. "Laura Gunn and Associates, P.C. Standing up for the rights of all women." It sounded like I was fulfilling my promise to Carly, but what had I done? The Book of Proverbs said, "He who troubles his own house will inherit the wind." The quote had been made famous by a play and movie, but had I done just that? Had I brought down a storm by the name of Gigi on my community?

I didn't have to wait long for an answer. I got a call within the

255

hour from the Chief.

"What the hell is going on?"

I checked my watch. It was just after noon. "Good afternoon, Chief. What can I do for you?"

"First I get a call from some hotshot San Francisco lawyer who says she's representing Carly. She busts my chops, sayin' I didn't Mirandize Carly. Know anything 'bout that?"

I rubbed my forehead. This could be the end of a beautiful friendship. "I called a friend from high school who said she'd help. She asked if I heard you Mirandize Carly and I had to admit I hadn't. What was I to do? Lie?"

The Chief didn't say anything for a moment. Then he huffed. "Of course not. But then Judge Bryant calls and says he has some concerns about the legality of the warrant. He *suggested* that I release her to you until they could be addressed. Then he mentioned a Mirandizing problem." He paused. "Look, I felt like crap arresting Carly. I agree it's not likely she did anything illegal. Well, except taking the Bronco and she had a good reason for that. I've been stalling booking her, so come get her out of my hair before the Governor or the President calls me."

"I'll be right down." I hesitated. "You know I had no choice. Like you said, it's my job."

"Yeah, yeah. We're cool. Just get down here before I change my mind."

After he hung up, I told Doris I'd be back soon and hopped in my truck.

When I got to city hall, I saw that the Bronco was gone, probably towed away for evidence. Carly was sitting on a hard plastic chair in the waiting room of the police department. She had her feet drawn up on the chair and was hugging her knees. When she saw me, she sprang up, ran to me and hugged me tightly. I tried to pull her off, but she just clung tighter.

"You saved me, Preacher-man," she mumbled. "You kept your promise."

Ann was staring through the window and I finally got Carly to let go. Ann motioned for me to go to the door by her window. I looked down at Carly.

"I have to do some paperwork with the police before we go. Will you be okay?"

She nodded, then took up her knee-hugging position in the chair.

Ann buzzed me in and handed me a clipboard. "Sign here, here and here," she instructed. "I already gave Carly back her purse."

I complied and handed the clipboard back. "Is the Chief here?"

She almost suppressed her smile. "No, he said he needed to check out the town. I think he's a little ashamed of all this. He really did try to stop the warrant when he got it, but you called and said you were coming in with Carly before he got anything done. I've seen them come and go in my time, the good kids and the hard cases. Carly acts tough, but she'd have a rough time in county." She put out her hand. "You're a good man, Father Bruce, but be careful. These kids know how to manipulate you."

I shook her hand. "I try to be as innocent as a dove, but wise as a serpent."

As I walked out, I wondered if I were too much the dove.

Chapter 47

When we got back to the church office, Doris gave me a raised eyebrow, but wisely said nothing. I planted Carly on a chair at Doris' L-shaped desk right across from her. Carly unwrapped a dripping hamburger I'd bought her from the Buggy Springs Diner and dug in. I'd asked her if she was hungry when I'd picked her up from the police department and found she hadn't eaten for almost 24 hours. I'd have guessed that she was a vegan and would go for Sprouts, our local vegetarian deli. She chose the Diner and grease. Oh, well, she could use a few extra pounds.

Once in my office, I closed the door and made a few calls, checking on some of the congregation on the church prayer list and making sure the children's director was ready for the Nativity play the wee ones were doing at the early Christmas Eve service. She told me one of the parents had volunteered a live donkey for the program's Mary to ride down the church's aisle. I vetoed it for several reasons. One was that it would likely traumatize the little girl chosen to play the mother of Jesus. Another was that donkeys can be ill-tempered and might nip a parishioner or two. That would be a sure lawsuit. The last was that donkeys are not housebroken. Incense was the only aroma I wanted permeating the church on Christmas Eve.

Having dealt with the asinine problem, I moved on to a message I had to call Lisa Franks. I punched in her number.

"Hello, Father Robert."

Was I the only one without caller I.D.? "Hello, Lisa. How are you?"

"I'm good." She hesitated. "I hear that Goth girl was arrested for killing Todd."

How did she know that? "Not exactly. She's having lunch with Doris right now."

She gasped. "You're exposing sweet, little Doris to a killer?"

No one has ever described Doris as sweet or little. At least not to me. "Carly is no more a killer than you are. Whoever killed Todd dragged him out of his house and put him under his truck before dropping it on him. That's not something Carly could do. He was a big guy."

"Well, I think you're being naive. I'm sure she's got a lot of low-life friends who would help her."

She might be right about the friends, but I still didn't see Carly as the killer. "I'm sure the Chief is checking out all the angles, but I'll let him know your concerns."

"No need. I'll do it."

The line went dead. I sat for a minute thinking about what Lisa had said. I did not want Carly to be a murderer; however, I had to consider that she might have done it with some help. But I'd leave that line of investigation to the Chief. Meanwhile, my phone was ringing.

"St. Nicholas Church, Father Robert speaking. How may I help you?"

"By getting off your butt, Accident, and getting down here. He's at it again."

I sighed. "Hello, Sister Dearest. So nice to hear from you. I guess you're talking about Pops going for a cruise on his big boat."

"Hell, no. I'm talking about him buying a chalet in Switzerland to go off with some Maria Von Tramp. Didn't he tell you? I thought you guys were doing all that male bonding crap and left me out last time."

"No, I didn't know." Then it hit me. "How do you know everything he's doing with his money, where it's going?"

She hesitated. "This is a Confession, so you can't talk about it. I've got detectives watching him. They've . . . well, acquired sources on his finances."

"It's not a true confession unless you are repentant, truthful and plan to try to reform. You flunk on all counts"

"Listen, you little weasel," she hissed, "if you rat me out to Pops, I'll--"

"Put a hit out on me?" I interrupted with a chuckle. "You should keep in mind that weasels eat rats, so your terminology is flawed. However, I won't tell Pops. That's between you, him and your conscience." I paused. "What makes you think there's a woman involved?"

"Why else? He's always led around by his–"

"Got it." This conversation was rapidly degenerating. "I'll call him, but that's all. It's his money. By the way, Maria Von Trapp was Austrian, not Swiss, and an ex-nun who was not a tramp."

She hung up on me without responding. Never correct an alpha female like Janet.

There was a light tap on the glass door to my office. It was Carly. I motioned her in and she opened the door.

"What can I do for you, Carly?"

She clutched some papers and proffered them to me. "I, uh, don't know if these are important, but Todd had them stashed in a lock box bolted to the floor of his Bronco."

I unfolded them. There were four pages. They were printouts of emails. One was from Jon Franks to the law office of Evans and Anderson, saying that his son, Todd Franks, had been sexually improper with many women, including his half-sister, and that Jon wanted a new trust, excluding Todd. The next was an email to Jon from Evans and Anderson, which said that proposed changes to his trust "because of problematic sexual indiscretions" were attached. There were two pages that must have been that attachment, showing changes to the trust that left Todd in the cold. The email from Jon also said there was an important matter to discuss in person. What was it? Was someone else to be left in the cold or did it have nothing to do with the trust?

I looked up at Carly from my desk. "If these were in a lock box, how did you get them?"

"I figured he would use 7-3-3-4-6-8 for the combination."

I cocked my head. "Why would he use that?"

She smirked. "Check your phone's keypad."

I checked it. PDQRS-DEF-DEF-GHI-MNO-TUV. R-E-D-H-O-T. I laughed. "Very good. You should be a detective."

She shrugged as she walked out. "I just used a little logic and intuition."

I sat back in my chair. Why had Todd kept them locked away? I called the lawyer.

"Good afternoon. The law offices of Evans and Anderson, how may I direct your call?"

This is Father Robert Bruce. I would like to speak with Earl Evans, please."

"What is this regarding?"

Three murders? Too much information. "Jon Franks' trust."

"Hold please."

The hold music was typical. It sounded like a Brian Eno version of "Who Let the Dogs Out?" The receptionist came back on the line.

"I'm sorry, but Mr. Evans cannot talk to you about confidential client information."

I shook my head. He was one of my parishioners, albeit a little lax in his attendance. How should I phrase it? "Look, I don't want any information. All I want to know is if he sent a certain email. Tell him I will overlook him missing church for the last five months if he just answers my question."

"Please hold."

Was that Aaliyah's "Try Again," a la Eno? I couldn't be sure. My reverie in Muzak was thankfully interrupted.

"Hello, Father Bruce. This is Earl Evans. How can I help you?"

"Call me Robert, Earl. I just want to know if you sent a certain document to Jon Franks."

"I will help if I can, Father Bruce."

Keeping me at a distance, huh? Okay, I got the message: no special privileges. "I have copies of documents that might have been sent to Jon Franks regarding revisions to his trust and more to come. All I ask is that you tell me if they are bogus. Can you do that?"

"Any client communication is privileged, even if the client is deceased, because other parties are involved. I will do what I can ethically do."

Priests had loose lips compared to lawyers. "Okay, it's regarding eliminating Todd from Jon's trust. Can you help me? Three people have been murdered and more lives may hang in the balance." Yeah, a bit melodramatic, but it might get the information I needed.

The line was silent. I wondered if I had been disconnected before Earl spoke.

"The only valid trust left by Jonathan Franks did not disinherit anyone. Any other documents you somehow, possibly illegally, acquired from this office were never finalized and are invalid."

262

"Can you just tell me about any possible changes Jon planned to make?"

"If there were any, I can't describe them.   Are we done here?"

"It sounds like you are.   Thanks, Earl."   I paused.   "Hope to see you in church soon."

The line went dead.

I considered what I had learned.   The emails were probably real.   According to the documents, it seemed that Jon was set to disinherit Todd.   Were these what Emma had taken from the law office and given to Todd?   If so, why hadn't the trust actually been changed? What was the other change Jon mentioned?   I needed more information.   I had to call Emma and brave the wrath of Rainbow, but first I called the Chief.

Chapter 48

"Hello Robert. Are you still speaking to me?"

"Of course, Chief. Carly's out of jail and we can get back to solving some murders."

"We?" he growled. "You're the one that brought that hot shot lawyer and a judge down my neck."

"Oh, you weren't the one to throw an innocent girl in jail? Since you've already figured everything out, I won't bother you then about the changes that didn't get recorded in Jon's trust. See you 'round."

"Wait." He took a moment to swallow his pride. "Okay, things got out of hand. Let's work together. What are these changes you're talking about?"

"First, two questions for you." I leaned back in my desk chair and toyed with a pen in my free hand as we talked. "There was a printer in Todd's dump, but no computer. Did Sheriff Bob take it? You had the Bronco towed away. Anything interesting in it?"

"Yeah, a bunch of hamburger wrappers, empty chip bags and old beer cans. That and a lock box that we need to get into."

"Try 7-3-3-4-6-8 on the lock box. How about the computer?"

"Wait, that was 7-3-8-what? Where did you come up with that?"

"Write this down." I waited a moment. "7-3-3-4-6-8. Let's say a little angel told me. And the computer?"

"I checked the inventory Bob's guys took and nothing about it. And I can guess who your angel was. There was an old song about 'devil or angel.' You should keep that in mind. What about the changes to the trust?"

"Let's have a drink at Merry Monk's about six. I'll bring you some interesting papers. You can show me yours and I'll show you mine."

He sighed. "You pay for the drinks. That place is too pricey for me."

"Done."

After we disconnected, I called Emma's cell. Rainbow answered.

"What?"

"Rainbow, I need to talk to Emma."

"No way."

I rubbed my temples. This was not going to be easy. "Look, I've kept Emma's name out of this, but I need some more information so I can continue to do so. I need to know if she emailed some documents to Todd and, if she did, what they were."

"Wait."

I waited. Rainbow spoke to Emma in the background. Then Rainbow came back on the line.

"Is this recorded? By law, you have to tell me if it is."

I stifled a laugh. "No, with God as my witness, it is not being recorded and no one else is listening."

"Except the NSA. They listen to all telephone conversations."

I drummed my fingers on my desk chair. "Well, if the NSA is listening, I had nothing to do with it. Okay?"

"Okay. She sent emails from where she was working to Greg's cell and he sent them to Todd."

That was good. "You have Greg's cell, so you can give me Todd's email address."

"I destroyed it so none of this could be traced to Emma."

"You what?"

The line went dead. So did my lead. Sure, the Chief might be able to trace the email accounts, but it would take a lot of time, even if it were possible. One step forward, two steps back. Since Lenin wrote that years before he succeeded taking over Russia, maybe it wasn't a lost cause, but it wasn't going very well for me.

I had a lull in the late afternoon. First I made copies of the emails, then I decided to see what Carly had read about me on the Mensa directory. It took me a few tries before I remembered my password: scots1314. It was the year of the Battle of Bannockburn, the biggest victory of the Scots under my ancestor, Robert the Bruce, against the English. I'd entered "Graduate degree" and "Service-Clergy" for occupation, with interests in "History-European,

266

Music-classical, Religion." I sighed. I sounded dull.

Then I checked other Mensans with my zip code to see who was there. I clicked on Carly Nelson. According to her profile, she had "advanced accreditation," which I doubted, and worked in "service-other," where waitressing in a bar might fit, but so would call girl. For interests, she listed "Atlantis, Doomsday, Locksmithing, Magic, Monty Python, Nudism, Parapsychology." I wondered if she were actually interested in any of them. For languages, she claimed proficiency in Braille, Esperanto, Korean and Yiddish. I chuckled.

I went back to the directory and scanned the other names, eight of them. I knew two and was a little surprised they were there as well as by some who were not. Still, membership is optional and some people are not joiners. I clicked on a few of them that I didn't know. A quick look at their details did not ring any bells and I logged off when my phone rang.

"Father Robert speaking."

There was a lot of noise in the background, but I could hear Laura's voice. "Hey, Rob, pick me up at that meadow you call an airport in about half an hour, okay?"

I'd almost forgotten that I'd called down some hellfire and brimstone on our little town. I checked my watch. "I'll be there."

"Make sure you've got Carly with you and take us to your best restaurant."

"Of course." I was meeting the Chief not long after picking her up, so Merry Monk would have to do. Having the two of them at the same table was going to be interesting.

"Can't wait to play a little grab-ass with you," she growled.

"I, uh . . . ." But the line was dead. After making reservations at the Merry Monk, I rubbed the back of my neck. Like Bette Davis said, "Fasten your seatbelts. It's going to be a bumpy night."

Carly and I picked Laura up at the airport at 5:23 p.m. It's a small airport and the tower, such as it is, is closed at 5:00 p.m. in the winter. Laura was standing by her twin-engine plane with the door open so the interior light cast a soft glow over her. She looked great, even bundled in a fur coat, no doubt faux because of her PETA connection.

As I pulled the Beast up to her, Carly let out a soft whistle.

267

"You hooked up with her?"

"We dated." I opened the door and stepped down. "Nothing more." I closed the door.

I walked up to Laura and put out my hand. "Thanks for coming. You saved Carly."

Laura wrapped her arms around me, one hand grabbing my rear end. She locked her lips on mine with a probing kiss. Stunned, I did not react immediately and then she stepped back, still gripping my biceps.

"Damn, I've missed that." Then she grabbed a small overnight bag and headed for the passenger side of my truck. "Let's get out of here before some bear or mountain lion attacks us."

Carly climbed into the cramped seat in the back of the cab as we opened the doors. Laura smiled at her and tossed a small, leather bag in the seat beside her. "You must be Carly. I'm Laura and I'm here to kick some butt for you."

Carly just nodded, staring at Laura.

By the truck's dim interior light, I realized that Laura actually looked better than Nicole Kidman. Her coat had slipped open and she was wearing an ivory jumpsuit that draped along her body more sensuously than any skin-tight yoga pants. She had on high-heeled taupe boots that looked impractical, but sexy. As she flipped her shoulder-length brown hair back past a black-pearl necklace, she smiled at me.

"If you can stop drooling, let's head to the restaurant. I'm starved. I skipped lunch because of you." She dropped several business cards in the cup holder. "And those are in case you ever need a real lawyer again."

On the way to the restaurant, Laura monologued about cases she'd won and how she'd "kicked butt on the misogynist pigs." Carly said little, mainly oohing and aahing at the right time. I said even less. I remembered why Laura and I did not mesh.

Luckily, I found a place to park near the restaurant. Laura grabbed my arm and walked close to me along the sidewalk. It had not snowed that day and the city had done its job in clearing the previous snowfall. As I opened the heavy oak and glass door to Merry Monk and was hit by a blast of warm air, I saw the Chief at the long, mahogany bar. He raised an eyebrow when he saw me. Or maybe it

268

was at Laura, who had shed her coat and caused every male eye in the place to turn toward her. The way her silky jumpsuit flowed along her body oozed classy sex appeal.

We walked over to the bar. "Chief, I'd like to introduce you to Laura Gunn."

A dark cloud descended over his expression and his voice was as cold as the weather outside. "We've talked on the phone. Or she lectured and I listened."

She smiled and offered her hand. "So nice to put a friendly face with a name."

He hesitated before briefly shaking her hand. He unsuccessfully tried to force a smile.

I looked for the maitre d' and signaled to him. "We have reservations for four."

"This is going to be as much fun as passing a kidney stone," the Chief mumbled as we were taken to our table.

Chapter 49

After we were seated, our waiter appeared at our table. Maybe in his mid-twenties, skinny, clad in black jeans and matching tight Merry Monk T-shirt, and sporting a goatee, he brushed back his long, auburn hair and smiled.

"Hi, I'm Chad. I'll be your guide for your visit to Merry Monk's tonight. Can I start you with some drinks? Maybe a Merry Monk Fandango, which is our version of Sex on the Beach, but with gin instead of vodka."

Laura lifted an eyebrow and licked her upper lip as she glanced at me, but did not say anything outrageous. "I'll have a diet Coke."

The Chief lifted his glass and nodded toward me. "I brought this double Jack and Coke from the bar and he's paying for it. I'll have another as soon as it's finished." He glanced at Laura. "I have a feeling I'll need it and I'm close enough to walk home."

Carly stared at the table. "Double Johnny Black on the rocks with a splash."

I was mentally tallying the bar bill when Chad turned to me. "And you, Father Brown?"

"Brown? You mean Father Bruce."

He smirked condescendingly. "Sorry. I've watched him on TV and heard you're solving these murders in Buggy Springs. I guess you reminded me of him."

Typical small-town gossip. However, as I recalled, G.K. Chesterton had described Father Brown as rotund and "dull as a Norfolk dumpling." The TV series portrayed him the same, running around in a baggy cassock and carrying an umbrella. So I reminded Chad of him. Nice.

I managed a smile. "But I'm not Roman Catholic." I tried to ignore Laura's chuckle. She must have known about Father Brown, too. I focused on the charming Chad. "I'll have a glass of house chardonnay and I'll be taking the check."

The Chief took a healthy drink of his Jack and Coke. I hoped

271

that bringing Laura to town wouldn't make him an alcoholic. "So, Robert, you have something for me?"

I handed him a copy of the emails from Jon to his lawyer. He studied them. "Interesting."

Laura leaned forward. "What are those?"

The Chief glared at her. "Nothing to do with your client."

"Better hope not. You could get into bigger trouble by withholding information about her from me." She rested her elbows on the table, laced her fingers together and propped her chin on them, giving the Chief a cold smile. She reminded me of a praying mantis. A beautiful one, but one who would still bite your head off in an instant. "Besides, I will get them in discovery and this will all be a waste of time, time that will cost you."

The Chief's face reddened. If he didn't share them with her, she could make waves. If he did, he would look like he'd caved in to her threat. I handed her a copy to save face for the Chief. "There's not really anything earth-shattering here."

She accepted the papers and gently patted my cheek. "You always were smarter than you looked."

The Chief stood, finished his drink in one gulp and slammed his glass on the table, staring hard at Laura. "Sorry, Robert, I need to leave before I say something very rude to your guest, like where she can shove those papers."

I stood to try to stop him from leaving, but he was already to the door. Laura grabbed my hand.

"Let him go, Rob. He's going to be a lot madder when I file the papers for Carly's suit against him and the department."

My jaw dropped. "Suit? For what?"

She smiled smugly. "We'll start with failure to Mirandize and build from there."

I looked at Carly. "Is this what you want? Remember, you are the boss here, not her."

Carly's eyes were teary and she shook her head. "No way." She turned to Laura, her fingers interlaced and tightly clenched together. "I live here. These are my people. Chief Garcia was only doing his job and I'm not going to crucify him. If you don't like it, fu–" She glanced at me, than back at Laura. "Take a hike."

At that moment, Chad arrived with the drinks. "I've got the

Diet Coke for the foxy lady, the Johnny Black for my Goth beauty, and the economy chardonnay for Father Brown, but I saw my Jack and Coke storm out the door. Did you guys offend Chief Garcia?" He winked at us. "Careful, or he won't write off any more of your parking tickets."

Laura leaned back, throwing out her well-shaped bustline. "He needed to get some tourists' cars towed away. The city's income has been a little off this week."

"Uh, okay." Chad's stare was riveted on Laura's chest for a moment, then he snapped out of it. "What do I do with his drink? I can't take it back."

Laura smiled at him. "Don't worry. I'll take it."

After Chad left, she sipped the drink and sighed. "I wish it had Diet Coke." She looked at Carly and gave a small shrug. "You are the boss. But I could have made you a rich woman."

Carly shook her head. "Rich people aren't happy. Money's the reason everyone's killing each other. I've got more than enough to live on and I'd rather be a cocktail waitress with my friends than be a lawyer in a big city like you are."

Laura's smile sagged. For the first time, I noticed that Laura was getting crow's feet at the corners of her eyes. "You're wiser than I expected. You are the boss and I'll play by your rules. I also like your spunk, telling me it was your way or the highway."

Then the moment was gone. She picked up her menu and studied it. "Well, Rob, since there's not going to be any hefty contingency fee for a lawsuit, this meal is going to cost you dearly."

As long as the Chief and the city didn't get sued, I'd be glad to pay, I thought.

When the bill came, I wasn't as happy. True to her word, Laura ordered the most expensive items on the menu. A carpaccio starter, smoked duck salad and two lobster tails for her entree. I never knew they had lobster tail and, after seeing the price, I wished they hadn't. Although she barely touched the double Jack and Coke, she did order a Hennessy Paradis Extra 25 year-old cognac after dinner. I'd never heard of it and was surprised that Merry Monk's even stocked it. Since that one drink cost more than all our dinners, I hoped it was exceptional.

Laura leaned back in her chair, again proving her great form, and sighed as she sipped it. "Not bad, Rob, but I wish they had Cognac Maxime Trijol Rare Grande Champagne. Still, what do you expect in Smallville." With a sultry smirk, she said, "So, Rob, we ready to head over to your place? I brought my sheerest teddy."

My throat almost closed and I had a hard time croaking out, "I made reservations for you at the Union Hotel. It's not great, but it's the best in town."

Laura laughed. "Just kidding. Not about the teddy, but it's not for you. Anyway, you take off and leave me for a confidential conference with my client."

Relief washed over me. "Great. When do you want me to pick you up and take you to the hotel?"

Laura shook her head with a bemused smile. "You are naive. Doug's wife is away for the holidays and he's all alone. We're going to relive old times at his cabin up at Tahoe before I leave tomorrow. He'll pick us up and we'll drop Carly off at her place."

I realized she meant Judge Doug Bryant, who'd helped get Carly out of jail. From the pictures I'd seen of him in the paper, he must be at least thirty years older than she. "You don't have to do this. You said he already owed you."

"It's just going to be a bit of fun. Besides, it's what I do, make sure there's always credit in my account when I need it." Sadness washed over her face. "Don't judge me, Rob. I do what I have to do to save people. It's my job. You save souls, I save bodies."

"I try to do some of both. It's my job. Jesus said, 'Truly I tell you, whatever you did for one of the least of these brothers and sisters of mine, you did for me.'"

"Whatever. I don't have time for your pontificating. Just leave my overnight bag with the bartender when you go." She turned away from me and looked at Carly. "You ready to get down to business and make sure your butt doesn't get thrown back into jail?"

I hesitated a moment. Laura waved me away without even turning, so I left. After leaving Laura's overnight bag with the bartender, I climbed into the Beast. It was still fairly early, so I decided to see my parishioners in care facilities before calling it a night. When I turned on the radio, Paul McCartney's *Wonderful Christmas* came out the speakers. Totally inane.

What happened to beautiful carols like *Once in Royal David's*

City, Adeste Fidelis, and *The Holly and the Ivy?* I shut the radio off and I drove away, humming my beloved carols.

Chapter 50

My last stop was Golden Sunset Convalescent Hospital to see Imogene. She was the only one of my parish there on the eve of Christmas Eve. I had a poinsettia for her. It had been given to me the day before and, since I have a black thumb, I was regifting it to her to give the poor plant a fighting chance for survival. I also had a dozen red roses I had purchased earlier. In places like Golden Sunset, valuables had a way of disappearing, but flowers didn't. Plus Imogene loved them.

When I walked in, the only sign of Christmas was a plastic tree that looked as real as a politician's smile with cheap ornaments and a couple of strings of lights with only half working. Well, there was also a sign of red glittery letters strung together that read "Happy Holidays" across one wall that looked like it came from some dollar store. Golden Sunset had gone all out in decorating.

Julie was at the reception desk and smiled at me. "Happy holidays, Father Bruce."

"Merry Christmas, Julie. Is Imogene still up?"

"She's in the activities room." She fluttered her lashes. "Want me to take you to her?"

"Thanks, Julie. I know the way."

The activities room was inactive except for the TV screen, which had Jimmy Stewart running through the snowy streets of Bedford Falls. One dim lamp on a side table gave the only other illumination and only one person was in the room. Imogene was sitting in a well-worn tweed recliner, a threadbare robe pulled up under her chin. With her head back, mouth open and snoring, she looked very old.

I placed the roses and poinsettia on a TV tray in front of her and gave her a soft kiss on her forehead. "Merry Christmas, Imogene."

I was almost to the door when she snorted and muttered, "Bobbie?"

I went back to her. "How are you, Imogene?" I picked up the roses and handed them to her. "Merry Christmas."

"Oh, thank you." She took the roses and brought them to her face, sniffing them. "So beautiful."

"Beautiful flowers for a beautiful lady."

"For an old lady, but one who still likes to be called beautiful." She lowered the roses to her lap. "I remember when I was beautiful. The boys would come to my house and my father would shoo them away." She smiled. "But maybe they were there for my mother's piernik instead of me."

"Piernik?"

She rested her hand on mine and patted it. "It's a gingerbread and my mother was famous for it. It was part of Wigilia, the feast we had on Christmas Eve in Poland. The whole family would gather for a fine meal before Midnight Mass." A tear glistened at the side of her eye. "I never thought I would be all alone in those happy days. I have no family anymore. William has a new lady friend here and I'm just an old woman waiting to die."

I couldn't speak. I knelt beside her and wrapped her thin, boney frame in my arms. Tears ran down my cheeks.

She rested her hand against the side of my face. "Don't cry. It's okay. I've had a good life and I'm ready to meet my Lord."

I cleared my throat and regained my composure. "I can't do a Christmas Eve dinner because I have two services, but you are coming to my house for Christmas. I'll pick you up about noon."

"No, no." she smiled. "You'll have plans for that day. They will have turkey for us and that's fine."

I stood and waved my forefinger at her. "Be ready at noon or I'll take you in your nightgown. No arguments."

She giggled. "Oh, Bobbie, that wouldn't be decent. I'll be ready."

"I'll see you then."

As I turned to go, she called, "You missed Marilyn Monroe. She was here a little while ago."

Lisa? What was she doing here? "Did she talk to you?"

"Just a little. She's very busy. I hear her next movie will be out soon."

She must think the real Marilyn Monroe had been here. Obviously, this was not one of her good days.

"She was here the night Elvira passed, you know. She and

Gentle Ben."

Gentle Ben? Was that an actor, too? "Who's Gentle Ben?"

"You remember that TV show about a bear? Gentle Ben." She paused. "But he wasn't a real bear like Ben was. He was a big, hairy man like a bear. A red bear with a beard."

Todd? Had Todd really been here the night Elvira had been murdered or was it all in Imogene's imagination?

I patted her hand. "I'll see you on Christmas."

On my way out, I stopped by Julie's desk. "Julie, have you been on duty long?"

"Too long." She shook her head. "We lost a couple of caregivers and I've been pulling double shifts. Great pay, but I'm shot."

"Do you know if Lisa Franks has been here today?"

"I don't know who that is. Does she have someone in here?"

"No, but she's a blond, good looking, big, uh . . . bustline and--"

"That sounds like Mary MacDonald's daughter. She was here today. Her name is . . . ." She placed a long, red-painted fingernail on her chin. "Annette something. Kirkwall, maybe?"

This was unexpected. "Does she visit her mother often?"

She nodded. "Couple times a week. Really regular about it."

So Marilyn Monroe was not Lisa. So much for placing her at Golden Sunset the night Elvira was murdered. Dead end again. Bad pun.

I smiled at Julie. "Thanks. I'm picking up Imogene at noon on Christmas for dinner. Would you have her ready?"

She clapped her hands together. "That's so sweet. She'll be ready, promise."

"I appreciate it."

As I opened the door to leave, Julie called to me. "Thought you'd want to know that I'm off tomorrow and I'm coming to your church."

I glanced back. "I'll look forward to seeing you there."

As I drove home, I pondered what I had gotten myself into. I was no chef and had never attempted a Christmas dinner. I checked my watch. It was just after nine. The Solstice would still be open. I headed for it.

279

Fortune smiled on me and I found a parking place right in front of the restaurant. Charles greeted me at the door, dapper as ever in a vested tweed suit, tattersall shirt and burgundy-striped tie, knotted with the dimple perfectly in the center.

"Father Robert, how good to see you. We don't have any openings right now, but I'll work you in if you can wait."

"I'm not here for dinner tonight. I need a little help for Christmas dinner."

He gave a slight roll of his eyes. "You know we're not open on Christmas, Father. I am a member of St. Nicholas, you know. It's a high holy day."

"Of course, I know that." Way too brusque. I took a breath. Don't take out your exasperation with yourself on someone else. "And I am very glad you're closed then. I've put myself in a bit of a jam. I've invited a parishioner to Christmas dinner and I have no idea how to cook one. It's for Imogene Casper. She's at Golden Sunset and I just couldn't let her have that cardboard turkey they'd serve on Christmas." I paused. "But it's probably better than what I know how to cook. Can you give me some advice?"

Charles studied me a moment, then sighed. "Good guilt trip, Father. You'll have dinner for four delivered to the rectory. What time?"

I held up my hands. "No, no, Charles. I'm just looking for advice. Nothing more."

"Shut up and take my offer. Maybe God sent you to me so Imogene will have a decent dinner." He grinned. "Besides, I always buy too big a turkey and have leftovers far too long. What time?"

"I, uh . . . ." Maybe God had sent me there. He certainly knew I couldn't make a decent dinner myself. "One?"

"Done. Christmas dinner with all the fixin's at one in the afternoon."

"There's only going to be two of us."

He lifted an eyebrow. "Can you swear you won't invite some other lonely soul? Besides, I already feel guilty for not inviting you to dinner. You were going to be alone, weren't you?"

I shrugged. "Everyone thinks the rector is already going somewhere for Christmas dinner. What do I owe you?"

"Nothing. Thanks for letting me give a little something to you on Christmas.   It's a blessing for me."   He smiled.   "After all, it is more blessed to give than to receive, isn't it?"

I took his hand.   "Thank you again, my friend.   Christ's blessing upon you.   And Merry Christmas."

"And you, too, Father."

Chapter 51

As I got in the Beast, my cell played *God Rest Ye Merry Gentlemen.* I had changed the ring tone to match the season. According to the display, it was the Chief.

"Merry Christmas, Chief. Sorry about the dinner."

"Forget about it, Robert. I let her get under my skin. That's not why I called. I got a report from the sheriff's. They found some good prints at Todd's place besides Red Hot's. One set was on a lock-back knife, the type that clips on your belt. They found it on the floor near the door. Looks like it was dropped accidently. At first, they thought it might have been the one used to stab Todd, but it wasn't. But the prints on it were Choke's. Then they found a number of prints on the two drink glasses and the door knob. Those were Todd's and Carly's. There's a BOLO out on him, but the sheriff knows where Carly is and is keeping an eye on her."

My heart sank. Had they been working together? I'd dropped in to a rather hot reception at Beezer's after Todd's death and had to use a baseball bat to get out. Ben had been there and Chewy, but no Choke. I should have caught that.

The Chief continued. "Another thing is that they found other guns and a few boxes of 7.62 rounds at Todd's, but not the AK-47 that was fired at you. And that was the gun used in the Kansas bank robbery."

"So someone else has the gun. Maybe Choke."

"Yeah. Looks like it." He paused. "Go home. I'm sending a car to sit outside your house, just in case."

"Don't bother. Even if Todd popped off a few rounds at the rectory, I really doubt that Choke or Carly would. I'm no threat to them. But I'll be careful and have my 12 gauge side-by-side by my chair, just in case. Let your guys have some rest and be with their families."

I was almost home when I got another call on my cell. It was

Carly. Her voice was subdued, almost inaudible. "I need help."

"What's wrong, Carly?" Had Sheriff Bob arrested her again?

"I need a place to crash."

I paused. "What's wrong with your house?"

"Five-O trashed it."

"The police trashed your house?" I saw red that the Chief did this, especially not telling me when I'd just talked to him, but something didn't make sense. "What was the reason?"

"I dunno. Pick me up at Higgins Diggins. Better hurry, 'cause I'm working on getting hashtag smacked."

"Carly, I–"

The connection was dead. She'd ended the call.

I let out a frustrated sigh as I headed back to town. It was almost ten and I still hadn't finished my homily for the Christmas Eve services. It was hard to keep up your Christmas spirit when everyone else's troubles kept crashing on you, even if you were the rector at a church named St. Nicholas.

I made a call to the Chief while I got in the Beast, glad I had his cell number. He must have been expecting my call.

"I was just going to call you, Robert. I had nothing to do with that search at Carly's. Sheriff Bob found a judge who gave him a search warrant and executed it without even telling me 'til afterwards. I just heard about it. This is my city and I'm as P.O.'d as you are." He paused. "But there's another problem. They found a half-full box of 7.62 rounds in her place. If they find Carly's prints on the box, it could be bad. Bob's got it in for Carly 'cause your friend got her out before."

His honesty and innocence took the angry wind out of my sails. At least Sheriff Bob hadn't arrested Carly. Yet. "Thanks for the heads up. I'm on my way to pick up Carly now. They made a mess of her place and I've got to find somewhere to take her for the night. Maybe I'll put her up in the Union Hotel."

"Hmm. You know the health department closed their restaurant because of excessive rat droppings?"

"What?" Why hadn't the gossip mill, a.k.a. Doris, told me? "When?"

"It just happened today. Anyway, thought you should know. Also, word is that Sheriff Bob has been asking around about any connection between Carly and Choke. Looks like he's working on them as our local Bonnie and Clyde."

I rubbed my temples. "Thanks. But I don't think Carly robs banks or smokes cigars."

"Cigars?"

"It's a famous photo of Bonnie. Anyway, I've got to roll."

"Well, Merry Christmas, Robert."

"Yeah. Merry Christmas, Chief. At least I hope it will be."

Next I called Brandy Mazzoni, the only person I knew who might cope with Carly, and explained the situation. She was on duty at the hospital, but was off at ten and said I could take my Goth problem to her house.

By that time, I was unsuccessfully looking for a parking place in front of Higgins Diggins. I double parked, threw on my four-way flashers and ran inside. If I got a ticket, maybe the Chief would fix it.

As I came through the door, I saw Blondie in a low cut top and yoga pants with a tray of drinks. She gave me a wan smile, then came up to me.

"I, uh, guess you're wondering about me working here."

I had a good idea why. "It's because Todd fired Dwayne."

"Yeah. But it's all good now. Dwayne says he's gonna get the business now." She hesitated. "Or will, as soon as that lawyer gets it all legal."

I smiled. "I'm sure it will be fine." I wondered how Dwayne felt about her dressed like that in a bar like this. Did it make him angry enough to kill Todd? He knew about getting control of the business awfully quickly.

Carly was sitting at the bar, a half-empty drink in her hand. She didn't turn around when I walked next to her, but finished her drink. Her speech was slow and deliberate, the first signs of intoxication.

"Don't preach to me, Preacher-man. I can't even . . . ." She held up her empty glass. "I need another. Join me bustin' bottles?"

"Your limo awaits outside, double parked and begging for a ticket."

She rose unsteadily and grabbed a backpack from the floor. "That's mad gucci."

I looked to the bartender and pointed at her drink, ready to pay. He waved his hand. It's good to have friends in town. Carly put on her coat, then I took her arm and guided her outside to my truck. I got

285

her in the passenger side, then hurried around and hopped inside. At least there was no ticket on the windshield. Thank God for small favors. But it was beginning to lightly snow, something I would usually like at Christmas. I was just too busy this year.

As we drove to Brandy's, I tried to open a conversation with Carly.

"So, do you know Choke from Beezer's Bar?"

"Why?" Her voice was laden with suspicion.

"No reason. I heard that the Sheriff's office think there's a connection between you two."

She tilted her seat back and propped her feet on my dash. "Yeah, well, they asked me that and I cancelled, just gave them Laura's number."

"And that's what you're saying to me, too?"

She was silent for a moment. "He's a friend with no benefits. Period. No fam. This is low key, got it? He saved my butt one night when Todd grabbed me right outside of Higgins. Choke saw it and cracked the uncool's skull. We've been buds since and he's tight with that."

Although I got the gist, that Choke was a friend and nothing more, my head was beginning to hurt from trying to keep up with her patois. Alcohol seemed to make her vocabulary worse.

"Have you had any contact with him since you went to Todd's?"

"No."

"Did you know they found a box of AK-47 ammo at your house? Do you have any idea what happened to Todd's AK-47?"

"'Nuff of this crap." She turned away, towards the window. "I'm tired boots."

She rode in silence, feigning sleep, until we got to Brandy's. She hopped out, grabbed her backpack and staggered towards the door of the Mazzoni's modern log cabin. The porch light was on and the door opened as we got to it. I introduced her to Brandy as we stood on the doorstep.

"Want to come in for a cup of coffee?" Brandy asked.

I checked my watch. "Thanks, but I've still have a lot to do tonight."

As Carly started to walk inside, she paused and glanced back at me.

"Thanks," she muttered, then went inside.

Brandy smiled. "For her, that's a lot. I know. I've been where she is."

I shrugged. "I don't do this for the thanks. Have a Merry Christmas."

"You too, Father." She paused. "But think about letting go of this, if not for your safety, at least for the sake of your friends. Lotta people are getting hurt and more might."

As she closed the door and I headed to the Beast, I reflected that sometimes it might be nice to get a little more appreciation.

Chapter 52

Although I wanted nothing more than to go home and have a nice mug of tea, or maybe even a shot of single malt scotch, I still had some questions. Sheriff Bob had, no doubt, already shaken that tree, but I headed for Beezer's Bar.

When I parked in the gravel parking lot, there were only a couple of cars in it, with a dusting of snow. The neon sign over the door was off, but there were lights on in the building. It was hard to imagine why Beezer's wouldn't be open when it wasn't even eleven yet. As I got out of my truck, I noticed the aluminum baseball bat behind the seat. Should I take it? It didn't seem very priestly. But when I recalled how I had been received on my last visit and that I had no backup for the Christmas Eve services, I decided to speak softly and carry a big bat.

The front door was unlocked, so I went in. The barbeque wasn't burning, so there was no layer of smoke or smell of seared beef. Chairs and tables were scattered around, many upturned or on their sides. The only lights on were three behind the bar, which was littered with glasses of various sizes and empty or almost empty bottles. Only Chewy and Ben were seated at the bar, hunched over with a half-full bottle of amber whiskey between them.

"We're closed," Ben growled without turning around. "Git yer ass out o' here."

"I just have a couple of questions and then I'll leave."

Ben and Chewy both slowly turned and glared at me. Ben spat on the floor, which was a common hobby in the bar. "Ya got a lotta nerve, I'll say that." He eyed the bat. "Ya gonna take up where your cop buddies left off?"

The air was hostile, but not threatening, so I set the bat on the bar and took a stool several away from the father and son.

"If cops did this, they weren't friends of mine. Sheriff Bob, I assume?"

They turned back to their drinks, refilling them from the bottle.

289

"Yeah. Came in here like Rambos, pointin' shotguns at everybody. Said they was lookin' for Choke. Got all P.O.'d 'cause he warn't here and started checkin' I.D.'s and found some dumb 20 year-old kid suckin' on a beer and closed me down. Said I'm gonna lose my liquor license. So we figgers to drink the stock ourselves."

I leaned on the bar, resting on my elbows. "Maybe I can help, but you've got to help me. Deal?"

The old man glared at me. "You just wanna railroad Choke so's you can get that Goth chick off."

I shook my head. "I don't think Choke had anything to do with killing Todd. I have no intention of helping Sheriff Bob railroad anyone. But I can't help him if you won't help me."

He pondered this while taking a swig of his drink. "Okay. Whatcha wanna know?"

"Did Choke leave here on the night that Todd died?"

Chewy belched. "Sure did. He got a call and said he had to leave."

Ben glared at him. "Shut yer yap. I'll do the talkin'."

Chewy refilled his glass and stared at the line of bottles behind the bar. "I'll say what I damn well please. 'Sides, Choke ain't never done nothin' fer me."

Ben cuffed him on the back of the head, causing him to spill some of his drink, then turned to me. "'Nuff fer ya?"

"No, when did he get the call?" I needed to establish a time line, even though the snow ruined the chances of the coroner verifying the time of death.

Chewy shrugged. "Dunno. Maybe an hour before closing."

"Thanks." I pulled out one of the business cards Laura had left in my truck. "Call her and tell her I said to call. Tell her you're being harassed by the police. Say there's grounds for a lawsuit against the Sheriff's office."

Ben's eyes bulged. "Hell, I don't wanna sue the cops. They'll bust our chops every time we drive down the road."

"I know." I smiled. "I didn't say to tell her you'd sue them, just say there are grounds. And don't sound like a misogynist."

"Massagist? Hell, I don't know nothin' about that stuff." He paused and grinned, revealing yellow teeth with a couple missing. "That ain't quite right. I did have one of them massages in Sacramento

290

where she—"

"Stop," I interrupted. "What I mean is she's very much against men treating women poorly, so don't say anything like you were about to say."

He rubbed his grizzled chin. "Not sure I can do that."

"If you want your bar back, you'd better." I sniffed. "And take a bath before she gets here. Both of you."

Chewy grinned. "Only if she's purty."

I shook my head in disgust. "You make a pass at her, you'll lose the bar and end up eating through a straw for a year. Trust me on that."

I grabbed my bat and headed out. I'd done what I could, but I didn't have much hope for them.

I finally headed home to finish my Christmas Eve homily. The snow had turned to sleet that was melting, not very Christmas-like. Of course, there probably wouldn't have been snow in Bethlehem, but my European heritage yearned for it. Life's full of disappointments.

Once home, I fired up my computer and found some carols from the Cambridge Singers on my iTunes player. I had just settled in my desk chair with a wee bit of Bunnahabhain 25 year-old single-malt scotch whisky (a gift from Pops years ago that I doled out to myself on special occasions, like the Christmas season), when my phone rang. It was after 11:00. It would not be good news.

With a sigh, I answered. "St. Nicholas rectory, Father Robert speaking."

"Hello, Accident. Merry Christmas."

I rubbed my temples. I had forgotten to call Pops about the chalet in Switzerland. "Merry Christmas, Sister Dearest. What's he done now?"

"He invited all of us to join him on his boat for Christmas."

I sat in stunned silence.

"Did you hear me? Pops invited us to join him on his boat. We're heading to Maui tomorrow morning. You're probably invited, too, but I guess you've got that church stuff."

I chuckled. "That church stuff." She never got it. "Yes, I do have two services tomorrow night that I can't miss and I've invited one of my parishioners to Christmas dinner."

291

"Too bad. Is she hot?"

I realized my sister was talking about my dinner guest, who she correctly assumed was female. "Very, especially for an octogenarian."

"You're sick." She paused. "Anyway, I just wanted to tell you that the chalet was just a joke. He was trying to get my goat. And he did. But everything's cool."

"Good." I couldn't think of anything witty to say. "Well, enjoy your Christmas on the high seas."

"I will." She hesitated. "Robbie, I really wish we could all be together again."

I sipped my whisky. "I do, too, Jannie. I do, too. Have a very merry Christmas. And tell Pops Merry Christmas for me, will you?"

"I will. Have yourself a Merry Christmas, little brother."
She disconnected.

I scrolled down my iTunes list until I found what I wanted and put on Judy Garland singing, "Have Yourself a Merry Little Christmas." My family was going to be together for Christmas for the first time since my mother had died, but I couldn't be there. I was feeling rather down. I took another sip of my whisky.

I had just finished my homily when my phone rang again. It was almost midnight. Who would call at this hour? I needed to get caller I.D.

"St. Nicholas rectory, Father Robert speaking."

"It's Morg. You still awake?"

"No, I'm talking in my sleep."

She laughed. "Stupid question. I just wanted to see if you wanted me to check out anything before I left tomorrow."

"Can't think of anything." I closed my eyes and leaned back in my chair. "What do you do when your prime murder suspect ends up dead, also murdered?"

"My favorite detective used to say, 'When you have eliminated the impossible, whatever remains, however improbable, must be the truth.' Does that help?"

I thought about what I knew and what I'd surmised. Then I remembered when I'd checked out the Mensa directory to see Carly's profile. Another name had been interesting. "It just might. Would

292

you check out a Meliscent Stewart who lives in Buggy Springs?"

"Sure. What else do you have on her?"

"I, uh . . . not much. I found her on the Mensa directory. She says she has a doctorate and is interested in animals. You can go there to check her out. U-S-dot-Mensa-dot-org. My user name is my email address and the password is--"

"Don't need it. I can log on myself. Believe it or not, a lowly P.I. could be a Mensan, too."

Oops. Maybe I should have asked. "Sorry. I wasn't trying to put you down."

"Relax. I'm not upset. Just jerking your chain. But I bet you didn't know that 'mensa' means 'stupid' in Spanish, so the joke's on us." She laughed. "Anyway, I'll check this out and email you what I find." She paused. "I did find something interesting about your Cindy Wolfe, too. Her divorce from Todd was never finalized, so she's his widow."

I mulled it over. "Interesting. I wonder if she knows." I wasn't sure how it would affect the trust. Maybe she'd get a much bigger chunk. I'd have to call Evans again.

"I wondered, too." She paused. "So, what are you doing for Christmas?"

"Christmas?" Was she kidding? "I officiate at two services on Christmas Eve."

"Great. What time's the last one? I can probably make it. How about Christmas day?"

I was a little taken aback by her boldness, but rather liked the idea of her joining me for Christmas dinner. "Sure. Our last service is at 10:00 p.m. A local restaurant is cooking for me on Christmas, so dinner will be edible. Since it's just going to be Imogene and me, you're quite welcome to join us."

"Oh. Forget it." She sounded disappointed. "I won't force myself into your romantic dinner."

I laughed. "Imogene is a parishioner who's in a rest home. We're not exactly involved, but she is good company, if you're into old movies and their stars."

"Love 'em." She sounded happy. "Sam and I will be there in time for the service."

Sam? "That's fine. He's welcome, too."

She laughed again. "Sam's a she and she's my border collie.
Is it okay to bring her? I hope you're not allergic or anything. I
should've asked."

"No, no, it's fine. I love dogs. I had an Aussie until last year.
When I had to put her down because of cancer, I think I cried for a
week. I really miss her. Sam's most welcome."

"Great. Check your email in the morning for what I dug up.
See you tomorrow. Merry Christmas." She paused. "You really
miss your dog, don't you?

"More than you'll ever know. Merry Christmas, Morg."

She hung up and I leaned back in my chair. Christmas was
looking up. I finished my scotch and headed for bed.

Chapter 53

I awakened to the phone ringing. It was dark and I fumbled for the receiver.

"Rectory. Father Robert speaking," I mumbled.

"Sorry to call so early, Robert." It was the Chief. "I thought you'd want to know. Choke was shot about two this morning in Reno. He's in intensive care in St. Mary's. He might die."

I rubbed my eyes, trying to come out of the fog of a deep sleep, and glanced at the clock. 6:02 a.m. I'd been asleep just over five hours. "What happened?"

"Reno P.D. isn't sure. He'd been in the Lincoln Lounge, talking to the bartender about making a big sale. At this point, they're thinking drugs. He was found in a parking lot with a couple of bullets in his back about 2:00 a.m. It must have been right after it happened 'cause the guy who found him thought he heard a car backfiring, probably the gunshots, and then saw a dark SUV burning rubber out of the parking lot."

"I don't suppose he gave a good description of the SUV or got a license number."

He chuckled. "The guy was three sheets to the wind. It was lucky he stumbled back into the bar and got the bartender to call 9-1-1."

I pondered this. "He didn't attend St. Nicholas. So, why are you calling me?"

"The drunk who found him said Choke mumbled something about the killer wanting his AK."

"Todd's gun, maybe?" Something wasn't right. "Maybe he was selling that AK-47. But why kill him for it? Are they worth that much?"

"Not really. I've known junkies to kill over a dime bag, but it seems odd. Guns are bought and sold all the time in Reno and the detective I spoke with couldn't come up with one time anyone had been shot in a gun deal recently. Choke still had his wallet and keys on him, so he wasn't shot for his money or truck. That's why they're thinking it was a drug deal. A lot of people get shot in those."

I turned on my night stand light and swung my legs out of bed, wide awake. "Choke have any history with drugs?"

"None. He beat the crap out of a couple of guys doing a pot deal at Beezer's. That's one of his arrests." He chuckled. "I never said he was an angel."

"So Todd's AK was the reason he was shot?"

"We don't know that it was Todd's."

I sighed. "Give me a break. This isn't a court of law. Todd's AK-47 is missing and Choke was shot by someone who wanted one. It must be the same one and someone was willing to pay to get it. Or kill. This isn't rocket science here. The questions are who and why?"

"Problem is Reno P.D. recovered an AK-47 by the Truckee River this morning that just might be the gun. We'll know after a ballistics check. A homeless guy saw someone toss something over the Sierra Street Bridge about that time and went to check it out. The gun had missed the river and he found it. Took it to the P.D. and asked for a reward, so they're running prints on it. Any other ideas?"

"Too many and none of them worth mentioning." I had one, but it was so far-fetched I was loath to speak it, so I didn't. Accusing someone with nothing but a gut instinct wasn't wise. I needed to do a little more checking. "Did he have his cell phone?"

"I asked. Nada." He paused. "I should warn you that Sheriff Bob is going to look closely at Carly. I hope she has a solid alibi."

"She does. She was staying at Brandy Mazzoni's" I hoped she had stayed.

The Chief chuckled. "Well, if Sheriff Bob messes with Brandy, he's likely to end up in your churchyard. I know her reputation."

"Our churchyard is a planter, not a graveyard."

"So he'd literally be pushing up daisies, huh?" He laughed.

The phrase was familiar, but it took me a second to remember where I'd heard it. "You sound like Ralphie in *A Christmas Story*."

"Yeah, I just watched it with my grandson last night. Anyway, I just thought you'd want a heads up on what's happening."

"Thanks. Any word on fingerprints on the ammo box they found at Carly's?"

The Chief was silent for a moment, then spoke softly. "It's not my investigation, so I'll tell you. They found both Todd's and Carly's."

"On the box?"

"On the box and on thirty rounds of the ammo. The only reason Sheriff Bob hasn't arrested her is your friend, Laura. He's going to make sure his ducks are in a row before he throws Carly in jail."

Not good. I needed some answers from Carly. "Thanks, Chief. I do appreciate this."

"What? Telling you about Choke getting shot? That'll be in the newspaper. I don't remember telling you anything else."

I smiled. "That's what I was thanking you for, of course."

"Good." He hung up.

I called Carly's cell.

"Yeah?"

"Good Morning. It's Father Robert."

"Duh. Cell phones have caller I.D., ya know."

I took a deep breath and refrained from advising her on telephone etiquette. "Carly, I need to talk to you."

"So, talk."

The hostile, rude Carly was back. I needed to shake her up so I could help her. I was going to make some assumptions and hoped I was correct.

"Choke's been shot and might die, probably trying to sell Todd's AK-47 that you gave him in Reno. Are you ready to drop the tough-girl routine and talk to me?"

"Choke was shot?" She let out a soft sob. "It's all my fault."

I waited for more, but only heard her ragged breathing.

"Carly, I'm here for you. Do you want to tell me what's going on?"

There was a pause before she spoke.

"Pick me up here in twenty."

She ended the call.

I had a quick shower and shave before bolting down a bowl of oatmeal. I was almost out the door when the rectory phone rang.

"Rectory. Father Robert speaking."

297

"Hello, Robert. How are you?"

For a moment, I was speechless. He hadn't called me Robert for years, only Accident.

"Not bad, Pops. And you?"

"Getting ready for Christmas." He chuckled. "Not my normal routine. I guess your sister called you about the boat trip."

"Yes, she did."

I knew he wanted more from me, a blessing on his omitting me from his plans, but I was not ready to give it.

"Well, I guess you wonder why I didn't ask you to come along when I did ask her."

I remained silent.

He sighed. "I hadn't planned on asking her. When she called to rant about me buying a chalet in Switzerland, I had a moment of weakness. I remembered all those Christmases with your mother, when we were a family. I know I'm going to regret taking her and her block-headed husband on a two-week cruise in close quarters, but it's done." He hesitated and said nothing. "If you want, I'll hold up a day so that you can fly down and go with us. The boat has plenty of cabins. I would like having you on board." He chuckled. "Literally."

He was trying, which was far more than he had done for a long time. By using the silent treatment, I was beginning to feel like a petulant child. Time to change.

"I do appreciate the offer, Pops, but I have a couple of people coming for Christmas dinner. You go on your cruise and enjoy."

"I will. At least as much as I can with Janet's drone on my boat. If you get a chance, read about its role in the hive. It's really a fitting description of him, except he survived doing his part to create those two brats who will try to destroy my boat." He paused. "Anyway, do have a Merry Christmas. I'll be thinking of you."

"I'll be thinking of you too, Pops. Have a very Merry Christmas."

He hung up and I sat a moment, remembering Christmases past. Then I saw the time. I needed to get over to Brandy's house to pick up Carly.

Chapter 54

When I pulled in front of Brandy's house, Carly came out the door and ran to my truck. She was dressed all in black, as usual, with a hoodie hiding her face. Over the sweatshirt she wore a ski jacket. She climbed in and sat looking straight ahead, saying nothing. I couldn't see her face.

"Morning, Carly."

She grunted.

"Have you had breakfast?"

She shook her head.

"How about we go to the Side Street Bistro?"

She nodded. This was a one-sided conversation.

I put the Beast in gear and drove to the Bistro. It was on a side street off Main, hence the name. I always called it the greasy spoon, even though the cooks used far less grease there than they did at the Buggy Springs Diner. But the first time I walked in the door of the long, narrow restaurant, with the open kitchen along one side, and saw the two cooks, that's what came to mind. With two beefy guys frying food on a long griddle, dressed in sleeveless, black T-shirts that showed off their muscular biceps and many tattoos, their heads covered with American flag do-rags, it just seemed right. One of them turned and gave me a curt nod, with no smile on his lips under a Zapata mustache. Since the sign had said it was open for breakfast and lunch only, I had wondered if the place doubled as a biker bar at night. It turned out that they were bikers, both owning Harley choppers that looked like they'd roared off the set of the movie *Easy Rider*. But they did know how to cook. They made great Greek tofu wraps, spicy Chinese chicken salads and Mexican chorizo scrambles, as well as specials like Philippine longaniza, which was a spicy pork sausage, served with garlic rice, fried egg and a dipping sauce of vinegar. Eclectic is the best word to describe the menu, but not greasy.

We were seated on the hard, wood chairs across a small table from each other. Carly couldn't hide her face any longer or her reddened eyes. I leaned forward.

"Ready to tell me something?"

She stared at the menu. "I'll have the chorizo scramble with dry sourdough toast and fruit instead of the cottage fries."

I sighed. "That's not why we're here."

Unfortunately, our waiter arrived before she responded. He was a short, thin young man with long, blond hair and a three-day beard.

"Hi, I'm Jeff. What can I get for you two?"

I forced myself to focus. "I'll have the longaniza and a cup of coffee. She'll have the chorizo scramble with dry sourdough toast and fruit."

He cocked his head. "Fruit's extra, you know."

I closed my menu. "No problem. I just took a second out on my house." I looked at Carly. "Anything to drink?"

"Sierra Nevada Pale Ale." She tossed her menu on the table. "Two of them."

Jeff looked to me and I nodded. He shrugged as if drinking beer before eight in the morning was normal and left.

I studied Carly. "Are you ready to talk to me?"

She sniffed and wiped her nose on her sleeve. "Why the hell not? I killed Choke."

I leaned back in my chair. "That'd be a little difficult since he was shot in Reno and you're here."

"I didn't stop him." She stifled a sob. "He told me he'd got a buyer for Todd's gun who'd give him enough money to go to Mexico, so I gave it to him. It's my fault. I want you to forgive me for it, do that holy stuff."

"I don't forgive sins, only God can. But we'll go back to the church after this and go through the rite, if you want."

She violently shook her head. "No. No church. Do the God bit here."

I looked around. One good thing about a place like Side Street is that nobody cares what you do or listens in on your conversation. Perhaps it's like the paper houses in Japan, the only way to have privacy is to ignore what you might overhear. I pulled my stole out of my pocket, kissed it and put it across my shoulders. "Say this after me, 'Have mercy on me, O God, according to your loving-kindness; in your great compassion blot out my offenses. Wash me through and through

300

from my wickedness, and cleanse me from my sin. For I know my transgressions only too well, and my sin is ever before me. Holy God, Holy and Mighty, Holy Immortal One, have mercy upon me.'"

There, in the greasy spoon, we did the Reconciliation of the Penitent without any more of the liturgy, just her confession. Jeff gave us an odd look as he put Carly's beers on the table, but said nothing. In Buggy Springs, it was only a little unusual. If I'd been doing a Buddhist *puja*, it would have been considered normal.

"I found the AK-47 in Todd's Bronco when I drove it to get away from him," she told me in a whisper, as she leaned close. "Choke called me and said I'd killed Todd, but he'd taken care of it. I'd never get blamed. He said he was in Reno and had someone who wanted to pay big bucks for the AK and needed the money to get away." She broke into tears, but quickly got herself under control. "He was a good friend, there when I needed him, but never asking for anything back. So I took the bullets out of the gun and put them in the box before I gave it to him." Tears ran down her cheeks. "I killed him. He couldn't protect himself."

A gray-haired woman in a loose, knitted cap and garish, multi-colored sweater sitting next to us glared at me, probably thinking I was being cruel to Carly. I gave her a weak smile before turning back to Carly. "No, whoever shot him did it from behind. Even if his rifle had been loaded, he didn't stand a chance. He made a wrong choice, not you. Did he tell you who told him you'd killed Todd?"

She shook her head. "Just said he got a call from some dude with a weird voice, like a chain smoker. Said he couldn't tell me more 'cause he'd promised and if he did, I'd get arrested."

Our food arrived then. She blew her nose on the paper napkin and picked up her fork. Carly ate maybe half of her order, but polished off both beers and ordered another.

"Carly, you know drinking will not change what happened."

"Yeah, but if I get a good buzz, I won't care." She pushed the two empties to the center of the table. "And they're on your tab."

I slowly shook my head. "I'm just worried about you."

Her beer arrived and she downed half of it in one, long gulp. She belched and grinned. "Don't worry about me. See? I'm feeling better already."

I sighed. "Is there anything you remember that might help find

301

who shot Choke?"

"No." She thought a minute. "Maybe. He called me and said he'd put Todd under the truck to save me. How'd he know I'd been to Todd's and stabbed him?"

I leaned back in the hard chair. How, indeed? "Did you call him that night?"

She shook her head. "All I did was drive to Reno."

I pondered this. "Did anyone else know that Choke was . . . well, your protector?"

She gave an unladylike snort. "How about everyone in Buggy Springs but you?"

I try to avoid gossip, but it does have its uses. Especially when there's been a murder. Or two. Or four.

I dropped Carly back at Brandy's. As she got out of the Beast, she grabbed my hand.

"Have a Merry Christmas, Preacher-man. You're one of the good guys."

"You have a Merry Christmas too, Carly." I hesitated. "What are you doing for Christmas?"

She shrugged. "Higgins Diggins is open."

"No. I'm having a few people over for Christmas dinner and I'd like you to come."

Tears filled her eyes. "Really?"

"Really. Will you come?"

She could hardly speak. "When?"

"One o'clock." I smiled. "And don't be late."

She just grinned and nodded. Then she ran to the front door, pausing to wave before going in. I waved back. It felt good.

I drove to the church. Doris was off, of course, but I needed to check emails and phone messages. A priest doesn't get the day off on Christmas Eve.

The heat was at a low level and I didn't take my coat off when I sat at my computer. I went through all the normal junk mail and answered parishioners who were mainly making sure the services were at the normal times. If there is one thing you can count on in Episcopal churches, it's that the times won't change. Then I opened the one from Morg.

"Well, I'll be a son of a gun," I muttered. "I was right."

The question was, what to do with what I knew. I had no proof, but I knew. I could tell the Chief and see if he could find a way to use my information. That was a long shot. Or I could call the killer and say I knew everything, even if I didn't. Considering how many had died, a rash action. But, as I used to say when playing the board game *Risk* with friends when I was in high school, God hates a coward. I called on the church phone.

Chapter 55

"Hello?"

"This is Father Bruce. You need to confess."

A pause. "Is this a joke? Confess to what?"

"To killing Jon Franks, Elvira Murdoch, Greg Hartz, and Todd Franks."

Another pause. "Are you recording this?"

I wished that I knew how. "I swear by all that is holy that I am not."

Silence.

I drummed my fingers on my desk. "I've accumulated a lot of evidence, though, and I can just go to Sheriff Bob, if you want. He'll love it. He needs a flashy arrest."

"No." A pause. "I didn't really kill any of them."

"But you have committed grave sins. Maybe you didn't actually kill them, but you helped Todd kill most of them. That makes you an accessory. And you got Choke to kill Todd." A lie, but one to bring justice.

"I didn't start this. It was Todd's fault, his pride. Pride goes before a fall, you know."

Again with that misquote of Scripture. "No, pride goes before destruction. A haughty spirit goes before a fall."

"You're such a smart ass." A pause. "If you have so much evidence, why aren't you going to the police instead of calling me?"

Because I exaggerated, because what I mainly had were guesses and conjectures? Think fast. "I'm not a policeman. My job is saving the lost, not enforcing the law." True, even if a bit deceptive.

"Okay. You're calling from the church. Is that nosey Doris there?"

Caller I.D., no doubt. I needed that on my phone. However, this was probably a burner phone. "No, she's off today. It is Christmas Eve."

A chuckle. "So it is. Okay, you win. I'll make a confession.

305

Then you can't tell anyone. I'll be at the rectory in half an hour. Do you swear by the Father, the Son and the Holy Spirit that you will be the only one there and you won't tell anyone I'll be there?"

I hesitated. I did not take such oaths lightly. "I do."

"Say it."

"I swear by the Father, the Son and the Holy Spirit that I will be alone."

The line went dead.

For a confession to be valid there has to be true repentance. This, obviously, was not going to happen this time. Just in case this did not go as planned, I emailed the Chief before I left the church, keeping my promise not to reveal my caller's name.

Chief,

I am going to be having a meeting at the rectory. If anything happens to me, my GoPro will be recording and will be on my bookcase. Just so you know.

Father Robert

When I checked incoming emails, I found one from the Chief.

Robert,

Reno P.D. notified me that there were three sets of prints on the AK-47 they found. Todd's, Choke's and Carly's. It's also the weapon from the bank robbery.

Chief

This had to work.

After arriving home, I found my GoPro video recorder and put it on a shelf where it was not obvious, but would catch the scene. I would start it when I heard my visitor arrive. I should call the Chief, but I needed the confession or nothing would stick and if he showed up, there'd be no confession. I'm not a small guy and am in good shape, so I wasn't worried. Still, I set my aluminum baseball bat near the door just in case.

A nice cup of tea would help settle my nerves. I put the kettle on the stove to boil the water. As I was getting out the teapot, the doorbell rang. It was time. First I started my GoPro and then I went to the door, picking up the bat before I opened it. It wasn't much use. Lisa had a gun and it was pointed at me.

Dressed in baggy men's work clothes with her hair tucked up under a battered fedora, I wouldn't have recognized her at a distance. She smiled, reminiscent of a rattler about to strike. "Aren't you going to invite me in?"

I leaned the bat in the corner behind the door and opened it wider. "Of course, Mother Goose." I cocked my head. "Why do you have the gun?"

She shrugged. "Security. Never know what's lurking behind a door."

I stifled a grimace. She was sharp. "Come in."

As she came in, she glanced at my bat. "Planning on a game?" She snickered. "You should never bring a bat to a gunfight."

"You never know when you might hit a home run." Weak, I knew, but what could I say? "You didn't bring Walt? He must not know much about you."

She gave a short laugh. "That phony? When he found out that I'd lose my share of the trust if we married, he dropped me. Turns out he was just working for the mining company that wanted to reopen the mine, not the owner. It seems I'm stuck in this boil on the ass of the world as long as I live."

"It's really not a bad place to live." I stepped back. "So, you want to do the Reconciliation of the Penitent?"

"Not really. I can't say I'm sorry for what I've done." She looked around. "You know, this is not exactly an impressive place."

I thought it was rather nice. Not fancy, but tasteful and with some rather valuable antiques. "It's home. But you had something to say to me or did you just want to point a Colt 1911 in my face."

She glanced down at the handgun she was holding. "Impressive. I don't know much about them, but I do know how to fire one." She waved the Colt around. It was cocked and I winced. "I got this one from Todd."

A piece of the puzzle fell into place. "You stole that Colt and his computer, because the computer had emails to and from you. That was when you went to his house after he tried to drug Carly."

She rolled her eyes. "What an idiot. When he told me he was going to rape and kill Carly, I hurried over to stop him."

Another puzzle piece. "No, you didn't. While you knew about the trust, Jon never told you the whole story. When Todd killed Jon, you then found out that it made murder pay. As more die, there's more for the survivors. Todd told me to follow the money. So let Todd kill Carly, then kill Todd, right?"

Lisa awkwardly clapped her hands, dangerously waving the Colt. "Very good. Todd was a liability, a loose cannon. I warned him about you, but he gives you a big hint. Then he tries to kill you a couple of times and botches it. When the cops finally did figure out he was the idiot who tried, I knew he'd probably rat me out to save his skin. So, eliminate the vermin."

"And get a lot more money. But it didn't work out, did it?"

She rolled her eyes. "The jerk drank her drink and let Jon's bastard get away. I get there and he's whimpering about the little cut she gave him. Then he passed out."

"How did you kill him?" I paused. "As a vet, you got him the ketamine that he was going to use on Carly. But you didn't kill him with that, did you?"

"I am impressed. How did you know I'm a vet?"

"Was a vet," I corrected. "Your Mensa page. You used your birth name, Meliscent Stewart. I remembered you'd wanted Jon to get a kilt in the Stewart tartan. Dwayne said you had a different last name and also said you used to be known as Millie, but changed it to Lisa. They both fit your real first name. He also said you had been a professional and that's what you said on your Mensa bio, as well as saying you have a doctorate and are interested in animals and medicine. I knew you had lived in Oklahoma. A friend of mine did a little research and found that you had a DVM from Oklahoma State, but lost your license to practice after suspicious deaths of some dogs in your care when your pet hospital burned down. Ketamine is used in veterinary medicine."

She sighed. "I'm less impressed. Any half-wit could have figured that out with the information you had."

"Maybe." I shrugged off her insult. Sour grapes at being found out. Time to check out some of my theories. "However, if you put a 1000 piece puzzle in front of a half-wit, he's not going to put it

308

together. And that's about how many pieces there are to this puzzle. But I also know that you called Jon so that he would go to where Todd could knock him off a ladder and bash his head in with a rock. Next you taped open the door at Golden Sunset so that Todd could smother Elvira because she was going to tell me something about you. Then you killed Greg and tried to blame it on Todd by calling the hospital to report him running around there."

"I gave Todd diazepam to put in Jon's beers that morning, so killing him was easier than falling off a log." She chuckled. "Or off a ladder. A quick cremation burned up any evidence. Same with putting a pillow over the old woman's face. It was my plan and I gave her more of her sleeping pills hours before he did the job to make it easier. But Todd was scared off at the hospital before he took care of Greg. He called me and I had to do it. I thought I'd been seen there, so I called KMUCK about Todd to distract the attention." She flicked back a stray lock of hair with her free hand. "I am rather noticeable, you know, even in nurse's scrubs."

My suppositions proved correct. By not denying them, she also showed that she had no intention of leaving me alive. At least when they found my cell phone after discovering my dead body, they'd have proof. Thankfully, I did believe in eternal life, even if I were not actively seeking to experience it immediately. But I needed to make sure Lisa was convicted of murder.

"You knew you were going to kill Todd long before that." I remembered the second call from my anonymous caller. "That's why you called with the Exodus passage about the sins of the fathers. You had planned it all, then drove over to Todd's because you expected that Carly would be dead and then you would kill Todd for his share of the trust. You had planned it long before it happened, even down to shooting Todd. It was all in the nursery rhyme you riddled. Pop goes the weasel and that's the way the money goes, to you."

She shrugged. "When he told me he was going to run you over at Beezer's, I knew he was a liability. He had to go, but I had to be careful and not be implicated."

"That's why having him kill Carly was advantageous to you, so you gave him the ketamine for Carly. But how did you kill Todd? In fact, how did you kill Greg? It wasn't ketamine."

"By being smart." She smiled smugly. "I remembered an

309

article I read about Dr. Herman Sanders. He killed an old woman by injecting her with 40 ml's of air. So I tried it with Greg. I took out his I.V. and injected a shot of air from a 60 ml horse syringe I had from my vet days, then replaced the I.V. It worked like a charm. So I did the same for Todd, but right into his external jugular vein. He was out cold, so it was easy. Worked again. Problems solved."

So now I was the next problem to be solved. "But you made me a problem by calling me and taunting me after Jon's murder. I know it was you, but you did a great job of disguising your voice. Electronic?"

She nodded. "Bought a little voice-altering device at a shop in Reno. It was pretty cheap, but did the job."

"But why did you call?"

She was silent for a moment. "Because you always treated me like a dumb blond and avoided me. I wanted to show you that you aren't as smart as you think you are."

"I did what?" I didn't remember being unkind to her. "In what way?"

"When I flirted a little with you, you acted like I was some stupid slut and pushed me away." She glared at me. "I'm a Mensan, you know."

"Of course I didn't respond to your flirtations. You were a married woman, remember? How did I treat you like you were stupid?"

"When I asked you if Thomas Aquinas was right about the difference between a philosopher and a believer, you turned away to shake some old man's hand as he was walking out the church door."

I racked my brain, but couldn't remember the slight. No doubt she had said it while pressing her pair of advantages toward me, which had often happened. "I really don't recall ever doing that, but I apologize if I did."

She waved away my apology. "Too little, too late. When Todd and I were planning how to kill Jon, I went through the lectionary until I found the one about Saul's son, Jonathan. I almost laughed when I heard it. Too perfect. The mighty Jon had a great fall. All the king's horses and all the king's men couldn't put that bad egg together again. I couldn't resist making the call taunting you." She tossed back her hair and shrugged. "Too bad you figured it out. We

310

might have had some fun otherwise."

"You're telling me all this to try to prove how smart you are, to impress me, just like your phone calls." I paused, but was unable to resist. "But you haven't. I did figure it all out, just like I did your riddles."

Her eyes narrowed. She said nothing and kept the Colt aimed at my chest, but still didn't pull the trigger. I wondered why.

Chapter 56

There is an adage that where there is life, there is hope. My only hope was to keep her talking long enough that someone would come by my house. Since I didn't expect anyone, it was a slim chance, but better than none.

"Tell you what, riddle me another and see if I can get it."

She thought a few minutes, precious minutes. "Okay, solve this and you'll live. The Thomas Flyer gave a mathematician's story of childhood's end. Amazing adroit describes the game with no black men, that you'll get if you're leery. The journey is in the mind. Entitle me."

I rubbed my brow. Fortunately, I was a crossword puzzle lover, so convoluted clues were no strangers to me. "Give me a moment." The Thomas Flyer was the car that won the 1908 race around the world, from New York to Paris. *Childhood's End* was a sci-fi book by Arthur Clarke, but was he a mathematician? I didn't know. What game excluded black men? None that I knew of now, but there had been many in the past. Baseball? Journey in the mind. A dream? A novel? It didn't help that she was pointing a gun at me and had basically said she intended to kill me if I didn't solve her riddle. I played for time.

"Why kill Jon in the first place? You seemed to be well off and free to do what you wanted."

She laughed, without humor. "I had money, but no freedom. He hopped into bed with any and every woman who would have him, even my sister-in-law, and everyone knew it. It was humiliating. I had a few flings, discreet ones, and he was going to divorce me. The pre-nup I signed would have left me with nothing. So when Todd found out he was getting cut out of Jon's will, we became allies. I made the plan, of course, and he followed it."

Another piece of the puzzle fell into place and I snapped my fingers. "Jon told Elvira, his old schoolteacher and confidant, about the upcoming divorce, so she had to go."

313

She cocked her head. "You're getting better at this. I really didn't want to kill her, but the old bat told me when I visited her earlier that she knew Jon was going to divorce me, but that he hadn't even told his lawyer yet, so she had to go."

"But why shoot Choke? Was Todd's AK-47 that important, since you tossed it away in Reno?"

She shrugged. "No. Choke himself was the problem."

She leaned against the wall, gun still aimed at me. "After I killed Todd, I decided it would be better if it looked like an accident. My original plan was to go into his pigsty after Carly was dead and shoot him with his own gun." She waved the Colt. "Then put it in Carly's hand and fire another shot into Todd. I watch enough crime shows to know about gunshot residue. But Todd's incompetency ruined that. She got away before I killed him."

I shook my head. "Life's tough, especially when people just don't die the way you want."

Lisa chuckled. "True. So I figured that if Todd crawled under one of his junkers and it fell on him, there wouldn't be an investigation. I had no alibi, you know, and I do profit from his death. But Todd was too heavy for me to drag through the snow. It was falling pretty heavy by then." She glanced around. "Do you have a glass I could use? I'm thirsty."

She was cool and collected, that was for sure. I went into the kitchen, opened a cabinet and got her a glass. She filled it with water, never taking her eyes off of me. My knife set was out of reach. No opportunity there. So I kept mulling over her riddle. There was something about Thomas Flyer and amazing adroit that seemed to connect, but I couldn't quite figure what.

"Anyway," she continued, "Todd had told me about getting in a fight with Choke over Carly. Perfect. I called Choke and told him Carly had killed Todd when he was trying to rape her. I told him that I needed his help to keep her safe from prosecution. He came in like a knight in shining armor, dragged Todd out and dropped the truck on him. I told him to go home and pretend nothing had happened, that there was no way the police would know he was there, since I'd used a burner cell to call him and we'd worn gloves." She shook her head disgustedly. "But he fled to Reno instead. Then he called me, all worried that Todd hadn't really been dead and that the cops would

314

figure out what he had done.   He said he needed money to get out of the country."

Suddenly, my phone rang.   As I started toward the phone, Lisa shook her head and waved the Colt.

"Let it go, Robert."

"It might be important.   Let me answer it and find out."

She leveled the Colt at my chest.   "Leave it."

I heard my greeting, then the caller's voice.

"Father Bruce, this is Dwayne.   Something came up and I'm going to be about a half hour late getting there."   A pause.   "Do you have a cold or something?   Anyway, I'd be glad to give you that estimate on repairs and can make it to your place by 11:30.   See you then."

I looked at Lisa.   "You called him and asked him to come here at 11:00.   What was that about?"

She shrugged.   Her eyes never left me.   "Anyway, Choke said he'd talked to Carly and she had Todd's Bronco with the AK-47.   So I told him the gun was a real collector's piece and I'd give him the money if he got Todd's gun for me.   He was stupid enough to believe it."   She took another sip of water, hopefully leaving a lot of DNA in spite of the gloves she was wearing.   But that didn't seem to fit her careful planning.   "I killed two birds with one stone.   Or two bullets, I should say.   Got rid of the only witness that I'd been at Todd's place and put Carly under suspicion because she'd had Todd's gun.   I tossed it where it would be found, with her prints on it."

"And took his cell phone that showed his call record.   What did you do with that?"

She winked.   "My aim was better.   It's in the Truckee River."

She was taking another drink of water when I let my bombs drop, block-busters, even if one were a major exaggeration.   "Two problems, though.   First, Choke left a good set of prints on a knife he accidently dropped in Todd's house, so the cops are on to him.   Second, Choke's expected to make a full recovery.   He's awake and talking."

She choked on the news.   She was sputtering when she spoke.   "You lie.   If he were talking, the cops would be after me now."

"Probably are, but they don't know you're here.   It's over.   Killing me won't help you in any way."

"You're bluffing." She eyed me warily. "Even if you're not, all Choke knows is that he helped me put a dead body under a truck and that I offered to buy Todd's gun. He never saw me shoot him."

Then it hit me. "'White Rabbit' by Jefferson Airplane."

"What?"

"That's the title of the song you gave me."

She slammed her glass on the counter, sloshing water. "How the hell did you get that?"

I sighed. Maybe she would keep her word and not kill me. "I reasoned. Thomas Flyer is Jefferson Airplane and amazing adroit is Grace Slick, who sang the song. Thomas Jefferson and *Amazing Grace* were the keys. Lewis Carroll was the pen name of Charles Dodgson, an Oxford mathematician who wrote *Alice in Wonderland,* about a little girl he knew. The song is the end of Alice's childhood, getting into drugs, and it had the Red Queen, but no black chessmen. It's obviously about an LSD trip, or journey of the mind, advocated by Timothy Leary. Right?"

She nodded, but said nothing.

"My dad is a big fan of '60's rock and I heard that song a lot as a kid," I explained. "But what does that song have to do with anything?"

At that moment, my tea kettle started to whistle. I motioned at it. "Okay if I turn that off?"

She glanced over at the stove. "Do it."

As I turned and removed the kettle from the stove, I felt a jab in the side of my neck. I spun around to see Lisa with a syringe in one hand and the gun still in the other.

I pointed at the syringe. "What was in that?"

"Ketamine, of course." She gave a short chuckle, the Colt still aimed at my chest. "If you're so smart, why didn't you expect that?"

"Enough to kill me?"

"No, but the fire afterwards will. It'll destroy everything, just like it did when all the dogs they accused me of mistreating burned up at my clinic in Oklahoma. Everything except Dwayne's travel mug that I just planted at your doorstep. He'll arrive just in time to be a suspect." She laughed, like Glen Close playing Cruella de Vil. "Now you see what a song about taking a drug trip has to do with you. If you ever popped acid, this will be a lot like it."

"I've never even smoked pot," I muttered. "But you said if I

316

solved the riddle, you wouldn't kill me."

"I lied." She came close, pushing her breasts into my chest. "Aren't you sad you never got to experience the pleasures I can give?"

Colors started swirling. Objects became distorted. Lisa's breasts became enormous and her head small. I was losing it. I shook my head.

Lisa's small head leaned in and grew very large. Her voice was like she was inside a metal drum, hollow and indistinct. "Enjoying your last trip?" She grinned like the Cheshire cat.

My GoPro and all the evidence would be destroyed in a fire. I had to stop her. I still had my hand on the tea kettle handle. With all my waning strength, I swung it at her. The kettle hit the side of her head with a clunk and she grunted. Like a scene from a movie viewed through a fisheye lens, I saw her hit the floor, the water from the kettle flowing over her like a blue, steaming river as I held it. That was the last thing I remembered.

Chapter 57

I awoke lying on a hospital bed in the ER. I was familiar enough with it from visiting parishioners there to know where I was. An I.V. was in my arm, but I was still wearing the khakis and red flannel shirt I remembered putting on Christmas Eve morning. Was it the same day? I glanced around and saw the Chief in a hard chair, reading the paper.

"How long," I croaked.

The Chief looked up. "About three hours. I drove out to your place as soon as I saw your email. You did quite a number on Lisa, you know. So, did you have one of those eee-piff-any things while on your K-hole."

I shook my head, trying to focus. "I have no idea what you're talking about."

"After we brought you in here, I looked up that stuff Lisa shot you with, ketamine. Kids get high on it. It's called K-holing. Claim it's some religious, enlightening experience. Maybe priests should try it." He grinned. "Problem is you won't remember most of it if you had a strong dose. Do you?"

"Not much." I rubbed my temples. "What I remember had nothing to do with God, so it wasn't an eee-piff-any, as you said. Just drugs messing with my mind and I didn't like it. What happened to Lisa?"

He chuckled. "Well, you gave her a nice bump on her temple and then scalded her face and neck with boiling water. Second-degree burns. You're not her favorite person right now. She lawyered up pretty quick, too. Funny thing is that she tried to get your pit-bull friend to take the case and she was going to until Lisa told your friend that you were the intended victim. Maybe pit bulls do have a few scruples."

I smiled. "Maybe she does." I checked my watch. It was just after two in the afternoon. I would still make the children's service at 5:00. I swung my legs off the bed and started taking off the I.V.

"Hope that's all, because I'm short on time."

"Whoa, partner." The Chief held up his hand.

Just then Brandy appeared at my doorway and advanced toward me like a defensive linebacker, fire in her eyes. "Where do you think you're going?"

"You ask that of a priest on Christmas Eve?" I stood, a little wobbly, but not falling on my face. "To church."

Her expression softened. "You should stay overnight for observation."

"I have two services today and one is in less than three hours." I picked at the tape holding the I.V. needle in my arm. "I'm not staying."

She removed the I.V. and turned to the Chief. "You're responsible. If anything happens to him, I'll come looking for you."

The Chief held up his hands in surrender. "I'll do my best, but he's pretty bull-headed." He paused. "Just like you."

She grunted, but let me go out the door.

"Let's drop by the station," the Chief said as we walked down the hallway. "I found your GoPro recording, thanks to your email, but I still have some questions. This is a multiple-murder investigation, you know."

I headed for the front door. "Just drive me home and I'll answer anything you want."

On the way, I filled him in on everything he didn't know, leaving out Morg's unorthodox help. He looked at me oddly a few times, then asked, "Did you have any help at all?"

If he checked my phone records or saw Morg here in a few hours, it would look suspicious if I did not mention her. "There's a P.I. I met in Incline Village a while ago. She gave me some advice. Her name's Morg Mahoney."

"Morg? That's an unusual name." He scratched his cheek. "Is she from San Berdoo area?"

"No, from Long Beach."

"If her name is spelled M-O-R-G, that's her. I met her when I was on the job in Colton." He chuckled. "If she'd been here, we'd probably have to order a few more body bags. But I like her."

"Good. She's on her way up here and is going to be at the

320

10:00 service tonight."

"Really?" He stroked his chin. "Then I will be, too. Just don't tell her I'm coming. It'll be a surprise."

"Wait, you're Roman Catholic."

"Yeah." He chuckled. "Isn't there a joke about Episcopalians being Catholic-lite?"

"You mean, 'all the liturgy and half the guilt?'"

"Yeah, that's it." He grinned. "My wife is always saying I need to lighten up."

The children's service went off without a hitch. Well, our Mary did break down into tears when she forgot her line about the Son of God and one of the shepherds wandered along the aisle while the Gospel of Luke was being read, but that's the great thing about children's services: the only people there are mainly parents and grandparents. To them, everything is perfect. Since I had forbidden any live animals in the nave, I didn't have much clean-up afterwards.

My cell rang about 7:15. It was Morg.

"Robert, here. How are you, Morg?"

"I'm about an hour away from your thriving metropolis. Where are you?"

"I'm at the rectory."

"I have two questions. First, I need someone to watch Sam while we're at church. Do you have anyone?"

I thought a moment. "Not off hand, but let me see what I can do."

"Great. Second, do you have any food there?"

Nothing I'd serve a guest. "There're some great restaurants in town. I'll call you right back."

"Okay, but don't wait too long. It's a long drive up here and Sam and I just might go for road kill. I've seen some deer crossing the road. Venison anyone?"

I laughed. "I won't be long."

I called the best restaurant in Northern California.

"Solstice, Charles speaking."

"Charles, it's Father Robert. I'm desperate."

"I heard about what happened to you. Are you okay?"

It's a small town, after all. "I'm fine, but something

321

unexpected has come up."

"Let me guess. You have more than four people tomorrow and need to up the numbers for dinner."

"No, I have two of us tonight at about 8:30 and need to be out for the 10:00 service." I paused. "I'm begging you, Charles. Help me."

He sighed. "Be here and I'll work you in."

"Thanks, Charles." I hesitated. "She also has a dog and it's awfully cold tonight. Do you know anyone who can dog sit?"

"You're pushing it, Father. But I'm a dog person and one of my waiters has an apartment behind the restaurant. When you get here, I'll have him take your lady friend's dog to warmer quarters."

"I owe you big time, Charles."

He chuckled. "Yes, you do. But I'll probably never get to collect."

Chapter 58

Morg showed up at the rectory about 8:15. She arrived in a beautiful, gun metal grey Range Rover. At least it was grey where the mud wasn't clinging to it. She hopped out, wearing a beige, quilted, fur-lined parka, and designer jeans that looked good on her with furry boots that looked like Chewbacca's feet.

She grinned. "Hey Robert. Like my duds? Heather bought them for me in Incline Village when we met a couple of years ago.

"Very nice." I knew I needed to say more, but was at a loss for words. I was very happy to see her.

Her smile faded. "Did you find a place for the dogs?"

"Sure did. The owner of the restaurant helped." I paused. "Did you say dogs?"

"I mean dog. As in Sam." She opened the door to her Range Rover. "I'll follow you to the restaurant."

Charles was there to meet us, dressed in a tux with a red and green bow tie. No doubt, they were all from a famous designer. I introduced him to Morg and he called over a waiter who would take care of Sam while we dined. Morg went with him to her car and Charles seated me.

"Very nice." Charles gave a wry smile. "It's about time you found a special someone." He paused. "One who's polite."

"She's just a friend." I hesitated. "For now."

When Morg returned, Charles stood behind her and took her coat, revealing a rather form-fitting sweater and a great bustline.

"I'll hang this in our closet, if that's alright," he said with a smile.

Morg returned his smile. "Thank you."

Then he pulled out her chair with his free hand and, when she was seated, placed her napkin in her lap.

When he had left, Morg gave me a small smile. "He's quite the charmer, isn't he?"

"He's a class act." I glanced over at Charles. "In so many

ways."

Dinner was great, as expected, and all went well. I started with the tuna tartare with avocado, mango and Sriracha, followed by pan-seared sea scallops with wild mushroom risotto. Morg opted for a bibb salad with Asian pears, spiced walnuts, and gorgonzola for her starter and aged New York strip au poivre with Courvoisier cream. Since we obviously could not share a bottle of wine, we ordered by the glass, one for me and two for Morg. At least she didn't drink a whole bottle like my previous date nearly consumed. We both refused dessert, although Morg seemed torn for a moment when she saw the chocolate ginger ganache.

I leaned over. "Would you like the ganache? Please order it if you do."

She lifted an eyebrow. "If I ordered everything I wanted to eat, I wouldn't fit out the door."

After dinner, I ordered a Dow's Vintage 1963 port and Morg had a Jameson 18 year-old Limited Reserve. The meals were more than I would usually spend on eating in a month, but I owed Morg for her help and it was so nice to relax after all that I had been through, especially with an attractive woman who didn't go psycho or try to kill me.

After I filled her in on what had happened, we talked of things that had nothing to do with death and killers. Well, almost. We did talk of Shakespeare, Sir Arthur Conan Doyle, Dashiell Hammett, and Raymond Chandler, all of whom had a lot of death and killers in their works. Don't most authors? All too soon, the evening was getting late and I had to leave. I motioned to the waiter, who promptly came to our table.

"Yes, Father?"

"I need the check, please."

"There isn't one."

I leaned back in my chair. "What do you mean, there isn't one?"

The waiter glanced over at Charles. "The boss said to tell you Merry Christmas and next time give more notice."

On our way out, I went to find Charles, to tell him that I wouldn't let him pay my bill, but he had disappeared. I checked my watch. I owed him even bigger time than before, but I had to leave.

Once I was in my white vestments, I greeted those who came to the service.

Emma grasped my hand as she entered. "I heard you found Greg's killer. Thank you so much."

I didn't know what to say. "It was nothing."

Tears were in her eyes. "Bless you, Father."

There were a few surprises. When Morg saw the Chief come through the doors, it was momentary pandemonium. She jumped up and hugged him. Oddly, I was a little envious.

Julie sashayed in, wearing a long, red coat with a matching pillbox hat, looking like the 1950's, and shook my hand with a powerful grip. The real shocker was when the Zacharys, Ben and Chewy, walked in.

Ben even took his hat off and shook my hand. "I ain't much fer apologies, but you done right by us. Got word Choke's gonna live and that lady lawyer got the sheriff running with his tail 'tween his legs. Bar's gonna be open for New Year's Eve. Maybe this church stuff ain't all lies." He glanced back at Chewy, who stood there with his hair recently washed and slicked down. "Right?"

Chewy nodded, baseball cap in hand. Then they went inside.

Brandy and Tony came up the stairs to the front door, followed by Carly.

Tony glanced back. "I only came because of Brandy and Carly, so don't blow it." Then he grinned. "If you do a good job, I might be back."

Carly came up to me and hugged me. For a moment I was too surprised to respond. Then I returned her hug.

"Preacher-man, you're okay," she muttered.

Then she broke away and rushed inside before I could say anything.

Christmas was a "smells and bells" service, which means using incense in the processional at the beginning of the service and ringing small bells when the Host, or wafer, was raised during the Communion liturgy. We also had six lighted candles on the altar to signify a High Mass and I sang the liturgy during the first part of the Holy

Communion. Although we used Rite II, which was modern language, all the stops were pulled out at Christmas. I loved it, but it often made those from a non-liturgical background uncomfortable. Still, this modern age often left people feeling untethered and blown by any random, whimsical breeze, so I felt it gave an anchor that we need.

I looked around as I did the liturgy and saw no one looked unhappy. That was good. Christmastime is a time to be happy. Just as the Holy Communion part of the service began, Laura walked into the rear of the nave. She gave me a small smile, shrugged, then slipped into a pew. I glanced over at Morg, who was focused on *The Book of Common Prayer*. Laura was absolutely stunning while Morg was beautiful. Yet Laura was somewhat shallow, while Morg had great depth. A momentary sadness washed over me for Laura, but a joy for Morg overwhelmed it. Then I was back into the liturgy. I noticed that Morg came up to receive Communion, but Laura didn't.

When the service was finished and I stood on the top of the steps in front of the church to greet all who had attended, Laura was standing on the sidelines.

Morg came out and whispered in my ear. "I hope you have a king-size bed."

"I, uh . . . ."

She laughed and nudged me. "Just kidding. I found a B and B in town that takes dogs. You're safe. For now." She winked. "Did you know that you're cute when you blush?"

Everyone loved the service, or at least they said they did. Many of those who had played some part in the events of the last month or so greeted me. The Chief, Julie, Tony, Brandy and Emma came out the door and shook my hand, but there was no Rainbow. You can't win them all.

I missed Elvira's brutally frank, sometimes crude, assessment and advice that she delivered with honesty and no lies. Still, when Ben came out with tears in his eyes and grabbed my hand with both of his, that was honest. And when Carly hugged me so long and so hard that I needed to come up for air, that was not a lie.

Morg was at the bottom of the steps, her breath creating small clouds of moisture. It was cold. She smiled at me. I looked around for Laura, but she was gone. I felt a guilty sense of relief, but I had to try.

"Carly, do you know where Laura went?"

"She said something about needing to get back to San Francisco and that you were way too churchy for her." She gave me a pitying look. "Sorry, Preacher-man. She was one stone-cold fox, but not your type."

I smiled. "So true."

After everyone was gone, I walked down to Morg. She leaned up and kissed me on the lips. I made sure it was a long kiss. After a time, we finally parted.

Her voice was low, breathless. "Hey, sailor, buy you a drink?"

I laughed. "In Buggy Springs on Christmas Eve? Only the lowest of dives are open." I hesitated. "How about you come to the rectory for a scotch?"

She got an odd look in her eyes. "Okay. I just have to stop by the B and B to make sure Sam's okay. Give me ten or fifteen?"

"Sure. See you in a few."

True to her word, Morg was at my door in less than fifteen minutes. When I opened the door, she grinned and pointed at a black and white border collie. "This is Sam. Sit and shake, Sam."

Sam obeyed and I shook her paw, but my eyes were locked on what, or who, was behind Sam. It was a blue merle Australian shepherd, staring at me with the bluest of blue eyes.

Chapter 59

Morg nudged me. "Don't stand there gawking. Say, 'Hi' to your new best bud."

I turned to her, then back to the Aussie, speechless.

Morg sighed. "Blue, say, 'Hi' to this rude guy who won't talk to you."

Blue came up to me and I stretched my hand toward him, palm facing me. Blue sniffed it, then gave it a couple of licks.

I found my voice. "Hey, Blue dude. How's it going?"

"Finally, you talk to him," Morg said. "He's a rescue dog, so you two may have some adjusting to do. You can change his name, if you want."

I looked at Morg. "Why?"

"Change his name or adjust? The rescue people named him Blue and we don't know his background, whether he was abused or something. They only knew that they found him wandering the street and–"

"No, why did you bring Blue to me?"

She grinned. "Well, maybe anyone who only has an old lady and me for Christmas dinner needs a real friend. And you said you lost your Aussie, so I knew you liked the breed."

"I do." I knelt and Blue came up to me and licked my cheek. "Blue, this is the beginning of a beautiful friendship, even if your name isn't Louie."

Morg laughed. "Fortunately, I'm a big fan of *Casablanca* or I might not get that. After we talked, I called a guy who works with an Aussie rescue organization. *I* rescued *him* from a lawsuit about one of his dogs falsely accused of biting someone a few months ago, so he owed me big time. He stretched the rules and I got you Blue. If you mistreat him, I promised to shoot you, so don't. I keep my word."

I stood, my hand resting on Blue's head. "You made me believe in Santa again and made this a great Christmas. I would never mistreat this guy."

329

"Good. I'm low on bullets this trip."

I looked up at Morg. "Uh, do you want to come in for that scotch?"

"I'm really beat from the drive up here. Plus I'm not really into scotch." She turned and headed toward her car. "Just make sure you have some Jameson on hand for dinner tomorrow."

"Of course." I waved as she got into the Range Rover, wondering where I could get a bottle of Jameson so late on Christmas Eve.

I called Solstice, praying Charles would answer.

"Solstice fine dining. I'm sorry, but we're closed until the 27th. If you want to make reservations for New Year's Eve, please call back."

I breathed a sigh of relief. It wasn't a recording. "Charles, it's Father Robert. I need help."

He cleared his throat. "I'm already sending dinner for four to you tomorrow, so what now? You want caviar with it?"

"You're doing far more than I could ever hope, but I have a problem and you're the only one that can help. I need to buy what's left of that bottle of Jameson you served tonight. I'll pay you what it would cost if I were buying it by the drink in your restaurant."

"The bottle's almost full, Father. That's not cheap."

"I don't care. You've done more than I can accept, so I insist that I pay, but I have to have it. It's for the woman who was with me tonight. She requested Jameson and I can't let her down, but I don't have any."

"Look, Father, I'll send you a regular bottle of Jameson and charge you what I pay for it, okay? You don't want to know the price of the Jameson 18 year-old Limited Reserve."

"No can do." I paused. "Charles, she brought me a dog, an Aussie like the one I lost a couple of years ago. I can't cheap out."

He was silent for a moment. "You're lucky I'm a dog lover. I'll send the bottle and you pay me cost. Now I'm going home. It's been a long night."

"You saved my bacon. Thank you, and have a Merry Christmas."

"You, too, Father. Have a Merry."

After he hung up, I looked over at Blue. His long, lank body was curled up on the carpet, fast asleep. He was home.

Christmas morning dawned with Blue loudly shaking, tags rattling. At least it was almost dawn. He had followed me into my bedroom the night before and stayed there. I wished I'd known about him coming and could have bought him a present. With no family, it was a little sterile at Christmas. Santa hadn't visited the rector of Saint Nicholas. I prepared my oatmeal and found some canned salmon for Blue and put it in one of my bowls. I wasn't prepared to have a dog. I had no food, no dishes, and no bed. But when Blue looked up at me with those piercing blue eyes, I knew I would find a way to make it until the stores opened after Christmas.

I turned on my small tree's Christmas lights. Being a traditionalist, it hadn't mattered if I were the only one to see it. Now, I had four, no, three guests. Blue wasn't a guest. It finally felt like Christmas.

The first person to show was Carly, standing there with a wrapped package in hand. It was before noon and I was just about to pick up Imogene. Blue answered the door with me, his test.

"Hi, Preacher-man. I–" Then she saw Blue and dropped to her knees. "Oh my . . . . He's beautiful. How long have you had him?"

I glanced at my watch. "About 12 hours." Blue was licking her face. I guessed he wasn't a one-man dog. "Can you watch him while I pick up one of our guests?"

"Sure." She nuzzled Blue. "We'll be fine."

Stifling a little jealousy, I hopped in the Beast and headed to Golden Sunset. The staff had Imogene ready, so maybe my previous attitude had done some good. I took her out to the truck in a wheel chair, then lifted her into the seat.

"Ooh," she said. "You're like Hercules. Did I tell you I dated Steve Reeves?"

I smiled as I fastened her seat belt. "No, but I'd love to hear about it."

When I got back to the rectory and sat Imogene in a dining room chair, Carly had a large glass of amber liquid in her hand. I saw my bottle of Bunnahabhain on the sideboard, looking much reduced from

331

its nearly a third-full standing earlier. I almost said something about not taking that which wasn't offered, but reconsidered. The scotch could be replaced, but life could not be. I was alive and with wonderful people on the celebration of the birth of our Lord Jesus Christ. All was well.

There was a knock at the door and I answered it. Morg stood there, a large bag at her feet with a big, red bow and a wrapped package in her arms. She grinned.

"Merry Christmas, Robert."

Guilt washed over me. So consumed with solving the murders, I had not purchased presents for anyone. I opened the door wider.

"Merry Christmas, Morg."

She looked down at the bag. "That's for Blue. I figured you wouldn't have any decent food for him, so that's what he's been eating." She grinned at me. "If you change his diet, he may have some gastrointestinal issues, if you know what I mean."

"I do." Hopefully, the canned salmon wouldn't be a problem. I picked up the heavy bag and carried it inside. "My dog thanks you, my father thanks you, my sister thanks you and I thank you."

She cocked her head. "Cute. Been watching *Yankee Doodle Dandy*?"

I stopped. "You're pretty good on old movie lines."

She grinned. "Better than you, Bucko."

"Maybe, maybe not." I carried the bag into the laundry room and dropped it on the floor. Blue sniffed it. He knew what it was.

I turned to Morg. "How about one that describes how I'm, feeling. 'Today, I consider myself the luckiest man on the face of the earth?'"

She cocked her head. "That's a hard one."

I smirked. "Give up?"

"Are you kidding?" She glowered at me. "Let me think."

"We've got all the time in the world."

"That's easy. It's from *On Her Majesty's Secret Service*. Louis Armstrong sang it. Highly underrated movie because it didn't have Sean Connery."

I marked an imaginary line in the air. "You got that one, but you're still missing the big one."

She spoke softly, but distinctly. "I will get it."

Charles himself delivered dinner. "I couldn't ask any of my people to work on Christmas," he said.

After placing a box filled with cardboard containers, paper bags and the promised bottle of Jameson on my kitchen counter, he started to leave.

I grabbed his arm. "The bill?"

He sighed. "If you insist, I will email it to you. Right now, I'm heading to a dinner with old friends."

"Just make sure you do." I paused. "We may not be old friends, but I do consider you a friend, Charles."

He smiled. "And I you, Robert."

Dinner was wonderful. Thick slabs of white and dark turkey, chestnut dressing, creamy mashed potatoes, rich gravy, chunky cranberry sauce, green beans with caramelized onions and almonds, and some incredible sweet potato casserole with cream, brown sugar, cinnamon, pecans and a lot more. There were even four beautiful slices of pumpkin pie and of pecan pie.

Carly and Morg served the feast while I chatted with Imogene. She positively beamed. During dinner, she regaled us with tales of movies and movie stars. Some might have been true.

"I was a friend of Marilyn, you know," she told us. "She told me Jack was a great lover, even with his bad back. Said she made him forget it. She also told me about a mole by his . . . ." She blushed. "Anyway, she liked him a lot more than Bobbie. He was a lousy lover. Too immature."

We all looked at each other, knowing who she meant. Was this one true? We'd never know.

After dinner, where we had consumed almost two bottles of wine, I packed the leftovers in the fridge, we all sat back in sated satisfaction. Since my bottle of Bunnahabhain had been drained by Carly, who I obviously would be driving home that night, I opened a bottle of Sandeman 30 year-old tawny port I'd been saving to share with my guests.

Imogene tasted the port and smacked her lips. "That's good stuff. Almost as good as what Bogie shared with Lauren and me one Christmas when I was just a wanna-be actress. That man could hold

333

his liquor, you know."

Carly belched, clutching her glass. "You're a hell of a woman, Imogene. I hope I'm like you, if I live that long."

Imogene smiled at her, but said nothing.

Morg sipped her Irish whiskey and winked at me. "*Pride of the Yankees.* Lou Gehrig's bio with Gary Cooper. That's what you quoted. It took me a while because I don't give a damn about sports, not even the damn Yankees."

I leaned back in my chair. "That is amazing. How did you remember that?"

She touched the side of her head and grinned. "I relied on my little grey cells and they came through."

I laughed. "Of course, Poirot."

"Now that I won, open your present."

"Yeah." Carly pointed at the one she had brought that I'd put under the tree. "Open mine, too."

I opened Morg's gift, a pair of stainless steel dog dishes, a leash and a dog toy, a bright yellow stuffed water fowl with a squeaker. I held it in the air and Blue sniffed it, then grabbed it out of my hand.

I looked at Morg. "Thanks from both of us. That's just ducky."

Morg rolled her eyes. "Open your other gift."

I took Carly's gift, wrapped in black paper with black ribbon, from under the tree. When I unwrapped it, I found a bottle of Old Pulteney 35 year-old single malt Scotch whisky. I was speechless. I had no idea what it was worth, but it had to be hundreds of dollars.

I turned to Carly. "I can't take this. It's--"

"Shut up and accept your gift, Preacher-man. I drank your booze, so this replaces it. Now that one of Jon's heirs is dead and another is ineligible for the trust, I have way too much money." She leaned over and kissed me on the cheek. "If not for you, I'd be in jail or dead, so take it or I swear I'll drink it all myself, right now."

"I . . . I'll keep it here and we can share it, one drink at a time."

"Deal." She grinned widely. It was the first time I'd ever seen her do that. "Now open it."

But before I could reply, my phone rang.

"Merry Christmas. The rectory, Father Robert speaking."

"Hold on, Accident, this is a satellite phone." It was Sister

Dearest.

Then I heard a ragged yelling of "Merry Christmas" by several voices.

"Merry Christmas to all of you," I yelled back.

My sister came back on the line, without her Greek chorus. "Well, hope you're having a decent Christmas. Too bad you're stuck with that church stuff or you could've been on Pop's boat with us."

I thought about my complaining sister, her dull husband, her two brats and our sarcastic father. I looked around at my guests who had brought me so much pleasure this Christmas and at Blue, curled up by the fire next to Sam. I remembered the sheer joy of celebrating the Christmas services. I smiled. At that moment, I did consider myself the luckiest man on the face of the earth.

"Don't worry about me. I'm fine."

Made in the USA
San Bernardino, CA
24 June 2018